"Praise
The C

Finally Jazeer ha

He could see the man's finger begin to squeeze the trigger. Jazeer was expecting a bullet to his brain at any moment…but then the soldier screamed at him again. *"Hands out front!"*

Jazeer immediately laid his hands on the counter. He opened his eyes just in time to see the ax coming down. He saw blood, he saw pieces of bone…

Jazeer collapsed in shock. The American soldier stood over him and in perfect Arabic, hissed: "If you have no hands, you will be of no further use to Al Qaeda!"

Then the soldier threw a handful of playing cards on top of Jazeer and left.

One card fell next to where Jazeer's head had hit the floor. He could see it perfectly, through fading eyes. It was a photo of New York City's Twin Towers with the message: *We Will Never Forget.*

St. Martin's Paperbacks Titles
by Mack Maloney

Superhawks: Strike Force Alpha
Superhawks: Strike Force Bravo
(Coming soon)

SUPERHAWKS

★ ★ ★

STRIKE FORCE ALPHA

Mack Maloney

St. Martin's Paperbacks

For those who lost loved ones in
the attacks of September 11th

We will never forget

PART ONE

The Crazy Americans

Chapter 1

Tom Santos was scared.

He'd flown B-52s over North Vietnam. He'd seen entire squadrons shot down around him. He'd seen friends plunging to their deaths, 20,000 feet below. All of it terrifying. But nothing compared to this.

The doctor's office was cold and sterile. The yellow walls were devoid of anything but diplomas and awards. This guy had been referred to Santos as being the best in the business, that business being oncology. But he was having doubts. The diplomas looked too small and the awards too large, as if the guy had printed them up himself.

He'd been waiting here, alone, for 35 minutes. This after the nurse had told him the doctor would see him "in just a few." Ginny, his wife of 28 years, mother to his six kids, was down in the lobby, seven floors below. The torture of waiting for the results of the test he'd taken a week ago had exacted a toll on him, so Santos had asked her to wait downstairs. He didn't want her to see just how scared he was.

The door finally opened and the doctor walked in. He had a blue file with him and his eyes were downcast. He sat behind his desk, directly across from Santos, but didn't speak. He spent the next five minutes going over every paper in the file. Santos could barely breathe. He stared down at his hands, resting on his knees. His knuckles were pure white. His fingernails were digging into the flesh on his palms.

Finally, the doctor closed the file, looked up, and smiled faintly. That's when Santos knew. . . .

"It is not good news," the doctor said, with all the emotion of ordering a sandwich. "I'm afraid the problem has spread."

Santos didn't hear much after that. Terms like "near-complete metastasized" and "fifth stage" floated in one ear and out the other. The words "six weeks to six months" lingered a bit longer. It was impossible for him to know just how long he sat there, cold and stiff, in the hard plastic chair, eyes shut, heart pounding, his knuckles drained of blood. Somehow an envelope stuffed with brochures for chemotherapy treatment wound up on his lap. So did his insurance form.

When he looked up again, the doctor was gone.

Santos managed to stumble out into the hallway.

Stupid stuff began running through his head. He'd only been out of the Air Force a few months. Would the government still pay for his burial? What would happen to his pension? His mortgage? He had three kids in college.

Then came a crushing blow to his chest. *Ginny* . . . She was still downstairs, saying the rosary. They'd married the day they graduated from high school and he'd loved her more every day since. The bad times had been few with them, none of the horror stories most bomber pilots experienced after being gone from home for long periods of time. She'd never complained, never wavered. He loved her so much at that moment. How the hell was he going to tell her?

He collapsed onto a bench in the hallway. It squeaked when he sat down, and would not stop squeaking, no matter what he did. The hallway floor was filthy with spilled coffee, scuff marks, even drops of blood. A huge multimillion-dollar medical facility like this, you'd think they'd wash the floor every once in a while.

The nurses and doctors and administrative people strolling by all shared an air of privilege and self-importance. Meanwhile, the fluorescent lights overhead were so bright they hurt his eyes. Somewhere down the hall, a woman was laughing hysterically. She was telling someone about the repair of her new BMW and how she'd got the pickup date wrong.

How was he going to tell Ginny?

The bench squeaked again. But this time it was because someone had sat down beside him.

Santos didn't look up. It was hardly the time to make a new friend. With all his strength, he wished they would just go away.

"Colonel Santos?" a very unlikely-sounding voice asked. "Are you Tom Santos?"

Santos finally looked up and saw a very beautiful young woman sitting next to him. She couldn't have been more than 20. She was blond, big eyes, big mouth, absolutely stunning. Her skirt was short, her blouse opened several buttons too low. An angel, Santos thought. So soon?

"Who are you?" he asked her. "Do you work for my insurance company?"

"I'm a friend of a friend," was her reply.

She pulled a briefcase up to her lap and opened it. Inside was every personnel folder Santos had accumulated over his career in the Air Force. Several documents had TOP SECRET written in after his name. Others were bound with pieces of red tape. One clear plastic folder contained his old security badge, the one he'd been issued right after 9/11.

She took a file out from the top sleeve. It was a duplicate of the report the doctor had just read to Santos.

"What's going on here?" Santos demanded.

"I'm showing you these things so that you will believe what I am about to tell you comes right from the top—"

"Tell me what?"

"That, by presidential decree, you have been ordered to take part in a highly classified combat operation. . . ."

Santos looked back at her coldly. Was this the most poorly timed practical joke of all time?

"What are you talking about? I was just told that I'm dying, for Christ's sake. You've got the report right there."

She brushed the hair back from her eyes.

"Our mutual friend knows about your medical issues," she said. "He might be in a position to help."

Santos started to wonder if he was having a hallucination or something. This was crazy.

"How can *anyone* help me?" he asked, voice quivering.

She smiled, oh God, how sweetly, and then tapped his knee.

"You'd be surprised," she said.

She reached deeper into the briefcase and came out with a prescription bottle. It contained several dozen yellow pills. They were so bright, Santos thought they might glow in the dark. On the cap someone had scrawled the name "Bobby Murphy."

"Take at least one of these every morning," she told him, giving him the bottle, then closing the briefcase. "And make sure to eat a good breakfast right afterward. Then take as many during the day as needed for pain or depression. If the pills bother your stomach, drink some milk."

She stood up and brushed off her skirt. "Say nothing to anyone about this," she went on. "That includes your wife. Someone will contact you soon."

With that, she touched him lightly on the cheek and then walked away.

Chapter 2

The bomb was in the pastry truck.

It weighed 120 pounds and was made of the plastic explosive Semtex. Seven hundred two-inch roofing nails were layered inside it; they had been soaked in pesticide before being entombed. There was no timer. The bomb was set for manual detonation. An electrical charge from a car battery nearby would serve as the trigger.

The 1998 blue Toyota truck was parked on Fayed Terrace next to the side entrance of the el-Sabri function hall. It was almost half past noon, a Saturday, and the street was crowded with cars and other small trucks. A wedding ceremony was set to begin inside the hall at one o'clock. Guests were already arriving, some in limousines, many in SUVs. They were backing up traffic for blocks around.

This part of West Beirut was known as the Rats' Nest. The name came from the maze of alleyways that ran all around Fayed Terrace. It was a squalid neighborhood, still bearing the scars of a civil war that had ended more than a decade ago. These days it was home to many combat-hardened *mujahideen,* Muslim holy warriors from all over the Middle East. It was known as a very dangerous place to be.

This was no ordinary wedding being held inside the el-Sabri function hall, because the bride's father was no ordinary

man. He was Muhammad Ayman Qatad, supreme leader of
the Al-Hajiri *jihad,* one of the largest organizations in the Al
Qaeda network. Qatad was a financier of terror. He'd accumulated a fortune by running a string of bank-theft and
money-laundering operations from Lebanon to New Jersey.
The people in his organization, Algerians mostly, were experts at counterfeiting credit cards and manipulating ATM
machines. They stole as much as $25,000 a week from
money machines in Great Britain and France. The cash was
laundered by a web of Islamic charities also under his control and then deposited in secret bank accounts to be used as
needed. In this way, Qatad had supplied funds for suicide
operations on the West Bank and in Gaza. He'd sent *mujahideen* to fight in Chechnya. He'd paid for the boat and
motor used in the bombing of the *USS Cole.* He'd provided
airline tickets for the bombers of the U.S. embassy in Kenya.
His greatest accomplishment however, at least in his eyes
and those of his followers, was helping to bankroll the attacks on the World Trade Center and the Pentagon in 2001.
He'd provided nearly $200,000 to those operations alone.
Blood money, down to the last drop.

No surprise, the neighborhood was crawling with heavily-
armed men, local Muslim militia hired by Qatad to provide
security for his daughter's ceremony. They were stationed
along the streets and on the rooftops. Those on the street
were roughly handling any local Lebanese who were deemed
a nuisance or simply not moving along fast enough. As for
Qatad's personal bodyguards, more than a dozen were stationed inside the wedding hall itself.

It was now 12:45. More guests were arriving, a who's who
of the local Islamic underworld. Men were entering the wedding hall through the front door. Women were directed to a
door in the back. All the men were wearing *kaffiyehs;* all had
either beards or mustaches, symbols of strength in the Muslim world. The interior of the wedding hall smelled of oil
and cinnamon. At Qatad's request, the walls had been given
a fresh coat of paint.

The men took off their shoes and settled on their prayer mats. The women sat quietly off to the side. Each guest was offered watermelon and pastries while waiting. Lemonade was served. A small crowd had gathered on the street outside. Qatad's hired guards watched over it nervously as their boss arrived in an armored SUV and was hustled into the hall. He would be the last one allowed inside.

The wedding ceremony would be brief. As the clock struck one, the bride was led in. She showed no outward sign of emotion. She was wearing a *djellaba* and her hair was covered by a *hegab,* the traditional Islamic headdress. Her hand was clutching a rose. There was no music.

The bride took her place beside the groom. A prayer was recited by the men; then a marriage contract was produced. The groom made his formal marriage proposal and the bride responded three times: "*Kobul* [I accept]." Then she and the groom signed their names to the contract and put their thumbprints in the wedding registry. The ceremony was complete.

Qatad, the proud father, embraced the newlyweds, kissing each one three times on both cheeks. There was polite applause and others in the immediate families embraced. Then the bride and groom each ate a piece of fruit offered to them on a date palm. Then they kissed.

The bomb went off a second later.

The explosion was so powerful, the shock wave broke windows two miles away. At the instant of detonation the swarm of roofing nails went flying off in all directions, their tips ignited by the superheated pesticide, perforating everything within the wedding hall. In the same moment, a great wash of fire raced through the building, sucking up oxygen and vaporizing anything not made of stone. In seconds, a crimson cloud was rising above West Beirut.

When the smoke cleared, the wedding hall was simply gone. An immense crater now filled the space where the five-story building had stood. The hole was already awash in sewage, pouring out of pipes broken in the blast. Bodies were everywhere. Fifty-two people had been crowded inside the hall. Now, just a handful of survivors emerged from the rubble. They looked like wounded ghosts, bleeding and covered with plaster, stumbling out onto the debris-strewn street.

An eerie silence descended on the area. A deathly quiet, except for the crackle of flames. Then came the sirens. And suddenly the streets were filled with armed men again. All of Qatad's bodyguards had been killed in the blast—these soldiers were the local militiamen hired to watch the periphery of the wedding celebration. Through the smoke, many Kalashnikovs could be seen, moving around frantically, barrels in the air. Pushing the stunned survivors out of the way, the militiamen were looking, up, down, this way and that—but looking for what?

A group of them was immediately drawn to the wreckage of the pastry truck. All that remained was the chassis and the four tire rims. The militiamen were wise in the ways of truck bombings. It was obvious the blast had originated from here. They also knew the chances the perpetrators were still in the area were nil. But then a surprise. Shouts from two blocks away. Through the smoke and flames, two of their brethren were gesturing wildly.

"They are here!" they were both yelling. *"We have them cornered!"*

This seemed unlikely, but the small army of militiamen rushed forward anyway. The street was filling up with ambulances, fire apparatus, and men in Red Crescent coats. Barreling through these people, the militiamen reached their colleagues, and sure enough, at the other end of the alley, two blocks from the devastated wedding hall, they saw two individuals holding a small car battery and a handheld detonator plunger. They appeared frozen in place.

It seemed to good to be true—and it was. As soon as the militia raised their weapons, the men pushed the plunger again, and another bomb went off. A car parked nearby held the explosives this time. Six militiamen were killed in an instant.

For a few moments another surreal silence enveloped the

area. It was soon broken by the cries of those who had somehow survived this second blast. Those militiamen still standing made their way down the alleyway, now strewn like the
street behind them with bodies and wreckage. At the end of
this gauntlet, incredibly, they spotted the two bombers again.
Having discarded the detonation devices, the two men were
running even deeper into the Rats' Nest. The chase was on.

The militiamen found themselves fighting crowds of terrified civilians who, shaken by the two terrific blasts, were
fleeing the area before there was a third. This stream of humanity slowed their pursuit, yet the militiamen were still
able to keep the two fleeing bombers in sight.

The foot chase reached the center of the neighborhood, a
place known as the Wheel, for its circular marketplace. The
bombers were spotted ducking down a narrow alley to the
east. The militiamen followed quickly, knowing this particular alley was a dead end.

But after turning that one last corner, the militiamen
abruptly came to a halt. Before them was an incomprehensible sight. Hovering almost silently above the other end of
the alley, not 200 feet away, was a large black helicopter. It
had two ropes lowered from it and the two bombers were being lifted up into it.

More shocking, the helicopter was not unmarked, as might
have been expected in this case. Just the opposite. There was a
huge flag attached to its fuselage.

An American flag.

None of this seemed right to the militiamen, but they
started shooting at the helicopter anyway. This was a big
mistake. A gunner at the side door of the aircraft returned
their fire with a high-powered automatic weapon. It tore
through one group of militiamen, reducing them to pieces.
More armed fighters arrived on the scene. They, too, began
firing at the helicopter, one with a .50-caliber assault gun.
But suddenly another helicopter appeared above the alley.
This one was bristling with weapons. It fired two rockets directly into a second group of armed men, killing them all
instantly.

Chaos now ensued. The noise was deafening. Explosions, the sound of gunfire, the surviving militiamen trying to shout to one another over the racket. Another dozen gunmen arrived, their large open truck screeching to a halt at the end of the alley. They were armed with rocket-propelled grenades. One fired his weapon at the helicopter retrieving the bombers. The RPG shell missed high, exploding in the street one block over from the alley. Another RPG went off. This one went *right through* the rear cabin of the helicopter and out the other side, without exploding, an extraordinary piece of luck for those on board.

A third RPG was fired, this one at the helicopter that had unleashed the rocket barrage. Aimed way too low, the grenade smashed into an empty apartment building a half-block away. The structure went up like a box of matches.

The two bombers had been reeled into the helicopter by this time and the aircraft began moving away. Still, the remaining militiamen persisted. They were astonished that these were Americans doing this, astonished that it was happening so fast. But no matter. Shooting down one of the U.S. helicopters was now their priority.

So every man with a gun opened fire on the second helicopter. It took some serious hits along the fuselage and up near the tail. It began to stagger; a trail of smoke appeared. A cheer went up from those below. Suddenly half the neighborhood was shooting at it.

That's when the Harrier jump jet arrived.

It came out of nowhere as jump jets were known to do. It immediately opened up with its cannon, raking the alleyway from one end to the other. The militiamen went scrambling for their lives. Firing at helicopters with rifles was one thing; battling a jet fighter was quite another. The Harrier climbed, turned, and came back down again, cannon blazing once more. Another stream of explosions ran down the alley, tearing up the pavement and covering just about all the fleeing militiamen in concrete and burning rubble. This gave the second chopper enough time to safely move away.

Only then did the Harrier leave the scene.

Five hours later

The Mercedes had been speeding through the streets of East Beirut all afternoon, going in circles, a caravan of SUVs and Toyota trucks trying hard to keep up with it.

Slumped over in the backseat of the SE500 sedan was Abdul Abu Qatad, brother of the recently departed Muhammad Ayman Qatad. Abdul's chief bodyguard was lying on top of him, shielding him. After five hours of this, both men were very sweaty.

Abdul was lucky he was still able to sweat. Arriving late at his niece's wedding, he'd just climbed out of his SUV when the function hall blew up. Abdul had escaped with just cuts on his hands and face, but his young boyfriend had simply disappeared, caught by the storm of nails. His gore was still splattered on Abdul's robes. Abdul had served as his brother's right-hand man for the past 10 years. They had overseen dozens of *jihad* operations together, using their Algerian moneymen as their workforce. But never had Abdul imagined the horror he'd seen this day. And never had he come so close to being killed himself.

He'd been calling and calling on his cellphone all during this mad trip through the crowded streets, trying to contact anyone still alive in his brother's security organization. His fingers were numb from punching in the same numbers, over and over again. But no one answered. No one was left.

He finally ordered his driver to stop in front of a nondescript apartment building on the edge of East Beirut. The escort of SUVs and Toyotas, brimming with private security troops, roared up behind him. The armed men jumped from these trucks and surrounded the Mercedes. It was dark by now. The lights on the narrow street were very dim.

The chief bodyguard lifted himself off Abdul and opened the door. A mumbled request was translated into a quick order: the security men were not to look at their employer as he was being taken from the car. He was in such a sorry state, Abdul didn't want his hired guns to see him like this.

All eyes averted, the chief bodyguard gently eased his boss out and helped him through the apartment building's dilapidated front door. This was a safe house, a place Abdul had secured years before for just such an emergency as this. His bodyguard produced a key and turned it in the lock. The door sprang open.

Only then did Abdul straighten up. He wanted to enter the house with dignity; not to do so would be considered bad luck. He shook off the bodyguard and ordered him back to the car. "Watch the entrance until further notice" was the man's new order. The bodyguard hugged Abdul and departed.

Abdul stepped inside. Downstairs was only one room, small and dark, no running water, no electricity. It also smelled of sewage. But Abdul didn't care. The apartment was in such an obscure part of the city, no one would ever suspect he would flee here. Even his closest associates knew nothing about it. Nor did his wife or children. At last he would be safe.

He took another sniff of the air. What was that other strange smell? And that dripping sound? He retrieved his Bic lighter, located a candle, and lit it. Then he turned around.

They heard his screams out on the street.

The entire squad of security men started for the door, but the chief bodyguard stopped them with a shout. He pulled a pistol from his belt. Only he would go in—at first.

He walked through the front door and found Abdul doubled over, vomit covering his shoes.

Hanging above him was a body. It was a young man; his throat had been cut. The corpse was upside down and strung from the ceiling in such a way that Abdul must have looked right into the eyes upon discovering it. The man's pockets had been stuffed with wedding pastries. A pool of blood and crumbs had collected on the floor below.

The bodyguard stared into those dead eyes and then vomited himself. The body was that of Abdul's youngest son, Hamiz.

But how could this be? Hamiz was in Jedda, studying at a

madrassa under an assumed name. Who could have done this? And who could have known about this place and hung his body here?

Something had also been stuffed into the dead boy's mouth. The bodyguard retrieved it with shaking hands. It was a playing card. On one side was the ace of spades, except it was colored in red, white, and blue. On the other was a photograph of the World Trade Center in flames.

Scrawled below the Twin Towers were the words: *We will never forget.*

Mogadishu, Somalia
Two days later

The place was called the Olympic Hotel.

It was an infamous building, six stories, whitewashed top to bottom. Nearly a dozen years before, a horrendous battle had been fought near here between U.S. Special Forces and gunmen loyal to local warlord Mohammed Farrah Aideed. Months earlier, Aideed had stolen just about all the food the United States had delivered to the desperate city of Mogadishu. In a place where starvation killed nearly a thousand people a day, food was power. And Aideed wanted power.

On that early October day, a top-level meeting between Aideed and his henchmen was in progress in the building next to the hotel. The U.S. troops, including members of the United States' premier special ops unit, Delta Force, as well as many Army Rangers, had descended on the building in a swarm of Blackhawk helicopters. Their orders were to capture Aideed alive if possible, or, at the very least, bring in some of his high-level associates.

But Aideed's gunmen had been tipped off that the Americans were coming. They were waiting when the Blackhawks arrived overhead. Aideed's soldiers were no ragtag army. Many were in league with al-Itihaad al-Islamic, also known as the Muslim Brotherhood. They'd been trained extensively by veteran Al Qaeda fighters and were armed to the teeth.

Aideed's men waited for the right moment, then opened up on the fleet of American choppers. Two of the Blackhawks went down almost immediately; many others were driven away. The majority of U.S. troops that had already rappelled to the ground found themselves trapped. It took them a day and a half to fight their way out of the hostile city. Eighteen Americans never made it. One was butchered by an armed mob and dragged through the streets.

These days, the Olympic Hotel was a shrine of sorts. Because of what happened here, the Muslim Somalis got what they wanted: the embarrassing withdrawal of U.S. troops from their country. A mission that had begun as one of mercy, to feed the millions of starving in Somalia, had ended in a humiliating failure. The hotel still served as the not-so-secret headquarters of al-Itihaad al-Islamic, the people responsible for the killing and desecration of American servicemen that day. At any given time, several dozen Al Qaeda–trained soldiers could be found inside, too. It was here that tax money collected from the city's miserably poor was kept and counted. It was here that the terrorists sold *qat,* the narcotic leaf chewed by Somali men. It was here that top-level Al Qaeda operatives transiting through Africa could lay low and know they would be protected and safe.

Until this night.

It was 10:00 P.M. and the electricity in downtown Mogadishu had gone out for the night. Candles and cooking fires were lit in most of the rooms at the Olympic, as well as the building next door. The noise from battery-operated radios blared through the open windows. Drunken laughter, too, along with muffled praying and the sounds of sour music.

This was all broken by the growl of helicopters, approaching in the dark. There was no advance warning this time. No tip from the Italian peacekeepers to Aideed's men. This was unexpected. A complete surprise.

Fittingly, it was two Blackhawk helicopters that showed up first. No soldiers would be lowered by fast ropes this time. This was not an insertion operation or a high-level smash and grab.

This was simply payback.

The pair of Blackhawks dived for the hotel, miniguns firing, rockets flying off their underbellies.

One aircraft stayed in the lead; it was the gunship of the two. The second copter was packed with soldiers. Held in with safety belts, many had their weapons thrust out of openings on the right side of the aircraft. This second Blackhawk slowed almost to a hover, allowing the soldiers to fire their weapons directly into the windows of the hotel's upper stories. The first Blackhawk meanwhile launched two rockets and a TOW missile into the bottom floor. There was a trio of explosions and suddenly half the building was on fire. Many within instantly perished. Others died leaping from the rooftop and windows. Cluttered and rancid, the building next door caught fire, too.

The attack went on for 10 minutes. Crowds gathered in the streets surrounding the hotel; some were armed fighters who'd rushed to the scene but were not sure what to do. A few RPGs, the weapons that had proved so fatal to the attack back in October of 1993, were fired at the helicopters. But they all missed the Blackhawks because this time they were fired from the streets and not from the rooftops, as in the previous action.

The Blackhawks finally did depart, only to be followed by a jet fighter suddenly streaking low over the neighborhood. Its noisy arrival jolted many thousands from their sleep. The fighter—a Harrier jump jet—did not drop any bombs. Instead, it swooped down on the mob of gunmen and dusted them with a light green powder. This was barium sulfate and pepper acid—superitching powder. Once on the skin, it was near impossible to get off. It would plague the victim with incessant itching and bloody rashes for up to a year. The jet made two passes; then it, too, disappeared over the horizon.

Only then did the ancient air-raid sirens begin to wail

across the city, but they were too late on this good night. Rumors that the raiders would soon be back were shouted from the rooftops. Panic washed through the streets. Angry mobs began hunting down Muslim fighters and hacking them to death—they'd been the cause of this! No medical personnel ventured out into the madness. Nor did the police or the Army.

And no one bothered to put out the fire at the Olympic Hotel, either.

It burned to the ground.

Port of Aden, Yemen

Hamini Musheed hadn't yet heard about the attack in Mogadishu the night before. And he'd read only a brief story in *Al-Quds Al-Arabi* on the incident in Beirut that past Saturday. Which was good for him. In his position, some things were best left unknown.

He was a lawyer. A very wealthy one. His office, extremely luxurious by Yemeni standards, was located in a rebuilt villa, overlooking the harbor. He handled all kinds of legal matters within the city, everything from wills to criminal defense. He was well connected with the local authorities, all of them, like him, highly corrupt. It was a rare occasion that he even went to court. For the right price, he could get his clients out of just about anything.

Musheed also belonged to a group called the Islamic Relief Fund. It was a charity fronting for the main Yemeni cell of Al Qaeda. He was the treasurer, responsible for moving up to $10,000 a week to an Al Qaeda–controlled bank up in the United Arab Emirates. Musheed had also been responsible for hiding the terrorists who had transported the explosives used in the attack on the *USS Cole,* in this very same harbor, several years before.

Though, on the face of it, there seemed to have been cooperation between the Yemeni government and U.S. authorities in searching for the perpetrators of the *Cole* attack—which killed 17 sailors—Musheed had escaped the dragnet. Even when the United States eventually managed to track down many of the players in the *Cole* bombing, eliminating them, Musheed had remained unscathed.

He was just too connected to get into trouble.

He'd just sat down to his morning yogurt and tea when there came a knock on his office door.

His two secretaries were missing this morning—both had sent messages that they'd be late. Musheed was a large man, weighing more than 350 pounds. It took a lot for him to get up and answer the door himself. So he called out that it was open.

Two men came in. Non-Arabs, very white. Musheed knew immediately they must be Americans. They were wearing civilian clothes: jeans, T-shirts, and ball caps. They were also wearing black combat boots. Highly polished.

The two men were carrying bags that Musheed would never have recognized: they were baseball-bat sleeves. The two stepped into his office and calmly shut the door. Musheed asked them what they wanted. They didn't respond.

Musheed was pinned behind his desk; he couldn't move. The men reached into the bags and came out with two M-16s equipped with silencers. They both fired twice. Two tap shots each. Four bullets right through Musheed's head.

He hit the desk with a crash, landing facedown in his bowl of yogurt.

The two men packed up their weapons and departed. They were out of the city by the time Musheed's office help arrived 10 minutes later.

Twenty minutes after that, they were out of Yemen altogether.

Chapter 3

The palace looked like a California beach house on steroids.
Whitewashed walls, miles of blue roofs, large windows everywhere. It had 116 rooms, on six floors, each floor bearing three levels. Six living rooms, six dining rooms, and six kitchens were on every level, all with separate areas for men and women. There were three dozen bedrooms and just as many bathrooms. The palace also had a fantastic indoor garden, a zoo, a gigantic atrium, an aviary, and two pools, both Olympic size, both with intricate Arabesque detailing throughout, both indoors. Everything inside was huge—except the place set aside for prayer. It was located on a tiny patch of sand near the edge of the indoor garden.

The palace was one of seven Prince Ali Muhammad al-Saud owned within the Kingdom. He had yet to set foot in three of them.

Out back, where the compound met the desert, there was an entirely different structure. It looked like an Arabian tent but was as immense as a circus big top. It was made of canvas and concrete, with a lot of steel ribbing everywhere. It, too, was all white and had gold flags and those of the Royal Family flying from its peak. It was large enough to hold several thousand people.

This was Thursday night, the Evening of Favors, and the tent was crowded. Every week at this time, ordinary Saudis could come to the palace and make requests of the Prince. These came mostly in the form of written petitions, though some were put to music and sung. Frequently the Prince himself would be on hand, collecting the requests and allowing each petitioner to kiss him on the right shoulder. The most common favor asked of the Prince was to intercede with the government on behalf of someone seeking a passport. Other petitions sought money for a doctor, tuition for a child, or funds to bury a loved one.

More than 3,000 people were waiting for him this cool night, but Prince Ali was already two hours late. Only the captain of his household staff knew where he was, the same place he'd been all day: in his master bedroom, on the top floor of the palace, sitting on pillows with two close colleagues, watching CNN.

These were troubling days for Prince Ali, if anyone worth $20 billion could be troubled.

He was a fabulously wealthy man; a direct bloodline to the House of Saud was all it took. By King's decree, Ali got a percentage of every large construction contract signed within the Kingdom. He also owned the Pan Arabic Oil Exchange, which handled about 10 percent of the unrefined crude leaving the Persian Gulf. Through this, combined with his accountants' daily manipulation of bond prices and metals futures and plain old currency fraud, Ali saw about $4 million flow into his coffers every day.

He was 40 years old and while not a handsome man, he didn't have to be. He had 22 wives, all of them gorgeous. Two had been Miss America finalists, one had been Miss World. He also owned a fleet of U.S. and British sports cars, two Gulfstream jets, and a yacht the size of a destroyer.

But like the recently vaporized Muhammad Qatad and the Yemeni lawyer named Musheed, the Prince was also a moneyman for Al Qaeda. Many of those Islamic charities that Qatad and Musheed had been funneling money to ran right through the offices at the Pan Arabic Oil Exchange in downtown Riyadh. There the donations were mingled with Ali's own money, then secretly distributed to the *jihad* cells worldwide. Two thousand people worked at Pan Arabic; almost a third were somehow involved in financing Muslim terrorists.

The Prince's wealth and power were rooted in the Saudi business establishment, something the extremists claimed they wanted to tear down. Why then would he be involved in the backdoor financing of the terrorists? What did he share with the *mujahideen* hiding in the caves of the Pershawar or the sleeper agents living in the squalor of Manila, East London, or Jersey City?

Actually, very little. There was the obligation of every Muslim to help promote Islam, of course. There was also the respect he received from those holy fighters in the mountains and in the U.S. slums; they had been led to believe that Ali was spending millions of his own money on them. Then there was the dream of the Caliphate, the uniting of the entire Muslim world under a single entity. And the fact that if men in his position within the Royal Family didn't help the terrorists, the martyrs would soon be blowing up their planes, their ships, their houses.

But the real reason was simpler: Prince Ali detested Americans. He detested their lifestyles, their attitudes, the colors of their skin. He detested their freedoms, their diversity, and the way their women walked. He detested McDonald's, Chevrolet, Kodak, and Coke and the way Americans always seemed to have something on their minds and were never shy about spitting it out. He hated their ruggedness, their TV shows, their blond hair, and their big blue eyes. *He hated them.*

The Prince could really work himself up over this, too. There was a lot of anger inside him: strange, because he derived more than half his fortune from products purchased directly by Americans. The oil he sold today would be refined and pumped into American gas tanks in three weeks. He was rich *because* of America.

The irony did not bother him. But if Prince Ali ever decided to lie down on an analyst's couch, something he would never do, a not-so-surprising deeper truth would come out: that like many of his countrymen, rich or not, he hated Americans simply because he was not one of them.

He'd heard about the bloodbath in the Rats' Nest an hour after it happened. It was a very disturbing event. Not only was an important layer of Al Qaeda's organization wiped out, but also the attack had come with absolutely no warning, out of the blue. The same was true in the leveling of the Olympic Hotel, an even bigger surprise, because the target seemed so unlikely. Nearly half of the Muslim Brotherhood leadership had been killed as a result of that attack. Dozens of operations inside Africa were now in disarray. As far as the cold-blooded killing of Musheed, their legal connection in Yemen, went, the cut was even deeper. Musheed had been Prince Ali's third cousin.

"Praise Allah, I still think these were Israeli operations," one of the Prince's companions said now. He was Adeen Farouk, 50, fat, bald—and another third cousin. "Israelis—with their aircraft painted like the Americans."

"I cannot accept the boldness, either," the second friend said. He was Abu Khalis, the brother of one of the Prince's 22 wives. He shifted on his pillow in the middle of the vast bedroom. "This willingness to so openly show their flag? To make so much noise? No—these were tricks. It is not them. The Americans just aren't like that. They always come with a hammer, not a scalpel."

"It *had* to be them," Ali replied harshly. "The Jews don't have equipment like that. Plus we have the calling card stuffed into the mouth of the young nephew. Who else would have a dispute with Brother Qatad or our friends in Somalia? Or our dear fatso, Mr. Musheed? Yes, these were the Americans—and they were making a point. A *big* point. And that disturbs me."

"Praise Allah," the other two men said together. All three were furiously fingering their worry beads.

"But if it was the Americans, where did they attack from?" Farouk asked. "There is no American base or aircraft carrier within a thousand miles that our Chinese friends don't have some kind of surveillance on. We have eyes near their special operations bases; we have ears on their phones. Yet we heard nothing about any of these things."

The Prince replied: "What I am most concerned about is why we did not read about these attacks coming two weeks ago—in the *New York Times*. We know how the Americans are. It is impossible for them to keep a secret. As you said, they are almost pathological when it comes to telegraphing their next move. The sound of the giant's feet *never* reaches us before the sound of his tongue does."

"And they always pretend to be so careful about anyone seeing them," Khalis said. "But this thing in Lebanon, it was not just some Predator drone shot. It was done in the bright light of day, by real soldiers, helicopters, and jet fighters—"

"Yet still nothing on CNN," Farouk added, glancing at the wide-screen TV hanging on the far wall. "Nor on Fox. The BBC. Anywhere. . . ."

This was true. The Rats' Nest incident had been reported briefly as a gas line explosion. The attack in Mogadishu had been called civil unrest. Musheed's killing barely made the local papers. No one in the media seemed to be making the link that the three incidents were related, that the perpetrators might be the same. But then again, only people within Al Qaeda would know enough to connect all the dots.

The three men sipped their tea. This was all *very* mysterious.

"Let's say these *are* the Americans then," Farouk said worriedly. "Could this be their way of finally taking it directly to us? I mean, they seem more like a hit squad than a military unit and they seem to know who to hit and when. Could they have picked up *our* scent?"

Not so long ago, such a comment might have invoked laughter from the three men. They were so high up in the royal Saudi hierarchy, they once believed themselves invincible. But not so now.

A knock came at the door, startling them. It was the captain of the Prince's household staff. He asked Ali if he should tell the three thousand people waiting in the Tent to go home.

"Tell them to be patient," the Prince said, waving him away. "I will be there."

He stood up to go. "Brothers, we might be getting concerned over nothing. After all, the giant is still a giant. And praise Allah, this giant never acts both quickly *and* fruitfully on anything, as our brothers in Baghdad will attest. I feel this will be especially true after doing something like this. The perpetrators are already back home, I'm sure, in their beds, where it is safe, awaiting their medals and apple pie.

"In any case, we can't allow these things to interfere with any of our future plans. We would be fools if we did."

Chapter 4

Genoa

The buses had been arriving at the dock all morning.

Eighteen tour groups, flying in from all over Europe and the United States, were pouring off the airport buses and climbing aboard the *Sea Princess,* one of the newest cruise ships in the Mediterranean.

At 1,100 feet long, the *Sea Princess* was also one of the largest. It had 15 passenger decks, 1,700 cabins, 12 restaurants, four swimming pools, four health clubs, four casinos, a movie theater, a golf range, a skeet range, two nightclubs, two dozen bars, and a bowling alley. It could carry nearly 3,400 passengers.

By noon, the ship was 80 percent full. The passenger list was almost exclusively American, with many elderly Jewish couples onboard. It was soon learned that a plane carrying French tourists had been mysteriously delayed at Orly. They would not be boarding the *Sea Princess* in Genoa after all. Still, including the crew, there was nearly 4,000 people onboard.

The cruise liner went out with the tide around 1:00 P.M. Its itinerary included a sail of the Aegean lower islands, a stop in Cyprus, and then on to Israel.

As it left the harbor, two seagoing yachts began shadowing it. One was riding very low in the water.

. . .

The *Sea Princess* traveled down the coast of Italy, making a comfortable 18 knots. It passed through the straits of Medina during the night and was in the Ionian Sea by morning. The pair of sea yachts was still tailing it, staying about a mile behind. When the ship stopped at the Greek port of Corfu around noon, the yachts stopped, too. Some of the crew noticed them at this point but failed to inform the captain. When the liner pulled anchor later that day, the pair of yachts left as well.

Night fell again. At 11:45 P.M., the liner was about twelve miles off the coast of Greece, heading for the straits of Kithira. It entered the narrow passage shortly before midnight, slowing to five knots, a necessity in shallow water. At this point, the yachts were spotted again; they were now just 500 feet off the stern.

Finally the captain was notified. He was furious upon learning the yachts had been detected earlier, but he hadn't been told. Now he wasn't sure what do to do. In the old days, yachts would occasionally tail cruise liners, thinking they would lead them to the best spots in the Med. But this hadn't happened to the veteran captain in years, and certainly not in this new era of terrorism.

A small panic swept the ship. Word of the mysterious yachts spread quickly. Many passengers moved to the stern, gathering on three tiers of lower aft railings. Many brought their video cameras; some were equipped with low-light lenses. Through them, the passengers could clearly see activity on the two yachts, now riding just 200 feet away. The vessels had been lashed together and men in ski masks could be seen loading boxes wrapped in electrical wire and tape onto a small rubber raft that was hanging off the back of one of the yachts.

Once loaded, the rubber raft was put off the yacht, with two men in ski masks aboard, its outboard motor already turning. It hit the water with a splash, churning up a geyser of spray and smoke. The raft circled the two yachts once and then turned toward the cruise ship.

Passengers started screaming. It was obvious the rubber boat was filled with explosives and those driving it intended to ram the cruise ship. Some ran for the lifeboats. Others fled to their cabins. But many remained on the aft railing, simply stunned. Some continued videotaping the scene.

The captain hastily tried to increase speed, hard to do for such a large ship. He turned to starboard; the nearest land was still eight miles away. His communications officer was frantically sending out messages saying the cruise liner ship had an "extraordinary emergency" and needed assistance immediately. Meanwhile, up on the front promenade deck, with no one noticing, some members of the crew were trying to lower themselves into lifeboats.

The raft began to circle the *Sea Princess*. Keeping up with the liner's course change, it was clearly building speed. A Klaxon went off aboard the ship. Too late, the call went out for all passengers to don their life vests. Then the captain ordered all lights doused. He was hoping to make it difficult for the men in the raft to see their target, but this was sheer desperation. It would be very hard to miss such a large ship. The sudden blackout only caused more panic among the passengers.

The rubber boat circled one more time. Then with a growl from its engine, it began heading right for the middle of the cruise liner.

But suddenly there came another terrific roar, mechanical and powerful. A jet fighter flew out of the night an instant later. It was painted black and had a long spit of flame trailing behind it. Flying very low, it went by the ship and then rocketed over the speeding rubber boat at tremendous speed, not 15 feet above the water. Whether by fright or confusion, this caused the two men on the suicide boat to kill their engine. Big mistake. Momentum carried them forward another 50 feet or so before they went dead in the water. Then the jet fighter appeared again. This time it was hovering right above them.

Few people on the cruise ship realized they were looking at a Harrier jump jet. It seemed able to do impossible things.

But while the strange plane was attracting so much attention, almost no one noticed that another aircraft, this one a black helicopter, had emerged from the darkness and had slipped down next to the rubber boat. A sniper with a night scope was hanging out of the helicopter's side door. He raised his weapon at the two masked men and pulled his trigger twice. Two perfect head shots. Two dead terrorists. Both toppled overboard.

Now another helicopter appeared. It, too, was painted black and was virtually without noise. Three soldiers rappelled down ropes to the rubber boat below. They worked quickly, hooking up a trio of hoist lines and connecting them to a pull cable beneath the helicopter. The men on the boat then gave the pilots a thumbs-up and the helicopter lifted the rubber boat out of the water, explosives and all. The helicopter lurched forward and disappeared back into the night. The Harrier vanished as well.

The first copter now turned its attention to the two yachts. It positioned itself parallel to the vessels, flying about one hundred feet off their starboard. The yachts were no longer tied together, but neither had they diverted from their straight-ahead course. Shadows aboard both vessels could be seen scrambling for their radio equipment. Others were pointing, but not firing, assault rifles at the silent black aircraft. The helicopter was waiting for something. . . .

This went on for about a minute, the final act in the drama unfolding for the passengers still crowded onto the cruise ship's rear decks. The yachts never attempted to get away. The helicopter simply kept pace with them.

What the cruise passengers didn't know was that a communications expert aboard the helicopter was listening in on radio traffic coming from the yachts. Both yachts were sending out frantic messages, in English and Arabic, detailing what had just happened. Shrill voices in the night, they were screaming into their radios that the attack on the *Sea Princess* had been thwarted by two helicopters and a fighter jet. The men on the yachts were desperate. They were requesting that somebody, somewhere, give them new instructions immediately: *"What should we do? Withdraw? Surrender? Ram the cruise liner ourselves?"*

Finally the radio expert aboard the helicopter gave a signal to his pilots. Just as long as the men on the yachts got word back to their superiors that the attack had been stopped by the trio of aircraft, that's all the terrorists' leaders had to know.

The helicopter increased power and turned 90 degrees. It was soon facing the first yacht. The men onboard knew they were trapped. They had no defense against the helicopter's huge gun and no place to seek cover. So they stood there, feet frozen to the deck, unable to move. The helicopter's minigun opened up on them from just 100 feet away, engulfing the yacht in a vivid orange glow. The three men were simply blown away. Still, the helicopter kept firing. Its cannon shells eventually found the yacht's fuel tank, causing an explosion so powerful the boat was thrown into the air. When it came back down, it was in thousands of tiny pieces.

The second yacht had killed its engines by this time. The men aboard knew what was to come, knew it was senseless to run. Illuminated by a powerful light beamed from the cruise liner's mast, the three men tore off their ski masks— they were Arabs—and, one after another, dived overboard. The helicopter fired three rockets into the yacht and it went up in three simultaneous explosions. The helicopter flew through the wreckage cloud and, using its own powerful searchlight, found the three terrorists in the water. It came down to just about sea level, almost as if it were going to rescue the floundering men. But the helicopter crew was not in the business of showing mercy. The marksman with the night-scope rifle took up his position again. The pleas from the terrorists could be heard all the way back on the *Sea Princess,* but they were in vain.

One by one the man with the rifle picked them off. The cruise ship passengers cheered as each one was hit. It took five shots in all, as one man tried his best to stay underwater. But soon enough, he was shot, too.

The only noise now was the incredibly soft whirring of

the helicopter's rotor blades. The incident seemed to play out over a lifetime for those who witnessed it. Yet it took only two minutes from beginning to end.

The cruise passengers were awestruck. They had been saved at the last possible moment from certain death—but by whom? Certainly not the Greek military. When the spotlight on the ship's mast finally caught the American flag emblazoned on the side of the helicopter, they had their answer. One man on the aft railing let out a great cheer. Then came another. And another.

In seconds, all of the passengers on the lower railings were cheering. Hundreds of seniors, pumping their fists in the air. Then those on the upper railings began cheering, too. Soon the entire ship was chanting: *"USA! USA!"*

The helicopter went over the top of the ship, fast and low. The cheering grew. The Harrier reappeared and roared over seconds later. The cheering got even louder.

In fact, the passengers were *still* cheering 30 minutes later when a Greek patrol boat finally arrived to escort them to the nearest port.

In all the excitement, few noticed the rusty containership *Ocean Voyager* passing close by in the night.

Chapter 5

The Harrier put itself into hover mode. Automatically . . . no buttons pushed, no levers thrown. All was ready for landing. The ship below was pitching wildly, the wind and rain growing fierce. But he was lining up his approach just right. And he was feeling good. The cannon on his airplane was empty. All his missiles had been fired, too. He'd played the Wings of Death game again last night and had loved every second of it. He was descending now, a large platform of gleaming metal his landing place. It was surrounded by a perfect circle of sailors, wearing dress blue uniforms and holding incandescent flares above their heads. They were not getting wet, though. The wind didn't seem to be blowing on them. He eased the Harrier down farther. Twenty feet to go. The sea spray grew vicious, but his descent was unnaturally smooth. This wasn't the way it was supposed to be. At 15 feet his headphones exploded with chatter. Something *was* wrong. He was supposed to be doing this in total radio silence, but the voices in his head were shouting, *Look at the front of the ship! Someone is standing up there!* It was the absolute worst thing to do, but he took his eyes off the controls and looked to the bow. And there she was . . . on the railing so far away, smiling and dry, wearing the same red dress, beckoning him to join her.

If only he could.

When he looked back down again, the ship and sailors were gone. There was nothing below but the sea. He hastily went to full-power ascent throttle, but instead of going up, he was going down. He hit the water, full force. The sea rushed into his cockpit, soaking him. He tried to unfasten his safety harness, but the snaps had rusted shut already. He was trapped.

And sinking like a stone. . . .

He woke with a start.

He sat up too quickly, cracking his skull on the bunk overhead. His heart was pounding. He was drenched in sweat. *Where the hell am I?* He wiped his eyes and looked around. . . . Slowly the surroundings fell into place. The tiny gray room. The double-tiered bunk. The metal bars holding canvas over the only window. *Oh Christ yeah, I know where I am.* Not a prison cell. It was his billet, aboard the containership *Ocean Voyager.*

The ship suddenly lurched to starboard. He grabbed the sides of his bunk and held on. He was Col. Ryder Long, U.S. Air Force. He didn't like ships. Especially this one. It was big and square and built to be overloaded. Nothing but bull rings and lashing bars held everything in place. If the sea got the least bit choppy and all that weight began moving back and forth, the ship would start to roll.

And it was rolling now.

He fumbled for his watch, hanging off the bunk post, staring at it through bleary eyes. 0730 hours? He'd been asleep for 90 minutes? It felt more like 90 seconds. He fell back on his sweaty bedsheets. He'd dreamed about his wife again. She came to him almost every night, popping up somewhere, always smiling, and always in the same red dress. For the life of him, he could not recall ever seeing her wear it before. *That was always strange. . . .*

He waited, lying still. Maybe the ship would settle down again. Maybe he could even go back to sleep. *Just five more minutes,* he thought. *Just let me close my eyes for five more minutes*. But then the ship's foghorn went off, loud enough to wake the dead. And the ship pitched back to starboard, knocking his shaving kit off the sink. The foghorn went off again. Something clanged loudly overhead. Then the ship rolled back to the left. That was it. He gave up. He crawled off the bunk and finally got to his feet.

The sink in the corner was rusty and gross. Still he drew some water from the faucet and splashed it on his face. It did no good. He began a slow, tortuous ritual of cracking bones and unknotting muscles. His back was a mess, his fingers and wrists always stiff. Common complaints of a Harrier pilot; it was not the easiest plane to fly, and he wasn't a kid anymore. But at least last night's mission had been a success. The mystery men at the bottom of *Ocean Voyager* had been tracking the Genoa-based terrorist cell for weeks, listening to their chatter, following their money, knowing they were planning to attack a large floating target sometime soon. The snooping paid off. The plot was uncovered, the timetable revealed. Nine terrorists KIA, four thousand people saved, mostly Americans. Not bad for a few hours' work. Ryder's only regret: he'd didn't have a chance to pop a couple of the mooks himself this time. But that was OK. There'd be more to come.

The ship moved again; he leaned against the wall for support. He ran his hands over his graying close-cropped hair. This was how most mornings started out these days. Thinking about Maureen, cursing his aching muscles, seasick, and wishing he'd been deeper into the body count the night before. Not exactly a bowl of cornflakes and the sports pages.

He climbed into his overalls and sneakers and made his way up to the deck, three levels above. It was foggy and the sea was choppier than he had thought it would be. Negotiating an obstacle course of ropes and steel cable, he reached the outer railing at midships. Where the hell were they now? Still in the Aegean? The western Med? Or heading back toward the Suez? He couldn't tell, and at that moment, he really didn't care. He lit a cigarette and took a long first drag. The ship's foghorn blew again, perfectly synched as he exhaled. He would never forget the scene last night. The passengers on the back of the cruise liner, cheering and waving, old people pumping their fists. That took some of the pain away.

Another drag and it began to rain. The ship rolled to port. He fished two amphetamine pills from his pocket and swallowed them dry. They were supposed to help with seasickness, but he always felt like he could use about ten more. The ship fell to starboard and then back to port again. It began raining harder. He was getting soaked. He power-puffed the Marlboro, then flicked the butt overboard.

So much for breakfast, he thought.

If homeliness and rust were the perfect disguise, the *Ocean Voyager* would have been invisible.

It looked like a typical containership. Eight hundred feet long, 105 feet wide, with a 60-foot drop from the top deck to the bottom of the cargo bay, it weighed 30,000 tons. When it was first built by Maersk back in 1981, its top speed was barely 15 knots.

There had been no need for glamour in the ship's original design and its builders had stuck to the plan. The deck was a nightmare of winches and tie-offs and thick rope strung tight everywhere. There were dozens of things to trip over, crack a knee on, or get crushed by, especially up near the bow. The recessed deckhouse offered a great view . . . of the smokestacks, the ladders, and the railings and, of course, all those containers on deck. They stretched out in front of an observer like a railroad yard somehow lost at sea.

Flat and boxy and dirt-dog ugly, the ship looked no different from hundreds of container carriers plying the world's oceans; dozens could be found at any time in the Mediterranean, or the Indian Ocean or the Persian Gulf.

But *Ocean Voyager* was not a containership. Not really.

Officially, it was an Air-Land Assault Ship/Special.

A warship. In disguise.

It was the British who first came up with the idea of launching jet aircraft from a containership.

During an era of drastic defense cuts in the 1970s, the

Royal Navy thought about putting heavy-load platforms
onto ordinary containerships from which their VTOL Harrier jump jets could operate. It was considered a cheap alternative to building a new generation of aircraft carriers.

The *Ocean Voyager* took the Brits' idea further. Much further. Two elevators, of the same type used on U.S. Navy aircraft carriers, had been installed side by side in front of the
deckhouse. They could move a load of several dozen tons up
from the cargo bay to the deck or vice versa. They were, in
essence, movable launch and recovery pads and had more
than enough muscle to handle a fighter jet or a couple helicopters. When the elevators were not in use, six empty containers
were rolled on top of them, hiding them from prying eyes.

And this was how the people on this ship had been able
to pull off the string of deadly counterterrorist attacks in
Lebanon, Somalia, the Aegean, and Yemen. The raids had all
originated from here, a moving, floating air base with the
perfect disguise. No one knew where they had come from
and no one knew where they went, because the Harrier jump
jet and the two Blackhawk helicopters and all of the raiders
they had carried to battle were hidden in the bottom of this
innocuous-looking ship.

But *Ocean Voyager*'s assets did not end with its tiny air
force and assault team. The ship also had its own naval warfare section, a huge internal logistic operation, and an intelligence station unrivaled anywhere on the globe. It could
both track and attack terrorists, almost at a whim, and in
complete secrecy. The team onboard had been set up to be
totally self-sufficient, able to run missions on its own, inde-
pendent of any oversight, and unencumbered by international law. In many ways, it was not unlike a "cell."

Concealed inside the containers on deck were the things
that could sustain such an operation. A full deck, meaning
about two hundred containers, could support the jump jet,
the rotary craft, and the small army of assault soldiers onboard for 45 days without need of resupply—except for the
aviation gas. The containers were painted as if they belonged
to different shipping companies, such as Sealift, BDT, and

Ocean Transport of Britain, to maintain the ruse. They seemed to be stacked in no particular order on the deck, but actually each was in place by means of a strict priority. A color coding system on the access door determined what was within. An orange stripe meant aircraft support: spare parts, control change-outs, tires, spare engines. Blue meant ammunition. Green was electronics. Yellow meant general support, the things needed to keep the ship itself running. White meant human support: drinking water, food, soap, T-paper, the essentials of life at sea.

There were also eight containers with red stripes on their doors. Two were bolted down at the front of the ship, two more were on each side at midships, and two more were located aft. These crates did not contain food or ammo or a spare mouse for someone's computer down below. Inside these containers were CIWS guns, modern, remote-controlled Gatling guns, fierce weapons that could spit out 600 rounds *a second*. With the ability to drop the sides of their containers at any time, these guns were on hand to prevent the ship from being hit by an antiship missile or anything else unfriendly, if its disguise should fail someday.

The ship was extremely high-tech. It had a Combat Control Center sunk into the first level of the deckhouse that would rival any found on a modern warship. Everything, from the CIWS guns, to the over-the-horizon radar, to its hidden satellite dishes, was run from here. The ship's controls were all automated; they, too, had come from a U.S. Navy aircraft carrier. Its original Mitsu engines had been torn out and replaced by four GE F110-400 gas turbines, the same engines that powered the Navy's F-14 Tomcat fighter. If they ever had to push it, these powerhouses could get the ship up to an astounding 40 knots or more.

It was at the bottom of the ship though, on the keel level, that the real treasures could be found. This was the heart of the listening station, four interconnected compartments known as the White Rooms. The crew called the people who worked down here Spooks. The compartments—air-conditioned, environmentally controlled, and virtually dirt

and dust–free—were crammed with some of the most sophisticated eavesdropping equipment ever conceived. In the
space of three 12-by-36-foot containers were devices that allowed the Spooks to intercept just about any E-mail sent
over the Internet, and just about any fax, telegram, or wire
cable, too. Satellite-relay stations in one container could tap
into the National Security Agency's ultrasecret Echelon system, meaning just about any telephone call made anywhere
around the globe could be tracked, recorded, listened in on,
or even altered. The containers also housed facilities where
CDs, hard drives, official documents, photographs, videos,
and DVDs could be manufactured or counterfeited. Fake TV
news reports could be broadcast from here, pirate radio pro-
grams created, newspapers and magazines replicated.

There was also a Dirty Tricks section where just about
anything from superitching powder to a nuclear warhead
could be conjured up.

It was in one of these rooms that the bombs used to level
the Rats' Nest had been built.

Whose idea was all this?

No one was really sure. When the ship first set sail for
the Middle East two months before, the 43 people onboard
had been told to keep the chatter among themselves to a
minimum. This was not such an unusual request in the
world of supersecret ops, where most people operated on a
need-to-know basis only. Everyone onboard had done a
good job keeping his mouth shut. Of course it was a relatively easy thing to do. There was no recreation room onboard, no TV room, no game hall. The only common
meeting area was the forward mess, and it was huge. The
crew ate in shifts, and usually everyone sat at his own table.
Between this and the long hours of training and doing mission preps, there really wasn't much opportunity for interac-
tion or information exchange.

This did not mean, however, that there were no rumors
onboard. Military ships floated on scuttlebutt, and just about
everyone aboard *Ocean Voyager* was military to some degree.

And everyone was familiar with the name of at least one person behind the mystery ship, and maybe the only one. That name was "Bobby Murphy."

How did they know this name? Because it was plastered just about everywhere on the ship. It was hard not to turn a corner, come to a bulkhead, or work on a piece of equipment anywhere onboard without seeing *Bobby Murphy Approved* scrawled in yellow chalk somewhere near it. From the bow to the stern, from the top of the deckhouse to the floor of the keel, anything that had been installed, refurbished, repainted, or rewired during the ship's transformation from hulk to secret warship had been given a stamp of approval by Bobby Murphy.

But *who* was he?

The *Ocean Voyager*'s commanding officer was a Navy captain named Wayne Bingham, "Captain Bingo" to everyone onboard. Bingo's CO had actually met Murphy shortly before the ship sailed from Newport News, Virginia, the site of its secret refitting. It had been a brief encounter, but the CO had told Bingo a few details of the chat. This was where the scuttlebutt began. A whisper here, a chance meeting there, and things get passed along, even on a ship full of sealed pie holes. After a few weeks at sea, the story of Bobby Murphy had been retold so many times, some variations bestowed an almost mythical nature on the man. He was a genius. He was insane. He possessed "a beautiful mind." He was a drunk. He was a highly paid government clairvoyant. He didn't exist.

The most often repeated story had Bingo's CO first asking Murphy just who he worked for. CIA? NSA? DIA? NIO? Murphy claimed he didn't know himself. He indicated that he'd spent time in all of these agencies, the DIA being his most recent. But, he also claimed, he'd been shuffled around so many times between them, due to his status as "a spy, par excellence," apparently sometimes he *didn't* know exactly who he was working for.

He knew a lot of people in Washington but quickly added that, in his case, this was not the same as having a lot of friends there. He claimed to have been called into secret trials to give testimony relating to the Middle East and Muslim terrorists, and indeed, Murphy was supposedly a walking encyclopedia on terrorist groups, and especially on the ways of Al Qaeda. Murphy had also bragged about having many friends in other countries' intelligence agencies, especially the European ones.

Though he'd claimed he was married, he admitted he wasn't sure where his wife was these days. She was not as in love with the spy game as he. He claimed to have a cadre of beautiful, highly paid prostitutes in place around the world, women he used to get what he could not get by other means. Supposedly a dozen of these beauties were working for him in the United States alone.

But how did the whole *Ocean Voyager* concept come about? It was another murky story, one with holes big enough to sail a battleship through. The most accepted version went like this: After the September 11th attacks, Murphy spent days browbeating his bosses at the DIA to do something—*anything*—to strike back at Al Qaeda. The DIA turned him down: they gathered intelligence; they didn't run operations, which he knew was a lie. He then went to the CIA and pleaded with them to let him plan a mission similar to Jimmy Doolittle's raid over Tokyo in the dark early days of World War II, something that would lift the morale of all Americans in the wake of 9/11. The CIA sat squarely on their thumbs for weeks, then months; no one wanted to take responsibility for OK'ing such a plan, no matter what form it might take. Murphy then went to Naval Intelligence, Air Force Intelligence, even the National Security Agency. All of them turned him down for the same reasons: too much risk and the fear of insulting both Arabs and allies around the world.

Time passed, but Murphy could not be deterred. He finally prevailed, so the story went, when by sheer pluck he managed to get a sit-down with the President himself. What he told the Chief Executive during the course of their 30-minute meeting was apparently known only to the President and Murphy himself. One account said Murphy promised to hunt down and eliminate every Al Qaeda operative connected to the attacks on 9/11, whether they be foot soldiers or financiers—and grease any other bad guys he found in between. Whatever the case, by the time he walked out of the Oval Office, Murphy had been given a blank check to essentially do his thing.

The assurances to keep it *ultra*secret were all there, too: The President promised absolutely no oversight, no justifications, no receipts. No micromanaging from Washington, no reports to be filed, no debriefings needed. Murphy had been given access to whatever military resources he wanted. He had a lengthy shopping list. The 18 helicopter troops came from Delta Force, America's best-trained, most secret special operations group. The Blackhawk pilots were from Air Force Special Ops, the best at driving copters in and out of tight spaces. The ship itself was run by a company of handpicked U.S. Navy sailors, each one given the highest security clearance possible. A Marine Air maintenance squad took care of the aircraft hidden below. Murphy claimed that he'd personally selected every person for the secret unit himself sight unseen and as proof rattled off for Bingo's CO the names of just about every soul who would eventually come onboard.

Murphy got everything he asked for and more—and as a result this was no ordinary secret ops team. There were no uniforms. No IDs. All orders were given verbally. Nothing was ever written down. The ship never took a call or a radio message from Washington or any U.S. government agency. They never spoke with the Pentagon. They communicated, only when they had to, with a top-secret NSA computer site, located in a typical house in a typical suburban neighborhood somewhere in New Jersey known as Blueberry Park. The only way information could be sent and received from this location was via a porn site chat room on the Internet.

So the operation wasn't being run by the generals or the admirals or any U.S. intelligence agency or even by the White House itself. It wasn't being run by anybody. Again, this meant the team would not encounter any red tape when planning or executing an operation. It would be under no constitutional restrictions as to what it could do, when or where, or to whom. *That* was the beauty of Murphy's idea. The unit was self-contained. On its own. And so hush-hush, even the President himself didn't know all the details, if any at all.

Bingo's CO supposedly left him an E-mail that summed up Murphy this way:

A highly educated loose cannon. A very hands-on, very patriotic guy. He'll get things done either quietly or with a bang. He's brash, cocky, unpredictable, cold-blooded. He's out for revenge against the Arab terrorists, and seems almost maniacal in that pursuit. He's vowed not to rest until every mook connected with 9/11 has been taken out and appears as fanatical as they are in fulfilling his goal.

Now, if you give a guy like that a billion dollars these days, what do you get? You get a guy who secretly buys a containership, turns it into something from a James Bond movie, arranges to get Harriers and choppers and Spooks and even some Delta guys onboard, all so they can go out and get down and dirty with Al Qaeda. To get down and fight at their level, with no political correctness bullshit to get in the way, and then disappear once the deed has been done. Is it a good idea? Who knows? Either he's nuts or I am.

• • •

How did Ryder get involved in this?

Sometimes he wondered that himself. He'd had an interesting military career up to this point. Originally doomed to flying C-130 cargo planes after completing Air Force flight training, he somehow got slotted into fighter jets. He became so good at it, he was tapped as part of a secret program to be one of the first Air Force guys to go through the Navy's famous Top Gun air combat school. He performed so well there, more covert assignments followed. He excelled at flying tough and keeping his mouth shut, and soon he was involved in some of the darkest secret operations ever undertaken by the

U.S. military. The stories he could tell would make Ian Fleming's hair curl.

In between all the black ops, Ryder did airframe testing at Edwards Air Force Base, including the VTOL version of the new F-35 fighter. Later on he flew new plane tryouts at Nellis AFB, which was just outside Las Vegas and practically a stone's throw from his front door. He was transferred to the Reserves to free up his schedule and finally started giving the black op opportunities to younger guys. Then, at the age of 44, when he had 20 years' service staring him in the face, he got an offer to test fly for Boeing. He'd be a civilian, but it was more money than he'd ever dreamed of making.

Then, September 11th. The day his dreamworld came to an end.

His wife, Maureen, was an on-air TV reporter. Beautiful, blond, and smart, she'd done local news in Las Vegas but had been featured on many national spots as well. She'd flown to Boston earlier that week to do a report on a massive highway project there called the Big Dig. Her assignment wrapped up a day early. She got a seat at the last moment on United Flight 175 to LA. It was the plane that hit the second tower. Back home in Vegas, Ryder had fallen asleep on the couch the night before, typically with the TV on and his cell turned off. He woke up just in time to see it all happen in living color.

No good-byes. No final phone call.

His wife was simply gone forever.

How do you live after that? How do you walk or talk or breathe? He stumbled around his house for days, smashing his phone to bits and telling the local media horde pounding on his door to go to hell. How could they ever understand what he was going through? Her running shoes were still waiting by the back door. Her tiny garden out back needed weeding. The dresses in her closet. A sweater left on the bed. He didn't touch any of it. He couldn't.

Weeks went by. He didn't work. He didn't sleep. Eventually he moved out. He went to a motel on the other side of town and it was here, alone, that he went through the

predictable stages of grief. Denial, anger, depression—
wrenching, all three. But he missed one. The last one.

Acceptance. . . .

That was the hurdle he just couldn't get over. The fact that
she was really gone. Just couldn't. Booze. Sleeping pills.
Even prayer, an embarrassment on his knees. Nothing
worked. In his stupors, he began wondering if maybe going
to heaven wasn't a crock of shit after all, maybe it was a way
to see her again, and whether it was better to go slow by the
bottle or quick via the muzzle of his hunting rifle.

That's when the phone rang. It was very early in the dark
morning, but Ryder recognized the voice from the past right
away. It was a guy named Lieutenant Moon. He'd been in-
strumental in getting Ryder involved in many black ops over
the years. Moon knew about Ryder's loss and, in a very short
conversation, solved Ryder's problem of getting over the
last stage of Maureen's death. How? By presenting him with
another option. By giving him the opportunity to leapfrog
over that fourth stage of grief, that big sticking point, that
deepest of human emotion, and go on to a fifth: *Revenge*.

"A friend of mine is starting a program . . ." was all Moon
had to say. Ryder didn't even let him finish the sentence. He
just asked him where and when, and Moon told him.

He was packed and gone by noon.

Ryder returned to his cabin now, took a shower, and did his
morning business. Then he walked to the forward mess hall,
looking to find some coffee. The mess was a cavernous
place, low-lit and gloomy and, like his cabin, a study in dirty
gray. There were a half-dozen people scattered around the
20 or so tables. No one was talking to anyone.

Ryder took a seat in the corner, near a covered-over
porthole. A galley sailor was at his side a moment later. He
put before Ryder a huge platter bearing two tenderloin
steaks, a baked potato, and a half a loaf of hot bread. A cup
of coffee and a stick of butter also materialized. Ryder
stared at the meal. His pep pills, free for the asking at the

sick bay, were just beginning to kick in. Did he really want to eat all this?

"Those are the orders," the sailor told him. "Everyone on-board gets steak today."

At that moment an Army officer strolled into the mess. His name was Martinez. He was a full colonel and an obvious up-and-comer, as he was at least 10 years younger than Ryder. Martinez was tall and rugged, with a dark complexion and movie-star looks. He was rarely seen without a cigar hanging out of his mouth.

Martinez had two jobs. He was the commanding officer of the Delta group and the intelligence officer for the ship. He did all the planning for the unit's counterterror strikes, he coordinated the land, sea, and air assets, he researched the targets, and he made sure everyone got back in one piece. Martinez probably worked harder and slept less than anybody else onboard, Ryder included.

The team owed a lot to Martinez already. For the first 30 days of the mission, *Ocean Voyager* had sailed in circles around the frigid South Atlantic, far away from the sea-lanes, burning gas while everyone onboard got their act together. Their objective was to become nothing less than in-visible, at least whenever they were leaving or returning to the ship. Delta and the Air Force pilots trained endlessly during this period, especially in how to load up their special Blackhawks and take off quickly. The Marine Aviation guys also drilled hard at keeping the two choppers and the Harrier in top condition, bombed up and ready to go, 24/7—not an easy task in the salt-heavy marine environment. Ryder himself constantly practiced landing the jump jet on the moving ship, in all weather conditions, day and night, at 5 knots or 20. (This was not so easy, either. The Navy liked to brag that landing a supersonic jet on an aircraft carrier was the most difficult thing a combat pilot could do. "Like having sex during a car crash," they said, because when you hit that arresting wire, you went from 120 knots to 0 in two seconds. But getting the temperamental Harrier to set down exactly where it was supposed to, in rough seas, at night, with no radio, no lights—that could be like a car crash, too. Without the sex.)

It was Martinez who'd run these unorthodox training sessions. He proved to be a whiz at directing the movements of big machines flying close to each other. Gradually, the team came together. By the end of that first month, Delta could load into the choppers and be airborne inside five minutes, while Ryder could get his jump jet into the air in half that time. And upon their return, they could all get belowdecks in three minutes flat, lowering their exposure to the outside world to the barest minimum. What might have seemed impossible at first—disparate units working as one—became routine. Much of the credit had to go to Martinez.

So, even though Martinez was younger than him, Ryder had come to respect the Delta boss, at least from a distance. He was a by-the-book type certainly, but out here, all alone, that was the best way to be. Martinez also had a certain bearing to him, proud and refined. If you ever insulted him, though, it would be no surprise if he drew a sword and challenged you to a duel, right there on the spot.

Because of the edict that team members refrain from too much fraternization, Ryder and Martinez had talked infrequently since coming aboard, and only about operational stuff. Ryder knew nothing about the Delta officer's personal life. The only clue was a tiny badge Martinez always wore over his shirt pocket. Inside was a photograph of a pretty 18-something girl, bordered by a black ribbon, obviously a very personal item.

As far as Ryder knew, no one had the balls to ask Martinez whose picture it was.

Upon entering the mess, Martinez walked directly to Ryder's table and sat down.

"What do you want?" Martinez asked him.

"To kill mooks," Ryder replied without hesitation.

"No, I mean for your steak," Martinez said. "It's from Japan. Kobe beef. Most expensive in the world. Murphy sent it to us."

Ryder just shrugged. "They got A-1 here?"

Martinez motioned to someone in the galley. A coffee cup full of steak sauce appeared. Ryder dumped it all over his meal.

"Good work last night," Martinez told him. "I just saw the mission tapes. Can you believe all those old dudes video-taping the whole thing?"

Ryder looked back at him strangely. This was already the longest conversation he'd ever had with the Delta officer.

"We'll be playing on four thousand VCRs back in the states inside a week," Ryder finally replied with his first bite. "Not to mention all the news shows. I thought the idea was to stay secret."

Martinez waved his concerns away. "That's all been taken care of," he said mysteriously. "How's the cow?"

"It's excellent," Ryder replied honestly. "I'm glad Murphy is so concerned about our appetites."

"Keep that happy feeling then," Martinez told him. "Because today is your lucky day."

"It is? Why?"

"You're getting a wingman. Murphy's decided two jump jets are better than one."

Ryder was mildly shocked. He'd just assumed he'd be the lone fixed-wing in the unit.

"Can the air techs really handle *two* Harriers? Keeping mine in shape seems to be a full-time job already."

Martinez laughed. "Hey, they're Marines—they're sup-posed to be able to handle anything."

Ryder took another huge bite of steak. "Do you know the new guy's name? Or have we already fraternized for too long?"

"We probably have—but I'll tell you anyway," Martinez said. "His name is Gerry Phelan. I don't know his age, ori-gin, or rank. He's just out of the Marines' hot school for Har-rier training, though I understand he's actually in the Navy Reserve."

Ryder thought about this for a moment, then went back to his steak. The ship started rolling again.

"That's great," he said dryly. "If you've got to be on the water, you can never have too many Navy guys around."

Ryder was back up on deck 30 minutes later.

The sun had come out and the sea had settled down again. He was able to enjoy a smoke for a change. They were still in the Med; he could tell by the color of the water. They were heading west, though, which meant Sicily was most likely just north of them and Algeria or Libya just to the south. An interesting part of the world. . . .

A handful of Delta guys jogged by him. The highly trained special ops troops were constantly running around the ship, lugging weights, staying in shape, working on their tans. They looked like teenagers. *Bastards . . .* Ryder thought. A few weeks ago, he'd been caught in a traffic jam in a passageway with several of the Delta operators. One collided with him unintentionally and apologized by saying, "Excuse me . . . *sir.*"

It was like someone twisted a knife in Ryder's chest. The way the soldier had said that word—*sir.* Ryder knew he wasn't using it in the vernacular of officer and enlisted man, more the way a young student would address his elderly college professor. *Excuse me . . . sir.* Ryder had noticed his hair getting a little bit grayer every day after that.

He glanced up at the open bridge. The Navy guys were making their breakfast. Or was it lunch? Or dinner? It was hard to tell on the ship. With so many schedules, and people dealing with events in so many different time zones, the ship had no real set time of its own. In any case, the Navy guys had a big grill on the upper deck where they would prepare food while on duty, usually bacon and eggs or grits—but today definitely steak. You could smell it all over the ship. That aroma was the unofficial start of the day for *Ocean Voyager.*

But it was really closer to 10:00 A.M. His new partner was due any minute.

No jet driver would ever turn down a wingman. Another set of eyes and ears could only help when up on a mission. But not just anyone would do.

Ryder had had some great second bananas in his career. A guy named J. T. Woods stood out among them. He'd been a superior flier, all nuts and guts, and had been a good friend, too. Officially, he'd been lost in action during a very black op about 15 years ago. Ryder looked around the massive undercover ship now. What would old Woody have thought of this?

A bell up on the bridge started ringing. This was a very low-tech early-warning system the Navy guys had rigged up. They had an ultraadvanced over-the-horizon radar installed in the combat center that could spot anything flying within 20 miles of the ship dead-on, even something that had been dipped in stealth paint. Whenever a bogie was picked up on this radar set, someone would ring the bell. This meant anyone who wasn't dressed like a Filipino crewman had to clear the deck immediately, as something was about to fly overhead. The bell always set off a predictable scramble, with those crewmen wearing battle fatigues going down the chutes as if they were in a U-boat that had been told to dive, sometimes carrying their breakfasts with them. The deck could be cleared in under a minute this way, usually in plenty of time for everything to become "normal," at least looking down from above.

But this time Ryder didn't bother to move. He knew the sound of a Harrier engine by now—at least he thought he did. His ears had been bothering him lately, too. He waited and the noise got louder. Then finally he saw it. A jump jet, coming out of the south, starting to curve into a long elliptical orbit around the ship.

Someone in the combat control room was talking to the pilot by now, he was sure, not on the radio but on an SCP, a satellite cell phone. For security purposes, this was how the ship communicated with its tiny air force. Cell phone mikes and speakers had been installed in everyone's crash helmets; the dialers had been sewn into their flight suit knee pads. Landing instructions, responses, and replies were all set in code, using words heard frequently during shipping operations. On special occasions, or when things got too hairy to speak in code, the SCPs also had a scrambler mode, which could distort any two-way conversation for up to 30 seconds. This quickly drained the phone's internal batteries, though, and was used only as a last resort.

The incoming Harrier got a 20-mile clearance, too, meaning nothing was within 20 miles of the ship in any direction. This was the designated time frame in which a jump jet could land or take off from *Ocean Voyager*. Anything closer and the pilot would have to fly away for a while and wait until he was called back for another try.

But the all-clear was sounded, via the ship's equally low-tech foghorn, once the CAC got a visual and confirmed that this guy was a friendly. The Harrier glided over the ship with admirable precision just a minute later. Ryder straightened a little. This speed jockey looked good, thank God. This was not a mission to have a wet noodle watching your six. Three containers had been rolled away and one of the aircraft elevators appeared from below. It arrived with a whoosh of clean hydraulic power. Following hand signals from a trio of Marine Aviation guys, the Harrier slotted in perfectly above the mobile landing platform, known to all as the pancake. As Ryder well knew, matching a hover with the speed of a moving ship was an art that would take even a test pilot a while to master. Yet this guy was doing it with ease.

The plane started coming down. Like Ryder's Harrier, this jump jet had been "ghosted," upgraded in the area of radar avoidance. The plane had been coated with a thick black and gray paint to absorb unfriendly radar signals. Movable heat deflectors had been installed to cool its various jet exhausts. All the plane's sharpest angles had been smoothed over, and anything that had been previously hanging off the fuselage or wings was now recessed inside them. The plane even had a specially tinted canopy, nearly opaque from the outside. In other words, the jump jet was now stealthy, and, ironically looked more like the original British version of the plane, than the current U.S. model.

Ryder stepped back; so did the Marines. They'd seen

Ryder land enough times to know that whenever a Harrier came down there was a bounce and then a flare of hot thrust deflecting off the pancake. The new pilot didn't need their help anymore, so they'd moved off to safer footing.

But this Harrier came in so perfectly, it touched down without anything remotely resembling a thump. Nor was there any hot kick-up. This, too, brightened Ryder's spirits. The person behind such a smooth landing *must* have had at least as much flying time as he, possibly more. Chances were good he was a real veteran, in both service and age.

"This guy will be ancient," Ryder predicted aloud.

The Harrier shut down, its canopy popped, and the pilot climbed out. Ryder took one look at him and nearly fell off the boat.

He looked younger than the Delta guys.

They met at the edge of the pancake. He was short, as many fighter pilots were. Maybe five-seven on a good day. He took off his crash helmet to reveal a cross-cropped surfer dude haircut. He also had a pair of Walkman-type earphones wrapped around his neck. The wire led into his left-side breast pocket, where a mini–CD player was located.

Ryder introduced himself and they shook hands. Phelan was a lieutenant, Ryder was a colonel, but there was no need to salute here.

It sounded like a line from a movie, but Ryder just had to ask him. "How did you learn how to fly like that?"

Phelan smiled—it was a Pepsodent smile. "Well, the Navy paid for it, but the Marines were the ones who taught me, sir. . . ."

There was that word again.

Ryder pointed to the earphones. "And you listen to music in the cockpit, Lieutenant?"

Phelan was looking around, taking in his new surroundings. "Had to do the jump in radio silence, sir," he said plainly. "So why not?"

Ryder started to say something—but stopped. What was there to say, really? The kid came across not so much cocky as supremely self-confident, in that rookie sort of way. Typical of the Top Gun, Navy jock, Tailhook crowd.

He reminded him of someone, though. His mannerisms, the attitude.

But try as he might, Ryder just couldn't remember who.

Chapter 6

That night

There was one drawback to the Air-Land Assault Ship/Special concept.

It had to do with the aviation gas. A Harrier could go through tons of it, literally, in just a few flights. A bulked-up stealthy one burned that much more. The helicopters were also gas guzzlers, but nothing compared to the jump jet. The problem was, the ship could only keep so much JP-8 av fuel onboard. Space on *Ocean Voyager* was at a premium despite its size, and there were safety concerns as well. There had been no good place to set up a fuel reservoir big enough to meet just the fixed-wing asset's needs, so the copters and the jet had to draw from the same tank, an uneven feeding. (The ship could carry just about enough gas to keep the three of them flying off and on for 14 days.) The rest of the available tank space was taken up by fuel needed to run the ship's turbine propulsion engines.

Keeping the gas supply up then was an ongoing concern. It wasn't like they could get a hose boost from a passing Navy fuel ship anytime they needed some extra fuel. Nothing would blow their cover quicker. So Murphy had devised an alternative system. On prearranged nights, Ryder would take the jump jet up to meet an in-flight refueling plane. These aerial gas pumps were almost always USAF KC-10

Extenders, usually flying out of bases in Europe or the Middle East. Their crews knew only that an American Harrier needed a drink, nothing more. If Ryder wasn't going on a mission, he would fill his internal tanks and some spares on his wing. He'd float back down to the ship and the Marine Aviation guys would drain the extra fuel off into auxiliary buddy tanks for use later on. To have a four-day supply of gas dedicated just to the jump jet was considered optimum. Now that Phelan was onboard, though, that requirement would have to double.

Ryder had run the nocturnal refueling drills several dozen times since the *Ocean Voyager* started operations. They weren't growing on him. The flying part wasn't bad. It was finding the tanker. The Extenders were usually on time and at the right altitude. But locating them on the vertical plane took both skill and luck, especially in bad weather.

And it all had to be done without any lights and, of course, no radio.

It was 2350 hours when Ryder and Phelan took off. They were going out on a mission, their first together, even though they hadn't spoken more than a few words to each other since the junior pilot came aboard. Ryder had barely introduced himself to the young pilot when the typical workday aboard ship kicked into gear. They were both summoned to the CAC by Martinez to be briefed on what would prove to be a long night of multiple assignments. A lengthy airplane prep came next, then a few hours to nap, another to suit up, and the final premission brief. Then it was time to go.

The long night had to begin with one of the aerial fill-ups, though, as both Harriers were low on gas. They'd been told the weather above the ship was clear up 5,000 feet, but after that it would be solid overcast for a while. They went through the first cloud layer with no problems. The cumulus was moving fast, as it always did above the Med at night. They were promised a full moon after 12,000 feet. The tankers always flew at 20,000.

They were going nearly straight up, Ryder out front,

Phelan off his right tail, exactly where he was supposed to be. They had reached 11-5 when suddenly an enormous silver shape came out of the night and went over their heads. It was moving so quickly, Ryder and Phelan had no chance to react. It was not the tanker. It was an Italian airliner, Alitalia Flight 7544, Rome to Tunis. Ryder and Phelan had come within 500 feet of it—but it never saw them because the Harriers were ghosts; their signatures would barely register on a military radar. Never would they show up on an airliner's screen.

This crisis passed only to be followed by another. They popped through the cloud layer at 12,000 feet but found no moon. Wrong forecast? Wrong time? Wrong altitude?

Nope. The moon was being obscured—by an oncoming sandstorm. A big one.

The Africans called them *haboobs*. Clouds of desert sand and dust that looked like gigantic fists, rising with the wind and the heat of the day. Blowing unobstructed across the Med, they could make flying very unpleasant.

Ryder had ridden out two of these monsters already and he wasn't looking forward to a third. He guessed that the sandstorm would arrive in their part of the sky in about ten minutes. They still had to find the gas truck, hook up, get a drink, and split. Was it possible to do all that in such a short amount of time?

They climbed to 20 Angels and found the tanker just a minute later, right where it was supposed to be. How Murphy was able to arrange these secret refuelings no one knew, but the tankers had not failed them yet. It took another minute for the Harriers to get the right speed and altitude, communicating only through the quick blinking of their navigation lights. The KC-10 could only serve one ship at a time, so Ryder hooked up first. He was full in three minutes. With one eye on the sandstorm, he unhooked and drifted off the nipple.

Phelan went up and in and fucked the duck. But then the Extender started shaking, and Phelan started shaking with it. The windspeed at 20,000 feet had suddenly doubled. Phelan was smart enough to break off contact and then reinsert once the big tanker settled down. But the turbulence came again, not once, but twice. Ryder was riding right alongside Phelan, but there was little he could do except watch his wingman bounce all over the sky, a long nasty stream of fuel spurting from the Extender's boom. Phelan kept his cool, though. He finally hooked a fourth time and hung on long enough to take a full gulp. Then he flashed his lights once and disengaged.

The tanker immediately banked south, its ordeal over, and disappeared into the clouds, intent on escaping the worst of the *haboob*.

Ryder and Phelan turned north.

Chapter 7

The huge explosion rocked the tiny village of Sardarno just after midnight.

The village police chief was thrown from his bed by the force of the blast. He landed in the far corner of the bedroom, a dresser smashing against the wall next to him. His wife, all 327 pounds of her, was also hurled to the floor, their modest bed stand collapsing on top of her. Every window in their house blew out instantly; their kitchen ceiling came crashing down. Outside, half their flock of pet geese died on the spot—of heart attacks. All this in just a few seconds, and the ground was still shaking.

The chief—his name was Roberto Tino—thought it was the end of the world. Anything less wouldn't have sounded so loud.

He slowly got to his feet, stepped over his wife, and retrieved his eyeglasses. He pulled the torn curtains from the bedroom's broken window and looked out.

The night sky was on fire. A red-and-orange spire of flame was rising out of the west. Tino wiped his glasses clean and then realized the flames were coming from the top of Monte Fidelo, the tallest peak in a line of remote hills outside Sardarno. Monte Fidelo was nearly 2,000 feet high—and four miles away from Tino's farmhouse. Yet the glow was so intense, his roosters were crowing. It was that bright outside.

Tino finally had gone to help his wife when the telephone rang. Stepping over her again, he picked it up to hear the very anxious voice of the village mayor on the other end. The mayor was 91 years old but still a pistol. Tino couldn't believe he'd been able to dial his phone number so fast.

The mayor had also been thrown from his bed—and he lived inside the village, more than five miles from the peak. He asked if Tino's house was still intact; the explosion had been so violent, he'd assumed everything between the village and Fidelo had been leveled.

Tino replied that his house was still standing, but that it looked like the summit of the Fidelo was engulfed in flame. Was it an *eruzione,* the mayor asked him urgently. An eruption of a volcano? That's what everyone in the village thought. People were fleeing toward the sea, many still in bedclothes, expecting to be overtaken by lava at any moment.

Tino didn't think this was a volcanic eruption. A plane crash, maybe. Nevertheless, the mayor ordered him to get as close as he could to the hill and investigate. Tino began to protest. They'd received an order from the *Carabinieri,* the Italian national police, earlier that very day telling them to stay away from Monte Fidelo and keep any civilians away from the peak as well. (This was not a hard thing to do, as the area was very isolated and only one dirt road ran in and out.) No official reason was given for this order, but the national police had been adamant.

"Maybe this is why they didn't want us to go near it," Tino reasoned to the mayor. He knew a little more about Monte Fidelo than he was letting on.

But the mayor couldn't have cared less about the *Carabinieri*. He was convinced Monte Fidelo was erupting and he wanted Tino to go up there and prove him wrong.

Tino just shrugged and hung up. Orders were orders and the mayor was his boss. So Tino slipped on his boots, grabbed his rifle, and headed out the door. As he passed over his wife, still on the floor, he heard her gently snoring.

No reason to wake her up now, he thought.

Tino jumped into his Toyota jeep and began driving west, toward the glowing hill.

There was a villa at the top of Fidelo. It was very old, with 12 rooms and a spectacular view of the Mediterranean, a mile over some very rough terrain to the south. In telling Tino to stay away from the hilltop the *Carabinieri* had also asked him to report any unusual activity around the area, but again they never said why. Just after receiving their communiqué, Tino had called a friend at the state police base in Palermo asking if he knew what it was all about. He did. The villa had recently been leased by 16 men of Middle Eastern descent. They'd all claimed on their rental application to be "physicians and religious students." Their previous address had been a rooming house in Genoa. The national police suspected these men were terrorists and that the villa was rented as a staging point for their operations. Plus, something strange had happened in the Aegean Sea the night before that might be connected with all this.

The *Carabinieri* higher-ups in Rome were going to move on this information very soon, Tino's friend revealed. He suggested it was best that the police chief obey their order.

"Questa non e una cosa da coinvolgeri," his friend had told him. "This is nothing to get mixed up in. . . ."

Tino arrived at the bottom of Monte Fidelo ten minutes later. The flames shooting out of the peak had intensified. But he didn't see any lava or whatever else might come rolling down the side of a volcano.

He checked his rifle. It was loaded, but only with birdshot. Not much of a punch, but it would have to do. He looked to the summit again and blessed himself. The glow was even brighter. The air around him was getting hot. He vowed to ask the mayor for a raise after this.

He put his Jeep into low gear and started up the hill. It was more than 1,900 feet to the top. The villa was located just below the peak, on the south side. There was a huge abandoned vineyard directly in front of the main house. Thick woods and rock covered the other three sides of the hill.

Tino quickly passed the 500-foot mark but had to slow down as he neared 1,000 feet. The Jeep's engine was breathing hard and the road went nearly straight up from here. The flames were climbing even higher as he reached the 1,500-foot point. He pulled to the side of the road and stuck his head out the window. He could hear the roar of the fire, the crackle of wood and old vines burning. The smoke was getting thick.

But he pressed on.

His Jeep was just about to quit when he reached the 1,800-foot mark. Here he found a trail leading to the villa.

He got out, locked his doors, and checked his rifle one more time. Then he started walking cautiously toward the flames. The wind was blowing clouds of glowing sparks all the way to the ocean, a mile away. That's why the sky seemed to be on fire. Tino had never seen anything like it.

He walked out of the woods and onto the pathway leading directly to the villa's front door. The door was still standing. But the rest of the villa was gone.

Tino was shocked. There was *nothing* left. The villa had encompassed five separate houses, one of which had been four stories tall. But everything was just . . . gone. There could be no doubt about this: an explosion had taken place up here, one so powerful, it had blown the compound into dust.

The flames were coming from the cellar, the only portion of the main house still intact. Between the path and where the house used to be Tino spotted the remains of six adults. Their bodies were twisted into grotesque positions; all had been horribly burned. They'd been running from the house when the blast went off.

Several nearby residents now arrived on the scene. They'd been about a minute behind Tino in climbing the hill. Tino did not order them away. This was a vision of hell up here, and at the moment he welcomed the company. He did, however, stop them from entering the field where the bodies were located. He asked them what they had seen or heard prior to the explosion. Two reported seeing low-flying helicopters in the area just minutes before the blast but claimed they could not hear them. Tino discounted these reports right away: helicopters always made a racket; he knew of none that could fly silently. Another villager, an Army veteran, told him the wreckage spray indicated an enormous blast must have originated *above* the main house and not inside it. He pointed out that all of the villa's walls had been blown downward before they were vaporized. His guess was a large cache of explosives had been detonated just a few feet from the villa's roof, literally blowing the structure into the ground. Tino's conclusion: someone had bombed the suspected terrorists occupying the house. But who?

There was only one clue. It came with a strange discovery made by another villager who had driven up to the scene but had parked lower on the hill. Walking through the abandoned vineyard, he came upon something very puzzling. Those up near the burning house heard him shouting and made their way to his location. They found him studying the wreckage not of a car or truck or even an aircraft, but of an outboard motor, the type typically used on a large speedboat. It was embedded in a bramble of old vines and was still too hot to touch. Obviously, it had been thrown here as a result of the blast.

But this didn't make sense. The Fidelo was nearly a half-mile high; the villa was at its summit. The only means of land access was by four-wheel drive, and the road was so steep it was impossible to tow anything up. Plus the nearest deep water was a mile away—and a long way down.

How then did a speedboat motor get way up here?

The place was called Ben Annaba.

It was a small oasis village about fifteen miles in from the Algerian coastal city of El Kala.

Ben Annaba was the headquarters of a terrorist group

known as the Holy Islamic Army of God. They were part of Al Qaeda, though one of its smallest components. The government in Algiers wasn't Muslim enough for the Holy Army, so they had vowed to change it. To do this, they had taken to attacking isolated desert towns and butchering the occupants. Men, women, children—everyone got chopped up in the name of Allah.

Traveling on motorbikes and in high-speed desert SUVs, the Holy Army was always long gone before the Algerian military could arrive on the scene. They moved so fast, in fact, sometimes the military didn't bother to come at all.

Bobby Murphy had somehow come upon a videotape shot inside the stronghold at Ben Annaba. Using the secure porn site in New Jersey, he'd fed this footage to *Ocean Voyager*'s White Rooms in bits and pieces, disguised as mpgs. The tape showed the Holy Army's command facilities in the center of the town, with the terrorists' living quarters and training areas on its periphery. Murphy had also drawn a map of the camp, which he sent as a jpg file. The drawing was so detailed, it looked like a photograph.

The videotape keyed in on one barracks marked: *BAYT ASHUHADA,* loosely Arabic for "House of Martyrs." This was where Al Qaeda members stayed when visiting their *mujahideen* brethren at Ben Annaba. Murphy's information said up to 20 "martyrs" were in residence at the camp, along with their families.

Then there was another building, located next to the main command hut. It was covered with crude drawings warning against bringing any open flames near. Murphy was certain this structure was the Holy Army's ammunition dump.

Ryder's primary mission tonight was simple: put a thousand-pound bomb into the House of Martyrs and another into the No Smoking building. If he had any time to spare, he should strafe the encampment as well.

The trip up to Sicily went off without a hitch. The Blackhawks had ingressed at their assigned point, one of them carrying the raft full of explosives picked up during the rescue

of the *Sea Princess* the night before. The planning for the
terrorists' attempt to sink the cruise liner had indeed taken
place inside the villa atop Monte Fidelo. The explosives that
were eventually packed aboard the suicide raft had been kept
inside the villa as well. This had been confirmed by cell-
phone intercepts pulled down by the Spooks in *Ocean Voyager*'s White Rooms. Once the information was in hand, no
one was in the mood to wait for the Italian national police to
act. Besides, returning the explosives, raft, engine and all to
their point of origin was a message to other terrorist cells:
We know who did this and this is how they paid for it. And
when we find you, you'll pay, too. . . .

Once the Blackhawks were safely over land, Ryder and Phelan turned back over the Med and went their separate ways.
Ryder would have no wingman for the second half of this
night. Phelan went off to a point southeast of *Ocean Voyager,*
to fly a sort of flanking picket duty. Ryder meanwhile had
headed southwest, toward Algeria.

He went under the Algerian radar net with no problems.
His radar signature was less than that of a bird. Once over
the coast, finding the target was easy, thanks to the coordi-
nates supplied by Murphy and his hand-drawn map. The
camp was in the middle of a large, bare valley, bordered on
three sides by coastal mountains. There were about twenty
buildings sitting on the edge of the large oasis, most of them
pink stucco structures, set low among hundreds of palm
trees and other North African fauna.

Ryder came over the top of the mountain 15 miles north
of the camp and went down to 200 feet. No one would hear
him coming, not until he made his first pass over the camp.
He clicked on his FLIR mount. This device gave him a
thermal image of the camp, now just 10 miles away. He
could see the smoke from a few campfires and some thermal ghosts, actually a bunch of guards, sitting at the edge
of the oasis. A quick scan of the rest of the compound
showed no SAMs in evidence, no big antiaircraft weaponry
at all.

· · ·

He screeched in at treetop level and put the first bomb right on target. He would later swear he saw the 1,000-pounder go through the front door of the House of Martyrs. The bomb exploded and the building blew apart. The kinetic energy alone of a half-ton of steel hitting something at high speed could cause an enormous explosion. This was a half-ton of high explosives. The fireball was so intense, it flicked Ryder's tail as he climbed out and exited to the east.

All hell broke loose inside the camp. Suddenly people were running everywhere. And lights were coming on all over the village, not a smart thing to do when someone was bombing you at night. Heart pounding, Ryder went up and back and over. He boosted the FLIR screen. All he could see now was the flare from the huge fire he'd just started, with many thermal ghosts running through the flames. He located the second target—the No Smoking house—and locked it into his weapons delivery computer. He left the FLIR hot this time, allowing him to stay on target despite the thickening smoke.

Many people were running near the No Smoking house, but no one was running out of it. So Murphy had been right; this was the Holy Army's ammo locker. Ryder prepped the second bomb drop. He put his speed at 245 knots, a fast approach guaranteed to knock some socks off. He queried the weapons release system; it came back as green and ready. He was now 10 seconds from target. He checked his airspeed again and then looked back down at the FLIR screen. Something had changed. . . . Now there *were* heat images pouring out of the No Smoking house. But they weren't adults. The images were too small. They were kids, dozens of them. They were scrambling out the door, climbing out the windows; they were even coming out of the roof. Ryder froze. *Why were kids sleeping in an ammo locker?*

The bomb went off his wing and slammed into the building a second later.

. . .

He pulled up and out but saw no secondary explosions behind him. He roared over the target again, taking some
small-arms fire but seeing nothing but flames coming from
the second building. Had this been the Holy Army's ammo
bunker, it would have been blowing up like a fireworks display by now.

He buzzed the camp twice more, strafing with his cannon
and making sure the Holy Army's fleet of SUVs and motorbikes was reduced to cinders. He took out the water tank and
some water pumps, too. He wanted these guys to know what
it was like to be out in the middle of the desert, all cut up, under the hot sun, with no way out and no one coming to help.

Finally, he pulled out and turned north. Once up to 200
feet, he shut down his weapons computers and snapped off
the FLIR. Only then did he have a moment to think. Had
Murphy been wrong after all? Could the second target have
been marked a no-flame zone not because it was an ammo
locker but because it was a kids' nursery?

Damn. . . .

He sucked in some oxygen, hoping it would settle him
down. It did. He surprised himself by not plunging immediately into a deep black depression, back to the blackest part
of his soul, though the image of the building just before the
bomb hit would probably be burned onto his retinas forever.
He swallowed a pep pill and gulped some more O. This was
war. He had to remember that. And in just five minutes he'd
put more hurt on the Army of God than the Algerian government had in 15 years. This wasn't a screwup. This was another good night's work.

But kids? What were *they* doing there? And how many
did he actually kill?

Another deep gulp of oxygen. From his lungs to his
brain, he calmed down again. The dark landscape streaked
by below him. The Med was in sight up ahead. Those kids
never knew what hit them—and that was a blessing. How

much warning did the passengers onboard the 9/11 planes
have? At some point, they all knew they were going to die.
How long did Maureen have to sit there, terrified that this
would be her last day?

Fuck them, Ryder thought, surprising himself again.
What would those kids have grown up to be anyway? What
airplanes would they be snatching in 10 years? What ships
would they be trying to sink?

Or would they just walk into Macy's with a belt full of
explosives wrapped around their waists someday?

Fuck them. . . .

It was better to rid the world of them now.

Ryder passed over the mountains and, still hugging the terrain with his fingernails, was back out over the coast 90 seconds later. No one was in pursuit.

He flew about thirty miles out to sea and turned northeast,
back toward the ship. It was now 3:00 A.M. He opened his
communication link and started monitoring *Ocean Voyager*'s
radio frequency. It was down near the end of the short-wave
band, the domain of the mid-Mediterranean's secondary
shipping.

As usual, these airwaves were a traffic jam of voices, lan-
guages, accents, and static. Ryder was waiting for a sequence
of phrases purportedly about the weather, broadcast by a
prerecorded tape loop from *Ocean Voyager*. A good weather
report would tell him that everything was OK and he could
make a normal return to the ship.

But instead of clear skies and high-pressure areas, he
heard a report of fast-moving thunderstorms, and maybe a
squall. This sequence was used to indicate that one of the
team's aircraft was in trouble. A chill went through him.
They'd been operating full-time for six weeks and nothing
had ever gone wrong. Until now. . . .

He had to switch communication devices immediately.
He turned down his radio, reached into his boot, and came
out with his Nokia sat-cell telephone. This was the most secure way for the team to speak to one another in a crisis,

though some code phrases still had to be used in the non-scramble mode.

He slipped the phone into position on his right leg knee pad, then switched on his helmet speakers. He hit the first speed-dial button—this was to the Blackhawk gunship. There was no answer.

Second speed dial: the Blackhawk troop mover. The pilot picked up on the second ring. He was an Air Force captain named Ron Gallant.

"Are you having car trouble?" Ryder asked him.

"Not us," Gallant replied. "We're about to put the car in the garage. It's your brother."

Ryder cursed under his breath. In this language of double-talk, his "brother" meant Phelan. The new guy was in trouble.

"How do you know?" Ryder asked Gallant.

"Because he just called," was the reply. "He said something about the cops trying to pull him over."

Ryder didn't need a codebook to decipher that phrase.

Phelan had been spotted by unknown aircraft and they were trying to chase him down.

Ryder hung up and pulled out his mission book. Phelan had been tasked to fly a CAP—a combat air patrol—50 miles southeast of *Ocean Voyager*. Essentially he was to put himself between the secret floating base and Libya, which, despite a recent thawing in relations, was still the most probable source of any mischief during the night. Running a CAP was a smart thing to do if the team's air assets were out on separate missions. Having a jet already in the air should trouble arrive was better than trying to launch one when it was probably too late.

Ryder followed procedure and called the ship directly; Martinez was soon on the line. They had a difficult conversation, spoken in the imprecise and impatient language of decidedly American code words and phrases. As best as he could understand, Phelan had reported at least two jet aircraft flying in the vicinity of *Ocean Voyager*. There was no mention of whether these planes were "unfriendly" or not. But there was no need. *Every* aircraft the team encountered had to be considered unfriendly until proven otherwise.

Ryder disconnected from Martinez and tried calling Phelan. His line was busy. He tried again. Same result. No more time to waste. He swung around to the southeast and pushed his throttles forward. In seconds he was streaking toward where Phelan was supposed to be.

It was a coordinate about 45 miles off the coast of Tunisia and now just 22 miles south of *Ocean Voyager*'s position. As Ryder approached the invisible point in the sky, he knew he was facing a real concern here: How would Phelan react his first time under pressure? Everything Ryder had seen so far indicated that the kid was a good flier; his cool while hooking up to the Extender was proof of that. And so far Bobby Murphy had a 1.000 batting average when selecting the right people for this unusual job. Still, Ryder was dealing with an unknown quantity, not the best of circumstances when combat might be imminent.

He arrived at Phelan's last known coordinate three minutes later to find the sky empty. He slowed, circled, went up, went down—nothing.

He called the ship again. They were in the process of recovering the two Blackhawks—both running low on fuel—and had shut off their hot radars to avoid suspicion. They'd heard nothing further from Phelan. As Ryder was talking to Martinez, his cell phone got a beep. Someone else was calling him. Ryder pushed the talk button. It was Phelan. He said just four words: "Look out behind you."

In the next second the sky around Ryder's aircraft lit up bright as day. The blue-orange flash told the tale: someone was firing a 23mm cannon at him.

He peeled right and let the bottom drop out from under him. He yanked back on his throttle and lowered his variable jets. In a jump jet, this was like stepping on the brakes. His forward thrust was immediately directed downward; Ryder heard everything but the screech. The aircraft shooting at him roared by a moment later.

It was an Su-24 Fencer, a huge two-seat Russian-made fighter-bomber similar to the American F-111. There was an enormous brown-and-green emblem plastered on its side.

The plane was a Libyan. No surprise there. They were just 20 minutes' flying time off the Khadafi Coast.

Now this was an interesting problem. The Harrier was a great airplane in many ways. Versatile as hell, and this stopping on a dime thing couldn't be beat. But it was not a dogfighter. It wasn't a fighter at all. It was an attack craft. Something best suited for carrying bombs to a target. During the Falklands War, the Brits rigged their jump jets with air-to-air missiles and the woggies paid the price. But Ryder wasn't carrying any air-to-airs tonight. The big Libyan plane, however, had a half-dozen slung under its wings.

Ryder pushed his plane into forward flight again. He saw the big Fencer, bathed in the light of the full moon, pulling out of its attack dive a half-mile away. It looked like a city bus trying to take a wide corner. Ryder sucked in some oxygen, his old friend. It had been years since he'd seen anything resembling air-to-air combat, but some things never change. The immediate confusion and body rush. Heart pumping, palms sweaty. He'd dodged the Libyan's first barrage, though, thanks to his wingman's warning. That meant his chances of survival were now up to about 50 percent.

The phone rang again. It was Phelan. He was using his scrambler this time.

"We've got at least two of these guys up here," he told Ryder directly, no need for doublespeak now. "I've been dancing with them for ten minutes. I don't know what they are up to. But when they came upon me, they were heading directly toward the ship. And now they're chasing me around in circles."

Phelan had done the right thing. His job up here was to protect the exposed flank, and when he saw two mooks heading toward *Ocean Voyager* he'd exposed his position and distracted them. Then he warned the ship. Two correct moves in a pressure-packed situation.

But both Blackhawks had to be down and hidden safely belowdecks by now. So while the delay had protected the ship's cover from being blown, Ryder and Phelan were still up here, involved in something like a dogfight, causing a ruckus that they would have been better off avoiding.

Ryder asked Phelan to give him his position. He followed his directions and saw him blink his taillight once about 500 feet off to his right. Meanwhile the Libyan fighter had finally recovered and was now climbing again. Even though he and Phelan were stealthy, there were in such close quarters, the Fencer pilots might get a visual on them at any second. And that would not be good. If the big Sukhoi switched off its cannon and started throwing missiles around, they'd be in real trouble. Even if they turned and ran, it would be difficult to get away from a well-placed missile shot.

The next decision was easy. If the big plane was climbing, there was only one direction the Harriers could go: down. Down to the deck. Phelan read Ryder's mind. He started diving even before Ryder did.

But then another complication. As Ryder was falling through 1,000 feet, he saw another flash go by, down near 500. It, too, was a large warplane, the second of the duo Phelan had encountered earlier. But it was not the same type as the first. This was a MiG-25, a grandfather in the twenty-first century but still a formidable warplane. The strange thing was the MiG did not have a Libyan emblem emblazoned on its fuselage. Instead it was wearing white-and-yellow meatballs on its wings. What country was that?

Phelan came back on the phone. *"Sillakh Al Jawwiya As Sudaniya,"* he said in perfect Arabic. "Translation: the national air force of Sudan."

"Sudan?" Ryder exclaimed. "Since when are we near *Sudan?"*

Both Harriers slowed their descent and let the big MiG go by. If its pilot saw them, he never made any indication of it. He stayed down close to the water and disappeared into the night.

So now they had two jet aircraft, from two different countries, flying around in the middle of the Med and acting very strange. Had they been fighting each other when Phelan came upon the scene? Or had they been doing some kind of joint operation?

But just then something *else* caught Ryder's eye. Right

below him he saw a group of cargo ships, moving northwest. They were sailing in a straight line, very close to one another. It was like a scene from a World War II movie—but it didn't make any sense. When was the last time cargo ships had to travel in convoys? An odd thought came to him: Could these two fighters, from two different countries, be up here acting as aerial bodyguards? Were they riding shotgun for the half-dozen ships below?

Ryder always carried a small low-light camera in the cockpit with him, just in case he came upon something interesting to show the boys back in the White Rooms. He pulled the camera out and with one hand snapped six quick shots of the convoy. Then it, too, vanished into the night.

Meanwhile, the big Su-24 had looped and was bearing down on them again. And off to the right, the MiG-25 had turned toward them as well. Clearly, it was time to go.

Ryder got Phelan back on the phone.

"I think the only way we lose these guys is to scare them," he said through the scrambler.

Phelan replied: "Roger that."

They both waited until the big fighters were within 2,000 feet of them. Then, on Ryder's count, they opened up with their cannons. The twin spray of 25mm shells lit up the night—and no doubt scared the piss out of the Su-24 pilots, as well as the guy flying the MiG. The plan worked. The two Arab planes quickly peeled off to the left. Ryder and Phelan quickly went right. They booted up to full power, a real kick in the pants, and were soon rocketing away from the area, flying as fast and low as possible.

Only when they were a couple miles away did Ryder strain his neck to look back to see if either of the bigger, more powerful fighters was in pursuit.

But for whatever reason, neither of the Arab warplanes chose to follow.

Chapter 8

Evansville, Indiana

Tom Santos had packed three bags.

One contained essentials. Underwear, socks, pajamas, shaving kit, deodorant. The second held his suits, his ties, his shirts, his good shoes. Bag three held his Air Force dress uniform. He hadn't worn it in almost a year. It still fit; in fact, it was a little loose on him, not a good sign. He'd been told to bring it with him.

He carried the three bags down to his front door and checked the time. It was nearly 10:00 A.M. He would be leaving soon.

Ginny had run to the drugstore, to fetch him his pre-chemo medication, which he wasn't using. She still knew nothing of this. Knew nothing of the girl he'd encountered in the medical building last week, knew nothing of the man who had waylaid him in the very same drugstore, the day before, and handed him a list of things he had to do to continue in the very strange, secret government project.

That's what he was involved in, the stranger in the Wal-greens explained to him. Top-secret. Level Five security. The details of the operation would be given to him only on a need-to-know basis. The man also handed him another bottle of the bright yellow pills. They tasted like candy, but they *were* help-ing, Santos was convinced of that. *Take as many as needed,* this label said, and he'd been following those instructions. Anytime he felt a twinge, he'd pop a pill and the twinge would go away. Simple as that. Was this some secret government cure for his kind of cancer? A reward for the service he was about to provide for them? Santos really didn't know, and on a certain level, he didn't care to know. He was willing to keep an open mind about the whole matter. The bottle of yellow pills was never very far from his reach.

The man in the Walgreens didn't tell him much more than that. He provided him with the itinerary and it called for Santos to pack the required items and be ready for a car pickup at 10 o'clock this day.

Again, he was to say nothing to anyone.

It was two minutes to ten.

Santos took a long look around the house. The kitchen walls needed painting. The lawn needed a good weeding. Ginny's car needed a wax. No problem. He would do all these things when he came back home.

The car pulled up at precisely 10 o'clock. Santos wasn't sure why, but for some reason he'd been expecting a limousine. What he got instead was a cut-rate five-year-old Chevy Impala, obviously a vehicle from a federal government car pool.

But Ginny wasn't back yet. She was about twenty minutes overdue. Edict or not, he just couldn't leave without explaining a little of this to her. Without saying good-bye.

Two men in bad suits walked up to his porch and pushed his doorbell. It didn't work; he'd fix that when he got home, too.

He opened the door; they flashed IDs that might have said Air Force Intelligence—or might have been library cards.

"Ready to go, Colonel?" one asked.

Santos straightened up. It was good to hear it again.

Before he could reply, though, the second man grabbed his bags and started for the car.

"There's a screwup with our airline tickets," the first guy said. "The whole Midwest system went down. We have to hurry to rebook."

Santos didn't know what he was talking about, and at the moment, he didn't care.

"I have to at least leave a note for my wife," Santos told the man directly. "Something just to tell her I'm OK."

But just then, Ginny pulled into the driveway. She saw the men, the car, and the packed bags. The men looked like police officers. Santos met her halfway across the lawn.

"Tom? What's going on?"

He suddenly found it hard to speak.

"I have to go away, just for a while," he told her.

"Go away? Go away where?"

"I'm not sure," he said. "It's a government thing. Something they want me to do."

Ginny looked at him like never before. Her eyes said it all. She thought he was losing his mind.

"Tom—you can't go anywhere," she said. "You're sick—"

He held up his hand, cutting her off. "Correction," he said. "I *used* to be sick. . . ."

She was frightened now. "Tom, let's go in the house, please."

But he leaned forward, kissed her quickly, and started to walk away. She dropped her grocery bundle. The contents spilled out on the grass. Santos climbed into the backseat of the car with the second man and began to drive away.

Ginny was just one breath away from hysterics. She looked down at her feet and saw Tom's prescription, just refilled. She picked it up and screamed after him: "Your medication!"

He rolled down the window, waved, and yelled back: "I don't need it. Not anymore!"

Chapter 9

The six Gulfstream jets arrived, one at a time, at the private airfield outside Manama, the capital of Bahrain.

The island nation off the coast of Saudi Arabia was the most liberal of the Gulf states. It wasn't Sodom or Gomorrah, but there were nightclubs here and some sold liquor and beer. There were women here, too, women who didn't keep the faces covered and would share a drink or two, with the right person.

There were many private clubs on the island as well, and these were even more risqué. One was the destination of the passengers in the six private jets. The club was located close to the airport, convenient, as most guests flew in from other places. It was built of plastic and mortar; its design was that of a huge futuristic Bedouin tent. The gaming tables were on the first floor; the women were on the second. Few of them had ever seen a *burka*. In fact, none were Arab. They were Eastern European. And they were all beautiful. They accepted money or chips, for favors.

The six jets parked at the far end of the field; they'd taken the same flight path from Riyadh. Two F-15 fighters from the Saudi Royal Air Force had escorted them right down to the runway. The skies above the Gulf could be dangerous, especially at night, so the six travelers welcomed the airborne bodyguard. And the protection did not end there. The two fighters would remain on alert, ready to scramble, whenever the six men decided to return.

This was Prince Ali Muhammad al-Saud's gang, he of the 116-room palace back in Riyadh. His close friend Farouk was there, as was Khalis Abu, his twenty-second brother-in-law. The three other men were board members of the Pan Arabic Oil Exchange, Ali's $4 million a day business. Like the Prince, they were all involved in the financing of *jihad* operations. Farouk and Khalis Abu had hand-carried funds to various cell members in the past; the Prince's colleagues at Pan Arabic had helped in laundering charity money as well. (Indeed, some *jihad* groups called Pan Arabic "the diamond mine.") The six men flew to this place once a week, usually on Saturday night. But they never all flew in the same plane together, or even in one another's airplanes. They didn't trust one another enough for that. . . .

Once landed, a separate limo picked up each man and transported him the half-mile to the club. The six were all wearing their best flowing-robe ensembles. Ali, as always, was dressed entirely in white. Finally gathered in one place, they were ushered through a side entrance and brought up to a suite on the second floor.

This place was gigantic, with huge curved windows, very low Aladdin-style lights, and gold fixtures everywhere. Many satin pillows were strewn about the floor. A dozen servants were stationed at various places around the room, Filipinos all of them. A case of champagne was waiting on ice. The six men rolled out their prayer mats and, led by Prince Ali, quickly recited their evening prayers, even though they were several hours too late and none of them had the faintest idea whether they were facing Mecca or not. This done, the club manager was signaled. He clapped his hands softly and a side door to the room opened. A line of girls appeared. Clad in negligees and bathing suits, they were paraded before the six men as they lounged on their pillows and drank *Dom Perignon*. Every girl was blond and busty. They were mostly German and Czech, with a few

Russians thrown in. There were 30 in all. The oldest one was 20.

Each man picked two, except the Prince, who took three. The rest were dismissed. Those girls selected were led to another room and told to wait.

The men got around to ordering their late-night dinner. All six chose the beef *l'orange* with french fries, and chocolate cake for dessert. Then they gathered their pillows together and had a serious conversation.

They were worried. The mysterious, and undoubtably U.S. unit had struck again, breaking up the *Sea Princess* operation, killing every member of the Genoa cell, and then bombing the Party of God headquarters—all in just 48 hours. And this just days after the attacks in Lebanon and Somalia and the assassination of their rotund Yemeni brother, Hamini Musheed.

"The Crazy Americans are *not* going away," Farouk began. "And this could be very bad for us. They have got under my skin. I think about them constantly."

"They knew exactly when our friends in Genoa were going to hit the liner," Khalis Abu, the-brother-in-law, said. "You might say they just got lucky. But I ask you, have you ever known the Americans to be *that* lucky?"

The others shook their heads no.

"I tell you, brothers, they are listening in on *us*," Khalis went on. "From our lips to their ears. . . ."

Ali raised his hand, as if to slap him across his face.

"No!" the prince screamed. "They would not dare. We are too important for that. *I am* too important for that. . . ."

But Farouk persisted. "What if they do have us bugged, my brother? Our homes. Our jets. This place. *This room?*"

Again Prince Ali tried to wave their concerns away, but not quite as dramatically. The Algerian Party of God had nothing to do with his activities; he couldn't have cared less about them. But he *had* sent money to the Genoa cell just days before it was wiped out. The plan to sink the cruise ship had been in the works for months, in absolute secrecy, but somehow the Americans had sniffed it out. The attack on the Si-

cilian villa was even more disturbing. Its location had been
so secret, even the Prince was never told where it was. The
dark humor of dropping the raft loaded with explosives on
the house was also unsettling.

Stranger still, the attempt on the cruise ship had received
scant coverage in the media, as had all of the recent American actions. Fox called it "a failed attempt at terrorism by
amateurs." CNN didn't cover it at all. This was so perverse.
It was as if the news networks were intentionally downplay-
ing the kind of events they usually trumpeted. This was as
baffling to the Prince as the shadowy U.S. strike team itself.

He knew many people in the U.S. military; he met with
them frequently at receptions and diplomatic gatherings.
He'd talked to several at a luncheon earlier this day. As sub-
tly as possible, he'd brought up the subject of the recent incidents. Each U.S. officer he spoke to seemed to draw a
blank on the subject; a couple said they'd get back to him.
Were they as much in the dark as he was? Or were they setting him up?

All this only made him worry more—and when Ali worried, he tended to drink heavily. If he drank too much, he
would get angry and sloppy—and drink more. Sometimes
this behavior would lead to the dark areas of his ancestors,
to violence and blackouts, the curse of many with blood on
their hands.

After that, just about anything could happen.

The night passed with lots of food and more champagne—
and no further talk about the recent troubles. Prince Ali ate a
lion's share of beef *l'orange* and french fries. But anytime he
began enjoying himself, his thoughts went back to the Crazy
Americans. Who were they? What were they going to do
next? Would they ever really come knocking at *his* door? It
was too much worry—as a result, he'd consumed two bottles
of champagne and a dozen shots of *sake* along with his meal.
The alcohol did not dull his uneasiness, though, and neither
did the food. Ali was not by nature a strong individual.

Around midnight, five of the men retreated to their individ-

ual suites along with the female companions they'd selected
for the evening. The Prince had been the last to retire. Those
who'd seen him remembered he was in a foul mood when he
finally staggered to his private chambers just before 1:00 A.M.
Noises were heard coming from the room about a half hour
later, not all of them pleasant. The sky grew particularly dark
at this moment, and the winds began blowing fiercely.

By 2:00 A.M., though, everything was quiet again.

The Prince was the first of the six to leave the next morning.
He encountered a floor manager as he was going out the
back door. Ali told the man to take care of the mess in his
private bedroom. The manager went to the suite and found
two of the three girls who had spent the night with the Prince
cowering in the corner of the bathroom, crying and in shock.
On the king-size bed lay the third girl. She'd been beaten to
death.

The manager just shook his head.

"Not again . . ." he whispered.

Chapter 10

"It's fruit. . . ."

Ryder leaned over the technician's shoulder and studied the blue-tinted TV screen. It looked a little fuzzy without his reading glasses.

"Fruit?" he asked. "Are you sure?"

"One hundred percent. . . . Looks like lemons, oranges. Watermelons. . . ."

Ryder was at the bottom of *Ocean Voyager,* inside one of the White Rooms. It wasn't so much a room as a long, narrow chamber, the same size as the containers up on deck. Inside was definitely white, though, and spotless. It looked like the control room of a TV studio or something at Cape Canaveral. There were dozens of video monitors hanging off the walls and ceiling. Jammed in between them were banks of shortwave radios, satellite receivers, fiber-optic lines, faxes, and computer screens. Most of the TV monitors and PC screens were displaying not satellite imagery or IR read-outs but pornography. Streaming videos, Web sites, chat lines, Triple-X rated, all of it.

There were ten guys working inside the White Room. They looked like high school students, all lab coats and glasses. On first coming aboard the ship, Ryder had been told not to insult this group by asking if they were CIA.

They were actually employees of the NSA, America's largest, most secret intelligence agency. Their primary job was to eavesdrop on the terrorists and then try to locate them on a map. How good were these kids and their listening equipment? They could hook a suspected terrorist by the simple act of his turning on his pager. Once he was tagged, they could electronically tap his phone, intercept his E-mail, even hear messages on his answering machine. The trick was to connect what they were hearing to a warm body and then get a location so the Delta guys could go and grease the bad guys. Down here they called it Spooks versus Mooks.

And all that porn? Just like Bobby Murphy, the terrorists used Internet porn sites to communicate. They spoke on dirty chat lines and porn-based bulletin boards, and through erotic-picture newsgroups. Some of the most sensitive gear inside the White Rooms allowed the Spooks to monitor up to 1,000 of these sites, around-the-clock.

But this was not porn Ryder was looking at. In front of him was a 3-D photo analysis computer. The guy working the machine for him was Gil Bates, Head Spook, the top man down here in the White Rooms. He was tall and reedy, with tiny eyeglasses, spiked hair, a goatee, and earrings in both lobes. He'd been a child prodigy, earning a Ph.D. in Military (C-3) Theory from MIT at age 16. The government recruiters swooped in right away. By 18, he was a senior systems analyst for the NSA. He was now just 20 and had nine other eggheads working under him. He was supremely confident in his abilities but had a reputation for being a bit of a wiseass. He also had a thing for extremely bright Hawaiian shirts.

Displayed on the screen was a digitized version of one of the photos Ryder had taken over the Med the night before. It showed three of the seven ships he'd spotted in convoy formation during the encounter with the Arab warplanes. The Spooks had developed his film, run it through a computer enhancer, and then fed it into this 3-D imaging machine. Bates's conclusion: Yes, the ships seemed to be following one another in a convoy. However, the crates on their decks and in their holds contained nothing more than fruit. In fact, that's how all of the crates were marked.

"But how do you know that they aren't just fruit crates with weapons or explosives inside?" Ryder asked him.

Bates shrugged. He was so young he made the Delta guys look like retirees.

"Materials used in weapons or explosives give off a heat signature completely different from organic matter," he explained, slowly, so Ryder's prehistoric brain could absorb what he was saying. "Even from belowdecks, we'd get a whiff of it. Now, we can't get a real heat read off your photo, of course. But we are able to have the enhancer break down the spectro-magnetic image. Then, for every color in the spectrum we can assign—"

Ryder cut him off. "OK, Einstein, I believe you."

This was a disappointment. Ryder had convinced himself the Arab aircraft were, for some reason, riding protection for the line of cargo ships. But if the ships were only hauling fruit, what would the point be?

"Tell me this then," he asked Bates. "Why were those ships sailing the way they were? All in a line. . . ."

"There'd just been a squall through the area," Bates replied. "Small ships like to sail within sight of each other in bad weather. Safety in numbers. . . ."

"But seven ships? All in a row? How big was this squall?"

Bates clicked his mouse button. A weather map showing the area the night before popped onto the screen. Another click and Ryder could see what looked like a microscopic hurricane about sixty miles off Tunisia. He scratched his graying head. He hadn't seen any bad weather up there last night.

"OK, I give up," he said finally. "But can you keep all this on a file or something? You know, hang on to it for me?"

Bates clicked his mouse again and said: "Forever and ever, *sir*. . . ."

Ryder left the White Rooms and began the long climb back up top.

He'd really thought he'd had something, with the ships

and the two planes from two different countries—a movement of weapons or the like. But he had to concede that just because it *looked* funny didn't necessarily mean that it was. Sometimes his gut *could* be wrong, he supposed, though in all those black ops he'd been involved in years ago he really couldn't remember his gut being wrong about anything.

Maybe it was another sign of age. Maybe he was losing his touch.

He reached the seven deck—just five more to go—when his cell phone rang. It was Martinez.

"Find your little buddy and meet me on the fantail," the Delta boss told him. "There's something I've got to show you."

Ryder hung up and trudged up the next three levels. Something seemed different, though, when he reached the upper decks. He could hear a lot of activity on the ship. Voices, carrying down the passageways. People shouting. People laughing. And was that someone singing? This was very strange. Usually the ship was as quiet as a convent.

Phelan's cabin was just four doors down from his own. They'd still not had a substantive conversation since the young pilot came aboard. After the bizarre encounter the night before, both Harriers were recovered and brought below, even before their engines were turned off. Martinez met them in the ready room and did a so-called ship's debrief, a verbal report of actions taken by the team, the details of which would never meet a pen or paper.

When this was over, Phelan went directly to his cabin, as did Ryder—only to fall into another troubled sleep, with another visit from Maureen, this time casually saying hello to him as she passed by in the rain with a bunch of Arab kids in tow, many wearing bandages, a harbinger, Ryder was sure, of many bad dreams to come. Phelan had not been out of his room since. So after 24 hours, Ryder had not talked anything but business with the young pilot, and it had been very little of that. Orders or not, this was very unusual. Even on the most secret of missions, a pilot and his wingman were supposed to be tight. Like the way two cops on the beat were tight.

Or at least that's the way it used to be.

He reached Phelan's cabin and knocked twice. No reply.
He tried again. Still, nothing. Ryder toed the door open and
peered inside. Phelan was lying on his bunk, amid a pile of
CDs, headphones on, writing a letter. A strange way to pass
the time, Ryder thought. There was no way to mail anything
off the ship.

The young pilot finally saw him. He took off his headgear
and Ryder told him they were wanted up on the tail. Phelan
asked what it was about. Ryder said he didn't have a clue.
Phelan quietly put his letter away, closed his CD player, and
grabbed his hat. While he waited, Ryder's eyes floated down
to a framed picture Phelan had attached to his cabin wall.
It was a photo of a beautiful woman, blond, sweet eyes, shy
smile, great body, taken on a beach somewhere.

Unconsciously Ryder said: "Nice rack. Is this your girl-
friend?"

Phelan looked at Ryder, then at the photo, and then back
at Ryder again. He was clearly appalled.

"Dude," he said. "That's my mother. . . ."

They walked up to the fantail in silence.

It was almost sunset. The horizon was bright orange; the
sun looked like an ember, falling into the water. A great
abundance of cumulus was scattered around, making the sky
almost heavenly. They were heading east again. Back toward
the Suez.

Martinez was leaning against the rail, puffing on his cigar. He was smiling, for a change. It was odd that the Delta
boss wanted to meet them up on deck, and especially at this
time of day. Team business was usually conducted in the
morning, down in the ship's combat planning room.

There were no salutes as the two pilots approached. Ryder
simply asked him: "What's up?"

Martinez gave them both the once-over. "Can you two
keep your mouths shut?"

"Of course," Ryder told him.

"I've done nothing but," Phelan added.

Martinez never stopped smiling. "OK—but this is *really* top-secret, right?"

He was standing over a metal grate. It covered a steel tub sunk about three feet into the deck. This was the aft line locker. It was used to store extra bull rings and rope, the products of the spiderweb crisscrossing the cargo deck.

Martinez lifted the grate with his foot. There was no rope or rings inside. Instead the tub was filled with ice and cans of Budweiser.

"Wow!" Phelan cried.

Ryder was caught speechless. He hadn't had a beer in nearly three months. *"There's been beer onboard?"* he finally exploded. *"All this time?"*

It really was a beautiful sight. Ice cold. The red-and-white cans gleaming in the glorious sunset.

"Where did it come from, Colonel?" Phelan asked anxiously.

"The Spooks," Martinez replied. "They found it this morning at the back of one of their supply containers."

Ryder did a quick count. He could see at least four dozen cans chilling down. There were 42 people on the boat. That was one can per man, with a few left over. . . .

But Martinez saw what he was doing and just shook his head. "They found more than a *hundred cases*," he revealed. "All of them wrapped in long-term cool-paks."

"Wow . . ." Phelan said again, this time in a whisper.

"The Spooks gave a bunch to the Marines," Martinez went on, proudly, like a miner who'd just struck gold. "And the Marines gave a bunch to me."

From behind them came the unmistakable sound of one of the ship's forklifts. The propane-fired engines gave off a very distinctive hiss. One was heading in their direction along the rail, carrying two men and a metal toolbox on its fork. This box was also filled with beer; two cases, still wrapped in cool-paks. Riding on the little truck were Red Curry and Ron Gallant, the U.S. Air Force Special Operations pilots. They were the guys who drove the Blackhawks. Both were captains.

Curry was an odd duck. He was from Staten Island, real

New York Giants country, yet he was a die-hard fan of the
Oakland Raiders, a team located a continent away. He was
never seen without his black-and-silver ball cap and matching T-shirt, appropriate, as he had the face of a linebacker.
He was early thirties, married, with three kids, rugged, and
stocky. He always seemed on the verge of throwing a punch
at somebody, anybody. The last angry man syndrome.

Gallant on the other hand was real cool. He looked like
he'd fallen off a brochure for the Air Force Academy. Tall,
rock-jawed, clean-cut, blemish-free. Except for the throw-
back 1950s-style glasses, he was a real Clark Kent type, as
restrained as Curry was volatile. He had an air of hipster so-
phistication, too. His hero was Miles Davis, not Al Davis.

They made for an odd couple. Yet both had been brilliant
so far in handling of the team's helicopters.

They screeched to a halt in front of Ryder, Phelan, and
Martinez. They looked into the rope tub and saw the stash
of Bud and ice.

"You guys, too?" Curry asked.

"And ours is colder than yours," Martinez replied with an
amusing puff of cigar smoke. "And we got more of it. So,
lucky us."

"Colonel, the whole ship is floating," Gallant told him.
"Your guys are jammed into the forward anchor chamber
with about ten cases of this stuff. And the Marines are down
in their locker room with even more. The Spooks spread it
around to everyone."

On cue, they heard a burst of laughter from the front of
the ship. Then a blast of awful music from down below.

Gallant turned to Ryder and said: "The Marines are really
into their Metallica."

"Who?" Ryder asked.

Phelan spoke up. "Excuse me, but moving around all this
beer—is it really authorized?"

The Air Force pilots laughed at him. So did Martinez.

"What makes you think *anything* we're doing out here is
authorized?" Curry asked him. "Shit, man, if we were any
blacker we'd be picking cotton."

Again, from the forward decks came the sound of many voices raised in laughter. And more music was blasting from below. The ship itself seemed to be rocking, most unusual.

"But what about 'the order'?" Phelan insisted. "About not fraternizing with each other. This won't help that situation."

It *was* a quandary. They had all this beer; it was found in one of their supply containers. But did that mean they could actually drink it?

"What else would it be here for?" Gallant reasoned. "It isn't like we're going to drop it on the mooks."

"And it ain't poison, because half the ship would be dead by now," Curry added. "Besides, you can't plant a couple thousand cans of Bud onboard and not expect people to drink it. And you'd be crazy to think they won't blab about anything while they're doing it."

"I've always thought the 'no-talking thing' might be a test," Martinez revealed. "They told us to stay quiet just to see how long we could keep it up."

Ryder caught himself licking his lips. He'd heard enough.

"Well, if it's a test," he declared, "then I just flunked."

With that, he reached down, grabbed a Bud, popped it open, and took a long, noisy swig. It was his first beer in a hundred days. It seemed more like a hundred years. It went down like spring water from the Fountain of Youth.

That was it. The rest of them grabbed their own cans from the tub—they *were* colder—and opened up. Curry meanwhile dumped his beer into Martinez's ice.

They didn't toast; they didn't know one another well enough for that. But they did drain their cans with the precision of a drill team. Caught in the brilliant orange of the sunset, for a moment, they looked like actors in a beer commercial. No sooner had they finished their first than each man grabbed a second.

Curry was already loose. "I always thought it was a POW thing," he said, with a burp. "They didn't want us talking to each other because if any of us got captured and they tortured us, we wouldn't know anything. They can't beat out of us something we don't know."

The other four just stared back at him.

"Thanks for that assessment, sunshine," Martinez said dryly. "Let's make you the morale officer."

"It *is* strange," Gallant said. "All this beer, hidden way back in the container—almost as if Murphy didn't want us to find it until now. . . ."

"Or at least until our training was complete," Curry said. "He didn't want us shit-faced in the middle of the South Atlantic."

"A wise man then . . ." Ryder said, adding: "We should have looked for it earlier."

They all finished their second beers in record time. Martinez passed everyone a third.

"Do we ever get to meet this Murphy guy?" Curry wondered, opening his with a whoosh. "I have a few questions I want to ask him."

Martinez relit his cigar. "How do we know he even exists?" he said mysteriously. "Bingo's CO might have been full of shit. Or he might have been ordered to intentionally mislead us. Now, I see Murphy's name on a lot of stuff. And I've e-mailed and been in secure chat rooms with him. But is he a real guy? I have not seen anything I could call definitive proof."

The rest of them opened their new cans of beer. Someone changed the subject . . . and they began to talk. About everything. Sports, the military, women, the military, and sports again. The predictable arc of men their age and profession.

The conversation continued into dusk and then early evening. As the sun finally sank and the stars came out, the ship maintained its party mood. Music, laughter, people talking.

The mountain of beer slowly got chipped away.

Sometime after 9:00 P.M., Gallant asked Curry what seemed to be a simple question: "How did they contact you to join up?"

They'd burned their way through a case of beer by this time and were already deep into a second. Ryder let the others talk. He spent much of the time looking up at the stars and imagining they were moving into elaborate celestial formations over his head.

"They called me in the middle of the night," Curry replied. "I'll never forget it. It was the day they found my brother."

"Found him?" Martinez asked. "Found him where?"

"In the rubble of the World Trade Center," Curry replied simply. "He was a lieutenant in FDNY. He was one of the first guys to go in. He just never came out." He raised his beer to the sky. "For you, Jamie. . . ."

"But wait a minute," Gallant stopped him in midsip. "Your brother was killed on Nine-Eleven?"

Curry nodded.

"We've been flying together six weeks—why didn't you ever tell me that?" Gallant asked him sternly.

"Because we weren't supposed to talk to each other, remember?" Curry answered. "Besides, what's the big deal?"

Gallant's reply was totally unexpected.

"Because *my brother* was killed that day, too," he said. "He was a commodities trader. He worked in the North Tower."

Martinez dropped his half-finished beer. The can rolled away, spurting foam all over the deck. He ripped the badge from over his shirt pocket. The one with the picture of the pretty girl inside. He held it up for them to see.

"This is my daughter," he said, his voice filling with emotion. "She was on the plane that hit the Pentagon!"

Absolute stunned silence from the others.

How strange was this?

Ryder quickly told them of Maureen's death. But this left them even more perplexed.

They turned to Phelan. "My dad was killed aboard the *Cole*," he said quietly. "He was a CPO, a fill-in . . . on the ship for less than a week."

Phelan angrily whipped his beer can off the end of the boat. It seemed to fly for a mile before it hit the water.

"They told me he was getting coffee when it happened," he said. "A lousy cup of coffee. . . ."

They all just stared at one another, dumbfounded.

"We've *all* lost someone to the mooks?" Gallant asked with no little astonishment. "Could that be? Really?"

Each man repeated his story. Each confirmed that he'd lost someone close because of Al Qaeda.

"This is giving me the creeps," Curry said. "Unless it's some weird coincidence."

"It's no coincidence," Martinez said. "Someone wanted to get a bunch of psychologically pissed off guys together, guys who wouldn't sneeze at some of the stuff they want us to do. And we're it."

"Man, *someone* did a good job picking out us Indians," Curry said.

Gallant replied: "Yeah, someone named 'Bobby Murphy.' "

Another hour passed—and another case was drained.

There was music coming from several different locations now. Ryder was too old to recognize any of it.

They talked about Murphy, but it was all just speculation. They talked about the missions they'd run, especially the one in the Rats' Nest, their nastiest affair so far. They talked about the mooks they'd greased and the bombs they dropped.

Then, inevitably, the conversation came back to the ones they'd lost. Curry barely made it through a story about him and his brother skipping school one day and seeing the Mets and catching a foul ball and getting on TV and making the *Sports at Five*—and getting caught red-handed by their parents. Gallant told a moving account of his brother's last minutes and how he saved dozens of people in the North Tower by forcing open an elevator door, loading it with handicapped employees—and then going back for more.

Martinez spoke of his daughter and her school play; the last time he'd seen her she was onstage, dressed as an angel. Phelan talked, a little, about a car he and his dad rebuilt. Whether it was the beer or not, the young pilot was the most affected of them all. Ryder retold an abbreviated version of his own personal hell—their house, her garden, he and his gun in the motel room. He skipped over the part about his peculiar dreams.

He was literally speaking the last word of his last sentence when the bright moon suddenly broke through the clouds right over their heads. The sky above them had turned from deep black to deep red. Suddenly an eerie glow came over them.

It stayed for only an instant; then it disappeared. *What the hell was that? Do they have Saint Elmo's Fire in the Med?* Ryder thought. Or was it just that someone up on the deckhouse was fooling around with the ship's searchlight and had locked them in its intense beam for a drunken moment or two?

He couldn't tell. But then just as suddenly, Martinez stuck his right hand out, fist balled, and held it there, strong and steady, in front of them. Way off in the distance, thunder crashed. Lightning lit up a faraway cloud. Phelan was the first to catch on. He touched Martinez's fist with his own, tapping it twice and leaving it on top of his. Then Curry joined in, two taps, then adding his fist to the pile. Gallant followed.

Ryder completed the ritual by laying his fist on top of them all. Then they all drained their beers with their free hands and quite spontaneously let out a great, *"Whoop!,"* something between an Apache war cry and a drunken coyote call. Then they exchanged high fives all round.

Then Ryder asked: "What does this mean exactly?" He was really lit. They all were.

"It means we are now *familia,*" Martinez said, in an exaggerated Latin accent. "Brothers. We now fight as one. . . ."

"We're family, all right!" Curry yelled. "Family—as in the Mafia. . . ."

He tapped each one of them twice on the head, draining yet another beer at the same time.

"Yeah, we're the *new* Mafia, baby . . ." he went on. "And those ragheads better watch out for us. . . ."

The Marines played their Metallica; the Delta guys played poker. The Spooks watched real porno. And the officers on the fantail just talked. Around 2:00 A.M., the Navy guys fired up their grills and started making everyone a very early breakfast.

Just before dawn, they collected all the empty beer cans around the ship and threw them overboard, more than 300 in all. Divided roughly among 42 people, that was more than a six-pack each.

When the sun came up, it was a new day aboard *Ocean Voyager*. The ship had a new vibe. The top-secret team was now a close-knit one as well. The sound of people talking was now heard throughout the ship, up on the deck, in the passageways, even way down below. Many conversations, endless and nonstop, all rolled into one. Phelan turned out to be especially loquacious. A case would be made that from this point on, he never really shut up.

As for the order that the team members refrain from too much fraternization during the mission . . .

That went overboard with the cans.

Chapter 11

The ship entered the Suez Canal and traveled all night.

It was *Ocean Voyager*'s third passage in two weeks. They were in radio contact with various people connected with the canal, many employed by the Egyptian government. Most of these communications were handled by Captain Bingo. He'd perfected a nondefinable Middle Eastern accent. The aim was to blend in as one of many. They stayed clear of military ships, paid attention, and followed procedures. And people left them alone.

They reached the Red Sea by sunrise and sailed all that day. When the sun went down again, *Ocean Voyager* was off the west coast of Saudi Arabia, near the city of Yambu. Mecca, the holy Islamic capital, was a hundred miles to the south.

At 11:30 P.M., a radar sweep of their area indicated there were no ships or aircraft within 20 miles of them. Their window of opportunity was opened. A new mission began.

Martinez was up on the bridge, lording over the launch operation. He'd spent all day planning the night's mission, working on intelligence from the White Room Spooks. Now it was time to watch it fly. Below him, the two enormous elevators lifted the pair of Harriers to the deck. Ryder and Phelan were already strapped in, their engines running. The

Marine air techs ran one last check of the jump jets' external
systems; everything looked good. Ryder got his thumbs-up.
He hit his throttle and was off. Running without any lights,
he vanished into the night. Phelan followed him seconds later.

As the two jets climbed to meet the refueling plane, the elevators went back down and retrieved the pair of helicopters.
Their engines were turning, too. The team did not fly ordinary Blackhawks; some people called them "Superhawks."
They were not as streamlined as a typical UH-60, being eight
feet longer and six feet wider. But every sharp angle on the
fuselage had been stretched out and every edge smoothed
over, like on a Stealth fighter. Their paint job was basic nonre-
flective black, the same as a stealth plane, too. Any heat
sources, especially around the engines, had been dampened
off by thick metal cowlings. Most important the specially
adapted engines helped keep the choppers' noise down near
zero. Even now, Martinez could barely hear them.

The helicopters' call names were *Eight Ball* and *Torch*.
Eight Ball was the gunship. It carried eight big weapons.
A GE minigun was sticking out of its nose. Twin five-inch
rocket tubes were mounted on either side of the cockpit.
Twin .50-caliber machine guns were located at both doors in
the open-air bay. Secured to a slot and pivot on the right side
of the bay was a Mark-19 40mm grenade launcher. Essentially a machine gun for throwing grenades, it could fire 60
explosive rounds a minute, earning it the nickname *Grass
Cutter*. The helicopter's extra-heavy-lift turbo engines helped
get all this, plus the crew of five, into the air.

The *Torch* ship was dedicated to carrying the Delta guys.
It could hold up to 16 troops, fully equipped, plus its own
flight crew, though many of the Delta operatives could fly the
aerial troop truck in a pinch. There was a single .50-caliber
machine gun at each door of the *Torch* and, like the *Eight
Ball,* it had rocket launchers set up on rails on either side of
the belly. Each aircraft also carried a large American flag,
folded under its front seat for display at appropriate times.

Once the helicopters were properly heated up, a line of
Delta troopers appeared from a nearby hatch. They hurried

across the pancake, in single file and climbed aboard the *Torch* ship with practiced haste. The Marine techs were holding green fluorescent glow sticks to help light the way. The lights gave the proceedings an eerie feel. Once Delta was in place, the Marine techs loaded the strange cargo the *Torch* chopper would also be carrying this night: four metal cages, each holding a twenty-pound pig.

Another radar sweep confirmed no other ships had wandered into their security zone. The helicopters could launch. Up on the forward bridge, Martinez asked for a GPS check. Bingo's nav guys came back with a good read. They were where they were supposed to be. A phone call from Ryder confirmed the jump jets had successfully hooked up for gas. Martinez put his fingernails to his teeth and went through an imaginary list. This mission had a high probability of being a nasty affair. Had he crossed every *t*? Dotted every *i*? He was sending out 27 guys who might not come back if he fucked up anywhere along the way.

He touched his daughter's picture and did a gut check. The feeling came back as OK.

He gave the deck officer two thumbs-up.

The helicopters took off.

U.S. Army Sergeant Dave Hunn was riding in the jump seat of the *Torch* ship. There were two squads in the Delta package, eight operators each. Hunn was the squad leader of the first team. He was six-three, 225, a large individual, with less than 2 percent body fat. He looked more Marine than Army. A jughead, with a chiseled chin, beady eyes, and a low brow. He was sporting a goatee and deep tan.

He was wearing the standard Delta ops uniform: a Nomex flight suit, a black Fritz helmet with headphones and a sat-cell phone attached, a pair of shatter-proof goggles, armored shorts to protect his groin, GORE-TEX boots, and a Kevlar vest.

He was carrying an M16A2-CAR-15 specialized assault rifle, the black ops version of the standard M16. It had a collapsible stock, a shorter barrel, held a 30-round magazine,

and was equipped with a silencer. The rifle could also carry
an M203 40mm grenade launcher under its barrel and any
number of special ops gadgets on the top, from low-light and
thermal-imaging systems to laser pointers.

Everyone in the squad was equipped with one. Hunn's
team also worked with bayonets attached to their weapons.
Few things could demoralize an enemy faster than to see
nine inches of razor steel coming at them.

Hunn was from Queens, one of eight kids. He'd been a
member of Delta for four years. He'd started out as a "door
kicker," typical of someone good at hand-to-hand combat.
He'd gradually advanced to Squad God. Seven guys took
orders from him. He was the team's demolition expert, its
backup medic, and its interrogator. He also spoke fluent
Arabic.

His youngest sister had been on a job interview at the
Twin Towers on 9/11. The last time anyone saw her, she was
getting on the express elevator to the top floor of the North
Tower, going up to see the view before sitting down with her
prospective employer. She'd just turned 18 years old.

She was among the youngest victims that day. Hunn lost
it when he found out. A sweet little kid who wanted to be a
professional dancer gone, her body never found. The Army
put him into a precautionary five-day psychological aware-
ness group the day after the attacks, this instead of allowing
him to go home. Hunn told the shrinks all the right things,
though. It was a huge blow, he said, but life must go on. "Are
you sure?" the shrinks asked. "Positive," he told them. Truth
was, he wanted nothing less than blood to avenge his sister's
death. Whose blood? Anyone from the Middle East would
do. He didn't tell this to the shrinks, of course. Somehow he
felt they knew. They let him out two days early.

Time went on, and it was tough. But then he was given
the opportunity to volunteer for this unorthodox program.
It promised few regs, lots of action, and no PC bullshit.
The two civilians in bad suits who came down to see him
that warm night at Fort Bragg couldn't have been more

blunt. "Want to kill some sand monkeys?" they'd asked him.

Hunn jumped at the chance.

Hunn tightened his seat belt as the Blackhawk rose into the night. The pigs squealed on takeoff but then settled back down again. Being the end guy, Hunn had a great view. He watched the strange containership fall below as the copter began to climb. There was no moon this night and the deep water of the Red Sea looked particularly black.

Up to 1,000 feet and well clear of the ship, the helicopter made a long, slow bank to the east and headed for the coast-line of Saudi Arabia, barely visible on the horizon. Hunn watched *Ocean Voyager* disappear behind them. It looked like it vanished into thin air. A nice trick.

He glanced down the bench. Each of his men was as bulked up as he. In addition to the unit weapon, two were carrying muzzle-mounted grenade launchers. Two more were lugging a half-sized TOW missile unit. Two others were loaded down with field sacks full of incendiary grenades and taser stun guns. One was packing a Mossberg automatic shotgun. They were all wearing the same patch on their right shoulder. It showed a silhouette of the World Trade Towers, with the letters NYPD and FDNY printed above them and an American flag behind. Below was the team's motto: *WE WILL NEVER FORGET. . . .*

Hunn slipped a pep pill into his mouth and let it dissolve slowly. One of the pigs let out a plaintive cry. Even though the helicopter's engines were quiet enough to have a con-versation inside the cabin, no one spoke a word during the ride in.

The village of Ubal-Sharif was located along a wadi, at the base of the Hejaz mountains, thirty miles south of Yambu. Only 200 people lived here. But many farmers from outlying areas frequented the village, as its marketplace was the largest in this part of Saudi Arabia. On Mondays, there could be as many as 3,000 people in town. Today was Monday.

There was an apartment located near the center of the village, three rooms in the back of a tea shop. No plumbing, no stove, and just one outlet for electricity, which worked infrequently. Five men were jammed into the front room of the flat, all of them sitting on the bare dirt floor. It was 5:00 A.M., but these individuals never slept at night. They could barely sleep during the day.

Two were playing runes. Another was watching an American dance show on an ancient TV. A fourth was cleaning his Kalashnikov assault rifle. The fifth was trying to get his cell phone to work. They were surrounded by boxes of fruit and extension cords, all feeding into the lone electrical socket.

The five men were members of Al-Habazz *Jihad,* a Saudi terrorist group considered among the most fanatical within Al Qaeda. Members of Al-Habazz carried the money for the 9/11 attacks out of banks in the Middle East and to banks in Europe. They also bought all the tickets for the 9/11 hijackers when they first flew to the United States. The group had a reputation for being smart, loyal, and ruthless.

In intelligence terms, these five men were "cutouts" for Al-Habazz, go-betweens that acted as the group's conduit to the bin Laden hierarchy. Cutouts were very valuable cogs in the *jihad* machine. They handled money, weapons, information. They provided martyrs. They were also responsible for keeping smaller cells in line, especially when it came to funding their operations. Al Qaeda was notoriously tightfisted.

They had gathered here to await copies of a CD-ROM being sent to them directly from Al Qaeda's provisional HQ. The CD held plans for what some people called the Next Big Thing, a huge operation that promised to dwarf 9/11 and anything since. Talk of this impending attack had been making the rounds for almost two years. Now its time was very near. Al-Habazz had already been told that it would have a major role to play in the mission. They would be among a select few to see exactly what Al Qaeda planned to do next.

The man with the cell phone finally got it to work. The others gave him a fake round of cheers. He quickly dialed the number of another cell phone in the United Arab Emirates.

His call was answered by another cutout, a man he'd never met. The man told him, in code, that the CD had been sent out that morning by armed courier and should arrive at any minute. They were to study the CD and then instruct their cell members accordingly. The five were also warned not cause any kind of disruption for the next few weeks. Planning for the big operation was at a critical phase, and no one at the top wanted anyone at the bottom screwing things up. The man with the cell phone said he understood and hung up.

Then he turned to his colleagues and said: "The day of falling sparrows is almost upon us. . . ."

Dave Hunn burst through the apartment door a moment later.

He came in firing, silencer in place, tracer rounds going off everywhere. One round shattered the room's only light-bulb, plunging the apartment into darkness. Hunn threw his body into the two men playing runes, slamming them to the floor. This cleared the way for the rest of his squad to flood in.

The man with the Kalashnikov turned it toward him—foolishly, because it was not loaded. He got the butt of Hunn's rifle in the mouth. Teeth went flying in the dark. Hunn's number-two man, Corporal Zangrelli, pulled his stun gun and tasered the man in front of the TV to the point where he began convulsing. By the time Hunn reached the man with the tele-phone, the entire squad was inside the room. They began vi-ciously beating and stunning the terrorists. All five were soon writhing on the floor.

The duct tape came out and a binding process began. The five men were being made prisoners and this suddenly frightened them. They had heard about this mysterious American unit with the Twin Towers shoulder patch, heard what they did to just about any Arab who crossed their paths. The man with the cell phone was especially terrified. He knew they were all going to die soon, at the hands of either their captors or their employers. They'd screwed up royally.

Each man was taped across his mouth and then bound with his hands behind his back. The Delta guys then tossed the apartment, finding a treasure of fake IDs, passports, and credit cards. The search was complete in two minutes, with an absolute minimum of noise.

Hunn took out his sat-cell phone and hit the flash button twice. He heard the slight whirring of both Superhawks passing over the top of the apartment building. The choppers had been waiting at their landing site about a half-mile outside the village. They were now moving in for the pickup. Hunn was expecting to hear two return clicks in his earphones, the signal from the pilots that the way was clear for the squad to extract itself and the prisoners they'd come to get.

Instead, Gallant came on the phone. Trouble was approaching.

"You got a deuce-and-a-half truck, nearing in your location," Gallant reported. "It's a military vehicle. Approximately two dozen mooks hanging off the back. They are armed."

"Damn it," Hunn cursed. "Who the hell are they?"

He could almost hear the copter pilot shrug. "I don't know," Gallant replied. "The Saudi Army maybe?"

"Do those guys even have a fucking army?" Hunn cursed again.

"They do now," Gallant said. "Because a pair of APCs just came over the hill, too. They'll be at your location in about thirty seconds."

Christ . . . Hunn thought. *A party.* . . .

He signaled his men to deep freeze; do not move a muscle. Two Squad was up on the roof. He hoped they were smart enough to freeze, too.

He moved over to the window and calmly closed the shutters, hiding the recent damage inside. He left a crack to see through and immediately spotted the *Torch* ship. It was hovering, quietly, in the shadows a block away. The *Eight Ball* was close by. Hunn looked up the street. A moment later, the Army truck rumbled into view, the two APCs right behind it.

The sky was brightening; sunrise was about twenty minutes away. Not the best time of day for a gunfight. Hunn looked back at the leader of the five mooks. He'd gone nearly white when he heard the small Army detachment was heading their way. Hunn's intuition kicked in. These troops were coming here not as enemies to the five terrorists but as friends. That's what his gut was telling him. Whatever the case, there was no way the Delta team could be caught here like this. As with the pilots over the Med the other night, anyone they encountered out here was an "unfriendly."

The troop truck drove up to the house and screeched to a stop. It belonged to the Saudi National Guard. An officer climbed off the truck, checked his watch, and then walked up to the front door. Hidden in a secret pocket in his hat were five CD-ROMs. He knocked three times, paused, and knocked twice more. The prearranged signal.

When the door opened, he found himself staring at the muzzle of Hunn's 16A2-CAR-15, clicked to its shotgun mode. The officer put his hands to his face. Hunn pulled the trigger.

The man's skull blew apart, hat and all. He fell backward into the street. At the same moment, the TOW team on the roof fired a missile into the middle of the troop truck. It went up like a can of gas. The soldiers began jumping or falling off, some on fire, some not. Two Team started mowing them down.

The APCs arrived. They came to a halt about a half-block away. One crew believed the gunfire that had blown up the truck had come not from above but from farther down the street. They opened up with tracer fire that went whipping right by the apartment where the Americans were holed up.

The crew of the second APC wasn't so dumb. They turned their weapons directly on the small apartment and opened fire. Instantly the apartment's walls were blown away by huge 5.61 cannon shells.

Hunn yelled for his crew to hit the deck, but they needed no prompting. The window exploded in a blast of glass and dust. Suddenly Hunn was looking directly into the street. He could see the burning truck and the smoldering bodies of the soldiers blown out of the back of it. The APC firing on them was just 30 yards away. There were so many tracers coming from its muzzle, it looked like it was throwing pure flame. The first APC was turning toward him as well. He could hear Two Squad above him on the roof, desperately scrambling for cover.

This was not good. . . .

Then came an earsplitting roar, and suddenly the first APC just wasn't there anymore. One of the Harriers had come out of the night and laid a laser-guided bomb right down its turret. A storm of shrapnel hit the apartment house a heartbeat later. The Delta troops flattened themselves further into the floor, certain the whole building was going to come down on top of them.

The second Harrier appeared. It walked a cannon barrage up one side of the second APC and down the other, splitting the APC in two. It blew up a moment later. Once again, the building was hit by a wave of flaming jagged metal this as the jump jet vanished into the murk.

Hunn had seen enough. On his order, the team got up and went out the back door, dragging their prisoners behind them.

By this time the tiny village had been shaken from its sleep. People ran into the streets, crying and panicking. They had no idea what was going on. At the same moment, people from outlying areas were materializing out of the morning fog, pulling wagons full of vegetables and cloth to the marketplace.

Hunn's men poured out into a narrow courtyard separating the apartment from the next building. The last two guys threw three incendiary "joysticks" behind them. The first floor of the apartment house exploded in flames. Hunn bit down on a pep pill, then fired two more grenades into the building, lobbing a third into the doorway on the opposite side of the courtyard, for good measure. The simultaneous explosions were so powerful they ruptured the cement beneath their feet.

Hunn kept his guys moving. The *Torch* ship was hovering above him. Looking up through the narrow space between buildings, he saw it had its fast ropes already extended and the rooftop squad already aboard.

His first two guys reached the street. The *Torch* ship floated over their heads. They secured the fast ropes, and then the five prisoners were hurried out. They were quickly tied onto individual ropes and hoisted up. A barrage of gun-fire back near the burning apartment building distracted Hunn. He fired a grenade in the direction of the gunshots; it went off with an extra-loud *bang!*

When he turned back, he saw the five Arab men had been pulled into the *Torch* ship, even as its door gunner was firing furiously at someone or something farther up the block.

Hunn yelled into his microphone: "Mooks out! Everyone else—*let's go!*"

Hunn's pep pill kicked in at that moment. The noise and the confusion suddenly doubled. He was still in the court-yard and pieces of debris from the apartment explosion were falling on his head. Fire and dust were everywhere. He could hardly breathe. Was this anything like the day the towers crashed? Could it be about one-millionth the horror? He be-gan screaming. A door opened off to his right. A middle-aged man, holding either a gun or a cane, emerged. Hunn emptied a half a clip into him.

Another explosion went off to his left. Hunn screamed again, firing his weapon into the flames and smoke. The *Eight Ball* gunship came overhead, minigun going nonstop. The squad's incendiary guys were now off the ground, with the Big Fifty guys just latching onto the ropes.

Hunn's whole squad had made it up. Now it was his turn. He slid out onto the main street; the fast rope was just ten feet away. He was about to latch on when he heard a screech. An old, broken-down bus had pulled up not 15 feet behind him. The driver's face showed pure fright—he couldn't be-lieve he'd just blundered into the gun battle. Hunn could see the bus was loaded with Arab men. But were they civilians or more terrorist types?

He didn't wait to find out. He fired two grenades into the vehicle. They went through the windshield and exploded

halfway up the aisle. Then he began spraying the bus merci-
lessly with his rifle on full auto. Someone began yelling in
his headphones. It sounded like: *"Everyone is out! Time to
go!"* Hunn kept firing. The bus burst into flames, filling the
morning air with screams. *"Right now! We got to go!"*

Hunn never stopped shooting. Even as he connected to
the fast rope, he was raking the bus from one end to the
other.

And as he was being lifted out, he was firing at it still.

Al Fujayrah, United Arab Emirates
The next night

The FedEx truck pulled up to the green stucco house on the
edge of the village Al-Ruyah.

The driver was also the village's plumber, so he knew the
people who lived here. They had no problem accepting a
package from him.

It was an overnight envelope, containing a videotape and
nothing else. The owner of the house plugged the tape into his
VCR. About thirty seconds into it, he realized this was something he did not want to see. He jumped in his Fiat and drove
at full speed to the nearby city of Jubai. Here he had a hasty
conversation with the chief of police. The chief took possession of the tape and ordered the man, his first cousin, never to
speak a word of this, or he'd be relieved of his tongue.

The chief then drove 20 miles to another small village,
this one near the coast. He knocked on the door of a man
named Abdul Zoobu. Zoobu was high-up Al Qaeda. He was
the man who had spoken by cell phone with the Al-Habazz
go-betweens the previous day, just seconds before Hunn and
his Delta guys dropped in.

Zoobu knew the police chief. The chief knew what Zoobu
did for a living. The chief handed him the videotape; Zoobu
handed him a hundred-dollar bill. But first, he drew it across
his throat. The message was clear. . . .

The chief departed and Zoobu put the tape into his VCR.

He was more mystified than anything. He communicated with the terror network three or four times a day, using a different cell phone each time. This tape had not come to him from them. It had reached him by way of a too-roundabout route; plus he would have been told to expect something.

The tape began with a minute of static. But slowly came a close-up shot of his associate in Saudi Arabia, the man with the cell phone. His mouth was sealed with duct tape. His hands were tied behind him. The camera moved to the left and showed another of the Al-Habazz cutouts crouched next to the first. He, too, was bound with tape and gagged.

The camera pulled back to reveal the three other cutouts, also tied up, crouched beside them. They were on the edge of a high cliff. It was daybreak. Several pillars of smoke could be seen rising in the dawn's early light, across the desert a few miles away.

Next to the men were four small pigs, each in a metal cage. They were squealing loudly and seemed as terrified as the Saudi prisoners.

The camera zoomed in again and focused on the face of the oldest of the group, the man who'd been cleaning the Kalashnikov. A wanted poster showing his picture was thrust into the camera frame. It gave a long list of his crimes and in large print identified him as a friend of Al Qaeda. The camera lingered on him for a long moment and then—*pop! pop!* Two buttons of blood suddenly formed on his brow, one right between his eyes. He fell backward out of camera range. Zoobu was shocked. Someone had just pumped two bullets into the man's head.

The camera became shaky but then settled on the youngest man in the group, one of the runes players. A wanted poster detailing his offenses came into view, then again, two loud pops—and the younger man joined the older, dying and bleeding on the ground. Two more of the men were executed in the same gruesome manner.

The camera shut off for a moment. When the tape resumed, some time had passed. A large hole had been dug in the soft earth of the cliff. The four dead terrorists had been thrown into it. The pigs' squealing became most unnerving. Four American soldiers then walked into the frame, faces covered, bayonets in hand. They were each holding one of the pigs. One by one, they proceeded to cut the pigs' throats in the most disturbing fashion. Bleeding profusely, the pigs were thrown into the grave with the four dead terrorists.

Zoobu nearly threw up. Burying a pig with a Muslim was a sign of infinite disgrace. According to the Koran, it guaranteed that man would never see Paradise. This grisly segment ended with the sound of two more loud pops.

When the next scene began it showed the only prisoner not yet buried. Zoobu's cell-phone friend.

His body lay crumpled near the now–covered over unmarked grave, two bullet holes in his forehead. His cell phone had been stuffed into his mouth—sideways. Flies were already landing on his body.

"Praise Allah," Zoobu whispered. "But these Americans *have* gone crazy. . . ."

But for him, the worst was yet to come. Just before the tape ran out, one of the American soldiers wrote something on a piece of paper and held it up to the lens.

This time Zoobu did throw up.

The message read: *You're next. . . .*

Chapter 12

One week later

The storm clouds began building west of the Persian Gulf just after dawn.

Dark cumulus forming high over the desert—unusual weather for this time of year. A cold, hard rain was coming, though. Ready to soak the Empty Quarter, the dry plains at Al Haditha, to cover Riyadh, and then to play havoc on the waters off Arabia itself. A monsoon of sorts. In the desert.

Strange. . . .

Already it had been a morning of whispers around the Gulf. Distressing words, pressed lips to ear, rumors in the shopping malls and the casbahs. Something bad was blowing in, from the west, the traditional direction of poor luck. Strange things spotted in the early-morning sky and then again at noon. The waters of the Gulf were beginning to stir.

The sound of thunder, off in the distance.

But getting closer.

Jet fighters from Oman and Muscat had scrambled several times during the day. Unidentified aircraft had been spotted flying over their borders and above the Gulf. An air-raid siren went off in Bahrain. The lights blinked in Dubai. Reports came in of ships off the coast vanishing in the morning fog and of Maydays from vessels that weren't really there.

What was going on? That's what all the whispering was
about. No one was sure. It was known throughout the region
that a large U.S. Navy battle group was on its way to the
Gulf. A 22-ship armada led by the aircraft carrier USS *Abraham Lincoln* was coming to beef up the already-mighty
Fifth Fleet. This was not unusual, though. The Gulf was all
but an American lake these days. But some people thought
the false alerts might be connected with the battle group's
imminent arrival. Its airplanes and secret weapons, being
sent out in advance.

The truth was, the battle group wouldn't be in the Gulf for
another week.

The dark clouds were still pouring out of the desert by midnight, covering the Gulf by 1:00 A.M. The heaviest overcast
was across the upper regions, above eastern Saudi Arabia
and the countries of Bahrain and Qatar.

Out of this murk, two Harrier ghost jets arose. It was Ryder and Phelan. They'd been responsible for at least some of
the anxiousness across the region this day. The skies were a
bit more crowded here than above the Med or the Red Sea.
Even the slickest flying couldn't hide you completely, not
from the naked eye. But their sudden appearance made it official. A bad wind *had* blown in.

The *Ocean Voyager* was now in the Persian Gulf.

Ryder and Phelan were up here looking for gas.

It had been four days since they'd flown a refuel mission; bad weather and bad positioning had caused three
aborts. The reserve of jet fuel on the ship was so low now,
the Harriers barely had the gas to take off and get some
more. The next few nights were going to be busy. This fill-
up was critical.

They got airborne just after midnight at a point east of
Qatar. Their windows of opportunity to land and take off were
squeezed dramatically in the traffic-clogged Persian waterway. They'd sat in their jets belowdecks for nearly an hour,
waiting for a half-dozen supertankers to pass *Ocean Voyager,*

all of them heading south for Hormuz. When it came time for them to take off, they had to do it inside a 90-second time frame. This included starting engines and being hauled up to the deck. Test piloting was not as exciting as this.

They saw the KC-10 Extender break through the thick clouds. It was hard to miss, huge and silver, this one with the emblem of Pegasus—the Mobil Oil flying horse—painted in red on its tail fin. Even though the tankers were always from different squadrons and different bases, they were always on time and in the right place. In fact, this one had waited up here for them. Another touch of Murphy's magic.

The jump jets moved in quickly to hook up. Ryder went first, then waited as Phelan got pumped. The winds were bad, flying along the edges of the thick clouds. The hookups were shaky. But nothing they couldn't handle.

The glitch came when they phoned down to the ship to say they were coming back. The ship replied that they could not be cleared for landing.

A fleet of fishing boats had wandered into the 20-mile security zone. Martinez thought the fishermen were out of Qatar, but it made no difference. Just about every fishing boat in the Gulf carried a cheap video camera these days. Why? Because certain intelligence services around the Arabian Rim bought videos showing the movement of U.S. warships or anything else suspicious. Usually the local fishermen were gathering more than nets.

What all this meant was the two Harriers couldn't land back on the ship until either the fishermen cleared out or Bingo decided to turn the ship 180 degrees and head south again. (The waters north of their current position were like an LA traffic jam.) But with the fuel situation not being good, the Harriers couldn't fly around burning up precious gas, waiting for all this to happen. And another refueling mission couldn't be scheduled for at least 24 hours.

"So what's Plan B?" Ryder asked Martinez.

"Stay by the phone," Martinez replied.

A minute went by. Ryder's phone beeped. It was Martinez again. He was on the scrambler. So was Phelan.

"Bahrain," Martinez told them.

"What about it?" Ryder asked.

"You have to land there—at the same base your tanker calls home. Catch up with him and follow him down. You're about ten minutes away."

Ryder and Phelan couldn't believe it. They asked Martinez to repeat the order even though their sat cells were being drained in the full-scrambler mode. "You want us to *land*—in an Arab country—where someone *can see* us?" Phelan asked him incredulously.

"That tanker is out of a very high-security zone on the northern tip of the country," Martinez came back. "And Bahrain is a friend of the U.S. And they run black ops out of this place all the time. It will be OK. . . ."

But Ryder disagreed. He thought they were taking a big risk and said so. "We're not just a couple of typical Harriers floating around up here," he told Martinez. "We look different. We fly different. We might not even show up on their radar screens. Someone is going to know something is up."

"Who got the authorization for this?" Phelan wanted to know.

"I got it straight off the screen from Murphy himself," was the Delta officer's no-nonsense reply. "That good enough for you? Now get going—he's already contacted them for you. . . ."

Still Ryder was feeling uneasy. "But what should we tell them we're doing there? Shouldn't we have a cover story or something?"

"Murphy said make one up," Martinez replied.

" 'Make one up'? Like what?"

"Like you're ferrying those planes to Diego Garcia. . . ." Both ends were losing their scramble functions now.

"And we are landing at this base, even though we just got filled up?" Ryder fired back.

"Look, it's an *Air Force* base," Martinez said firmly. "No one will care what the hell you're doing there. . . ."

With that, he hung up.

After a few seconds, Phelan called over to Ryder.

"That guy's a regular James Bond," he said.

They set down 10 minutes later, one behind the other, coming in for a conventional landing but using only half the runway.

The airfield might have been a secret place, but that didn't necessarily mean there was anything secret here. It was really just a tanker farm out in the middle of nowhere. Dozens of huge KC-10 Extenders, KC-135s, and even a few naval-designed A-6 buddy ships, wearing USAF insignia, were parked here, a strange sight. Bahrain was such a tiny country, it would have seemed impossible to be so isolated. Yet there weren't any other humans within 50 miles of the place.

Ryder and Phelan steered their jump jets past the maze of refuelers, all the way to the end of the base. A beat-up Jeep was waiting here to meet them. The pilots followed it to a pair of hardstands far away from the rows of tankers. As soon as they stopped, the vehicle disappeared. A strange thought went through Ryder's mind: Maybe that was Murphy himself behind the wheel of the Jeep. He seemed to be everywhere else.

Ryder and Phelan shut down and popped their canopies simultaneously.

"How's your pee bag?" Ryder yelled over to Phelan.

"I missed it completely!" Phelan yelled back.

A ground crew appeared out of nowhere and began to chock off both jump jets. The mechanics all seemed to be Arab.

Phelan squirmed in his seat. "Are they authorized to do this?"

Before Ryder could answer, two USAF techs walked out of the dark and gave the pilots a lazy thumbs-up.

The message was clear: It was OK to have the locals around the airplanes.

The pilots climbed down and had a brief conversation with the American ground crew. These were specially refitted Harriers and they were transiting to Diego Garcia after a refueling training mission, Ryder tried to explain—but Martinez had been right. The air mechanics couldn't have cared less.

"If you can find us, then it you're OK to be here," one told Ryder. He pointed to the badge over his left breast pocket. It was colored red. High-security clearance.

"Capeesh?" the guy asked him.

Ryder just nodded back. "Yeah, *capeesh.* . . ."

The mechanics started to walk away, leaving the two Harrier pilots standing alone in the middle of the huge parking area. Ryder estimated they had at least two hours to kill before Martinez gave them the OK to return. He sure didn't want to do it waiting way the hell out here.

Ryder called out to the mechanics: "Where do you guys go on your lunch break?"

The mechanics both pointed to a particularly dreary part of the base.

"Just walk that way," one said. "It will be the first thing you bump into in the dark."

The base club was called the OFF-1.

Ryder and Phelan found it after a 20-minute walk along the edge of the enormous shadowy base. It was an old Quonset hut, painted black and set back near some enormous sand dunes. There was a sign on the front door that read: "Due to restrictions against alcohol in the Muslim religion, we're not really here."

Ryder and Phelan walked in. It wasn't exactly the bar at the Ritz. It was a long metal rail with a Formica top, a few tables and chairs, and a broken karaoke machine. There were fewer than a dozen people inside.

They took seats at the table farthest away from the front door and right next to the bar. An E-5 airman was slinging drinks.

"What do you serve here?" Phelan asked him.

"Beer," the bartender replied.

"What kind of beer?"

"Cold beer. *Wet* beer. . . ."

They ordered two beers. It turned out to be real crappy Spanish stuff, making them long for their Made in America Bud. Ryder vowed to limit himself to just a couple pops, three tops. He would be back up flying soon enough.

They drank quietly. More people came in but ignored them completely, which was good. But then Phelan spotted a slight commotion at the other end of the bar. Two Arab men were waving at them. Both were wearing USA T-shirts, blue jeans, and New York Yankee caps turned backward.

"I think your fan club tracked you down," Phelan said to Ryder.

The two men made their way across the bar and were soon standing right behind them. The Arabs could barely contain their excitement.

At that moment, a USAF pilot walked in. He ordered a beer, wandered over, and had a brief chat with the two Arabs. Then he approached Ryder and Phelan.

"You guys the AV-8 drivers?" he asked.

Ryder and Phelan just nodded. There was no sense in denying it now.

The pilot stuck out his hand. "Marty Noonan," he said. "I just filled you up."

It was the tanker pilot. The guy they'd just taken a drink from. Phelan automatically ordered him a beer and invited him to sit down.

"Fascinating place you got here," Ryder told him.

Noonan just laughed. "Busiest gas station in the Gulf," he said, adding in a low voice, "especially if you're pushing a couple dozen B-2s around."

The B-2 was the famous Stealth bomber. The all-black Flying Wing was the most expensive airplane ever built. Price tag: $1 billion each. Probably the most advanced plane to ever leave the ground, too.

"They've deployed that many B-2s this far over?" Ryder asked Noonan.

"Where've you been for the past two months?" the tanker pilot replied. "They've got entire squadrons of B-2s up there, flying around, all night long, doing God-knows-what. And that's just the beginning. They've also got JSTARS planes. SEASTARS planes. Pulse planes. Laser planes. . . ."

He stopped—it was clear he couldn't really say much more.

"Just keep your eyes open up there," he concluded. "It can get pretty crowded sometimes, especially when a new carrier deployment comes through. . . ."

The two Arab men were still standing on the periphery of the conversation, still acting giddy.

"Are these guys waiting to clean our table?" Phelan asked.

Noonan feigned insult. "Hey, that's one-twentieth of the Bahraini Air Force Pilots Reserve you're talking about," he said.

"*Those* guys are *pilots?*" Ryder asked him.

"Who do you think you were hooking up to up there?" Noonan asked.

"Please tell me . . . not those guys," Ryder replied.

"Those are the rules," Noonan said. "Any plane that takes off from here has to have a Bahraini pilot onboard. It's both a cross-training thing and a political one. Makes them feel involved and so justifies us being here."

The Arab men were now pointing to their T-shirts and proudly displaying their Yankee hats, turned round straight.

"And you should return their greeting," Noonan added. "It's the thing to do around here. They *love* fighter pilots. Plus their families have more money than God."

"Hey, maybe they'll adopt me," Phelan said.

Ryder finally saluted the two Arab pilots. They approached and shook hands aggressively with him and Phelan.

The two men couldn't speak English—so it was a short encounter. Just hello and good-bye, then the Harrier pilots turned in their seats and effectively gave the two men the brush-off. They eventually wandered away. Once they were out of earshot, Phelan leaned over to Noonan.

"You don't really let them do anything up there, do you?" he asked the tanker pilot.

Noonan laughed again.

"Ever hear of the twelve-thousand-dollar coffeepot?" he asked.

Ryder and Phelan nodded. Years before, government whistleblowers had caught the Pentagon buying $12,000 coffeepots for some of its aircraft, an extravagance of days gone by.

"Well, we got one onboard," Noonan said. "And we let those guys use it to make our coffee . . . and believe me, nothing else."

Ryder and Phelan didn't get the call to return to *Ocean Voyager* until six that morning.

In that time Ryder had drained four beers but also drunk four cups of the strongest, thickest *Arabic kaffee* imaginable. It gave him a buzz that made his pep pills seem like Chocks. Phelan had matched him on the beers but managed to down a half a dozen cups of the hot black glue.

They passed the time jawing with Noonan. They were all too smart to ask for specifics about one another's missions, so the conversation touched on everything but what they were doing out here, in the middle of the Persian Gulf, on this night of dark, thick clouds.

Noonan filled them in on some recent events up in Iraq and other places. Nothing earth-shattering, but suffice to say, the region was always hopping with U.S. military activity. Another round and they started hauling out old "war stories." Mishaps in training, fuckups by officers. Close calls. The universal language of military fliers.

Then they started talking about their hometowns. It was strange. Ryder learned more about Phelan during this part of the three-way conversation than in any talk he'd ever had with him one-on-one. Phelan had grown up in San Diego, and not only had he been very close to his father, the old man had been grooming him to be a major-league baseball player. Phelan was attending San Diego College, doing NROTC and playing shortstop for a championship team, when his father, *his hero,* was killed in the attack on the

Cole. He immediately dropped out of school, went into the Navy, earned the rest of his wings in less than a year, and volunteered for the nastiest duty the fish could find for him.

Such dramatic requests usually went unfulfilled. The Navy wasn't in the business of making its officers—its pilots—into instant heroes. But when what he called in Noonan's presence "our little club" was started, Phelan's name popped up somehow. A fast course in flying Marine Harriers, a jump to the Naval Reserve (to avoid typical assignments), and the rest was history. The shortstop in the cockpit. Soft hands. Pinpoint landings. Good wingman potential.

But this was just the tip of the iceberg with the young lieutenant. He also revealed, in the most conversational way, that he was an accomplished musician, in guitar and viola. Berklee had wanted him, but he chose to fly jets instead. He also had a slew of girlfriends back in San Diego, owned a rebuilt 1981 Corvette, was a championship motocross racer at age 15, and at 4 was the youngest person to ever ride a hang glider solo.

Then, there was one more thing: before she got married, his mother had been a Playboy playmate.

Miss August 1978. . . .

It was six-thirty the next morning when the two Harriers returned to the *Ocean Voyager.*

The ship had wound up turning 180 degrees—twice. Ironically, Ryder and Phelan found it in nearly the same position as when they left, just off the coast of Qatar.

They landed almost simultaneously, each plane using its own separate pancake. The Marine techs were practically pulling them out of the sky, obviously anxious for them to land. The elevators were going down even before Phelan's wheels touched. Ryder felt sure the rush-rush had to do with the security window closing.

Actually, another aircraft was coming in.

He and Phelan rode one of the pancakes back up to the top. They arrived in time to see Martinez and Bingo descending from the bridge house. Ryder and Phelan joined them on the railing.

They spotted the incoming helicopter. It was an elderly Huey, painted white and blue, a bad imitation of something that might belong to a private oil company or a cargo-handling firm. There was a long stream of black smoke trailing behind it, and the copter's engines were backfiring mightily as it circled the ship.

"Oh God," Martinez said. "They're trying to kill him. . . ."

Somehow the Huey made it down, landing with a great thud, not on a pancake, but on the ship's aft-end, little-used static copter platform. The side door opened and a passenger stepped out, carrying two suitcases and a briefcase.

He was short, thin, with large ears and gray thinning hair. He looked in his early sixties. He was wearing golf slacks, a red cotton shirt, a light jacket, and holding a baseball cap with an American flag stitched above the bill. He had a befuddled look about him and seemed confused by his new surroundings. It was almost as if the copter had scooped up an American tourist wandering through Disneyland and deposited him here. The guy seemed very out of place on the dirty, oily undercover ship.

"Who the hell is that?" Phelan finally asked.

Bingo laughed. "Who the hell is that?" he said. "Son, *that's* Bobby Murphy."

Chapter 13

The man in the bad Yemeni suit had been waiting patiently for two hours.

His name was Abdul Kazeel. He was 37, short and seedy, with dark eyes, one much larger than the other, a thin mustache, and a chronically unshaven face. He'd come to Saudi Arabia by way of motorboat from Iran earlier in the week. This morning, a taxi carried him from the coast to here, the soaring, futuristic Pan Arabic Oil Exchange building in downtown Riyadh. He smelled of four days of travel.

Kazeel was now sitting in a holding room on the seventh floor, just outside the office of Prince Ali Muhammad.

The Prince was not expecting him.

Kazeel killed his first man at the age of nine. A dispute over a cup of goat's milk in the village square left an old man with his throat slit. Young Kazeel was never charged with the crime. He hadn't stopped killing since.

He was born of a Palestinian mother and a Kuwaiti father. His village was near the border of Saudi Arabia and Iraq. His uncle, a Syrian, was the mayor and strongman of his village and a man connected throughout the Saudi Kingdom. *This* is why Kazeel had never been arrested in his life. He grew up protected from the inconvenience of the law.

His second victim had been a paid hit—at the age of 13. The target was a rival of his uncle. When the man answered the door, Kazeel shot him twice in the groin; then as he lay dying on the floor, Kazeel shot him again in the head. All this happened in front of the man's wife and seven children.

For this job, and others performed by Kazeel at the bequest of his uncle over the next seven years, he was able to get a passport and gain admittance to al-Azhar Religious College in Cairo. Here Kazeel studied radical Islamic law and, naturally, turned to terrorism. Dalliances with Hamas and the Palestinian Authority followed. Both organizations were impressed with his brilliance and ruthlessness. He was also an expert in planning large suicide operations.

Kazeel's talents quickly became known in the terrorist underworld. In 1999, he reached his peak. That's when the boy who'd once killed a grandfather over some squirt from the village goat became one of the top mission planners for Al Qaeda.

Fifty feet from the waiting room, behind two locked doors, Prince Ali Muhammad was sitting at his desk, a stack of documents in front of him.

He had important business to conduct this morning. Pan Arabic dealt in oil lease futures; they could be traded like stocks or bonds, with tankers full of crude being moved about the globe like chess pieces. Most of the oil Pan Arabic handled was heading for the United States. As president of the company, Ali had to sign these weekly leases and have them time-stamped to lock in the price of the crude.

The lease purchase agents were waiting for him in the next room. At exactly 10:00 A.M., he began taking them one at a time. He signed his name to 23 total leases, more than $200 million in business transacted in 15 minutes. Sums like that sometimes called for a celebration, a lunch or at least some tea with the customers. This time, though, Ali dismissed them all with the wave of his pen.

He was in no mood to celebrate anything these days.

• • •

At eleven o'clock, his male secretary announced a dozen visitors were still waiting to see Ali. The second half of his business day was about to begin. Just like the *jeebs* who showed up in his backyard every Thursday night, a small group of oil ministers and police officials appeared at Pan Arabic every Wednesday morning. They were looking for handouts, too, and for the most part, Ali was obliged to pay them. Keeping these people happy made Ali's life run easier. They helped his business; they protected his home life; they cleaned up his indiscretions, like the one over in Bahrain a few nights before.

He still had a hazy memory of the incident, one that was not going away quite as fast as he had hoped it would. With similar occurrences in the past, all thoughts of his actions would have faded by now. Such things certainly weren't rare among his kind these days. And those girls really should be more careful! Besides, what was the life of one person—or two or three—worth compared to that of someone who had billions? Ali, too, was a killer. He'd just started later in life.

Usually the psychic hangover lasted 48 hours at the most. But earlier this day Ali had discovered something that would make this memory linger even further. He had foolishly worn his best white robe ensemble to the casino club that night; they were the same clothes he was wearing today. On his shirt, at a spot right over his heart, was a tiny drop of blood. Blood that was not his.

The outfit had been laundered by his staff, yet the spot had remained. He didn't realize this until he'd already arrived at his office. He'd caught himself looking at the crimson spot many times since, *obsessing* on it. He'd tried to wash it out with warm water and clear tea, several times. But nothing worked. The spot defied all means of removal. This was not good for someone who fretted as much as he.

He despised the distraction of worry.

Ali finally signaled his secretary to begin the second ritual of the day.

The usual suspects were led in, one at a time, asking about the Prince's health, the health of his children, even talking about the weather—this while Ali was less-than-graciously handing them envelopes stuffed with money. Each one went out the way he came in, bowing and scraping. In 20 minutes, Ali had paid out more than $500,000. A drop in the ocean.

The last man through the door was not from the oil world or the government, though. Nor was he from the national police. It was Kazeel, the planning minister for Al Qaeda.

Prince Ali knew him well. But he was very surprised, and a little nervous, to see him.

Kazeel did not bow and scrape like the others. He kissed Ali twice on his cheeks and then flopped into the chair across from his desk. Ali was nearly staggered by his body odor. Kazeel said: "I am happy for the happiness of my brothers." It was a rote Arabic saying that Kazeel delivered without an ounce of emotion.

Ali tried to recover. He sat behind his desk and leaned forward, hands open.

"Why are you here, my brother?" he asked Kazeel gently. "We had no meeting prearranged, did we?"

"This could not wait, praise Allah," Kazeel replied. He looked around the luxurious office. "Can we talk safely here?"

Ali nodded. The office was soundproof and bug-proof. The entire Pan Arabic building was.

Kazeel got right to the point.

"We have come up with a foolproof plan," Kazeel said. "For a very big hit. Very, *very* big."

"Allah be praised," the Prince whispered. He wasn't quite expecting this.

Kazeel went on. "The objective will be most prestigious. Most visible. Most symbolic to the Americans. Our friends around the world will view this act as great and holy retribution—and a gigantic production."

"Can you tell it to me?" Ali asked.

Kazeel reached into his pocket, where he would normally

carry a pistol, and came out instead with a CD-ROM. He handed it to Ali. "It's all in there, praise Allah. The names of our operatives. Their rendezvous points. Our distraction ploys. The many planes we intend to take. Protect that with your life."

He then reached into another pocket and pulled out a small copy of the Koran. This, too, he gave to Ali. The Prince started to refuse, but Kazeel forced it on him. "I know you have many already," Kazeel said. "But you will need this one especially."

Ali's hands shook slightly when taking the Koran from Kazeel. "Is there anything else I need to know about this, brother?"

Kazeel winked his bad eye. "Just to remember the favorite words of our father, the Sheikh himself, and be frugal always. . . ."

Ali nodded, then locked both the CD and the Koran in his top drawer. He began pulling his chin whiskers to approximate deep thought. Kazeel, of course, was not here to bring him into the loop. He was here for money. There had been talk of this next big hit for some time now. It was to top all previous attacks and again put pressure on the United States to remove its troops from the holy lands. Ali had already funneled nearly a quarter-million dollars into the initial planning for it.

"This will kill thousands of Americans, guaranteed," Kazeel went on, lowering his voice. "Many more than September Eleventh. And, I should say, we might even find a way that we can split their own atoms, right under their noses. And who knows what side effect that will have?"

Ali found his eyes going back down to the bloodstain on his shirt.

"But, my brother," he said, "it sounds like you are about to embark on an enormous undertaking. Getting just four airplanes under our control on September Eleventh took so much time and effort. Am I to understand that for this to work, you will require so many more?"

Kazeel nodded. "Yes, up to twelve, as a matter of fact."
Ali was stunned. "*Twelve?* Where will you ever get them?"
Kazeel smiled again.
"Leave that to us," he said.

PART TWO
Murphy's War
Chapter 14

Illinois

The interior of the flight simulator could get very warm in the afternoon.

It was the electronics, Tom Santos supposed. The panel lights, the read-out screens. The false pressurization devices. They all contributed to a temperature rise that Santos guessed was 10 degrees or more.

At least, that's what he *thought* was making him perspire so much.

He was somewhere in one of Chicago's suburbs, in a Boeing facility. He knew this because all the techs wore coveralls of Boeing Blue. He'd been here five days, living in a Ramada Residence nearby. The men who'd picked him up that day at his house were now occupying the rooms on either side of him. He still did not know their names. He was given all his meals, but they had to be taken in his room. He had access to a large-screen TV, free HBO, a Jacuzzi, and a free minibar, but he could not use the phone.

At night, when he got tired of TV, he would write letters to Ginny. Many recalled some special place they'd visited early in their marriage, a certain restaurant, a certain beach.

A certain bookstore. Each letter ended with a promise to visit these places again very soon.

He could not mail the letters of course. But that was OK—he'd deliver them personally when he got back home.

He was being taught how to fly a jet airliner. What type didn't seem to matter. The simulator had such extensive software, it could mimic any number of passenger jets, such as the Boeing 747 and 777 and the smaller MD-80, even a DC-10.

But his training was going slow. Santos had flown B-52s for most of his military life, but there was a big difference between driving a Hog and flying a 747. The Stratoforts he used to fly were nearly as old as he was at the time. True, they'd been constantly refitted and upgraded, but they were still not like modern airliners. He tried to explain this to his tight-lipped hosts, but they didn't understand. To them a big plane was a big plane. It was obvious they thought his tutelage would be easier than this.

So he worked hard to learn what they were trying to teach him. There were similarities, of course, between what he used to do and what they wanted him to do now. Roll time was crucial. Weight of aircraft, wind across the runway. Making sure every control was set properly. The flight checklist for a B-52 was a lengthy affair. So was the one for a 747.

In real life, most airliner takeoffs were done by computer. But Santos had been told he would have to learn how to do a takeoff manually, and this is what took the time. Whether the controls were too fast for him or he was losing his reflexes or a combination of both, he'd "crashed" on takeoff a number of times the first couple days. This did not make his hosts happy.

But he had always been persnickety when it came to learning how to fly a new bird, and nothing had changed. He was very methodical, very cautious. Very slow. In the back of his mind he imagined that he was soon going to be called on to take off with a cabin full of passengers. He wanted to be a fully prepared when that time arrived. What was the biggest difference between taking off with 250 people in the back and a load of nuclear bombs? The passengers were counting on you to get them back down again.

So he was trying to be careful. But again, his hosts were getting impatient. They had a clock ticking, though Santos had no idea just what it was ticking down to or where or why. He was just doing his duty, something his government had asked him to do.

He was doing it to the best of his ability.

When the simulator got hot in the afternoon, Santos would begin to sweat. In minutes, his shirt would nearly be soaked through. When his hosts saw this, they would reluctantly, but gently, suggest he take a break. He welcomed the time-out. He would visit the rest room, then be taken to a small adjoining suite that was air-conditioned and had a TV. There was a glass of ice water and one of his yellow pills waiting for him whenever he walked into this room. There was also a couch and a pillow if he wanted to catch a few winks.

He could take as long a blow as he wanted. But there was a training quota that had to be met every day. If it meant him staying until 10:00 or 11:00 P.M. to get the required number of hours in the simulator, well, that's how it was going to be done.

But then, even after his training session was over, he still had to go under a tanning lamp for two hours. This, too, was mandatory.

By the end of the first week, Santos was exhausted. And losing more energy by the day.

But he had a hell of a tan.

Chapter 15

The Persian Gulf

Ryder had never been inside *Ocean Voyager*'s captain's quarters. He didn't even know the ship had one.

It was located on the top level of the bridge house, above the glassed-in control deck where Bingo's guys actually ran the ship. The CQ was huge but also amazingly elegant. It had leather chairs, leather couches, large windows, Oriental rugs, and artwork covering the walls. A very ornate and valuable wood desk sat in one corner. A satellite TV, several CD and DVD players, and a Bose stereo were also on hand. A long dining table dominated the center of the room. Two dozen people could eat dinner here and look out on the sea at the same time. A nice touch.

This place was now Bobby Murphy's cabin.

It was high noon and *Ocean Voyager* was moving north, toward the upper Persian Gulf. Murphy had summoned the strike team to his compartment to sit and speak with him. Everyone was there: the Marine techs, the Delta guys, the Air Force chopper pilots, and the Harrier drivers. Many were drinking coffee. Ryder was drinking a beer.

Murphy was at the head of the table. He didn't seem like much of a mystery man in person, and hardly a master spy. He seemed more like a guy who sold life insurance or ran the local hardware store. An uncle. A neighbor. He seemed . . . *ordinary*. Yet somehow he'd put together this extraordinary thing. How? *That* was the mystery about him.

Murphy introduced himself and explained why he was here. He spoke with a soft southern rasp, a voice that would have sounded perfect narrating a documentary about the Civil War. Head down, hands flat on the table, he looked like an elderly history professor on his first day of class. He did not appear to be particularly brainy, though, or endowed with ESP—or insane, or a booze hound for that matter. He seemed shy, out of place. Nervous. Not the John Wayne everyone expected him to be.

Yet he knew the intimate details of every mission the team had run so far. And he knew every man in the room, too, and had addressed each of them by his first name. He'd also walked the ship from stem to stern an hour before, reciting volumes about each of its components, from the pancakes to the hidden CIWS guns. If it was tied down somewhere on the ship, Murphy knew where it was.

He also knew, intimately, the people they were out here to kill.

"We are up against a very devious enemy," he told them. "Al Qaeda is tighter than the Italian Mob. Their version of *omerta* is to cut their *own* tongues out. Why are they so good? Because they have what all the other terrorist groups have lacked. They have *organization*. In fact, they are an *organization* of organizations. That's their secret. They can pull members in from other groups. When the job is done, they separate again. Oily bastards. It makes them very hard to catch.

"And as you know, they work in cells. The cell members are given a mission and are trained to do it. A cell can hold five to fifteen guys; the number doesn't matter. None of them know each other. They don't know any personal details about each other. They don't even know each other's real names. They are told not to discuss personal issues or even have idle conversations. This is how they handle their security. In many ways, they are strangers acting in concert."

Some curious looks went around the table at this. Every one seemed to be saying: *That sounds likes us. . . .*

Murphy went on: "They seem unbeatable, or that's what a lot of people think. But every enterprise reaches its peak, and then, in one defining moment, something happens that causes it to go back downhill again. Sometimes that defining moment comes from a punch in the stomach, sometimes a kick in the nuts.

"As we all know, our aim out here is to pop anyone we can find whose hand was in Nine-Eleven. Despite everything that has happened out here since, this is still our noble job to do. I understand we've already rid the earth of a load of these bastards—and their families. In my opinion, that's great. I hope I don't sound cold when I say that. If I do, I'm sorry—but don't cry for me, Argentina. Those people attacked our homes, our country, our citizens. Our neighbors. Our friends. *Our* families. It is up to us to exact some blood in return. It's really as simple as that. If we teach one terrorist a lesson or, better yet, change one's mind by what we do out here, then it will all be worth it.

"So maybe at least we can lay the groundwork for that defining moment. That's why we always have to hit them hard and quick and never let them know how we are coming at them next. And you people have performed that mission brilliantly so far, and I'm here to tell you how proud I am of you all."

A sip of water.

"But I am out here for another reason, too. Something just as important. Simply put: Something big is coming. Really big. The mook chatter is off the charts. We are intercepting five times the usual number of phone calls, and they are clogging up the porn lines. There's been a run on cell phones all over the Middle East. And one thing we know about these guys: when they start talking like a bunch of old hens, smoke will soon become fire.

"I believe they are talking about the Next Big Thing. The next big attack. As we know, they are constantly trying to outdo themselves in getting their 'message' out. That's another of their traits. So we can never underestimate them. They might act small sometimes, but they *always* think big, and so should we.

"Now the chatter our friends downstairs have picked up tells me the mooks are already spreading the word to their cells about what and when this Next Big Thing is going to be. So we all have to be on the lookout while running our missions. Especially you guys on the ground. Keep your eyes peeled for anything that can carry information from one mook to another. Tapes, computer disks, even CD-ROMs. Anything that might give us a clue as to what they are up to.

"For every mission we run, and for every mook we take down, we get closer to the head of the snake. And we are going to continue this. Word is spreading about us and we will not let up. In the next few days we will be delivering some 'messages' to them that will have their heads spinning, guaranteed."

Another sip of water. Or was that gin?

"But one thing we must always remember: At the end of the day, these guys don't run on bombs or bullets. They run on money. Their network is like a corporation; that's what makes it so tough to crack. But just like any other corporation, they have a lot of people they have to support. Their expenses are very high. It costs them fifty million a year just to keep everyone fed, and paid, and still many of these cell members are put in slum conditions, just to save money. Now, you might have heard that at one time the Original Big Cheese was a billionaire. That's not really true. His *father* was a billionaire. The guy himself inherited only forty million or so. And by the way, he's not the type to spend his own money on all this, no matter where he is. In fact, the whole organization is as cheap as they come."

"They're *cheap?*" someone asked.

"They're oily cheap," Murphy confirmed. "Here's an example: They figured it would cost five hundred thousand dollars to plan and execute the hit on the World Trade Center. It wound up costing about four hundred and eighty-five thousand dollars. The day after the attack, NSA picked up a phone message from the Big Cheese to the guys who were still alive inside the Nine-Eleven cell, the very bastards we are out here looking for. What do you think the Cheese said to them? 'Congratulations'? 'Good job'? Nope. The first thing out of his mouth was, 'Where's the fifteen thousand?' His plan to kill scores of Americans had just succeeded beyond his wildest dreams—and he's looking for the leftover fifteen grand. That tells you a lot about the whole *jihad* organization."

Ryder looked about the room. Any initial skepticism had all but drained away. He could see it in the faces of those around him. It wasn't so much what Murphy was saying but how he was saying it. There was a sincerity in his voice that made you want to believe him. And it was hard not to like him. He was a funny little guy with big ears, but he also had seriously big ideas. After just a few minutes, he had everyone in the room hanging on his every word.

In a strange way Ryder knew this was exactly what the team needed; another part of the puzzle fit into place. The team had bonded in their beer ritual a few nights before. They were tight like fingers in a fist now. But the brains of the operation had always been somewhat remote. Until now. Finally, they were getting a leader.

"We were blindsided September Eleventh," Murphy went on. "Absolutely sucker-punched. Why? Because our institutions let us down. The CIA? Slower than hell, and when things go wrong they're the first to run for cover. The FBI? Useless. They practically had every one of the Nine-Eleven hijackers delivered to them on a platter months before the day. They did nothing. Homeland security? Are you kidding? And what about our political leaders? Back when this thing should have been nipped in the bud, they were more concerned about whose bud the Chief Executive was nipping. You see, this is the problem. *These* are the people everyone is counting on to get back what was taken from us. To prevent it from ever happening again. Well, God help us, because we're going to need it.

"Our country changed that day—how many times have

you heard that? But it's true. That's the sad thing. A guy goes to work, trying to provide for his family, trying to get ahead, and now he's got to worry about some asshole flying an airplane into his building? Or poisoning his water, or his mail? That is *not* the way America is supposed to be. Maybe that's how some people like it, living in their little shithole countries, but not us. We are Americans and we are special. Don't let anyone tell you different. We went to the goddamn moon and we saved Western civilization three goddamn times in the past hundred years. But damn it, we have got to learn how to take care of our own! And we can't leave that up to the CIA or the FBI or anyone else, because history shows they'll just get it wrong. *That's* why *we* are out here. This is our job. Take the gloves off and put it right on their doorstep and see how *they* like it. Very few people back home know it, but we're the ones they are counting on. And we've got to do what we can. For them. For everyone who died that dark September day. Thank you."

Murphy closed his briefcase and put his glasses down on the table. He was finished.

Ryder looked around the room again. He saw tears in many eyes. It was amazing. Every man at the table was a battle-hardened special ops guy. They'd been to places few people would ever want to go. They'd seen it all. Heard it all. Done it all.

Yet at that moment Ryder believed every one of them would have taken a bullet for Bobby Murphy.

Himself included. . . .

Chapter 16

The Burjuman marketplace was a crossroads of the world.

It was a huge open-air bazaar, four blocks around, located on the edge of a city known as *Imarat al Arabiyah al Muttahidah el 'Ajmani* or, more simply, 'Ajman. Sneakers from South Korea were on display here, next to radios made in Germany. Russian shawls were for sale next to Mexican herbal tea. South African ice cream, Colombian coffee. Shamrocks. Cactuses. Poppies. And everywhere, all things American. Computers, watches, TVs, VCRs, DVD players, baseball caps, record albums, CDs. T-shirts. Shoes. Socks. Underwear. There was a McDonald's at one end of the marketplace, a KFC at the other. Huge Coke and Pepsi signs hung high overhead, dominating the square and providing the few patches of available shade.

Among the crowd of shoppers, Bassar Jazeer saw the man named Abdul Zoobu walking in his direction. Zoobu had been slowly making his way across the crowded marketplace for the past half hour, looking over his shoulder, scowling at anyone who came close. Finally, it was time to do business.

Jazeer owned an electronics shop right in the middle of the square. His was one of the few establishments in the Burjuman that actually had a roof overhead. It was a very busy place. The shop owner knew Zoobu from previous transactions. He was hard to forget. Tall, perpetually dirty, with one eye frozen deep in its socket, Zoobu was also known to be unstable. He was one of the few Arabs Jazeer had met who carried a switchblade; it was hidden under his robes. Zoobu was also in thick with Al Qaeda. He was a top mule, someone who delivered VIP messages, orders, or information to the lower cells. Ordinary people avoided him. On a whim, he could make a person disappear.

At least that's how it used to be. The word around the marketplace lately was that Zoobu had become a marked man. Someone was gunning for him, and they were packing more than switchblades. His imminent elimination was said to be taking a toll on him. He was even more unstable than before.

Zoobu finally stepped into Jazeer's shop. He lingered near some Singapore-made boom boxes while Jazeer took care of a customer. Once the customer had gone, Zoobu approached. Jazeer knew he was here to buy cell phones. Again.

"How many this time?" Jazeer asked him.

"Twelve," Zoobu said urgently "But they must be clean."

Jazeer was astounded by Zoobu's appearance. The man looked terrible, as if he hadn't slept in weeks. And he really smelled. Jazeer wished he'd never done business with Zoobu. He was a dead man walking. But he was here now and he was known to carry that shiv, so Jazeer reached under the counter and took out a box of new cell phones. Each one was in a vacuum-packed, tape-sealed plastic case. For further "cleanliness," no two were made by the same manufacturer. Zoobu studied each package as a jeweler would study a rare stone, except with shaky hands. It took several minutes in the brutal heat before he was satisfied.

"OK, so they are clean," he said to Jazeer. "What is your price?"

"Fifty American each. . . ."

"Too high," Zoobu said. He was trembling. "I can find these things anywhere down here."

"Forty-five. . . ."

"I can get them for thirty," Zoobu countered. He was looking over his shoulder again.

"Thirty-five and I'll give you some calling cards. . . ."

Suddenly Zoobu's switchblade was against Jazeer's neck. Its owner's hand was shaking so much, Jazeer was sure his throat would be cut.

"Bastard!" Zoobu screamed.

But then he caught himself and thought a moment—and recovered his composure, such as it was. He was almost embarrassed. He put the knife away.

"OK," he said. "It's a deal. . . ."

Jazeer quickly threw the phones into a used Macy's bag. He would have given them to Zoobu for free at that point. He just wanted the man to leave. But he was a merchant and he couldn't help himself. He suddenly asked the terrorist: "And how will you be paying for them today?"

Zoobu growled lowly but then reached into his robes, farther down from where he kept his switchblade, to his credit card collection. He pulled it out, thirty cards in all held together by a rubber band. He selected an American Express Platinum card and handed it to Jazeer.

Jazeer studied it for a moment. "This, too, is 'clean,' I hope?"

Zoobu replied: "It was stolen in Brussels this morning."

That was good enough for Jazeer. He started the electronic transaction but then happened to look over Zoobu's shoulder to see a rather amazing sight: a helicopter was landing in the middle of the marketplace.

Now this was strange. It was not unusual to see helicopters flying *over* the bazaar. There was a military police base about twenty miles to the south in Dubai—and they had just bought a new copter. But to have a helicopter land in the middle of the square?

The next few seconds went by very slowly. The helicopter was black and there were soldiers in black uniforms hanging all over it. The helicopter was not making any noise. This was very odd. And there was another one hovering just above it. It wasn't making any noise, either.

Then one of the soldiers hanging out of the side of the helicopter jumped out and Jazeer clearly saw the patch on his left shoulder. It was an American flag.

That's when it hit. . . .

"Praise Allah!" Jazeer cried. *"No!"*

The Crazy Americans were here. . . .

The people in the square scattered, hundreds of them, all with great haste and in every direction. They didn't need a CNN News Alert to know what was happening here. The grapevine in the Middle East was quicker than anything Marconi or Bell ever imagined. They had heard about the Crazy Americans. They knew of the people they'd plucked from their beds in the middle of the night and killed horribly. They knew about their car bombs, their itching powder, and the grenading of the bus. Unlike their cousins in Lebanon, Somalia, Yemen—pick a place—the people of 'Ajman did not want to be an audience for this.

That's why the square was virtually empty just seconds after the helicopter finally set down. The rest of the soldiers bounded out of it and began running right for Jazeer's store.

Zoobu was waking up from a stupor as well, even though only a few seconds had gone by. He saw the chopper; he saw the huge soldiers with the patch containing the Stars and Stripes and the outline of the Twin Towers. That's when he knew beyond all doubt that these people were after him.

Jazeer saw Zoobu take a CD from his pocket and try to snap it in two—but, for whatever reason, he was not able to do so. He even tried biting it in two, but this did not work, either. CD still in hand, Zoobu screamed and then ran up the store's main aisle. Jazeer lost sight of him behind the racks of the used CD department.

The American soldiers arrived a moment later. Jazeer fell backward against the display holding his phone cards and lottery tickets. The soldiers seemed unreal to him. They were enormous. Their weapons, their helmets, their body armor. They looked right out of *Star Wars,* at least the black-and-white version. Oddly, two were carrying hatchets.

Six of then ran in. Two went into a defensive crouch, weapons up, right in front of his counter. The other four went down the main aisle, moving very quickly, splitting up, looking to surround the hapless Zoobu. They quickly cornered him near a huge stack of CDs. Jazeer heard some shouting and then the sound of metal viciously cutting flesh. Once, twice, five times. Ten. Twenty. Fifty . . . It went on for the longest time. Jazeer could hear Zoobu's body flopping about the loose boards at the rear of the store. The man's screams, terrifying. Meanwhile the second helicopter flashed overhead again, this time much lower. It looked like a battle tank in the air. Above it two fighter jets that seemed to have the ability to hang in the air were doing just that, hovering ever higher above the scene.

Finally all was quiet at the back of the store. The American soldiers started exiting. The helicopter outside was kicking up a cloud of dust now. It was hard to see inside the store. The first two soliders departed; then two more ran by Jazeer. They were carrying Zoobu's butchered body in an unzipped body bag.

Another soldier rushed by. He was yelling something into his radio. He didn't even look in Jazeer's direction. *Just one more,* Jazeer thought. *Just one more has to leave before they can get on their helicopters and fly away.*

But the last guy out stopped right in front of him. There was a very disturbed look in his eyes.

He studied Jazeer for a moment and then looked at the copter waiting outside. The rest of his colleagues were already loaded onto the aircraft.

"You speak English?" the American soldier yelled at Jazeer, trying to be heard above the commotion.

Foolishly, Jazeer nodded yes.

"You knew this guy, Zoobu?" the soldier yelled at him.

"He was a customer!" Jazeer yelled back.

Suddenly the soldier's muzzle was pointed at Jazeer's throat. There was a bayonet on the end of it. The blade still had Zoobu's blood on it and now it was pricking Jazeer's skin as well, the second sharp object against his throat in less than two minutes.

"You know who he was buying those phones for?"

Jazeer had his hands up; they were flailing. He shook his head no—a lie.

"No?" the soldier screamed at him.

"No! No!" Jazeer was yelling back, even though tears were now running down his cheeks. Zoobu was not as crazy as this American.

Two of the soldier's colleagues jumped off the copter and ran up to him. Using urgent hand signals, they were telling him that they had to leave.

But he was ignoring them.

"You knew, didn't you?" the soldier bellowed at Jazeer instead.

Finally Jazeer had to scream. This man was going to kill him anyway. He could not die telling a lie.

"Yes!" he cried. "I knew. . . ."

He could see the man's finger begin to squeeze the trigger. The other soldiers were still shouting at him, but he was not paying attention. Jazeer was expecting a bullet to his brain at any moment, his last breath nigh. But then the soldier screamed at him again. *"Hands out front!"*

Jazeer immediately laid his hands on the counter. He thought the soldier was going to handcuff him. He opened his eyes just in time to see the ax coming down. It severed his hand just below the wrist. He saw blood; he saw pieces of bone. It just didn't register in his brain that these things belonged to him. Before he could leap away in pain, the soldier grabbed his left hand, forced it down, and proceeded to chop it off, too. Blood gushing again, the pieces of bone actually made a noise hitting the wall behind him.

Jazeer collapsed in shock. The soldier stood over him and in perfect Arabic hissed: "If you have no hands, you will be of no further use to Al Qaeda!"

Then the soldier threw a handful of playing cards on top of Jazeer and left.

One card fell next to where Jazeer's head had hit the

floor. He could see it perfectly, through fading eyes. It was a photo of the New York Twin Towers, with the message *WE WILL NEVER FORGET* printed beneath it.

Below that, scratched in pen, was written: *Dave Hunn, Queens, New York, was here.*

That night

The twenty-four prized horses were released into the corral to the beat of castanets and skin drums. Two trainers with whips began running the horses around in a clockwise motion. There was much snorting and crying coming from the Arabian champions, each as white as snow. As the taped percussion rose, the horses were made to run even faster.

All this was to the delight of six people sitting in the luxurious viewing box overhanging the huge yet virtually empty equestrian arena. This was the immediate al-Said Shaeen family. Two sons, an uncle, a mother, a grandmother, and a young daughter. Sitting in the middle was a seventh person, the family's patriarch. The man named Farouk. He was not so happy.

It was a rare occasion when the running of his prized horses could not cheer him up. It was usually the highlight of his week. But Farouk just could not enjoy it today, even as the trainers whipped the horses harder and they began to run at breakneck speed, butting and biting one another in a mad dash to stay ahead. Farouk was worried about his patron, Prince Ali. He'd been acting very irrational, more so than usual. The indiscretion over in Bahrain had been cleaned up, as the others had been, but these things were getting harder to do and more expensive all the time. Ali had also been missing office work at Pan Arabic in the past few days, putting valuable deals on hold. Worse, he'd been seen meeting with a known Al Qaeda minister right *in* the offices of Pan Arabic itself, a very dangerous thing to do. How many eyes were about, trying to link Pan Arabic and the Saudi establishment with high officials of the *jihad* organizations? This kind of behavior frightened Farouk, and it frightened Ali's other associates, too. They had many things going on. They had many secrets to keep.

The horses ran faster and faster and Farouk's daughter was yipping with delight. One horse fell in the scramble and broke its hind leg. The family cheered. The trainers were delighted, too. But Farouk hardly noticed.

His thoughts were still far away.

An hour later, they were all back in his summer palace outside Riyadh, Farouk in his own bedroom, his current wife in hers.

Farouk was tired, so he would forgo fucking one of his Filipino servants this night. He lit a cigarette and walked out to his balcony instead. The streetlights of Riyadh burned before him. What a dull place. . . . He felt a breeze at the back of his neck. *Must have left the door open,* he thought. He finished his cigarette and threw the butt off the balcony. His cleanup crew would dispose of it in the morning.

He walked back to his bed, took off his satin robe, and climbed in. No TV tonight, either, he thought, tying a rubber band around his long chin whiskers. He would just go to sleep.

He laid his head on the thin pillow and thought about his horses. When one stumbles and falls and breaks a leg, it was no big deal. True, the animal would have to be destroyed, but he could always buy another one. Plus, he believed it made his other horses that much more competitive—hungrier to stay alive. More than a few of his other steeds were getting old, though. It might be time to actually sell some of them off. Of course, he would not sell the one named *Al Sayet*. It was his favorite, a huge white Arabian king, a direct descendant from the Prophet Muhammad's own herd. The rest could die tomorrow, but if *Sayet* survived, Farouk would consider himself a lucky man, favored by Allah.

He drifted off to sleep but was awakened after a while by the sensation of a warm fluid leaking under his body. Still groggy, he reached under his thigh and found something slightly sticky. He brought the substance to his nose and took a sniff. Had he peed the bed again?

No, the scent was not familiar. He reached up, turned on the bed lamp, looked at his fingers, and realized they were smeared with blood.

He threw the covers from him. His legs and rump were covered with blood. Farouk was horrified. He turned over and saw a pool of blood had gathered in the center of his huge water bed. It was leaking out from beneath a lump of blankets on the other side, nearly six feet away. Trembling, Farouk reached over and pulled back the rest of the bedclothes.

It was not the head of his favorite horse—as he had feared.

It was worse.

It was the butchered body of his great-grandnephew, Abdul Zoobu.

Sticking out of his pockets were dozens of playing cards bearing the likeness of the World Trade Center towers.

Stuffed into his mouth was a bloody American flag.

Chapter 17

Martinez found Murphy at the front of the ship, near the bow, sitting on a folding chair, staring up at the night sky. They were heading south again.

"Everyone OK?" Murphy asked him, eyes never leaving the stars.

Martinez lit a cigarette. "Message was delivered. They all came back in one piece."

Murphy let out a sigh. "We get lucky again," he said. "That's good news."

It was midnight. The successful raid to the marketplace and the follow-up trip to Riyadh had wrapped an hour ago. And it *was* all good news. The team had flown two missions over two separate countries, without anyone challenging them, following them, or even trying to track them on radar. Postmission satellite photos of both targets showed no military or police presence at either site. This could only mean one thing: the team's reputation was so widespread, the local authorities had become just as fearful of them as the populace. Like the Algerian government and the Holy Islamic Party of God, what the Crazy Americans left in their wake could be so horrible, no one wanted to search for the culprits too aggressively. Not when they knew it could be their throat next to be slit. . . .

So the team had finally hit its stride. They were operating with virtual impunity, shaking up a lot of mooks, nailing some supporting characters of 9/11—and still no one knew where they were coming from. Murphy should have been doing handstands by now. But as Martinez found him, he did not seem too happy. While the team was out doing its thing, Murphy had been down in the White Rooms, sitting among the young Spooks, staring at the NSA read-out screens and reading the latest chatter picked up between the *jihad* groups. It had not been a wasted exercise, but what he'd uncovered was a little deflating.

"The plan for the mooks' Next Big Thing is already floating around on a CD-ROM," he told Martinez now. "We just got a third-party confirmation of it a few hours ago. It's being distributed, very secretly, to their network as we speak."

"Just as you thought," Martinez said. "That's good to know."

Murphy wiped his tired eyes. "Maybe not," he said. "That's probably what those Saudi troops were doing the night we snatched the five guys for the pig cutting. They were delivery boys."

"So?" Martinez asked.

"So if we had just waited a little longer we might have been able to turn up one of these CDs."

Martinez leaned against the railing, blew out a cloud of cigarette smoke and thought for a moment. "We're not mind readers, Murph," he finally said. "From the sounds of it, there was no way we could have known about the CD coming that night. Shit, the five mooks probably didn't even know it themselves until the last minute."

Murphy's eyes were still glued on the Big Dipper. "Yeah, but then we knock off this mook today in the electronics store. *He* was one of the guys distributing the CDs. He might have had one on him when we spotted him. If only we had been a bit more subtle. Damn. . . ."

Martinez took another long drag of his cigarette. "No one is perfect. And besides, we're not out here to be subtle. The guys down below have so many mooks under surveillance, another one of them will crack soon. It's inevitable. And when he does, we'll be right on him. . . ."

Murphy just shook his head. "Yeah, but this Next Big Thing they're planning is getting real close—I can feel it. I'm talking two weeks. Maybe less. If we keep knocking these guys off one or two at a time, we could be old men before it amounts to anything."

He lowered his eyes to stare out on the black waves of the Gulf. "They know we are out here. And, sure, by now they know what it is we do. But they are still running faster than we are, and they're a tough bunch to slow down once they get going. So we've got to hit them again, right away, and make it somewhere they're not expecting it. It's got to be a real sucker punch, too. Something that will knock them off-balance, throw them off-schedule, and maybe give us more time to divine what they are up to."

"But what happens then?" Martinez asked. "Suppose we find out the whens and wheres of this 'Next Big Thing.' Are we telling anyone?"

Murphy finally looked over at him. "Let me ask you a question," he said. "If you knew about Nine-Eleven one hour before it began, what would you do? Tell the CIA? Or try to stop it yourself with the guys we've got on this boat?"

It was a tough question, especially for someone so by-the-book as Martinez. "I really don't know," he finally answered. "What would you do?"

But strangely Murphy wasn't listening anymore. His eyes had taken on a very faraway look. Suddenly, he sat straight up in his chair and clapped his hands.

Inspiration had struck.

"How soon can the jump jets go out again?" he asked Martinez urgently.

The Delta officer thought a moment. "They've got enough gas onboard to fly one mission—if it's relatively close."

"Are the pilots awake?"

"Probably not. . . ."

"Wake them up then," Murphy said. "And get everyone connected to air ops in my quarters in thirty minutes."

. . .

Ryder was in a Chinese restaurant, cleaning the fish tank. Maureen was waving to him from the corner. The waiter had a quick conversation with her, then walked over to Ryder and said, in Maureen's voice: "Murphy wants us topside."

Ryder shook himself awake. Phelan was hanging over him.

"They want us," the young pilot was saying. "In Murphy's quarters. Now."

Ryder's fingers were numb. The ship had been rocking again and he'd been holding on to his bunk, very tightly, in his sleep.

He looked at his watch. It was 1:00 A.M. *Christ,* they'd just got back from the last mission two hours ago. He'd been asleep for less than 30 minutes.

Phelan was dressed and ready to go. The beach boy seemed even more eager than usual. Ryder hated such enthusiasm at this time of night.

He got up, splashed some water on his face, and popped a pep pill. "What do they want us for?"

"All Martinez said was that Murphy wants to talk to us and he's really pumped."

Ryder yawned fiercely.

"Good for him," he said.

They climbed up top, past the darkened "breakfast" deck, to Murphy's quarters.

They found Murphy, Martinez, and Bingo inside, along with the chopper boys, Curry and Gallant. Gil Bates, the White Room whiz kid, was also on hand. His Hawaiian shirt seemed brighter than the sun to Ryder's bleary eyes.

Murphy was sitting at the head of the long table. Everyone was drinking coffee. He waved the pilots into the two seats next to him.

"Like I was saying," Murphy went on. "We know the mooks have a great organization. They are run like a corporation. It's not just one guy—or even a group of guys. It's a thing unto itself.

"Now this is what I've been thinking about all night. How can you really hurt a gang like that? You can't bomb them all. You'd have to know where they all are to do that. But according to the CIA, it's been impossible to infiltrate them. So how do you deliver a sucker punch to them? Something that's going to hurt them on another level?"

He held his finger up in the air. "I'll tell you how. You interfere with their money. *You affect their cash flow.* Sure, they have a great organization—but they've got a huge payroll, too. And if there was some way to squeeze them on that, who knows what would happen? Think of it. If Yasif in Jersey City doesn't get paid, all of a sudden driving that cab and living in a slum doesn't look so good anymore. His enthusiasm might waver. He might want to go home. Not good for morale. Not good for the corporation as a whole."

He pulled a map from his briefcase. It showed the city of Abu Dhabi, the largest of the states comprising the United Arab Emirates. It was about fifty miles down the coast from 'Ajman, the scene of the team's most recent big raid.

"Abu Dhabi is the federal capital of the UAE," Murphy told them. "It's an important place. The UAE parliament buildings are here. Federal ministries, religious institutions, foreign embassies, state broadcasting facilities, and most of the UAE's oil companies. So it's an affluent place, too."

They studied the photo map. The streets downtown ran in precise geometric patterns. They were either perfectly straight or beautifully curved. The buildings, too, soaring and futuristic. This was not the Rats' Nest, Ryder thought. This was an ultramodern city.

In the middle of the map, on what could only be called the main drag, Murphy had marked a building with an *X.*

"The terrorists do a lot of things in cash," he went on. "They have to. They have a payroll to meet, just like everyone else, but it's not like they can send some of their guys a paycheck every week. They use couriers and they use Barrat, that informal banking thing they have going. But the guy at the front end still *has* to have cash handed to him. Especially when he is dealing directly with Al Qaeda. So, they have places where they have lots of cash sitting around, waiting to be tapped."

He pointed to the building with the *X* on it. "That's one of them."

"What is it?" Phelan asked.

"The Abu Dhabi National Bank," Murphy replied. "1001 Sayeeb Street. Sixteen stories high. Built 1999. I happen to know the mooks have twelve million dollars in cash locked in its vault right now. The bank employees are under orders not to touch it. Not to even look at it. Twelve million . . . that's about a quarter-year's operating expenses for these *jihad* guys. A big chunk of their liquid capital is in that bank."

"Sooo," Phelan said. "What do you want us to do? Rob it?"

"No," Murphy replied simply. "I want you to bomb it."

For the next half hour, Ryder and Phelan drank coffee and worked up the details of a typical night mission.

There was nothing complicated about it: Get the ship as close as possible to the Emirates' coastline and lay a path for ingress to the target. As for the dropping of ordnance, the bank's vault was on the first floor of the building. A glassed-in lobby made up the exterior of this first story. The pilots figured they would each be able to drop a pair of 500-pound bombs on the target. The first two would be blockbuster iron bombs. They would go down through the second floor, explode inside the bank, and, it was hoped at least one of them would reveal the vault. If this happened and the pilots could flash a laser on the vault, they could send two guided munitions right into it on their next pass. If these munitions were made of high-penetration high explosives, the money inside the vault would burn to a crisp. And the timing? They could fly the job now and be back on the ship before sunrise.

Murphy loved the plan. "I don't even know what thinking out of the box means," he admitted. "But if this is it . . . then you guys are geniuses."

They went around the table. Martinez gave it a thumbs-up. Bingo, Gallant, and Curry did, too.

That's when Bates, the top Spook, spoke up.

"It's cool," he said. "But how would you like to make this hit, let's say, ten times more effective?"

Everyone looked up at him. "*Ten* times more effective?" Murphy said. "How?"

"By making a *real* impression on them," Bates replied, not quite smugly, but close. "I know a little about how things work in the Gulf, especially in the Emirates. I studied Islamic business philosophy back in school."

"High school?" Phelan asked innocently.

Bates pretended not to hear him. He pointed to the big X on the map. "Now you can go in and bomb that bank in the middle of the night. And yes, if their twelve million goes up in smoke, well, clearly, that's good sucker punch. But . . ."

"But what?" Murphy said.

"But what if we hit it in the daytime?" Bates asked.

Murphy was surprised. They all were.

"The daytime?" Murphy asked. "Really?"

"Bomb it at noontime and go in loud," Bates said emphatically. "Make it messy and you'll spook the hell out of them. These aren't the people of Berlin or Stalingrad or London we're talking about here. They might be ninety-nine-point-nine percent for the *jihad,* but they really don't want to get their robes dirty. They're living too good of a life down there—all while keeping twelve million of the Head Mook's money warm. Now, you do this thing in the daytime and make a mess, believe me, the entire bank will go under; Shit, the entire *block* will go under. And a lot of oil-money people will be very upset that a place like this was actually hit. Just like hitting the World Trade Center. Knocking down a building is not very good for business."

Bates turned to the Harrier pilots. "How much ordnance can you guys carry?"

"Enough . . . why?"

"Then increase your bomb load. Instead of carrying two five-hundred-pounders, try carrying two *two-thousand-pound* bombs each. You will definitely burn the money that way, but you might leave a big hole in the ground, too." Bates's voice suddenly cracked with emotion, very unlike him. His mother had been killed in the Lockerbie bombing when he was just six years old. So he'd lost someone, too. "I say, give *them* a Ground Zero to look at every day."

Murphy thought a moment, then turned to Martinez. He was the operations guy. The Delta boss just shrugged. "A sixteen-story building? Downtown Abu Dhabi? Noontime? You'll make a mess, our biggest by far, no doubt about that. But you'll have a body count, too."

Murphy drained his cup of coffee, thought a long time, then snapped his briefcase closed.

"That's why we're here," he said.

Chapter 18

Downtown Abu Dhabi was *extra* crowded this morning.

A large street festival was in progress, a celebration for the governor's daughter who'd recently announced her impending motherhood. Sayeeb Avenue was the focal point for this event. The expansive concourse in front of the National Bank was jammed with vendors and outdoor stands selling food, tea, and candy. Musicians walked the sidewalks nearby. Magicians and storytellers entertained the children. Thousands were on the streets this day. Normally there would have been just hundreds.

A group of European missionaries was visiting Abu Dhabi today as well. Many were members of the German Green Party, here at the invitation of the UAE parliament. There were seventeen women on the tour, plus a tour guide and a translator. The missionaries were among the guests of honor at the motherhood festival. Two were carrying video cameras.

At noontime, the people in the streets were serenaded by the clanging of bells and the sounds of flutes. The height of the celebration had arrived. One of the German tourists turned her video camera up toward the Clock Tower, an 80-foot structure that soared above the near-spotless city. Through her viewfinder she saw a flock of white doves explode out of the tower, as if startled by something. Then a terrifying black form filled her frame. What was that? It was moving so fast, she could not tell. Then came the noise. It was horrendous, earsplitting. Then a second black shape crossed her eyepiece,

On the videotape, someone asks: "What is happening?"

"They are *Luftkriegers*," the woman holding the camera was heard to reply. Jet fighters. She'd grown up in Bavaria in the 1970s. She was familiar with the sound of warplanes screaming over the countryside.

But these two had come out of nowhere. They were flying so low, so fast, and making so much noise, hundreds of windows were breaking throughout the city. A slew of car alarms along Sayeeb Avenue went off, triggered by the racket. The people at the festival watched as the pair of black jets climbed in perfect unison, turned over on their wings—and began heading right for the downtown.

Many in the street instinctively ran for cover. This was definitely not part of the celebration. The German woman with the camera held firm though. Somehow she kept the pair of aircraft in view as they passed back over the Clock Tower and flew right down the center of the avenue. The planes were no more than 100 feet off the ground and the wave of approaching noise they were creating was just tremendous. On the tape, someone could be heard screaming in German: *"They are going to bomb us!"*

The frightened crowd became a frantic mob. People, running in all directions. The woman with the camera was knocked over in the stampede. She fell on her back but kept the camera pointing straight up. The videotape told the tale from there. By pure chance, it caught the flight of the first 2,000-pound bomb as it passed over Sayeeb Avenue and slammed right into the enormous, two-story front door of the crowded bank. The bomb exploded on impact. On the tape the building seemed to rise a foot in the air before coming back down. Every window in the 16-story structure was instantly blown out.

The tape then caught a second huge bomb slamming into the building just a few feet above the first. There was a gush of fire, blinding the lens for a moment. Then three people ran in front of the camera; they were engulfed in flame. They disappeared just in time for the camera to catch sight of the two planes, out over the water, but turning again. They were coming back.

There came now much static and the images of people's feet running past the camera. Some were burned and shoeless. Others were covered to the ankles in blood. The two planes were suddenly over them again. The German woman tried to get to her own feet, camera still running, and caught the third 2,000-pound bomb coming in. It landed almost exactly where the first one did but kept right on going. It punctured the center of the massive vault and then exploded. The shock wave was so violent this time, the camera was blown from the woman's hands. It landed with a crash—but did not break. It was made in America. The woman was somehow able to pick it up, and in the confusion now she, too, was running. The tape showed that she was on the tail end of a huge crowd of people fleeing for their lives, some looking back, though not believing what they were seeing.

Then came the sound of the fourth bomb hitting the target. The laser-guided munition went through the top of the fractured bank vault like a bullet through a tin can, blowing up only after it had embedded itself in the building's foundation.

This was the biggest explosion of all. The ground began shaking and would not stop. The German woman fell again. This time, she stayed down. Either by accident or design, she turned the camera back toward the bank just in time to see the 16-story structure start to collapse. It went over to the north, away from the woman's position, but the smoke and dust were horrible and suffocating. The tape showed the rubble of the bank was fully involved in smoke and flames, as was the wide concourse in front of it. There were bodies burning everywhere. One of the jets rocketed through the smoke and screamed away. The second jet was right on its tail. The German woman somehow used her zoom lens and caught, in full view, something that was painted on the side of the second departing jet.

It was an American flag.

The woman could be heard screaming in thick English: *"American bastards! Murderers!"*

Then the tape ran out.

Ryder and Phelan were circling above *Ocean Voyager* twenty minutes later.

The ship was only a few miles off the coast of Abu Dhabi, still moving south. They got lucky, as the vessel had sailed right into an adequate security zone, allowing both jump jets to land with no problems.

The airplanes were quickly brought below and all evidence of their retrieval covered over. Ryder and Phelan went down with the pancakes and then headed for their makeshift ready room, an unused cabin next to the crews' galley. They shook hands—a postflight first. Things had gone that well. They talked extensively, one-on-one, about the mission, another first. It was just as a flight leader and wingman should be. The adrenaline was still pumping in both of them. Neither had done anything like this before. They'd flown the job flawlessly, and they'd returned in one piece. It would take a while for this buzz to go away.

They changed quickly and went up to the combat center, knowing this was where the rest of the team would be. But instead of the expected case of beer and congratulations all round, they walked into a dry room, with some very startled faces hidden in the dark.

No one spoke. Martinez just clicked a remote and CNN blinked on a nearby TV screen. The first thing Ryder saw was his own jet passing above the burning bank back in Abu Dhabi, Phelan's jet right on his tail. A female reporter was halfway into a Breaking News Report on the bombing. The German missionary had been killed, the newswoman reported breathlessly, but her camera had been found and immediately turned over to the local TV station, who immediately sent it to the Al Jazzier Arab TV network as a raw feed. Al Jazzier had it on the air even before the Harriers were back on the ship. CNN had picked up the footage from there.

And this was not the dark, shaky camera work confiscated after the *Sea Princess* incident. This was clear and focused and disturbing. The damage was incredible. The noise. The fire. The carnage, appalling. And now it was being broadcast all over the world.

Ryder fell into the nearest seat. Phelan did, too.

"Wow," the young Navy pilot breathed. "We're on TV. . . ."

Chapter 19

The *Ocean Voyager* left the Persian Gulf the next morning.

They ran two hours out into the Indian Ocean and then began a series of slow 360s that kept them near the shipping lanes but not actually inside them. If a patrol plane, from any country, went overhead, the prewritten script would have Bingo and his crew claim they were doing rudder repairs.

Bobby Murphy had ordered the withdrawal from the Gulf. Things had changed a bit for his modern-day crusaders. Up until now, the American media had all but ignored the strike team's activities. (It seemed like Murphy had friends everywhere.) Most of the videotapes from the *Sea Princess* had proved as persuasive as UFO footage. Shaky, fuzzy, and shot at night, the best ones had been confiscated as soon as the cruise ship reached Israel. For the most part, the actions in Sicily, Somalia, and the western Saudi desert had been reported as "isolated terrorist acts" for which no one had claimed responsibility. Murphy couldn't have planned it better. By *chutzpah,* skill, and good luck, the team had become part of the Middle East's murky underworld of terrorists and spies, mooks and Spooks. It was a place where no one knew exactly who was doing what to whom or why. Chaos, unreported, but just under the radar.

The titanic destruction in Abu Dhabi proved too much

for the media to ignore, though. High-level friends or not, the footage shot by the German tourist had been playing on TVs around the globe nonstop. Enhanced and digitized, the bombing could be seen graphically clear, as could the two American-marked fighters carrying out the strike. More than 1,200 were dead.

Officially the Pentagon was investigating, but they had no idea what was going on. Neither did the CIA, the DIA, et al. The State Department reminded everybody that more than the British and Americans flew the Harrier. But no one could come up with a plausible explanation why the Indian Navy would want to bomb a bank in Abu Dubai and do so disguised as Americans.

So, the team had made headlines—and now half the world would be looking for them. The heat clearly on, Murphy decided to move to cooler waters for a while.

But the Harriers still needed gas. So on the third night following the bank bombing, Ryder and Phelan climbed into their jump jets again and took off for 20 Angels.

The night was clear over the water, a crescent moon just coming up between the mountains of faraway Pakistan. It was a beautiful time to fly, something that Ryder had not been able to appreciate of late. The stars were ablaze above them, and that bullshit about being able to reach out and touch the face of God almost seemed possible at the moment.

They reached 20,000 feet, on time, and at the right vertical plane.

Trouble was, the tanker wasn't there.

This had never happened before. The refuelers were always on time and in the right place. Ryder didn't have to call over to Phelan. The two were in sync by now. The young wingman banked right and Ryder banked left. They went looking for their gas truck.

In the past all the pilots knew about the refueling missions was that they could be flown by any number of U.S. tanker assets cruising the area. All had been classified as training missions, meaning the refuelers were getting practice in filling up Harrier jets. Tankers could fly great distances; the

Harriers could be gassing up over the Red Sea from a tanker that was based in Germany. Someone waiting over the Indian Ocean might have come from nearby Diego Garcia. Or as far away as Guam.

But wherever tonight's fuel hound was flying from, he'd missed his duly appointed round.

Ryder and Phelan searched the skies for nearly 30 minutes, but the tanker never showed up. They couldn't wait around any longer; they didn't have the gas.

Reluctantly, they headed back down to the ship.

They landed and the planes were taken below. The Marine techs told Ryder and Phelan that Martinez was waiting for them back on the aft railing. They should see him right away.

The pilots found the Delta boss on the ass end of the ship, gazing out on the wake. There was not a beer in sight.

They told him what happened up top. Martinez didn't seem very surprised, but he was obviously troubled by the news.

"While you were gone, a few of the screens up on the bridge blinked off," he told them quietly. "A few more in the combat room went dark, too. Communications and navigation stuff mostly, but the discreet line to the U.S. Middle East Security Command also went down—and that's like our lifeblood. Bingo's guys are trying like hell to get it back, but so far, it's been no dice. It doesn't look to have been caused at our end, either. It seems that the other end just stopped transmitting to us. Like someone flipped a switch and everything getting fed to us just went away."

Ryder felt his heart hit his feet. The *Ocean Voyager* was secretly wired into the same networks U.S. Navy ships used for navigation and communications. This included advanced GPS, SeaSatComm, the Navy's global weather system, the works. Without these things, they were just another ship plowing through the water, with little more than a shortwave radio and reports from the local maritime weather service. Ryder had assumed the tanker no-show was a screwup on the part of the refueling corps. But now, with the ship's nav/comm gear shutting down, too, could there be a connection?

"You're the Delta God," he said to Martinez. "What do you think is happening here?"

Martinez hesitated a moment. He was very good at being evasive; that's what his by-the-book training had taught him to do. But he was also an emotional guy, hot-blooded. Sometimes, when asked a direct question, he couldn't help but answer it straight.

"Maybe someone is trying to tell us something," he finally said. "No tanker. No nav/comm support. Some of the sat phones are blinking out, too. We made a lot of noise the other day. Who knows what the bounce-back will be."

"We made too much noise, you mean?" Ryder asked.

Martinez just shrugged and lit his cigar.

"But is that possible?" Phelan wondered. "I thought bigger was better?"

"I did, too," Martinez said. "But one thing I've learned in this business: the rules can change at any time—and usually it's the boots on the ground that are the last to know. Besides, just about *anything* is possible with Murphy and the guys who helped set him up. I mean, we're deeper than deep. Blacker than black. We're not supposed to exist. I don't think being on CNN is exactly what they had in mind."

Just then Gallant came walking along the rail.

"Precisely the people I'm looking for," the copter pilot said to Ryder and Phelan. "Murphy wants to see you two. Up in the CQ, chop-chop."

"Just us?" Phelan asked him.

"Just you."

Ryder didn't like the sound of that.

"Were you just up there?" he asked Gallant, nodding toward the bridge house where Murphy's quarters were located. "What's he doing? Sitting in the dark?"

Gallant laughed. "Actually, he's going over a computer file of yours."

"A file of mine?" Ryder asked, surprised. "Which one?"

Gallant winked at Martinez and Phelan.

"Everyone calls it 'The Fruit File' . . ." he said.

Ryder and Phelan walked up to Murphy's cabin and knocked twice.

Murphy yelled for them to come in. Ryder opened the door to see that Gallant had been right. The cabin was hardly dark. In fact, every available light inside was blazing at maximum intensity. There was no funeral atmosphere here.

The long dining table was covered with maps, charts, credit card read-outs, cell phone logs, and many, many satellite photos. Murphy was nearly lost behind this mountain of data. He was hunched over one of his six laptops, drinking a huge cup of coffee. He was wearing a ball cap that had DON'T MESS WITH TEXAS embroidered across the bill. Three small TVs, all tuned to CNN, were just an arm's reach away. Each was replaying footage of the Abu Dubai incident. Different angles, different enhancements, slow-motion, stop-motion, all it needed now was its own music score. Ryder tried to ignore it. He'd seen the video a hundred times already, and even though he was in it and it was now the center of a huge international controversy, he'd grown tired of it a long time ago. Phelan, however, couldn't wait for a chance to see it again.

Murphy waved them in and pointed in the direction of his bar. *At least there's beer up here,* Ryder thought. He and Phelan each took a Bud and joined Murphy at the table. The funny little man was looking at a pile of jpg photos through a huge magnifying glass.

Ryder felt compelled to tell him the bad news first. He recounted the aerial tanker's no-show and their unsuccessful search for it. Murphy listened, patiently. But he was more concerned with studying the photographs in front of him.

"I'll look into it," he said offhandedly.

Ryder glanced over at Phelan, who just shrugged. "You also heard that some of the nav/comm gear shut down?" Ryder told Murphy quietly. "Some of the sat phones are blinking out, too."

Murphy never took his eye from the magnifying glass. "Stuff happens," he said. "Especially when you're far out to sea."

Ryder finally leaned over and looked at the photographs that had so captured Murphy's interest. Just as Gallant had hinted, they were the pictures Ryder had taken of the "convoy ships" that night over the Med, the ones carrying all that fruit.

"I wish I'd known about these earlier," Murphy said, sounding more enthusiastic than ever. "This is really dynamite stuff!"

Ryder was puzzled. Of all the things going on, why was Murphy so hyper about his so-called Fruit File?

"The Spooks told me it was just a bunch of ships, carrying lemons and grapes," he told Murphy. "What's the big deal?"

"It's lemons and grapes, all right," Murphy replied. "But want a guess *whose* fruit it is?"

"Chiquita Banana's?" Phelan replied.

"How about the Head Mooks themselves?" Murphy shot back.

"You're kidding," Ryder said.

"They're into peddling fruit?" Phelan asked.

Murphy flashed a smile. "I couldn't make something like that up—it's too good," he said. He unloaded his briefcase onto the desk. It contained more enhanced photos from the Fruit File.

"I had some of 'Norman' Bates' guys downstairs zoom in on the names of those convoy ships," Murphy said. "They could only raise two—but that's all I needed. I tracked them to this place."

He showed them a satellite image of a city in Libya called Qartoom. In the eastern part of the country, right on the coast, it boasted a large harbor with vessels of all sizes tied up at the extensive docks. Murphy pointed to a huge structure next to a loading pier. It was a cargo transfer facility, very modern, with roll on, roll off capability and many heavy-lift cranes. It alone took up about a third of the harbor.

"This is the shipping terminal for an outfit called 'Heavenly Fruits,'" Murphy explained. "Al Qaeda owns it; they are its sole investors. The Big Cheese started it as a corporation a few years back, one of his thirty-three legitimate companies. Most of them are small and slimy. But three of them are huge: A construction firm in the Sudan. A shipping company in Italy. And this place. Now, I know the Libyans are supposed to be our 'friends' these days, but any idea how much fruit they roll out of there in a week?"

Ryder studied the photo. It showed a lot of activity around the warehouse and sea terminal. There was a ship being loaded that was nearly as large as the *Ocean Voyager*. Many smaller cargo ships were lurking around as well.

"A couple dozen tons?" he offered.

"Try *four thousand* tons," Murphy told them. "Lemons. Grapes. Oranges. Watermelons—who knew mooks liked watermelon? That place works twenty-four hours a day, shipping fruit all over the Middle East. And only to Muslim countries, or at least that's the first stop. It's expensive stuff, too, for fruit, that is."

But Ryder was still a couple steps behind him. It showed.

"Don't you get it?" Murphy asked him. "What you saw that night were some of their fruit ships, in a convoy, with at least two Arab flyboys providing air cover. That shows you how *valuable* this business is to them and their organization. In fact, Heavenly Fruits generates a good chunk of the fifty million they need to keep the whole *jihad* thing up and running. Those grapes are more precious to them these days than a hundred ships loaded with weapons. No wonder they're protecting it on the high seas. Guns and bombs they have. It's money that they need the most."

Murphy sat back and took a sip of his coffee. Ryder and Phelan drained their beers and grabbed two more.

"Looking at your photos got me thinking," Murphy went on. "We took care of twelve million of their cash the other day. That was a real shot to the ribs. Now here's a way we can hit them with another punch, an even bigger one, right out of the blue. They'll never see it coming!"

But just as those words came out of Murphy's mouth, the three TVs next to him blinked off. Then all of his six computers shut down.

A moment later, the lights went off.

They sat there in the dark for the longest time, not talking, not moving. The ship started rolling; the wind outside was kicking up again.

"Well, this is weird," Murphy finally drawled.

The emergency lights blinked on a moment later. Now the room was extremely dim and dreary. Murphy picked up his intership phone, intent on calling the bridge. But the phone was dead.

Then came a knock at the CQ door. Murphy yelled, "Come!" and the person hurried in. It was one of Bates's guys, a very young-looking Spook. He'd obviously run all the way up from the bottom of the ship.

"Sorry to bother you," he said, breathlessly attempting a weak salute. "But we've just lost almost everything down in the White Rooms. Everything coming in from Echelon is gone. Everything coming in from Central Command is too. We even lost a lot of our Internet sites."

Murphy was stunned. Ryder and Phelan, too.

"Well, son, we just had a power outage," Murphy said to him. "Are you saying everything kicked off because of that?"

But the kid was shaking his head no.

"No, sir—that power spike was *caused* by everything downstairs shutting off at once. The sudden drop in power sent a volt-wash through the ship. When that happens, it's usually a—"

Murphy raised his hand, gently interrupting the young technician. He got the point.

"Can't you boot it all back up?" he asked him simply.

But the kid never stopping shaking his head. "When I say shut down, I mean everything has ceased transmitting from the other end," he told Murphy soberly. "We didn't kill it ourselves. Someone on the other end did."

This news landed like a 2,000-pound bomb. Murphy just

stared back at the kid as it began to slowly sink in. The tanker. The phones. The nav/comm gear. The TVs. Now this. A domino effect. Like someone flipping a switch. . . .

"OK, son," Murphy said, his voice very low. "You can get going."

The kid disappeared. Outside, the wind had started to blow a little louder.

They sat there in silence for nearly a minute. Finally Ryder pulled up a chair next to Murphy.

"Can I ask you something, off-the-record?"

Murphy was still dazed. "Sure. . . ."

"Did someone up top get pissed over the bank job?"

"Yeah, like super–pissed off?" Phelan added.

Murphy started to say something but stopped. He took a deep breath and then it seemed like all the air went right out of him.

"It wasn't as popular back home as I thought it was going to be," he finally admitted.

"But I thought there really *wasn't* anyone who could get pissed at us officially," Ryder said. "No oversight. No limits."

Murphy just held up his hands. "That only leaves the very large world of 'unofficially,' " he said. "Nothing is fool-proof. Not even this."

He nodded toward the dead TVs. "It didn't help that they were showing the video twenty-four/seven. The media can really call the tune these days, once they sink their teeth into something."

There came another uncomfortable silence as Murphy looked sadly around the room. Things were starting to fall into place for all of them. Like a championship football game, the momentum had flipped. Just like that.

"How bad do you think it is?" Ryder finally asked him.

Murphy took off his glasses and leaned way back in his chair. He had been keeping up a brave face after all. "I got a message from my 'friends' back in the states earlier today," he said. "On the secure E-mail site. They say we've been put on life support. They suggested we stay in place and not do a blessed thing."

He looked around the dim room again. "I've yet to reply to them—but they said the plug could be pulled at any time. Looks like they were right."

The ship shuddered once, making even the emergency lights blink.

Murphy's voice almost broke. "That's how it always goes, isn't it? You do the job too well, and the people back home wet their pants."

He studied his glasses. At the moment, he could have been a druggist or a dry-cleaning guy. Murphy just did not exude "spyness."

"You guys have been out here what, six weeks now?" he went on. "Well, I've been working on this baby *for years*. And now, just when things are getting interesting, they go south on us. Damn. . . ."

Ryder couldn't argue with him. He'd been involved in many black ops in his time, though never one quite as bizarre as this. By their very nature, some secret missions had very short half-lives. Some never got off the ground at all. And Murphy was right. The quick pull usually was a result of someone inside the Beltway having kittens because things were looking a little untidy.

But this was different. Most black ops come and go. *This one* started as a quest, a journey, one man's uphill battle. Sleepless nights. Endlessly banging on closed doors. A parched voice crying in the wilderness. A thousand days of hard work. It was all right there on Murphy's face now, along with the realization that it was probably slipping away, all in a matter of seconds.

"Well, we gave it a shot, I suppose," the little man said, symbolically closing his briefcase. "I hope someday the survivors of everyone killed on Nine-Eleven will know that at least."

Another silence. The ship rolled again.

Ryder tried to be philosophical. "It's not like we didn't accomplish anything out here," he said. "We could sail away tomorrow and they'd *still* be looking over their shoulders for us this time next year. We made that much of an impact, in a very short time. All because of you."

But Murphy was shaking his head no.

"And what happens when the mooks fly off to do the Next Big Thing?" he asked sternly. "And we could have been here to prevent it? I hate to tell you that no one back in the states has any idea what is about to happen. They don't want to hear it. They're still fighting about whose office is bigger and who's got the nicest window and who will have the biggest staff. Just like last time, the signals are all around them, but they can't see the forest for the trees. Do you know the Homeland Threat Warning is still stuck on yellow? They refuse to raise it up to orange. Why? Because it affects the stock market. It's bad for business. Not that it matters. People are so sick of the false alarms, they don't take anything seriously anymore. But *I know* something is about to happen. Anyone with half a brain and access to the information we have—or used to have—would reach the same conclusion."

He wiped his tired eyes.

"But if we're just going to get put out to dry . . ."

He let the words hang in the air. He'd said it himself just a few days before: *Every enterprise reaches its peak*. Those words were echoing inside Ryder's empty beer can now. Had Murphy really peaked so soon?

"I knew it would make you guys stronger, you know," he told them suddenly. He was wearing a weak but sly smile, barely visible in the dank light. "All of you, stronger."

"What's that?" Ryder asked him.

"Putting you together but telling you not to talk," Murphy said. "If you haven't figured out by now, that was a little test of mine."

"Well, it didn't work," Ryder said. "We've been blabbing like old ladies for weeks."

"As I knew you would," Murphy said. "But I also knew that it would show me something if you did: that working to-gether was more important than any asinine order to keep your traps shut. Yes, I set you up like a cell. I did just about everything the mooks do, including getting people whose families have been personally involved, shall we say? But unlike them, we had human hearts beating inside our cell. Sure, you broke the rules. But whether you know it or not, doing so turned you into something that you weren't before."

"A conspiracy of dunces, you mean?" Ryder asked.

"Nope," Murphy said. "It made you whole. It brought you together, to find common ground on your own. No holy book was needed here. All we needed to be was Americans. And Americans have souls. That's what I thought was most important. That's all I ever wanted. That's all I thought we'd ever need."

Murphy got to his feet, a little unsteadily, and walked over to the large picture window. His eyes had watered up. Hands clasped behind him, he stared out at the dark, troubled water below.

Ryder got another beer. He, too, needed some time in the dark. Phelan appeared to be deep in thought for a few moments as well. But then he slipped into Murphy's chair and started examining the pile of stuff in front of it. The young pilot had been unusually quiet for a while. That was about to change .

"You were going to run another operation soon?" he asked Murphy.

"I was thinking of it," Murphy called over his shoulder. "A pipe dream for sure. . . ."

"And now, you're KO'ing it—and you're just going to wait for the ax to fall?"

Murphy replied: "That's seems to be the only option."

Phelan took a long swig of his beer.

"It's been my experience," he said, suddenly sounding like he was three times his age, "that in times like this, people get pissed off very quickly. Call it stress or whatever. But I also know that crap like this sometimes goes away just as quickly, and eventually ceases to exist altogether. I think Buddha said it best: 'Just because it's bad doesn't mean it can't also be temporary.' "

Murphy turned and looked across the room at him. "What are you saying?"

Phelan picked up the photo and pointed to the fruit warehouse. "I'm saying run it anyway."

Ryder froze midsip on his beer. Murphy looked at Phelan strangely.

"Run what?" he asked him.

"The plan you were working on," Phelan replied. "This next mission. Do it anyway—and screw the people who are turning up the heat. You might even go down in the history books if you do."

Murphy was very puzzled. So was Ryder. Suddenly Phelan was back to being all mouth.

"Explain, please," Murphy asked him.

Phelan took another long swig of beer. "Didn't you ever take military history?"

Murphy shook his head, but then said: "Sure. . . ."

"Down through the ages," Phelan went on, "many commanders have won great battles, pulled off incredible victories, turned the tides of entire wars, all while they were under strict orders not to do anything. It's true. And you know how most of them got away with it?"

Murphy shook his head no.

Phelan lowered his voice a little. "They always said, 'I didn't get the message in time.' "

"Really?" Murphy asked.

"I can list at least ten examples off the top of my head . . ." Phelan replied. "Maybe more."

Murphy raised his hands as if to indicate the dim lights, the dead computers, the rolling ship, their suddenly isolated condition. "But how can I say I missed all this?" he asked. "This is a message, loud and clear."

Phelan smiled slyly. "But who says they know that?" he replied. "Did you reply to the E-mail they sent?"

Again Murphy shook his head no.

Phelan never stopped smiling. "Well, until you tell them otherwise, as far as they're concerned, everything here could be *status quo*."

Murphy looked over at Ryder, as if to ask: *What do you think of this?* But the senior pilot just shrugged. Nothing Phelan said surprised him anymore.

"Do you believe this next mission would hurt the mooks badly?" Phelan asked Murphy directly.

"Yes," was the firm response.

"And do you think it will zap a few of the people who were involved in Nine-Eleven?"

"Absolutely it will. . . ."

"And could it even help prevent the Next Big Thing?"

"Prevent or certainly delay it," was the reply.

"Then just do your thing, Mr. Murphy," Phelan told him. "And when they ask, just tell them it all got lost in the translation. You didn't know what they meant. 'I didn't get the message in time.'"

Silence. Then Phelan added: "I mean, what do you have to lose? They can't kill you twice."

Murphy took off his cap and pushed back his thinning hair. He stood up straight again. Then he smiled and all but sprinted back to the table. The pep talk from the unlikeliest source had fired new energy into him. Just like that.

"Shouldn't argue with history, I guess," he said with a wink in Ryder's direction. The lights dimmed again. The ship rolled heavily to port. "Though I think we shouldn't waste any more time, either. . . ."

Phelan pointed to the picture of the big warehouse. "Now, you want us to blow up this building, I assume?"

"Not exactly," Murphy said. "I think I've got an even better idea."

"Tell us then," Phelan said.

But now Murphy hesitated. He looked down at the notes he'd been taking and seemed to consider them for a while. He turned serious again.

He said: "Look, whatever we do, I want you to realize that from now on I'm the guy out front. I didn't get the message—it was screwed up in translation, OK, fine. But if it goes wrong, I'm the one who gets the blindfold and the last smoke. No one else."

Ryder was finishing his third beer. Or was it his fourth?

"What are you talking about?" he asked Murphy.

"What I'm saying is, you might not want to know very much about this next one," he replied, indicating his pile of notes. "That way, I'll be the only one in position to take the heat."

He looked up at the two pilots. "In fact, I'm going to ask you guys to do just one thing," he said.

He pointed to the map of Qartoom, to the roof of the warehouse itself.

"Just get me here, in one piece. I'll do the rest. . . ."

Ryder and Phelan sat down with pen and paper.

Both had planned air missions before, of course, but not one quite like this. Murphy wanted to go to Qartoom sometime within the next 48 hours—anything after that he thought would lose them the very last of their momentum. But the warehouse was nearly 500 miles away and there was not enough time to turn the ship around and simply sail there. Thus the need for an air operation. But it would not be an easy one.

The mission called for a helicopter. But someone would have to fly it across Saudi Arabia, across the Red Sea, up along the Suez coast, and then over to Libya. After that, it would have to sneak under the Libyans' noses, find a secure location near the target, if not right on top of it, put at least two men on the ground, then wait for them to return. Then they would have to fly all the way back to the ship again.

It would be more than 2,500 miles, round-trip. A long way to go in a rotary craft.

Ryder explained this to Murphy. Details upon details, five pages scribbled in his bad handwriting. It would involve complex flying, multiple fuel-ups, prepositionings of fuel, and total reliance on their stealthiness. And still, much would be left up to the fates.

But at the end of the briefing, Murphy had only one question: *Where are we going to get the gas?*

Ryder stood up and stretched. Phelan yawned loudly, too. It was the longest time they'd spent with Murphy, one-on-one, since the funny little guy arrived on the boat. Despite the intrigue and all the conflicting emotions, it was just about impossible to dislike him.

"Murph, if you *really* want to do this," Ryder told him, "we can get you the gas."

Chapter 20

Bahrain

Marty Noonan, tanker driver, was back from another mission.

This one had brought him and his crew over the familiar waters of the lower Gulf, near Hormuz. They juiced up some F-15s from Sultan Air Base, the semisecret U.S. facility found in the middle of the Saudi desert, then flew around while some Marine F-18s based in Qatar used them for target-tracking practice.

The mission had lasted 10 hours, a typical night's work. It was now 5:00 A.M. Noonan craved nothing more than a few beers at the OC, some chow, and then eight hours' sleep. He would need the rest, if not the food and beer. He'd be going back up again later that day, and every day, at least until the Fifth Fleet battle group arrived.

He taxied the big KC-10 Extender over to its appointed hardstand and killed the engines. He ran the postflight checklist himself. His radioman shut down their communications suite. His boom operator locked up the refueling bubble. His flight engineer shut down the airplane's environmental systems, and the Bahrani copilot cleaned up the coffee station and galley.

All this took 15 minutes; then Noonan dismissed the crew. He did the interior postflight walk-through and found

no problems. It was 0530 when he finally climbed down
from the big jet himself. He was always the last to leave.

With the long walk across the tarmac to the officers' club,
he began wondering if there might actually be something
good to eat at the bar this time of day. Suddenly a hand
grabbed him from behind. Another hand quickly went over
his mouth. Instinctively he began to struggle, but many hands
were grabbing him now. They forced him to the ground,
locked his arms behind him, and clamped his feet together.
The next thing Noonan knew, he was being carried away by a
half-dozen people dressed in black and wearing ski masks.

They trundled him up and over the nearby sand dunes,
dropping him to the ground in front of a weird-looking helicopter that had landed on the edge of the secret base undetected. Two men were sitting inside the copter's cargo bay.
There were 10 cases of Budweiser stacked between them.
They lifted their ski masks.

It was Ryder and Phelan.

"You guys?" Noonan cried out.

"Yeah, us," Phelan told him.

Noonan was totally confused. "What the hell is going on
here?" he screamed at them. "I thought I was about to be
killed."

"Sorry for the dramatics," Ryder said. "But we're in a
strange position here."

"What kind of strange?"

"You like Bud?" Phelan asked him.

Noonan eyed the cases of authentic American beer.

"Who doesn't?" he replied.

They were called buddy tanks, or BTs.

Huge, bomblike containers that attached under an aircraft's wing, they not only carried extra fuel for the host plane
but also had the ability to stick out a hose from its rear end and
let another aircraft get a drink, like a mini in-flight refueler.

BTs were usually a Navy thing, and they were rare at that.
But Ryder and Phelan had spotted some Air Force models
at the secret base during their first unscheduled visit here.

That's why they were back. They needed four buddy tanks, 600 gallons in size, all filled with aviation fuel.

Noonan was not a Boy Scout and it wasn't like it was *his* gas. Plus this *was* a secret base; people were stopping by asking for strange things all the time. A few BTs for some Harriers was not that big of a deal. But how were they going to get them off the secret base without anyone knowing?

Ryder and Phelan directed Noonan's attention to the next dune over. Here he saw an empty container, the size of a railroad boxcar, inexplicably sitting in the middle of the desert. It was stuffed full of packing, from fireproof blankets to Styrofoam peanuts, millions of them.

Before he could ask Ryder and Phelan how this thing had got here, he saw the answer himself. Hovering above the container, maybe 50 feet up, was another weird helicopter. It had a three-chain lifting brace swinging beneath it. Its engine was absolutely silent—that's why Noonan didn't see it at first.

"Now that's freaking weird," Noonan said. Seeing a chopper in flight that made no noise was almost a surreal event.

"If you can pack the BTs in that thing," Ryder said to Noonan, pointing to the huge red container, "we'll take it from there."

There was only one way they could make Murphy's new mission work.

Three aircraft had to be involved and each one would have to fly more than 2,000 miles. The BTs they'd received for the cases of Bud were mounted onto the Harriers belowdecks on *Ocean Voyager*. The jump jets would use one BT between them, in addition to the fuel they already had onboard. They would each carry another BT to take turns feeding the helicopter that would make up the third part of their three-plane flight. The fourth BT, carried by helicopter, would stay full. After finding a place somewhere halfway between the ship and their target, they would hide this tank temporarily. It would be their lifeline, the fuel they needed to get back.

The Harriers took off first on the night of the mission.
The Blackhawk quickly followed them into the air. It was
just sunset and the ship was rounding the tip of Oman, sailing west. The three aircraft hugged the coastline until they
got to the eastern border of Yemen, the Harriers going as
slow as the helicopter was going fast. They turned north,
staying low, at no more than 250 feet maximum altitude, and
dashed up to the southwestern part of Saudi Arabia. It was a
quick flight over featureless terrain. About 50 miles inland
from the top of the Red Sea, there was a small mountain
range called Al-Hibiz Zim. It was uninhabited and held the
distinction of having the most inclement weather on the Arabian Peninsula. The mountains were the first high ground after coming off the Red Sea, and thus clouds tended to form
in front of them and then spill over. Many times, these clouds
turned into rainstorms, or worse.

They hid the lifeline tank here.

The sun had gone down on Qartoom hours ago.

The activity around the port did not let up, though. This
was a 365-day operation, especially on the docks at Heavenly
Fruits. Two separate workforces changed places every eight
hours. A ship could arrive at three in the morning, ten at night,
or quarter to noon. It would be loaded, quickly, efficiently—
just as long as the ship's captain paid all his fees in cash.

Qartoom was also a naval base, a small one with two escort destroyers and a pair of harbor police boats. The police
slept during the day, but at night they patrolled the port's
three miles of inner waterways, letting their searchlights
randomly sweep over the piers. They were looking for animal smugglers mostly.

The two Polish-built DD-6 destroyers based here repre-
sented about one-tenth of Libya's tiny whitewater navy.
These ships rarely left port. They had been stationed at Qartoom Harbor as a favor from the Libyan government to the
owner of Heavenly Fruits and had yet to be withdrawn by the
"new" Khadafi. Their presence here added a substantial layer
of visible security. They were here as a deterrent to trouble.

That's why it was such a surprise when the commander of one of the destroyers was roused from his sleep to be told British jet fighters were about to attack their base.

"No Englishman is up this late," the commander said drowsily. But he climbed out of bed and got dressed anyway.

The destroyer captain did all the right things. He woke the rest of the crew; it was the sole man awake, the bridge watch officer, who had first alerted him. He sent his men to their battle stations. He ordered the ship's engines started and lines made ready to cast off. Only then did he get up to the bridge to see what all this fuss was about.

Two planes had flown up the main waterway four minutes ago, the watch officer reported. He had watched them pass overhead. They were Harriers; he was familiar with their silhouette. He'd just guessed at their being British.

Why had no one else heard them? the CO asked him. Why was work continuing on the docks all around them?

"The jets were very, very quiet," the watch officer replied.

The CO was close to accusing the officer of sleeping and then dreaming up the planes . . . when suddenly he couldn't see anymore. A huge, extremely bright explosion had gone off not 200 feet from the port side of the diminutive warship. Both the CO and the watch officer found themselves thrown to the deck by its intensity. It took nearly 20 seconds of feeling their way around in the darkness before their sight finally returned.

Strangely, there had been no sound.

The destroyer's captain got to his feet, just in time to see two jet fighters streaking by, no more than 20 feet off the top of his bow. And there *was* noise this time. It arrived just moments after the fighters appeared, and it was as deafening as the bright flash had been blinding seconds before.

The dual assault on their senses threw both men for a loop. It was all they could do to keep the two jet fighters in sight as they roared back down the inland waterway, two streams of hot exhaust getting smaller by the instant. Before the captain could give an order, the planes started dropping "bombs" again.

Except they weren't really bombs. They were flares. Dozens of them were spilling out of the back ends of both aircraft, lighting up the night.

This caused great panic on the docks. The tremendous noise, the blinding light. The Navy officers could see dock-workers taking cover everywhere as the flares floated down all around them. Some workers even jumped into the water to get away. A moment later, someone killed all the lights around the harbor. When the string of flares petered out, Qartoom was plunged into complete darkness.

The destroyer's captain ordered his ship's air-raid alarm to be blown. Among other things, he wanted to wake the crew of his sister ship, docked just a few hundred feet away. It seemed like a good idea. But in reality, the weird electronic crying just caused further panic among the hundreds of dockworkers now scrambling around in the darkness. The planes came back again. This time they released even longer, brighter streams of flares, and it seemed their engines were twice as loud. Amid the clamor of the jets and the ship's air-raid siren, small scatterings of return gunfire could be heard.

Four of the destroyer's crewmen charged up to the bridge; one turned on the ship's air defense radar. The captain was soon huddled over its read-out screen. The jets went by again—more blinding flares, more earsplitting noise. In the glow of the phosphorescence, the officer could now see utter chaos on the docks. Dozens of workers were plunging into the water, leaving crates of cargo wherever they dropped them. Gunfire, the air-raid siren, the screech of jet engines—the multiple dots of light burned into everyone's eyes, like flashbulbs at a wedding. All over the port, confusion reigned.

And yet the two planes were not showing up on radar.

"This is *so* strange," the destroyer's captain was heard to say. "Perhaps I'm the one still asleep."

While all this was going on, no one noticed that a helicopter had landed on the roof of the Heavenly Fruits warehouse.

The rain of flares was blinding even up here, a quarter-mile away.

Gallant and Curry were flying the Blackhawk. It was the *Torch* ship troop carrier, but all its external weapons had been removed and cans of aviation fuel had been bolted down in their place. Its benches, radios, and other nonessential equipment inside had been stripped out, too, making more room for more gas.

They were carrying two unlikely passengers with them. Sitting in the back was Bobby Murphy himself. Swimming in an overly large Delta operator's suit, helmet and all, he looked like a kid going out for Trick or Treat. Beside him, dressed just as foolishly, was a Spook named Benny Aviv. He was the mad scientist of *Ocean Voyager*.

Aviv was a nerd from central casting: Coke-bottle glasses, unkempt hair, a pocket protector to protect his favorite pocket protector. He was brilliant, though. A Russian Jew who came to the United States as a boy, he'd worked his way through Harvard and then MIT. He had lost someone, too. His father was employed as a clerk by the CIA. He was murdered in Beirut in 1982 by Iranian gunmen who mistook him for the U.S. Ambassador. Aviv was just 10 years old when it happened.

It had been Aviv's job to dream up new ways to make life miserable for the mooks. Working in his own container compartment at the bottom of *Ocean Voyager,* he'd built the nail-heavy Rats' Nest bombs, he'd concocted the superitching powder, he'd designed the trigger that allowed the raft full of explosives to detonate above the villa on Monte Fidelo. In the parlance of espionage, Aviv was known as a "brain man."

Murphy had told Aviv about the Heavenly Fruits warehouse and what he wanted to do there. The plan was *so* nasty, they'd actually engaged in a moral discussion about its implications, albeit a brief one. Aviv came back with what looked like a huge aerosol spray can, about the size of a household fire extinguisher. It was exactly what Murphy had wanted.

Aviv explained that in order for the can to work, it had to

be kept under 75 degrees Fahrenheit until it was ready to deploy. Then, five minutes before use, Murphy would have to heat it up by putting a cigarette lighter at a spot precisely three inches off the center of the big can's base. When the molecules inside were properly heated, a small red button would pop, up near the handle, just like on a Thanksgiving Day turkey. This meant the can would be ready for use. But then there was the matter of installation. ... It was at that point Murphy made an executive decision and told Aviv he was coming along for this 2,000-mile chopper ride.

Now, here they were. They had survived the long, bumpy low-level flight, over three hostile nations, to find themselves atop the warehouse building, with the huge spray can and brilliantly blinding flashes of light going off all around them. The Harriers were dropping flares, not bombs, because there just wasn't enough gas available for them to lug any heavy ordnance into the air. Neither did they have any cannon shells in their guns. They were here making a ruckus by shooting blanks.

Murphy and Aviv climbed out of the helicopter, unloaded their sensitive cargo, and bounded away, carrying the big can between them. They had to be very careful. The materials inside were extremely toxic. One drop in 100 gallons of water was enough to kill several hundred people. If the substance got into the bloodstream, it would be lights-out in three minutes, a buildup that included a minute of extreme paranoia, and then what was called instantaneous dementia. This was followed by heavy nausea and then, boom, you're dead. Should the substance get on your skin, it was the same result, about 24 hours later.

That's why both men were also wearing extra-heavy-duty gloves.

They scrambled over to the air-conditioning unit, a huge metal flaring in the center of the warehouse roof. Aviv pronounced it usable. Murphy flicked a Bic lighter and held it under the bottom of the can. The two jets roared by again; still dropping their flares up and down the harbor, they were now taking return fire from the destroyers.

Murphy swore softly, for the long five minutes, trying to rush the heating process. Finally the red button popped out.

The can was now "gasified." Ready to use.

They broke out their screwdrivers and began working on the circulation vent.

Gallant and Curry ticked off the minutes the two men were gone.

How crazy was this? They were sitting on a roof, inside Libya, and with two people who didn't really look like undercover agents running around with a big aerosol can, searching for the warehouse's air conditioner vents, God knows why. The copter pilots were too smart to ask Murphy if the big can was actually a small nuclear bomb, as had been speculated. They'd been warned in advance that the less they knew about this mission, the better.

To their surprise, Murphy and Aviv jumped back onto the copter at precisely 11 minutes, 10 seconds. Exactly the time Murphy figured the installation would take. Their silenced rotors had never stopped turning, so Gallant took off immediately.

"Did you do what you had to do back there?" Curry yelled to Murphy.

"Sure as hell did!" was his excited reply. He was nervous, but it was obvious that on some level he was also enjoying himself.

"*Now* can you tell us what's going on?" Curry asked him. "Bombing this place would have been ten times easier than all this."

"Like I said before," Murphy yelled back, "there are some things you just don't want to know."

Then he paused a moment and added: "But a word to the wise: Don't put any bananas on your cornflakes for a while."

They made it back to the Al-Hibiz Zim mountains before sunup.

They had squirreled away the fourth BT in a depression next to an ancient dry riverbed. Both the Harriers and the

Blackhawk were able to set down on the stone where water once flowed. The fuel was found in good shape, its canister camouflaged from above by mounds of dirt, sand, and debris.

They attached the BT to Ryder's Harrier. He had the most fuel onboard internally; Phelan and the Blackhawk would be able to refuel off him on the way back. It would not be like the journey out, where the three aircraft had to perform a complicated ballet of low-altitude hookups and precalculated fuel transfers. It was always about weight. The plane carrying the most fuel was also *burning* the most fuel, so it had to be refueled more frequently than the others, in order to preserve the fuel it was carrying for them all to use later on . . . things of that nature.

The flight back promised to be a breeze compared to all that.

They prepared to set out again. As usual the Harriers would take off first and regulate their speed to match that of the ascending copter. Then it would be a dash straight to the south, where *Ocean Voyager,* steaming madly to the west, would meet them at a point closer than where they'd had left, another factor added into the fuel transfer madness.

But just as Ryder was preparing to lift off, he saw Gallant waving at him madly from the cockpit of the Blackhawk. He was drawing his finger across his throat, telling Ryder to kill his engine. Ryder did so; he had to believe Gallant had a good reason for telling him to. All Gallant had to do was point westward, over Ryder's left shoulder, to the other side of the Al-Hibiz Zim mountain range. There it was, a huge fist of dirt and sand, rising as high as a thundercloud and swirling like so many dark brown tornadoes.

It was a *haboob,* the gigantic sandstorm guaranteed to ruin anyone's day. This was the birthplace for many of these things, so tumultuous that flashes of lightning could be seen crackling within the tempest. The team was not going anywhere, not with this monster bearing down on them. They hastily repositioned the Harriers so that they were hard up against the mountain wall. They used strapping and electrical cord to tie off the Blackhawk's rotor blades. Then they all climbed inside the helicopter and hunkered down to wait out the storm.

Luckily Phelan had packed some playing cards and candy bars, because they remained here, like this, for the next two and a half days.

The team returned to *Ocean Voyager* on the morning of the fourth day.

The ship had been loitering in the Red Sea for nearly 48 hours, talking to the stranded team sporadically via Phelan's sat phone, which was dying because they'd used the scramble function too often. They had ridden out the storm but then faced another entire day digging out the aircraft and "desanding" them, especially the Blackhawk.

When the three aircraft finally thumped back down onto the ship, the away team was beyond exhaustion. Martinez had left strict orders with the Marine techs and anyone else who might come in contact with the returnees not to show them any of the Internet newspapers they were still able to get onboard. Nor should they talk to them about the BBC news broadcasts they'd been monitoring since the raiders left.

No one was to say anything to them about what had happened in the past 72 hours, about how the world had turned over a little bit while they'd been away.

Not until the team got a good night's sleep.

Ryder was so tired when he climbed down off his jet, he accepted the six-pack of Bud tall boys from a curiously quiet Martinez, went back to his cabin, drank all six beers himself, and then fell on his bunk. He hoped he could get at least 12 to 15 hours of uninterrupted Zs.

No such luck.

He awoke to the sound of a great commotion directly over his head.

His bleary eyes read 11:00 A.M. on his watch. He'd slept

for no more than 30 minutes. Cleaning his grandmother's roof with a sponge, Maureen had waved good-bye as Ryder fell out of this abbreviated slumber. He thought he was still back in the desert, the sandstorm blowing through his ears. The noise that roused him was almost that loud.

The great racket was coming from up top. The ship was vibrating mightily. Ryder took a moment trying to figure out what was happening. Then it came to him. A helicopter was landing on the ship; in fact it was setting down on the deck right above his head, where the ship's little-used external helicopter pad was located.

Resigned to never sleeping again, he got up, splashed water on his face, and climbed up top.

He reached the outer deck to find a silver chopper sitting on the ship's helicopter platform. Its rotor was still turning. It certainly was not one of the unit's aircraft. This was a Huey, painted silver with a thick yellow line stretching from the nose to the tail. It looked like something from a spy movie. There were four armed guards surrounding it; they were in plainclothes.

"Can you tell what's going on?" he heard a voice from behind him ask.

He turned to see Phelan sitting on the ladder one level above him, his Mexican breakfast—a glass of water and a smoke—in hand.

Before Ryder could answer, the hatch on the landing deck swung open and Murphy stepped out. He was holding his hands tightly behind him, which looked odd. Murphy took two more steps before Ryder and Phelan realized he was actually in handcuffs—the old-fashioned steel kind. Two armed guys in jeans and T-shirts were in back of him. They were leading him to the waiting chopper.

Martinez came rushing up the steps at this point. Everyone else had wisely stayed below.

"What the fuck is happening here?" Ryder asked him.

"They've arrested Murphy," Martinez replied, his voice hollow.

"Arrested? *For what?*"

Martinez pulled out a newspaper headline they'd taken off the Net from the English-language *Arab World News* that morning. This was what Martinez didn't want them to know, not until they had to. The headlines read: "More than 1,700 Dead in Fruit Poisoning.... Authorities Fear More Biowar Deaths.... Distributor Shut Down."

Ryder stared at the headlines. Poison. Biowar. No wonder Murphy had been so tight-lipped about what he wanted to do in Qartoom. *Why didn't we just bomb the goddamn place?* Ryder cursed to himself. *Why did we talk him into doing this?*

"Murph got his wish," Martinez was saying to him now. "He shut that bastard down. But shit . . . this is nasty."

The next thing Ryder knew, Phelan had leaped completely over him, landing onto the helicopter platform with a clang. He went to throw a punch at the guy holding Murphy's left shoulder—but Martinez had dropped down to the platform right after him and expertly blocked the punch. It was a good thing, too. These guys were State Department Security troops, a little-known civilian force who would just as soon shoot you as look at you. They probably would have shot Phelan had he truly interfered.

A small scuffle did erupt though between Phelan, Martinez, and two of the guards who'd stayed by the Huey. It was Murphy himself who quelled the shoving match.

"Cool it!" he yelled at Phelan and Martinez. "There's no sense in fighting this. The jig is up."

Now Ryder found himself leaping to the copter platform as well. He blocked the guards from putting Murphy into the copter.

"Tell them, Murph!" Ryder yelled at him over the screaming rotor blades. "Tell these guys what's what, that everything here is OK!"

But Murphy just hung his head.

Ryder was confused. "Just tell them," he urged Murphy again. "The operation. This ship. How you got the President to OK it all. To fund it. How he gave you a free rein. . . ."

Murphy just shook his head. "I'm sorry, Colonel," he said

with a wan smile. "But, really, take a good look around. What President in his right mind would have authorized all this?"

With that, the guards threw him onto the helicopter. The door closed and the Huey lifted off.

And just like that, Bobby Murphy was gone.

Chapter 21

It was Thursday night and the plaster tent in Prince Ali's backyard was filled to capacity.

Nearly 3,000 Saudi citizens had been permitted inside for the weekly ritual of asking the Prince for favors—and there was some surprise among the Prince's staff when Ali actually showed up for the affair. He'd been acting very odd lately. Harsher than usual on the help, spending more time wandering his palace than at Pan Arabic, working his worry beads to the nub. He'd also become obsessed with how thoroughly his clothes were being laundered.

He strolled into the tent 30 minutes late, but here nevertheless. He sat on his gold-and-sapphire-encrusted chair and brusquely motioned his people to let the parade of petitioners begin. On the rare occasion that Ali was in a good mood for one of these things, mostly in his younger days, he would stand at his throne for several hours, having a word or two with just about everyone who passed by in line.

Not tonight. The parade of citizens became a kind of human assembly line. One security man was literally pushing people toward Ali's assistants collecting the petitions, who would then shove them along to the senior bodyguards, who would frisk each one before pushing him or her up to meet the Prince himself. Ali wasn't even shaking hands tonight.

The citizen had about one second in his presence before he was pulled along by another security man, given an orange or a lemon, and then told to leave the grounds immediately, as the Prince wasn't that fond of crowds.

This roughhouse system got the line of people moving quickly. Still it took Ali more than a hour to greet them all. Most just gave him a slight kiss on the right shoulder, a sign of respect for the Royal Family. No one detected the smell of alcohol on him simply because no one got close enough, long enough, to give him a good sniff.

Finally the last person in the line was in sight. When this individual reached Ali's security coterie though, the bodyguards took one good look at the petitioner and then backed away. Ali was horrified. What was going on? Then the man stepped before him and pulled the *kufi* from his face. Ali saw his features for the first time. His stomach did a flip.

It was Kazeel, planning master for Al Qaeda.

Ali was furious.

"Brother, what are you doing here?" he hissed at the man.

"Peace to you, brother," Kazeel replied in that threatening tone of his. "You should be braver, my friend."

"I don't need to be brave," Ali shot back at him. "I can pay people to be brave for me."

Kazeel just waved his comment away. "You are protecting that CD-ROM with your life, I hope?"

Ali replied: "I don't have any other choice."

Kazeel displayed his gap-tooth grin for a moment but then turned very serious. "We have a problem, my brother," he told Ali. "With the big plan."

Ali was not surprised to hear this. He'd been watching CNN nonstop for days. The bank in Abu Dhabi. The biopoisoning at Heavenly Fruits. The overdue acknowledgment that a rogue team of U.S. operatives had been carrying out vicious attacks on Arabs for the past month. Ali didn't need any further explanation for Kazeel's sudden appearance. He was here for money. Again.

But there was a real air of desperation about him this time. Ali studied him closely.

"Things are really not so well with you, are they, brother?" he asked him.

"The operation date is very close," Kazeel replied. "But we are experiencing a sudden cash flow problem, due to the recent events, of which I'm sure you are aware. These things have left us less liquid than we hoped."

"You have never been one to massage words, brother," Ali told him, a little defiantly. "We are friends. Tell me how bad things are."

"We are bleeding dollars," was how Kazeel chose to put it. "These crazy American gunmen have pushed us to the brink, and frankly, many sources of our revenue have dried up. My brother, you are now one of the few people on earth who know this sad information, and it is a secret I suggest you protect as vigorously as you are protecting that CD.

"But Allah is nothing if not truth—and the truth is this: the big operation is in jeopardy. As we have all been praying for this for so long, our brave *maji* are fanatically reluctant to postpone it or cancel it outright. To do so might adversely affect our standing with our many brothers around the world."

"I understand, my friend," Ali said. It was no surprise that the Al Qaeda planner had come to him. People in Ali's position were just expected to give, on a regular basis, as proof that their Muslim hearts were still "pure." Ali went a bit further than most by allowing the *jihad* organizations to use his offices at Pan Arabic to launder their money. All these things kept the terrorist group flush in their bank accounts, kept the black ink from spilling into the red, and kept them from going after targets within the Saudi Family itself.

"I will have an envelope waiting for you at my desk tomorrow morning," Ali told him—he just wanted to get rid of Kazeel at this point. "I will gladly double my donation to four hundred thousand dollars and, as always, my offices stand by to help you in funneling any other donations collected during this pressing time."

But Kazeel just stared back at him. "Brother, a million apologies," he said. "But you really *don't* understand what I am saying."

Ali felt something poking him just below his rib cage. He looked down to see the tip of a knife pointed at his stomach.

Kazeel gritted his teeth and whispered: "We need *two million* in cash immediately. To refuse means you have turned unfaithful—and that this blade will soon be inside you. And may I remind you that a belly wound is the most painful way to die."

Ali nearly lost control of his bladder. "But . . . you would die, too, my brother," he gasped. As always, Ali had a small army of bodyguards around him.

But Kazeel only pushed his knife in deeper. "I will die, too?" he asked snidely. "So what? It is my job to die."

Ali was suddenly terrified, and appalled. That it had come to this defied all that he'd believed in Allah, what little that was. And it was not the money. It was the fact that every dollar he gave to Kazeel further illuminated the path the Crazy Americans would eventually follow to get to him. Just like they got to Farouk's nephew and so many others.

Yet if he refused outright, Kazeel would gut him right here, on the spot. There was no doubt about that.

So Ali hastily wrote out a note with which Kazeel could withdraw funds from a blind bank account Ali had in Riyadh. He included the bank president's private phone number, ensuring that Kazeel would get the funds right away.

Kazeel took the note and read it. Ali's signature was as good as gold in Riyadh. Kazeel withdrew the knife and simply walked away.

No farewell. No thank-you.

"Sleep in peace, brother!" Ali called after him. "God knows, I won't. . . ."

PART THREE

The Next Big Thing

Chapter 22

The maids at the Royal Dubai were starting to complain.

They were an army of 20, all Filipinos, and they could clean every room in the ultraluxurious Gulf-side hotel in under six hours. But the guests had to cooperate. They had to allow the maids into the room some time before 2:00 P.M. every day. They had to present dirty linen in order to get the clean. And they had to return room service plates and utensils after every meal.

But the men staying in the penthouse weren't doing any of these things. They had been guests in the hotel for three weeks, their number fluctuating between five and seven. In that time they had not once allowed a maid to enter the expansive tenth-floor suite. They had not put out any dirty laundry, nor had they taken in such essentials as soap, shampoo, or toilet paper. The men had all their meals delivered by room service and requested the food trays be left outside their door. But they had yet to return any of the dirty dishes.

When the maids pressed their ears against the penthouse door, they always heard the same thing, day or night: a constant clicking sound, like someone continuously flipping a switch. This and voices speaking softly into telephones.

The mystery guests had shown another peculiarity. They'd

spent lavishly in their first two weeks at the five-star hotel. They'd indulged in many of the gourmet foods the kitchen had to offer. They'd purchased pay-for-view movies around-the-clock. They'd even bought a couple of laptop computers from the hotel's gift shop, at outrageous expense. They'd also run up huge bills for using the hotel's Internet access lines, and their long-distance phone charges were into the thousands of dollars after just a few days. But then the extravagant spending came to a halt. For several days the men ordered no food or drink at all. The six TVs in the penthouse were never turned on, or at least not to any of the pay channels. They'd made no long-distance phone calls and did not access the Internet once. It was as if they'd become penniless overnight.

Then suddenly they were flush again. One of them had returned to the hotel late Thursday night, after a day trip to Riyadh, and paid their bill in cash. He also secured the suite for five more days. Then he ordered nearly three hundred dollars in room service food brought up to the penthouse and the spending spree began again.

The hotel management was suspicious of all this, of course. But then again, this was the Middle East and high-priced hotels were always suspicious of their guests, especially those who paid in cash. Calling the Dubai state police was like placing a collect call to Al Qaeda, and no one wanted to do that.

So the hotel management simply issued a new policy: the maids should stop complaining, stay out of sight, and, for the time being, be less ambitious about keeping the penthouse clean.

Aboard *Ocean Voyager*

Ryder would never quite recall why they'd decided to gather in Phelan's cabin that night.

Their traditional hangout spot had been on the fantail, where a few beers and the sight of the ship's huge wake could have a calming effect at times. But that was the trouble—they had been doing nothing *but* hanging out lately. They'd been lifeless at sea for nearly a week, just drifting around the upper Indian Ocean, with nothing to do and not knowing what they should do next.

All the plugs had been pulled on them by now. Things had been flicking off all over the ship since a few days after the bank bombing. Even while the raid to Libya was in progress, their lifelines were being cut and a slow withering on the vine process begun. The last of the porn sites had disappeared that morning, killing the White Rooms' last link to the outside world. The ship was also running out of necessities as the 45-day limit on resources was suddenly upon them. The days of Kobe steak were long gone. Coffee was being rationed. The T-paper supply was getting low. And they were almost out of beer.

Meanwhile the world seemed to be falling apart all around them, due at least in some part to the bank bombing in Abu Dhabi and the bioattack on Heavenly Fruits. According to BBC broadcasts picked up on the ship's lowly radio, the ripple effect of the twin attacks had caused so much instability around the Persian Gulf, gas prices in the United States were soaring. This while the stock market was doing a new swan dive with every session. The food industry was reeling, too, as few people wanted to eat anything that didn't come out of a can these days. And gold had become a very precious commodity again, always a bad sign.

Most acute, though, the U.S. airline industry was on the verge of total collapse. About two weeks before, someone began quietly hacking into the computers of all the major U.S. air carriers and buying up huge numbers of tickets, sometimes using bogus credit card numbers for payment but many times not. Almost immediately after buying a ticket on one computer, the hackers would then cancel it on another, in effect putting the seat in limbo. At first the computers handled the purchases like normal transactions, as many came in just one or two at a time. But as the cyber-attack continued undetected, a domino effect slowly befell the airlines. Flights that had no real passengers meant airplanes full of empty, and ultimately unpurchased, seats. Every time an airline tried to rebook a flight, the hackers would simply override the security codes, delete the new ticket purchases, and reinstate the old ones, just to cancel them again. It took a while, but eventually the entire U.S. booking system became overloaded with this new kind of spam. It finally crashed several days ago. Attempts to revive it had been sporadic at best.

Making the situation worse, many U.S. airlines, and especially those that flew to Europe, had been in this same time period victims of a staggering number of bomb threats, to both aircraft and airport facilities. Many had been called in while the planes in question were in the air and frequently while they were over the Atlantic. The flood of false warnings not only resulted in many flights being cancelled, it caused U.S. airline terminals in London, Paris, Rome, and a dozen other cities, including all those in the Middle East to close. These shutdowns were wreaking further havoc with overseas flight schedules.

What did it all mean? No one knew. U.S. intelligence wasn't even sure if the two situations were connected.

But air travel between the Unites States and Europe was just 10 percent of what it had been just three weeks before—and was in real danger of disappearing completely.

"We could always go into business hauling freight," Gallant had suggested this night, after the usual suspects had squeezed into Phelan's quarters. "We've got the ship already. We've got the equipment. And we've got the crew. Who would ever know?"

He was only half-kidding, trying to lighten the mood in the crowded, gloomy cabin. But the others were in no mood to have their moods changed. It had been a lot like that lately.

They presented as a fairly sad bunch these days. Curry in his Oakland Raiders T-shirt, its colors fading and fraying around the edges. Gallant looking more like a very tired Clark Kent than his superhero alter ego. Martinez, eyes bloodshot and sunken, perhaps betraying years beyond his admitted 35. And Ryder, feeling every bit the old man at 44.

It was Phelan, though, who looked the worst. Normally, you couldn't shut the guy up. But he hadn't spoken more than three words to any of them in days. His sunny disposition had turned very dark, like a light had gone out upstairs. The others were worried about him.

"What's killing me," Curry said a few minutes into the bitch session, "is that Murphy was *so* close to cracking the mooks' Next Big Thing. After all the time he'd spent down in the White Rooms, he probably knew more about it than the FBI, the NSA, and the CIA put together. Now we'll just have to sit by and let it happen."

"What else *can* we do?" Martinez shot back.

They'd been over this a hundred times. They had no commanding officer. No orders. No mandate. They didn't have any of the intelligence that routinely bubbled up from the White Rooms; they were almost out of bombs and ammo. Plus, they didn't have any aviation gas. Or not much anyway. Both copters were below a third full. The Harriers had even less than that. They'd gone from a very effective fighting force to an almost nonexistent one in just a week.

Worse, they had no idea about their own fates. Who knew what Bobby Murphy had *really* got them into? His last words to Ryder still haunted the team. The thought that the entire enterprise never had White House approval was so disturbing, no one wanted to believe it. But as Murphy had managed to get himself arrested, they had no reason to think the same wouldn't happen to them at any minute. Just why they weren't all taken into custody along with Murphy was perhaps the biggest mystery of all.

Certainly their military careers were over. There was no mystery about that. They'd almost single-handedly plunged the United States into another depression—such things would not look good on their service résumés. Curry had made the suggestion earlier that they quietly sail to someplace like Mexico, dock the ship, and then scatter to the four winds. It was sounding more and more like their best option.

But something strange would happen this night.

A jolt of inspiration, again from a most unlikely source, would change everything. . . .

It came while the team was still crowded into Phelan's room, jawing away. Phelan himself was sitting on his bunk, looking very agitated. It didn't take a shrink to know what was bothering him. He'd failed his dad. *His hero.* He'd missed his only real opportunity to avenge his father's death. Somehow, the bad guys had won again.

As a way of venting, Phelan was taking his precious music CDs one at a time from their cases and methodically flinging them around the cabin, Frisbee-style. They were bouncing off the walls, the floor, the ceiling, the backs of people's heads, some breaking, some not. He didn't seem to be paying much attention to anything besides this until . . .

"Freaking used CDs!" he suddenly cried out.

The others looked at him as if he'd finally cracked.

"What did you say?" Ryder asked him.

"The CD-ROM, the one with the plan for the Next Big Thing!" Phelan replied, breathless. "I think I know where one is."

The others were immediately skeptical.

"How the fuck is that possible?" Curry challenged him. "That CD is probably the most valuable piece of intelligence in the world right now. How could *you* suddenly come up with a location for one?"

Phelan jumped off his bunk to the middle of the floor. "You remember how Murph was bummed out that we iced that mook Zoobu before we figured he was distributing the CD-ROMs?"

Everyone nodded.

"Murphy was convinced the guy had at least one on him when we whacked him in the electronics store, right?"

Again, they all agreed.

"But he was clean when we hit him," Phelan went on. "Which means if he *did* have a CD on him, he must have ditched it before Hunn's boys started chopping him up."

Everyone turned to Martinez. "Did that mook have enough time to hide something before he got stuck?" Curry asked him.

Martinez shrugged. "A few seconds maybe. But where would he hide a CD in just a few seconds? Especially in a place where he absolutely did not want it to be found?"

Phelan smiled. The light was back in his eyes.

"Dude—think about it," he said. "They killed him in the *used CD section*."

Martinez considered this for a moment. "Are you're saying he might have stashed the CD-ROM somewhere in that store?"

"If he had it on him and he saw us coming, can you think of a better place?" Phelan replied. "There's got to be hundreds of CDs in that place. And who could tell one from the other if they weren't looking for it? I'll bet he dumped it into one of the racks."

Martinez just shrugged. "It's a possibility, I suppose. But so what? What good does it do us now?"

"Dude, we can go get it," Phelan told him. "If we find it and crack into it, maybe we can throw a wrench into the mooks' plans after all."

Martinez just shook his head and laughed. "Whatever you're smoking, can you give me some? I need a good buzz right about now."

"Wait a minute," Gallant interrupted. "Maybe Phelan's right. Maybe the mook *did* dump it—and it's just waiting there to be found. If there was even a chance of that, I think we'd be crazy *not* to go back and look for it. . . ."

Clearly Martinez was astonished at what he was hearing.

"Do you realize what you are suggesting?" he asked them. "Do you know how unauthorized that would be?"

Now it was their turn to laugh at him. " *'Unauthorized'?* Are you kidding?" Curry roared back. "This whole fucking bad movie has been *unauthorized*. If anything, Murphy sure as hell confirmed that. Besides, they're probably fitting us for leg irons as we speak. So what the hell do we have to lose?"

"Are you actually proposing that we run an operation—on our own?" Martinez asked him sternly. "With no orders? No Murphy? No nothing?"

Curry, Gallant, and Phelan all nodded.

Martinez just shook his head. "You're all crazy. Don't you realize they started shutting us down right after the bank bombing? That was their way of telling us we're ghosts. We have nothing left. . . ."

He turned to Phelan. "And no offense, Lieutenant—but the last time you came up with an idea, it sent Murphy over the edge to Libya."

Gallant was instantly furious: "Man, that's unfair. . . . I would have told Murphy to do the exact same thing if he'd asked me."

"Sure it's a long shot," Curry said to Martinez. "But look at it this way: if we *were* able to finesse something here, we might head off another Nine-Eleven—or even something bigger. . . ."

"And maybe we can all avoid going to Leavenworth, too," Gallant added.

Martinez was at a loss for words. He was the straightest shooter of them all, the most military of the bunch. It was against his nature to go against the book, even though the book had been tossed overboard a long time ago.

So he turned to Ryder. The pilot had spent most of the discussion wedged into a corner, counting the cigarettes he had left in his pack and planning how he could make them last, because there were no more to be had aboard ship. Suddenly he was aware that the rest of the team were looking at him. Sad eyes, needing guidance as bad as he needed an extra pack of smokes.

"Well, what do you think, *Colonel*?" Martinez asked him, emphasizing his rank for the first time ever. "After all, you are the *senior* member here."

Ryder could only offer a weary shrug. He *was* getting too old for this.

"I don't think any of us will look good in stripes," he said.

Chapter 23

The Burjuman marketplace was nearly empty.

The huge open-air bazaar, hard on the edge of 'Ajman City, hadn't seen a crowd since the day the Crazy Americans came and killed the terrorist named Zoobu.

The underwear and the computers, the boom boxes and the shamrocks, now seemed glued to the shelves, slowly becoming encased in the fine desert sand. The huge Coke and Pepsi signs still hung high overhead, dominating the marketplace, but there was no one to provide shade for anymore. Many of the makeshift shops had folded up their tents, literally, and moved on.

Jazeer's electronics shop was still here, though only because he was still in the hospital, recovering from his hideous wounds. His sister's 12-year-old daughter was now minding the store, but she did not have near the enthusiasm of Jazeer. She spent her days sitting next to the cash register, her tiny body in an adolescent slouch, reading American comic books and 'N Sync fan magazines and barely acknowledging anyone who came in.

She was also rather dull upstairs, so when the black helicopter landed in the middle of the square a few minutes before her 10:00 P.M. closing time, she barely looked up from the interview with Justin T. Even when the five huge soldiers stepped off the chopper and began walking in her direction, she remained unfazed. She had heard something about a helicopter crashing into the square last week—was that how Uncle Jazeer got hurt?—but then someone had told her the Jews had been the cause of it, and she forgot all about it soon afterward.

But now the five soldiers were suddenly standing in front of her, and it was registering that they were much too large to be Arab. Or Israeli. And they were holding huge guns.

"Whatdoyouwant?" she asked them finally, in English.

The soldier closest to her raised his weapon. Delta had never been greeted quite like that before, and this trooper didn't like it. A three-bullet barrage would blow her apart; she was that small.

Someone's little sister, he supposed. *Totally clueless. . . .*

A tense moment passed. Then he lowered his weapon and said: "We are here to take all of your CDs. . . ."

"Take them? As in steal them?" she asked.

"Let's just say we are going to move them from one place to another," was the reply. "As a favor, for the guy who used to work here."

For some reason, this made sense to her. "For Uncle Jazeer, you mean?"

The soldier nodded wearily. "Exactly."

She went back to her magazine.

"Be my guest," she said.

Aboard *Ocean Voyager*

Abu Jazeer had a total of 721 used CDs in the back of his store.

They were all now sitting inside the container compartment once known as White Room #2, most of them in two gigantic stacks, swaying precariously with the rolling of the ship. There was several million dollars' worth of audio enhancement gear nearby, gadgets that could decipher the smallest of sound patterns or clear static from a line or tell which part of the world a cell-phone call was being placed from. But the strike team leaders were interested in just one device down here at the moment. It was a battered old computer with a cracked keyboard and a balky sound system attached.

Phelan was sitting in front of this PC now, loading one used CD into it after another, looking for a needle in a haystack of pins. It didn't help that all of Jazeer's inventory was illegal, songs burned onto blank CDs and then sold as "used." Many were packed into unmarked paper or cardboard sleeves rather than jewel boxes. And those that *were* marked had been done so incorrectly, with the cover sleeve not matching what was inside.

In other words, the only way to find out which one wasn't a music CD was to load each of them into the computer, activate the CD-ROM drive, and hope that one would start downloading information, instead of just blaring out some bad foreign music.

So far, it had been nothing but bad music.

In the two hours since returning to the ship, Phelan had fed more than 300 CDs into the elderly HP 900E computer, with no luck. Contemplating at least another two hours with 400 disks to go, the team leaders were becoming restless. They'd slipped back into the Gulf just as another foul weather front appeared. A rainstorm was brewing outside, making the interior of the dreary compartment damp and uncomfortable. The adrenalin high of so swiftly confiscating the load of CDs was now dissipating with each roll of the ship.

It didn't help that they'd received some bad news about ninety minutes into the process. It came from one of the Marine techs who'd hiked all the way down to the bottom of the boat to tell them the *Torch* copter was no longer be able to fly. While the marathon flight to Qartoom had taken its toll, the last mission to 'Ajman had been a backbreaker, he said. The copter's avionics were already ragged. Now its engines were shot and beyond repair, due to a lack of spare parts. The Marines had drained the last few precious drops of fuel from its tanks and the *Torch* was now considered OTB—off the books. Inactive. *Dead*. It was an inglorious end for the great aerial troop truck.

By the third hour, the team members began wandering away. Curry and Gallant left after nothing had been found in the first 400 CDs. The little bleats of music were horrible and loud, and after a while they all had earaches. Martinez eventually retired, too. Too exhausted to be the contrarian now, before he left the Delta officer gave Phelan a fatherly pat on the back, as if to say: *Nice try, son.* Outside, the storm grew worse.

Only Ryder remained with Phelan, handing him a new CD as the one before it went spinning across the room, to splinter against the far wall. The floor of the previously antiseptic White Room #2 was now thick with pieces of shiny, broken plastic.

Shortly after the fifth hour of this began, Phelan stopped for a moment, rubbed his tired eyes, and let out a long, troubled breath.

"We're screwed," he said wearily. "If Zoobu had stashed the CD-ROM in with all this crap, the chances are we would have found it by now."

"Well, it was worth a shot," Ryder told him; his spirits, too, had begun to fade. "And it's what Murphy would have wanted us to do, right?"

But Phelan just shook his head. The emotional roller coaster was clearly having the biggest effect on him. "What am I ever going to tell my mom?" he said quietly.

Finally it came down to the last 100 CDs. They'd all been taken from a bin marked: FRENCH ROCK AND ROLL.

"If Zoobu *really* wanted to hide it," Ryder said smartly, "this would have been the place."

Phelan put in the first CD. Awful music. The second—and the music was even worse. The third went beyond the description of bad. Then he came to a CD whose paper sleeve was marked BLACK TUESDAY in French. Phelan numbly fed it into the computer.

Suddenly the screen popped to life.

The two pilots couldn't believe it. An electronically distorted image slowly came into focus on the monitor. It was a man's face. He was an Arab, with three missing teeth, a pop eye, and a crooked turban. He was smiling but looked treacherous.

Phelan clenched his fists in triumph.

"Either he's a French rock star," the young pilot said excitedly, "or we just caught us a fish."

Inside five minutes, the rest of the team had rushed back to White Room #2. A new energy had blown into the compartment.

They all studied the picture on the screen. It was Martinez who recognized the dirty face first.

"Damn," he said. "That's Abdul Kazeel. . . ."

"Friend of yours?" Phelan asked dryly.

But Martinez remained dead serious. "He's only the top operations guy left in Al Qaeda. Next to Khalid Shaikh, he did most of the down-and-dirty planning for Nine-Eleven. Christ, he handed ticket money to Muhammad Atta himself."

"Jackpot . . ." Phelan declared.

"Let's hope so," Martinez replied.

Phelan quickly gave his seat to Gil Bates. Summoned from above, the young Spook Boss knew his way around a computer better than anyone else onboard. He thought he recognized the type of CD-ROM they'd found.

"This *does* look like a final briefing disk," he told them. "I've seen a few of them before. The mooks started using CD-ROMS right after Nine-Eleven for security reasons, especially when something big was about to happen."

He began banging away on the keyboard. "They set them up just like computer games," he explained. "This one's probably divided into a number of different levels. That's how they usually put these things together."

They all watched the first level play out. Just as Bates predicted, it served as the disk's introduction and like a computer game, opened automatically. The initial images were highly visual, the screen filling with weird Islamic effects, lines of text, and nonstop dissolves of *jihad* members, all backed by discordant Middle Eastern music.

"It looks like a bad religious program," Gallant said. "Something they show on cable at two in the morning."

"You haven't seen much Arab TV," Bates told him, his eyes never leaving the screen. "This kind of stuff passes for prime-time programming over here."

The visuals of the *jihad* fighters were handled not unlike the introduction of a computer-game sports team. Each terrorist was given about ten seconds of face time, with his photograph displayed prominently on one part of the screen and a video cut-in of him speaking taking up the other.

Kazeel meanwhile served as narrator for this first level. Babbling on and on, his voice was laid over a still photo of himself dressed in full camo battle fatigues which kept dissolving from one corner of the screen to the other. A total of 22 *jihad* types were shown. The last pair had their faces completely tiled out, an extraordinary security procedure, Bates said.

"Whatever the mooks are planning next," the Spook Boss concluded, "these are the guys who are going to do it."

But no sooner were the words out of his mouth than the first level ended and the CD froze in place.

"Shit . . . what happened?" Martinez cried.

Bates began banging on the keyboard again, but the visuals would not budge.

"I was afraid of this," he said, pointing to three blank fields that had appeared at the bottom of the screen. "We need to enter encryption codes into those three boxes in order to get into the next level. Codes we do not have."

With those words, all that new energy went right out of the room again.

"Isn't there a way you can figure them out?" Martinez asked Bates sternly. "You're supposed to be the whiz kid."

"Sure I can—if you give me a couple weeks," Bates replied. "But short of that . . ."

"God damn it," Ryder said. "You said this is like a computer game. Don't you have any clues at all? Something that might crack the codes?"

But Bates just shook his head. "The mooks really know what they're doing when it comes to encryption. It's like a challenge to them. Hacking into the Pentagon is a breeze compared to what they can put up."

A groan went through the compartment. Once again, they were back to zero.

Bates rebooted the PC and went back to the beginning of the CD-ROM. Kazeel's dark face soon filled the screen again. In between introducing the martyrs-to-be, Kazeel seemed to be reading from cue cards out of camera range. The team members all listened closely, but Kazeel's words, in Arabic, made little sense, even to those in the room who spoke the language. They sounded like disassociated religious phrases, repeated over and over.

"What the hell is he talking about?" Martinez finally asked.

Bates just shrugged again. "I have no idea. . . ."

But then came a phrase that outlined the proper way a Muslim man could kill his unfaithful wife.

"Now *that's* from the Koran," Bates declared, cleaning up the audio a bit. "And that could mean everything he's saying might be, too. That could actually help us."

"What do you mean?" Martinez asked.

"This Kazeel might be speaking in Koranic code," Bates replied. "Let's say each mook already had a specially prepared copy of the Koran before he received his CD. They might have a system in place that when they hear these repetitive phrases from Kazeel, they will make some kind of sense to them—and lead somehow to the encryption codes needed to open up the rest of the CD-ROM. That way, should the CD itself fall into the wrong hands, the mooks still have a measure of security in place."

"So what you're saying is," Martinez asked, "the Koran is actually their codebook?"

Bates nodded. "They might be using it that way. Possibly even as a double-code book."

"So this disk doesn't do us any good then?" Ryder said.

"Not unless we get one of their Korans," Bates replied. "And how we do that I don't know. But whatever we do, we have to hurry. . . ."

"Why so?" Martinez asked.

Bates finally took his eyes off the screen. "When I first joined the NSA, my group did a case study on Nine-Eleven," he explained. "We concentrated on communications NSA had intercepted from the mooks in the days just before the towers were hit. We learned that the most important element in their entire plan was the timetable. The mooks were slaves to it. I mean, they scheduled things right down to the very last minute. Now the final communiqué from the top came less than a week before the hijackings took place. This was their one last briefing before they went off to do the deed. I'll bet this CD contains the same thing. The final details. Their marching orders, so to speak. That's why they went so heavy on the security.

"Now if we can get into the next levels, and I'm guessing there are two more, then I'll bet we'll see all their operational stuff: hours, dates, meeting locations, targets, the works. We might even see details for any misdirection they are planning."

"That would be more than enough to head off this thing, for sure," Phelan said. "Whatever it is. . . ."

"Correct . . . but remember this," Bates went on. "This CD is already more than a week old. And they wouldn't let it go floating around out there for very long if they didn't have to."

"In other words?" Martinez asked him.

Bates just shrugged. "I think whatever they are planning is going to happen very soon, like in the next twenty-four hours. I'd stake my career on it."

Total silence. The team leaders became frozen to their spots. Suddenly it felt very cold inside the container—cold and dirty and gloomy.

"Twenty-four hours?" Phelan finally said. "Murphy thought we had a couple weeks to work with. But this thing is happening like *right now.* . . ."

"And we still don't have a clue as to what they're planning to do," Ryder moaned. "Or where. Or how."

"That's the trouble," Curry said. "We're in our own little
fucking world out here. We used to be so plugged in—but
now, we hardly know what time it is."

Martinez collapsed into a nearby seat. His face had
turned pale. He knew this had been a bad idea from the beginning. "Any idea how many mooks were on the distribution for this disk?" he asked Bates wearily.

Bates just shook his head again. "There's no way of
telling. Could be thirty. Could be fifty. It was distributed on a
strict need-to-know basis, I'm sure. But at this late juncture,
they're all pretty much gone to ground by now anyway. They
button up very tight right before they run an operation."

The ship started rolling again. The lights overhead began
to flicker, a common problem of late. Bates thought a moment, then added, "But maybe . . ."

He started pounding furiously on the keyboard again.
The images on the CD were passing across the screen in fast
motion, but somehow Bates's trained eye was able to sort out
order from the confusion. He stopped at the visual of each
martyr-to-be, studying the screen before moving on. Finally
he brought the CD to a halt on the picture of a young terrorist in the process of saying his last prayers. He was Martyr
Number 12. The guy looked no more than 18 years old. He
was sitting cross-legged with a cloth wrapped around his
head, a Kalashnikov in his hands, and two vacant eyes peer-
ing out at the world.

"Look at this guy," Bates said. "He might be a minor
player, because he only gets about seven seconds of screen
time in total. But check this out. . . ."

He started moving the CD forward in slow motion. The
young terrorist was seen banging a Koran against his chest.
There were documents floating by his head, courtesy of a
very cheesy special effects machine, making it look as if he
were sitting on a cloud. Most of these documents were hand-
written, farewell letters to his family, not unusual, as Al
Qaeda fighters frequently left behind substantial messages

to be used for propaganda purposes once they were dead.

"Look, right there," Bates said, freezing the screen again. "See it?"

The others gathered closer around. Bates was pointing to one document that was hovering over the young terrorist's shoulder. It was not a letter.

"It's a birth certificate," Bates said. "The mooks have been known to stick them onto their visuals sometimes, especially with new members, as a way to prove the *jihad* fighter is an authentic Muslim. This guy's name is Jamaal Muhammad el-Habini."

"Yeah, so?" Phelan said. "There's probably a million guys named that around here."

"But look at this," Bates replied. He was pointing to the certificate's stylistic printing. It was nearly washed out in the bad video production. But when he enhanced this part of the image several times, the third line of the birth certificate became clear enough to read.

"What is that?" Ryder asked Bates.

"Believe it or not," the Spook replied, "I think that's his address. . . ."

"Damn . . . really?" Martinez exclaimed.

"Where does he live?" Phelan asked.

"Where else?" Bates answered. "Saudi Arabia. A place called El-Qaez. I think that's somewhere south of Riyadh."

"What makes you think this is current, though?" Curry asked him. "He's probably moved a bunch of times since his birth certificate was written."

But Bates shook his head. "These guys don't go out and get bachelor pads once they reach eighteen years old," he said. "They stay in the nest until they either get married or get killed. At the very least, I'll bet his family still lives there."

"Well, we gotta go get this guy," Gallant said with renewed urgency. "He might hold the key to a lot of this."

But then Martinez spoke up. "After that excursion back to 'Ajman, we don't have enough gas to fire up a grill," he said. "Or sure as hell not enough to go up to Riyadh. . . ."

"But we just can't sit on this," Curry insisted. "Especially now that we know a clock is ticking here. . . ."

But Martinez was still shaking his head. "Look, we're tapped out. We did what we could, but we're at the end of the line. Last chapter. End of story. We can't do any more about this. It's time to give it to someone who can."

"What are you saying?" Curry asked him.

Martinez just shrugged. "I don't see any alternative but to contact Langley somehow and tell them everything."

The rest of the team let out another collective groan. Langley, Virginia, was the headquarters of the CIA—and those three letters were a four-letter word on the *Ocean Voyager*.

Phelan was especially upset. "God, the CIA . . . they'll take *weeks* to follow up on this," he said. "And that's even if they choose to believe us. Which they won't. We're blacker than black, remember? Look what happened to Murphy. If we call them, it's more likely they'll arrest us first than listen to us. And by the time they do hear us out, it will probably be too late."

Gallant chimed in: "I agree. We can't go to the CIA. You know how much Murph distrusted them. And with their history of fucking things up . . . I mean, they've had some hits here and there, but in your own experience with Delta, have you ever known the CIA to do *anything* right, or quick, the first time?"

Martinez thought a moment but then had to shake his head no. "If Murphy was right about one thing," he finally admitted, "he was right about that."

Phelan went on: "And how would you call them anyway? I don't think you can just dial them up on the shortwave. And even if we flagged down the nearest Navy ship, it would still take hours for this to go up the chain of command—and then more time wasted bouncing it over to Langley."

"*We've* got to be the ones to snatch this monkey Jamaal," Gallant said. "We're the only people anywhere near up to speed on this thing. And it's our last shot at doing something good—God, something that will mean something."

"But this *isn't* what Murphy intended," Martinez came back at him. "We were started as an integral component—one part of a process. But now all our support is gone. We're lifeless. We are as OTB as the *Torch* ship."

"I disagree," Curry said strongly. "I think this is *exactly* what Murph would want us to do. He put us together tough, so we'd stay tough. And damn it, if we've got to go, let's at least go kicking and screaming."

"But we're stuck here!" Martinez fired back. "Aboard this ship. With no fuel! We just barely made it back from 'Ajman. We *can't* go out again. . . ."

"Fucking gas," Ryder cursed. "Always the problem. Unless . . ."

"Unless?" Curry asked.

"Unless," Ryder said, "we go back to the well just one more time."

Bahrain

Marty Noonan was exhausted.

He'd flown double-ups for the past two days; that was four 10-hour missions in just 48 hours. Every muscle from his brain to his butt was aching now as he climbed down from his KC-10 refueler, post mission number four. In the last two days, they'd gassed up everything from F-15E Strike Eagles and F-117 Stealth fighters to entire squadrons of A-10 Thunderbolts and National Guard F-16s. At times, it seemed as if the big refueler was getting as tired as its crew. There was one benefit, though: after all this flying, his Bahraini copilot had finally perfected the art of making a great pot of coffee. This was good, because Noonan had certainly needed his share of caffeine in the past two days.

As grueling as they were, the double-ups had become more or less routine. All U.S. military units in the Gulf were on heightened alert these days, with any number of local trouble spots having the potential to pop at any time. Noonan's refueling squadron was tasked with saturating a specific area with tankers, whether it be the airspace above the Strait of Hormuz, the narrow passageway all U.S. Navy ships had to sail through in order to enter the Persian Gulf, or the waters off the Gulf's upper coast for operations inside Iraq, or even a bit to the east, for a secret bombing mission or two inside Iran. The idea was that if trouble happened in any of those areas, U.S. fighters would not have to go far to gas up.

The last mission had been so long, though, Noonan didn't even have the strength to crawl to the officers' club. He went directly to his billet instead, drained the last two cans in his Budweiser reserve, then collapsed on his bunk even before he could untie his flight boots. He was asleep inside a minute.

Being a pilot, he rarely dreamed. But this dark night, almost immediately, visions of people dressed in black and dancing around his bed made their way into his subconscious. They were prodding him, gently, not to hurt him but to get his attention. And they were asking him questions, asking him for help. Asking for something . . .

Suddenly he awoke with a start—and found he wasn't dreaming at all. There were a half-dozen figures standing around his bunk, all dressed in black, all lugging heavy weapons and wearing ski masks to cover their faces.

He just sat up and shook his head.

"Oh God," he moaned. "Not you guys again. . . ."

The village of El-Qaez sat directly south of Riyadh, a 20-minute drive along Al-Sultan Highway.

El-Qaez was quaint, if anything in the Middle East could ever be described that way. It was several dozen clusters of high-priced whitewashed brick houses, not palaces but sizable, most of them, surrounded by palm trees and small artificial oases and water springs. There was a certain amount of nostalgia running through the place. It had been designed 20 years before to look like a village that might have been here in the desert for centuries, if not longer. At least it seemed that way from the air. The closer one got, though, the more hints of modern life appeared. The most blatant were the abundant satellite dishes sticking out of the sand and the fleets

of Mercedes and Jaguars that roamed the streets of the tiny
village.

This was a place where midlevel Saudi oil executives
lived. One family, the el-Habini clan, resided at the end of a
cul-de-sac that wrapped around a clump of recently planted
palm trees.

It was now six in the evening. The sun was going down
and the heat of the day was finally drifting away. There were
13 people inside the el-Habini household. They'd just sat
down to their evening meal of lamb guts in yogurt when a
tremendous explosion shook their house. A palm tree came
crashing through the huge picture window an instant later.
Every other window on the bottom floor was blown out by the
concussion. Suddenly smoke and flames were everywhere.

Before the family could move, five armed men burst
through the front door. They fired their weapons into the
ceiling, causing pieces of plaster and glass to crash down
onto the dinner table. The children screamed. The family's
grandmother fainted dead away. This was a nightmare come
to life. The armed men were wearing an unmistakable stars-
and-stripes patch on their shoulders. Without a doubt, they
were the Crazy Americans.

Each soldier was holding a photograph of a young man
and shouting out in Arabic: *"Where is Jamaal? Which one is
Jamaal?"*

Jamaal el-Habini was off in a flash. He scrambled over
the dinner table, pushing his family members out of the way,
and tried to go out the nearest window. One of the huge
soldiers caught him by the shirt collar before he made it
halfway through the glass-free opening. He was dragged
back into the room and stood up against the wall. Two other
soldiers compared his face with that in the photo taken from
the CD-ROM. It was a match. They both kicked him in the
stomach. He doubled over and hit the floor hard.

Now more soldiers entered the house, shouting and waving weapons. They began kicking over furniture, knocking
things off the walls. They were screaming in Arabic: "Give
us your Korans!" Yet the women were pleading with them,

saying they weren't *that* religious; they had no Korans. Still the soldiers kept trashing the place.

As all this was going on, a jet fighter streaked low over the house, once again shaking it to its foundation. A fire was raging outside. The clump of palm trees in the middle of the *cul-de-sac* had been blown away, courtesy of a daisy cutter bomb dropped by the jet. This had cleared an area large enough for a single black helicopter to land outside. That aircraft was now sitting in the crater left by the bomb, its rotors still spinning, a thin perimeter of soldiers in place around it. Frightened neighbors were peeking out their windows, but anyone who lingered too long had his home sprayed with gunfire. Much shouting and crying could be heard throughout the neighborhood.

Not a minute after charging inside the house, the soldiers came back out. They were dragging with them not only Jamaal but also two of his brothers. All three were bound and blindfolded and thrown into the helicopter. The aircraft started to lift off even as the last of the black-uniformed troops were jumping onboard. Some were still firing their weapons.

The jet fighter roared overhead a third time, its mechanical scream only adding to the chaos.

Finally the copter rose in earnest, clearing the house and going straight up until it disappeared completely.

The snatch-and-grab raid had lasted less than 90 seconds.

Ten minutes later, the *Eight Ball* Blackhawk was cruising 12,000 feet above the darkened Persian Gulf.

The *Eight Ball* was no longer a gunship. All of its weaponry had been removed to reduce weight and make it more fuel-efficient. Its interior had been cored out, too. No more extra seats, no more redundant communications sets. The aircraft was now just a fuselage with a rotor on top and some huge shoulder tanks, filled with Noonan's fuel, hanging off the sides. It even had Delta guys at the controls, saving the weight of dragging the two Air Force pilots along.

Sergeant Dave Hunn was crouched in the back of the

copter, next to the three Saudi youths. They were still bound
by the hands but were no longer blindfolded. Jamaal was the
oldest. The other two were about seventeen and fifteen. Hunn
knew he didn't have much time; the Spooks back on *Ocean
Voyager* expected the terrorists to make their move as early as
daybreak the next morning. That meant they had less than 10
hours to stop the Next Big Thing.

Hunn turned to the first teenager. He was the youngest.
Hunn didn't bother to ask if the boy spoke English. He knew
they all did.

He got right in the kid's face.

"We know what you guys are up to!" Hunn screamed in
his ear. "You, Jamaal, and your other brother."

The kid shook his head no. He was absolutely terrified.

Hunn grabbed him by the shirt collar.

"Why don't you have a Koran in your house?" he demanded to know.

The kid just shook his head wildly again. Indeed, no holy
books were found in the el-Habini household; in itself, Hunn
found that suspicious.

"Tell me the codes!" he screamed at the kid. "If not . . ."
He drew an imaginary knife across his throat.

The boy grew more frightened but became defiant as
well. He tried to spit at Hunn, but the wind in the cabin was
so strong, the spittle blew back into his face. Still, Hunn became enraged. He picked the boy up by his shoulders and
threw him out the open door.

Then Hunn grabbed the second teenager and repeated his
demands: *"What are the codes? Where are your Korans?"*
This kid was trembling, too, but he just kept shaking his head.
Either he was being antagonistic or he didn't know anything.
It didn't matter. A mighty kick from Hunn's boot and he fol-
lowed his brother out the door.

Then Hunn turned to Jamaal. He'd already wet himself.

"OK, my friend," Hunn said, moving him a little closer to
the open doorway. "It's time for you to talk. . . ."

But Jamaal knew talk or not, he was already dead. He
decided to take matters into his own hands. He broke free of

Hunn's grasp and scrambled for the open doorway himself. He screamed, but his cry was lost in the high winds. Hunn lunged after him; two other Delta troopers did as well. But he was already halfway out the opening. Hunn managed to grab hold of his pant leg. It started to rip. Hunn tried to hold on tight, a very hard thing to do, as gravity and forward motion were battling him. The Delta guys flying the copter quickly reduced their airspeed, but this just caused the aircraft to start bucking all over the sky. Other troopers jumped in now, trying to keep Jamaal from going out the door, but it was just too much. Jamaal's pant leg finally ripped in two. Hunn made one last grab, clutching at the boy's sneaker. It came off—but Jamaal kept going. He fell, screaming, to the Persian Gulf two miles below.

"God damn it!" Hunn cursed, holding Jamaal's Air Jordan in his hand. *"You little muthafucker!"*

The other troopers couldn't believe it. Hunn had freaked again—and that meant they'd just come a very long way for nothing. Hunn was fuming. He collapsed in the corner of the cabin and started punching himself in the head. *What the hell had he been thinking?* He should have taken all measures to keep Jamaal alive.

But then he looked down at the sports shoe and noticed something. There was a square compartment cut out of the inside of the sneaker. Tucked snugly inside this hole was something wrapped in wax paper. *A bomb?* Hunn thought. Al Qaeda had used shoe bombs before. But he didn't think so. He took out his knife and pried the object free. He unwrapped the wax paper.

Inside was a tiny, abridged copy of the Koran, Arabic on one side, English on the other.

The name of the hill was Saal-el-Qazell.

The Blackhawk had landed here with a mighty thump 10 minutes after the terrorist Jamaal and his two brothers went out the open door. Though the Delta guys could fly copters themselves, they didn't quite have the touch of the Air Force pilots. Thus the less than gentle landing.

The hill was about one hundred miles southeast of Riyadh; the people onboard could see the Gulf coast from here. They'd set down for the same reason the copter was now just a skeleton of its previous self: to save gas. Noonan had come through with 1,000 gallons, but he'd made it crystal clear that the bar was closed after that. That's why only one of the Harriers had accompanied the stripped-down gunship on the Jamaal raid. That's why the fighter had carried only one bomb—and that's why it had already returned to the ship.

Not so the Blackhawk.

Hunn had put his men in a defensive perimeter around the aircraft. The hill was extremely isolated. Night was closing in and he was confident no one would see them up here. He had with him one of the few working sat phones the team still possessed; it had a dying battery and its scrambler was barely functioning. He was to use it only in an emergency or to report any bombshell information as a result of the Jamaal raid. Or to tell the ship they were coming back empty-handed.

All he had, though, was Jamaal's holy book, the abridged Koran. Did it contain anything that could help them at this late hour? Hunn would have to find out, quick.

He was sitting in the rear of the helicopter, holding the tiny copy of the Koran in front of him. It was about one hundred pages long and made out of paper so thin, one could almost see through it. Even its cover was made of thin paper.

He studied the book closely. Unlike most dog-eared Korans found in the hands of true believers, this one's pages had been hardly turned. Hunn thought this odd. If this was in Jamaal's possession, in such a secreted place, it seemed logical that it was one of the coded Korans Delta had been told to look for. But how could Hunn break the code sitting way the hell out here?

He tried an old counterspy trick. He held the book, pages up, about twelve inches above the helicopter's floor and then let it drop. He was hoping the book would fall open to a certain page, indicating a place its owner had concentrated on. But no such luck. Hunn did his experiment a half-dozen times. Each time the book fell open to a different page.

A few frustrating minutes passed. Hunn's mood grew darker. He called his first corporal, the guy named Zangrelli, back to the copter. They discussed every method they knew about spies and codes. But nothing seemed to click. The Koran was small, on thin paper, and hardly used. There seemed to be nothing else special about it. Hunn became further agitated. Something big was going down very soon, and due to his actions the one chance they had to prevent it was probably gone. He'd fucked up, big-time.

He lit up a rare cigarette and continued thumbing through the small book. Before Delta left the ship, Bates had provided them with many of the phrases Kazeel had recited over and over on the CD. Hunn began rereading a section where one of these phrases had been found. Exhaling a lungful of smoke, he noticed something. Some of the smoke seemed to be passing right through the page.

He tried it again. He blew a mouthful of smoke at the page—and some leaked out the other side.

"Fucking, hey!" he exploded.

He repeated the procedure for Corporal Zangrelli. Sure enough, they could see tiny wisps of smoke leaking out on the other side of the page.

Hunn turned on his flashlight and held the page in question up against its lens. Tiny shafts of light came streaming through.

"Well, I'll be damned," he swore softly.

He immediately called the ship. Martinez got on the line and Hunn explained what he had found.

"Pinpricks," the Delta officer told him. "I haven't heard of that one in a long time."

It was an old spy trick. Tiny holes had been punched above some of the letters in the words contained in the phrases Kazeel had spoken. The holes were apparent only when the page was held up to the light. They were just about impossible to see otherwise.

"The phrases Kazeel speaks at the beginning of the CD-ROM tell the mook where to look in the Koran," Martinez explained to Hunn. "When he finds the pinholes, he matches

the letters below them to form new words. Those words
probably lead to the codes that open the rest of the CD."

But they didn't have time for the copter to fly back to the
Ocean Voyager with the information. Hunn would have to
recite for those back on the ship every letter he could find
with a pinprick punched above it. He went through the
whole book and found more than two dozen such letters
above the phrases Kazeel had spoken on the CD. It took
more than an hour, this as the stars came out and the desert
hill became extremely cold. Toward the end, the cell phone
began seriously losing power. And because *Ocean Voyager*
was actually moving away from them, the reception became
weaker with each passing minute. But finally they were
done.

Hunn then asked Martinez what he and his men should
do next.

The Delta officer replied with just two words: "Sit tight."

White Room #2, aboard *Ocean Voyager*

Gil Bates lost no time putting his Spooks to work crunching
the information sent by Hunn.

They were all familiar with the pinprick spy technique; it
went clear back to the Middle Ages. But they knew it was not
as simple as the Delta guys hoped. Frequently the pinprick
technique was used as a double code, and that was the case
here. The letters found designated in Jamaal's Koran did not
automatically form the encryption words. That would have
been too easy. Instead the letters formed what amounted to
a huge Islamic anagram, 30 characters long. The real magic
words were hidden inside this jumble. It was now up to the
Spooks to find them out.

With all of their hot-shit computers disconnected long
ago, the Spooks were forced to decipher the long line of letters the old-fashioned way. Bates knew that three words, or,
more likely, a three-word phrase, would be needed to open
up the second level of the CD-ROM, this because three blank

fields had appeared at the end of the first level. He had his guys write each pinpointed Arabic letter on a large sheet of paper, along with its closest English equivalent. They strung a thin piece of rope across the room and these sheets were hung from it by paper clips. When done, they had a line of 30 movable letters in front of them. Now they had to make coherent words from these letters.

They began sliding the letters back and forth, arranging and rearranging them, trying to find which groupings formed actual words. It took a while, as the Arabic to English character translations were not exact, but they finally hit upon the words "many won't believe," which Bates recognized as part of a line from the Koran that went: "All will see the sign, but many won't believe." When he typed these three words into the three corresponding fields, the next level of the CD-ROM began to open immediately.

A cheer went up in the damp, darkened room. There were high fives all round. But one look at the new screen and suddenly the Spooks weren't feeling so good anymore. To their dismay, the second level didn't have any photos, pop-in videos, or elementary special effects. What it contained instead was thousands of lines of Arabic text. Reams of it, totaling more than 700 pages in all.

And the text did not spell out targets or time lines or meeting places and such. Instead, it contained nothing more than a set of maddeningly generic guidelines to be used by the *jihad* operatives who were about to carry out the big mission. Things like what an operative should pack when stowing away on a fishing boat, where to carry his money, and why he should neglect personal hygiene so as "not to raise suspicions." There were hundreds of instructions on what to do, who to talk to, and when and how. At first, the text seemed to go on forever, with no beginning, no middle, no end. It was saturated with slang and misspellings and had no punctuation marks. In other words, a nightmare of Islamic jabberwocky.

In the intelligence business, this was known as "backfill," information that was either outdated or irrelevant or both. Maybe the text contained secrets that would have been valuable to the American team days or weeks ago. But with the Next Big Thing just hours away, it was useless now. And the Spooks certainly didn't have time to plow through all 700 pages, just on the slim hope that a kernel of secondary intelligence might be found within. To them, it was all crap.

But Bates *did* notice something unusual: after a quick scan of the text he discovered it was not really one long document but actually a group of documents, 22 in total, one for each of the 22 martyrs-to-be. For some reason, the documents had all run together, making it look like endless boilerplate. Buried at the end of each document, however, there was also a list of what *not* to do. It consisted of things that each *jihad* operative should avoid: the local police, any military officials, anyone not Muslim, and so on. It also instructed the operatives to avoid big cities, such as Riyadh and Damascus, as much as possible. It told them not to eat in open-air cafés, as their faces might be recognized. It told them not to use any cell phone more than once, as they could be tracked by satellite that way. But while each individual document differed slightly from the rest, each had the same last entry on it, indeed, the very same last sentence. Roughly translated, it told the terrorists "that in order to keep our operation pure, at all costs, avoid having any contact, conversations, business dealings, or other interactions with individuals connected to the Royal Dubai."

What the hell did this mean? The Spooks gathered around Bates's station to discuss it. There seemed to be only one explanation at first: the operatives were being told to avoid contact with anyone connected to the Royal Family of the UAE state of Dubai.

But Bates was not so sure. "The real Arabic term for the Dubai royalty would go on for a paragraph of its own," he told his men. "And the mooks have no penchant for abbreviations."

"So what could it be then?" one of his men asked. "Some kind of establishment? A business, maybe?"

"Or another bank?" a second Spook offered.

"If it is a bank, the Delta guys will have to go in with pistols and masks this time," Bates replied.

Silence, for several long moments. The ship began rolling hard again; another squall had kicked up outside. Back when their equipment was still working, the Spooks could have pressed a few buttons and one of the most powerful supercomputers on earth would have done a Net search on this in a matter of nanoseconds. But that ultraconvenience was no more.

"Maybe there's another way we can find out," Bates said suddenly. He popped open his dying cell phone and simply dialed ATT International Information. A short conversation in French confirmed there was no bank listed as the "Royal Dubai" anywhere in the Persian Gulf region. Nor was there a religious center, royal palace, or mosque under that name.

However, there was another kind of establishment called the Royal Dubai in the area.

It was a five-star hotel.

Minutes later, Bates was standing in Bobby Murphy's old stateroom, out of breath from his long dash up to the bridge house.

Leaving the Spooks to their own devices, the combat team leaders were up here now, going over everything that Murphy had left behind in his sudden departure. They had all his papers and notebooks spread across the huge conference table, searching for any other clues he might have uncovered concerning the Next Big Thing.

Bates interrupted this task with his report on the CD-ROM's second level and the odd message about the Royal Dubai they'd found hidden in the miles of text.

"So what you're suggesting I do," Martinez was saying to him now, "is send my guys to a place where the mooks were told *not* to go?"

"I know it sounds crazy," Bates replied. "And maybe it is. But whenever any big operation is about to go down, we know the bad guys are under strict orders not to attract any attention to themselves at the last minute. So, by telling everyone to stay away from this Royal Dubai place, they might actually be tipping their hand to us—in reverse."

"But it's a luxury hotel," Martinez said. "I didn't think that was their style."

"It isn't. Not normally. But remember, some of the hi-jackers were staying at five-star hotels in Boston in the days leading up to the Nine-Eleven attacks. And we've tracked others passing through the best resorts in Europe in the past. I mean, some things you just can't do in a cave. And, hey, if you're heading for paradise, why not run the bill up a bit?"

"But what could they be hiding in this place?" Curry asked. "Weapons? Money?"

Bates shrugged. "Your guess is as good as mine. There's a chance it could be something really scary—like germs or gas—that they intend to pull out of their hat at the last minute, stuff they don't want even their foot soldiers to know about. I just don't know. But if the people who put the CD-ROM together don't want their peons going near the place, there must be a good reason."

Martinez checked his watch. It was nearly 10:00 P.M. Hunn and his men had been on top of the hill in Saudi Arabia, freezing, for almost three hours.

"How about the CD-ROM's next level?" he asked Bates. "How soon can you get into it?"

"We're working on it," the young Spook replied. "And now that we know the double-code key, we are hoping that deciphering the right phrase might not take much time. But figuring out what's actually inside the next level and whether it's helpful or not—well, that might be a different story. What appeared on the second level was a bit of a surprise, I must admit. It's not like anything I'd seen before. So, the next level might not tell us how, or where, or when, or even what their target is, after all."

He paused and felt the greasy edges of his Hawaiian shirt. A huge nautical clock on Murphy's wall was suddenly ticking very loudly.

"I wish I could tell you more, Colonel," Bates concluded. "But this 'Royal Dubai' thing might be as good as it gets for a while."

All eyes went back to Martinez. He was no fan of these extracurricular activities; that was obvious. And those were his guys out on that hill, risking exposure.

It would have to be his call all the way.

"Well, we're already halfway into this thing," he said finally. "So where the hell is this place?"

Chapter 24

Midnight

The senior night maid at the Royal Dubai was sneaking a smoke in the lunchroom when the two monsters appeared.

They were huge, wearing strange clothes and carrying bizarre, glowing weapons. Their faces were covered with silver glass and their heads had thin red halos around them. The maid froze in midpuff. They looked like something from a horror movie.

But then she saw the monsters had a strange emblem stitched to their shoulders. It was filled with stars and stripes and had an outline of two tall buildings. The maid was not an Arab. She was Filipino. But like everyone else in the Persian Gulf region, she'd heard of the Crazy Americans and knew they were far worse than anything from a horror movie.

They took one step toward her and raised their weapons. She dropped her cigarette, let out a cry, then fainted dead away.

When the maid woke up again, she found herself on the roof of the hotel. It was very windy and there was a lot of commotion going on around her. The notion that she might be somehow stuck inside a horror movie did not completely dissipate up here. Now she was surrounded by more of the monstrous soldiers, and their weapons looked even more enormous and unreal. They were trying to talk to her in both English and Spanish. They were asking her if any strange people had been staying in the hotel lately.

Finally she managed to catch her breath and reply: "Stranger than you?"

Two minutes later, Hunn and five of his men were in the corridor outside the hotel's penthouse door.

Once the maid became convinced she wasn't going to be eaten alive, she began gushing with details about the odd guests living in the tenth-floor luxury suite. Their peculiar spending habits, their unwillingness to show their faces, their gluttony, the weird noises they were making. Only six men were believed to be inside at the moment; the maid said the seventh man just seemed to come and go. She'd asked the Delta soldiers to explain the actions of these *des locos,* but Hunn and his guys had no good answer. They were as much in the dark about the men as she was. However, they seemed to be the only suspects that clicked with the information sent to Delta from the ship.

Hunn had his men arrayed now in a standard forced-entry position. There was no time for them to do this stealthily; it was going to be loud and quick. Closest to the door on either side were two troopers carrying Mossberg shotguns. They were the Pumpers. Both had wide-dispersal shells locked and loaded; both were crouched nearly to the floor. Behind them, standing straight up, were two soldiers with flash grenades out and ready. They were the Firemen. Against the far wall was Corporal Zangrelli lugging the unit's huge .50-caliber machine gun, complete with an extended ammo belt. Hunn was standing next to him, his M16A2-CAR-15 specialized assault rifle at his side. Each man had his face mask down and his body armor in place. Each also had light-enhancement goggles on and activated. In their full-battle gear they *did* look a little extraterrestrial.

Each man was also pumping with adrenaline. According to the people back on the *Ocean Voyager,* this might not be the cakewalk that interrupting the el-Habini clan during dinner had been. There could be just about anything on the other side of the penthouse door. Hard-core Al Qaeda members. Heavy weaponry. Vials of anthrax. Smallpox. A nuke or two. The troopers had the unenviable task of finding out just what.

Hunn did one last check of their position. His men were properly in place. The copter was secure up on the roof, at least for the time being. The surrounding exits were being covered by other Delta troops. The flight to Dubai had passed without incident; they'd landed atop the hotel unseen. But Hunn knew they only had about ten minutes before word leaked through the hotel that something was not right. Ten minutes to get business done. What happened after that was anyone's guess.

He checked his weapon's magazine; it was full, of course. He checked his guys again. Everyone gave him a thumbs-up. That's all he needed. He thought: *OK, one more, for Sis. . . .*

Then he sucked in a deep breath, let it out quickly, and made a running leap. He hit the door feetfirst.

It disappeared in an explosion of cheap paint and splinters. The result of 252 pounds of sheer muscle hitting the sweet spot halfway up the frame. Hunn fell to the floor as soon as the door shattered. The Pumpers jammed their Mossbergs through the opening and fired. At the same time, the Firemen tossed in their flash grenades. The combined result was like a very large fireworks display inside a very small place. Though Hunn had his tinted face mask down, his eyes were still stung by this blizzard of pyrotechnics.

Now Corporal Zangrelli rushed in, firing his gigantic weapon while expertly vaulting over Hunn. The grenade men and the shotgunners followed him through. They found themselves in a foyer; five larger rooms lay beyond. There were no lights on inside. Hunn jumped to his feet and sprayed the hallway with tracer fire, illuminating the murk. Two seconds of eerie phosphorus burned a snapshot onto his eyes. There was a man about ten feet to his right, pointing a gun at him. His face was terrified; his hand was trembling. And his weapon was not a Kalashnikov but a puny handgun.

Hunn could even see a glint of light coming off the cheap plated pistol.

The man never did pull the trigger. Hunn opened up again and a stream of tracer fire hit the man in the upper torso. His head and chest came apart simultaneously. The gun went flying off into the darkness.

As this was happening, the two Pumpers fired over Hunn's shoulder, striking another man hunched in the corner off to their left. He, too, had a small pistol in hand but never got the chance to fire it.

With the sound of the two shotgun blasts, Hunn flattened himself against the wall. Zangrelli landed right beside him. The Firemen rolled across the foyer away from them. The shotgunners were two feet behind. There were six men suspected to be inside the suite; two of them—probably guards— were now dead. Not bad in the first five seconds. But the squad still had five huge rooms to clear.

The Delta soldiers stayed in place and just listened. Ten seconds went by. Nothing. Hunn slowly crept down the hall and peered into the next room. It was dark, but he could see it was full of futuristic furniture and had many, many windows. He also detected piles of dirty dishes stacked in just about every corner. And computers. Laptops and PCs. There were at least two dozen of them set up on stands all around the room. On the floor, thousands of scraps of paper. All shapes, all sizes. *What the hell is this about?* Hunn thought. The place looked like the inside of a Wall Street stock exchange. Or a bookie joint.

Beyond he could see a double bedroom. Beyond that a bathroom, another living room, and another bedroom.

On his signal, the rest of the squad joined him at the far end of the hall. Once again, they remained still for several seconds. Then it came—just what they were waiting for. The sound of a short, troubled breath, a shoe against the floor, the clink of something metal. At least one person was in the next room. He was trying to slip away. And he was armed.

Hunn gave a hand signal to Zangrelli. Four fingers straight

up, his thumb moving back and forth. A flash grenade was needed here. Zangrelli nodded to one of the Firemen, who undid a flasher from his vest, pulled the pin, and tossed it into the next room.

The result was blinding, as advertised. The Delta guys didn't need to get the order from Hunn this time. They plunged into the room even before the last of the sizzling sparks died away.

A figure bolted out from behind a couch. Zangrelli fired once but missed, tearing up a wall in the process. Hunn saw the man fly through the air; again, what appeared to be a small pistol was in his hand and pointed in their direction. Hunn fired but missed as well. The man scurried across the floor, knocking over lamps and upsetting a huge glass table. Zangrelli fired again. This time he caught the man in the back of his head, blowing off the top of his skull. His body actually crawled for a few more steps but then collapsed to the floor.

Again the Delta team froze. They could see through the next two rooms, into the master bedroom beyond. More shadows were moving in the bare light. Hunn signaled the Firemen to stay put; then he, Zangrelli, and the two Pumpers moved forward.

They crept through the next room, a kind of lounge area with a sunken floor. It was nearly pitch-black within, but it, too, was thick with paper. Long white strips of it hanging on the walls. Wastebaskets overflowing with it. Thousands of crumpled sheets on the furniture and the floor. The troopers began moving very carefully through this sea of litter.

Suddenly from outside came something they did not want to hear: the sound of sirens approaching. Again, this had not been a quiet ingress for Delta—there had been no time to plan for that. Hunn knew if this was the local police, they still had a few minutes to do their thing. If it was the military, though, that time might be cut in half.

The four troopers reached the end of the paper room and stopped to listen again. Another whimper. Another sound of a knee unintentionally thumping the hardwood floor. Hunn turned to Zangrelli and held two fingers straight up, then pointed to his ear. He was asking his corporal if he heard two people in the next room. Zangrelli listened again—then replied with three fingers. He heard one more than Hunn. Hunn nodded, then put two fingers briefly across his eyes. Zangrelli got the message. He looked back at the Pumpers. Each man loaded two flachette rounds into his Mossberg.

Again, all four moved forward. The next area was a huge bedroom three-quarters walled in with huge glass windows. They could see the lights of the city and the waters of the Gulf beyond. On Hunn's signal, Zangrelli threw a small flash grenade to the middle of the room. It exploded—and in the glare they saw one man dive behind a couch while two others ran for the adjoining bathroom. Hunn fired his M16 at the floor in front of the couch, hitting the crouched man in the feet. He jumped up—and both Pumpers let go with a double blast. The flachette rounds exploded about halfway between the gun muzzle and the intended victim. The man was hit an instant later, essentially by a small cloud of supersonic shrapnel. The dual blasts went right through him—and vaporized the huge picture window beyond. The glass exploded like a small bomb. The sudden change in air pressure caused everything not tied down in the suite to be sucked up into a minitornado. Suddenly a tempest of paper was swirling all around them.

Zangrelli fired again. He caught the second man as he was trying to scramble through the bathroom. With half his back blown away, the man collapsed into the tub, dragging the shower curtain down with him.

Just one left now . . .

But this guy they needed alive.

Hunn checked his watch. They'd been inside the penthouse for two minutes—an eternity by the measurement of these things. And now it was getting hard to see with the wind whipping fiercely and paper flying in every direction. Still he silently ordered his men to split up. He and Zangrelli went through the bathroom; the shotgun men took the slighter longer route through a small hidden kitchen.

They trapped the last man in the master bedroom, the four Delta troopers converging on him from two different directions. They turned on their combat lights and directed them at the man, who was cowering in the corner, near the edge of a very unkempt bed. He was certainly not dressed as most hard-core Al Qaeda members usually were. He was wearing a white dress shirt, black pants, and highly polished shoes. He was clean-shaven, another rarity for the *jihad* gang. And his complexion was not as dark as some of the mooks Hunn and his men had come up against in the past. For want of a better word, this guy seemed almost sophisticated.

Christ, Hunn thought. *Did we even hit the right place?*

Zangrelli started speaking to the man in Arabic. He was explaining there was only one way he was getting out of here alive and that was as their prisoner. Zangrelli was a tough kid from Brooklyn, a young Sylvester Stallone look-alike. But he had a way about him, so just about anyone would feel him a kindred spirit. The man in the corner was frightened but indicated he knew what Zangrelli was trying to say. He actually straightened up a bit.

A surreal moment ensued: the four huge soldiers, looking like space invaders weighted down with their high-tech gear, standing in the lavish bedroom, the swirl of paper nearly blinding them, the slight, terrified man in the corner staring back at them.

Zangrelli kept on talking. They just wanted to ask him some questions, they would promise not to harm him, and they were sorry his friends had to die—all lies, of course, but comforting nevertheless. Yet just as it appeared that Zangrelli's words were getting through, the man calmly reached into his pocket and came out with a pistol, the same nickel-plated type his comrades had died with. The Pumpers immediately raised their weapons, but Hunn held up his hand, telling his men to hold their fire.

The man never pointed the gun at them. Instead he put it against his own head.

"I do not want to live for what is about to happen," he said in perfect English.

Then he pulled the trigger.

The bullet went through his left ear and came out his right

eye, striking the bedroom wall beyond. He stood there for a moment looking at the Americans. He mouthed just one more word: *Crazy* . . .

Then he collapsed, dead before he hit the floor.

"God damn, what's with these guys!" Hunn roared. Once again their chance to extract information from a living, breathing mook had been thwarted.

Zangrelli reached down and checked the guy's pulse. He was already cold. "They just know what's coming, Sarge," he said darkly. "Nothing more to it than that. . . ."

The four troopers just stood there, frozen in the moment. The bizarre whirlwind continued swirling around them, scraps of paper blowing wildly, a blizzard on a cool Persian night. Then Hunn nodded to Zangrelli and they made their way back to the large bedroom, the one where the big picture window had been blown out. It took both of them using all their strength to push its door closed, the wind was that intense. But as soon as the minitornado was confined, the storm of paper in all the other rooms settled down.

That's when someone finally hit the lights.

There was blood everywhere. And many more mountains of dirty dishes than they first realized. And the piles of dirty laundry stretched from one end of the penthouse to the other. But the troopers could see no huge guns. No test tubes full of germs or spores. No nuclear bombs. And certainly no one who looked like a top mutt in Al Qaeda.

Zangrelli checked the KIAs. The two dead men in the hallway were light-skinned Somalis. They had Muslim Brotherhood symbols tattooed on their forearms.

"We didn't kill enough of those assholes that night?" Hunn asked.

"Missed by two, I guess," Zangrelli replied.

More surprising were the other bodies scattered around the suite. They looked like no more than four dead waiters, each one in white shirt, black pants, high-polished shoes.

"Did these guys even fire back?" one of the Pumpers asked.

No one replied.

Zangrelli patted one body; it was clean except for a news-

paper clipping detailing the weather in the Persian Gulf and
a photograph made bloody from the fighting. The newspaper
had been printed in Algeria. The photograph was of Abdul
Abu Qatad.

"Isn't he the guy we wasted in the wedding hall?" Zangrelli asked Hunn.

"No, it's his brother," Hunn replied, studying the photo.
"The guy whose son we had tap-dancing from the ceiling.
Both of those assholes used Algerians as their moneymen.
And that's who these guys were. Their dogs. . . ."

Zangrelli couldn't believe it. "Damn, I knew they were
like one big family," he said. "But who would have guessed
this Qatad guy would come back to haunt us?"

Hunn checked his watch again. Just three minutes, 10 seconds had passed since he first kicked in the door. The sirens
were growing outside. More of them. He could also sense
heightened activity on the streets below and more noises coming from the bottom floors of the hotel itself. Whatever else
they had to do, they would be wise to do it quick.

But what had they stumbled upon here, if anything?

They finally turned their attention to all the paper scattered around the suite. Hundreds of sheets were still tacked
to the walls, moving like wash in a gentle breeze. Hunn pulled
down a handful and scanned them.

"You've got to be kidding me," he said suddenly. "Take a
look at this shit. . . ."

The troopers did as told. A couple examined pieces of paper that had now settled to the floor; others took more sheets
off the wall. Every sheet was the same: a computer printout
with lines of letters and numbers, all arranged in the same
format, all bearing the same kind of information.

It was that information that was so baffling.

"This doesn't make any sense," Zangrelli said after reading over a dozen sheets. "Does it?"

Hunn shook his head, then pulled out his sat phone and
quickly dialed the ship.

"The brass ain't going to believe this," he said.

Aboard *Ocean Voyager*

"Airline tickets?" Martinez was saying into the phone a moment later. "Are you sure, Sergeant?"

The team leaders were still in Murphy's cabin, still tossing the place. They'd been anxiously awaiting this call, though, so much so, Martinez grabbed the phone before the end of the first ring.

The Delta officer listened for a few moments, his face screwed up into first an expression of almost amusement, then disbelief.

Then he asked Hunn, "Any chance you're making a mistake?"

But Hunn was obviously convincing Martinez that what he was reporting was accurate.

Finally the Delta officer asked: "How long can you hold that position? . . . Can you make it ten minutes, please? . . . And stay by the phone."

Martinez hung up and turned back to the rest of them.

"There were no weapons or explosives in the hotel," he told them soberly. "No germs. No nukes. No Big Cheese. Just six guys—now deceased."

"What *did* they find then?" Phelan asked him. "Did you say tickets?"

"*Airline* tickets—or more accurately, airline ticket receipts," Martinez replied, the quizzical expression never leaving his face. "The kind of E-ticket you can buy off the Internet these days. There are thousands of them over there. For hundreds of flights, all over the world. All of them expired. All of them worthless.

"What the fuck is *that* about?" Curry asked, bewildered.

"The screwup with the airlines," Ryder said suddenly. "The thing that's been all over the news. Those mooks must have been the ones who hacked into the airlines' computers and kept booking reservations over and over again.

The rest of them just collapsed into their seats. "Man, that's got to be it," Gallant said.

"But what's it have to do with the Next Big Thing?" Curry asked. "Or is there any link at all?"

Martinez just shook his head. "The info about that hotel was on the CD-ROM," he said, still baffled. "There must be *some* connection. . . ."

Phelan said: "But is the Next Big Thing just a plot to screw up the airlines? Make so many reservations that all their tickets become worthless?"

"They've boasted about going after economic targets before," Gallant offered. "And the airlines are a multibillion-dollar enterprise. Between screwing up the ticket computers and calling in bomb threats, they've really put the whammy on them."

But Martinez waved these suggestions away. "Look, the airlines were fucked up long before any of this happened," he pointed out. "Plus, the CD-ROM clearly shows a bunch of guys ready to die. And I don't think they meant from airline food."

"Then why the room full of useless tickets?" Phelan asked.

Silence descended on the cabin. The wind outside was beginning to howl again. The five men were tired. Nerves were frayed, their supply of brainpower dwindling. Once again, they were facing another brick wall, another mountain to climb.

"Well, maybe not *all* of them are blanks," Ryder finally said, out of the blue. "Maybe in the pile somewhere there are some that still can be used."

"Used by who, though?" Gallant asked. "And why?"

Ryder shrugged. "Who knows?" he said. "But it might be interesting to find out."

Martinez thought about this for exactly two seconds. Then called Hunn back.

"Are you sure *all* of those receipts are for tickets on old overbooked flights?" he asked the Delta soldier. "Any chance some haven't expired yet?"

There was a silence from the other end of the phone. It lasted 10 long seconds. Then: "It might take us a while to check that," Hunn replied. "I mean, this place is knee-deep, wall-to-wall. And I think we finally woke up the neighbors."

"Well, you've still got to do it, Sergeant," Martinez told him. "And I mean *toot-sweet*."

The lobby of the Royal Dubai was in chaos.

Most of the building's lights had gone out. All of its electronic equipment, its computers, elevators, fire alarms, and telephones, had gone dead, too.

In the midst of this, the Dubai state police had arrived on the scene, alerted by nearby residents who first reported a helicopter had crashed onto the roof of the hotel. Fire apparatus had also surrounded the building.

Inside, the confusion turned to panic as guests came streaming down the staircases, many still in their nightclothes, wailing that the building had been taken over by the terrorists and that they were shooting all the maids.

Two miles away, the military district commander of Dubai City received a call from the police. On their suggestion, he ordered his one and only aircraft into the air to report on the unfolding situation. It was a sparkling new PAH-1 Tiger Eurocopter delivered to the Emirates not a week before. The French-built copter was on par with the dangerous U.S. Army Apache gunship. It carried a slew of high-tech weapons, many of which the two-man crew actually knew how to use by now.

It was this helicopter that the Delta troops on the hotel roof saw approaching just about the same time Hunn was hanging up from his last conversation with Martinez.

This was big trouble. There were only ten Delta troops on the entire mission, including the two amateur pilots. Six of those troopers, Hunn and company, were down below, herding up to a dozen of the hotel's maids into the penthouse. Two more troopers were watching the hallway that led from the roof to the door of the suite. That left just two on top of the roof itself, guarding the battered, stripped-down, unarmed Blackhawk helicopter.

As soon as they heard the Tiger gunship coming, the roof

men called down to the two soldiers guarding the hallway
and told them to get up top immediately. They had no way to
contact Hunn and no time to do it. Whatever was going to
happen with the powerful Dubai military chopper, it seemed
it would be these four men who would face it.

The Tiger was brimming with machine guns and cannons. A 30-second barrage could produce enough firepower
to shave an entire floor off the top of the Royal Dubai building. The same kind of fusillade would reduce the old *Eight
Ball* chopper to a pile of metallic dust, taking the four troopers along with it and effectively stranding the rest of the
squad in very hostile territory one floor below.

Thus the dire situation for the Delta operators. There
would be no rescue force coming to get them this night. No
Harriers, no *Torch* ship, no cavalry riding in at the last moment to save the day. In many ways, the Delta troops *were*
the cavalry. And tonight, they were on their own.

It was in the midst of this precarious situation that Corporal Zangrelli suddenly arrived on the roof. He'd been sent up
by Hunn to retrieve binding tape from the *Eight Ball* and,
not finding the two Delta guards in the hallway, double-
timed it to the top. He came on the scene just as the Tiger
was turning toward the hotel. It was still about two thousand
feet out, but moving in a very aggressive manner.

Zangrelli quickly took stock of the situation and what he
and the others had on hand to defend themselves. It was not
very much. They didn't have any of the heavy weaponry the
Eight Ball use to carry—again the weight factor had taken
precedence. No shoulder-fired SAMs, no RPGs. Each man
had just his M16 rifle and nothing more. They didn't even
have the big .50-caliber gun Zangrelli had used in clearing
the penthouse. He'd left it below with the Pumpers.

So it would be five men on top of a roof, with rifles,
against an attack helicopter that ranked up there with the
Apache and the Hind. Very bad odds.

"What should we do, Corporal?" one of his men asked him.

Zangrelli thought a moment and then replied: "Get the
flag from under the backseat. . . ."

The pilots of the Tiger gunship had been on the radio with their base from the moment they'd taken off.

Their commander had no idea what was happening at the Royal Dubai—and neither did the pilots. The military station was getting reports second- and third-hand from the managers of the hotel, from the state police, even from the fire department. Yet no two stories matched. The hotel employees were insisting that armed men were running wild through the hotel, massacring the cleaning staff and shooting guests at random. The police thought a robbery, possibly even a jewel heist, was happening, as all the activity seemed to be centered on the hotel's penthouse. Yet the fire department claimed they could smell gasoline in the lobby—and that terrorists were about to turn the building into a towering inferno.

The only thing that everyone agreed on was that whatever was happening, the perpetrators had arrived by helicopter and that aircraft was still sitting on the hotel's roof.

The Tiger gunship pilots reported that, indeed, a helicopter *was* visible on the northeast corner, partially hidden in the glare of the building's summit lights. For this reason, the Tiger pilots couldn't get a solid ID on its type, but that really didn't matter. Their commander wanted to justify his base getting such a powerhouse of a gunship. This would be the perfect opportunity to do so.

So he ordered his men to go in shooting.

The pilots began punching commands into their weapons computer, deciding to use the nose cannon, at least on the first pass. The Royal Dubai hotel was a valuable piece of real estate and they weren't in the business of doing any property damage. However, the aiming system on the cannon was so precise, they were confident they could take out the stationary helicopter without turning the 10-story luxury resort into a 9-story one.

With their weapons set, they reconfirmed the fire order with their commander. Once again, he told them to proceed.

The pilots were both anxious and excited; this would be the first time their new multimillion-dollar aircraft would fire its weapons in anger. They didn't want anything to go wrong.

They were about a half-mile south of the building when they rolled in for their attack. Their weapons computer had locked onto the helicopter on the roof and would open up automatically at 400 feet out. The pilots could see people on the roof, hastily moving around, but they were of no consequence now. They had their orders to fire and fire they would.

But at about seven hundred feet out, the pilots saw something else—and suddenly they weren't so keen on firing anymore. It was a frightening and incomprehensible sight. It also answered the question of just who had landed on top of the hotel and why they were causing such a ruckus.

What the Tiger pilots found themselves looking at was five soldiers, standing right on the edge of the hotel roof, weapons raised and pointing at their incoming chopper. They were lined up in a forward combat position, straight and true, almost like a firing squad. Behind them, draped on the mysterious black helicopter, was a huge American flag.

The five soldiers did not waver as the Tiger gunship bore down on them. Certainly they didn't really intend to shoot down the Dubai helicopter. This was little chance of that, as rifle bullets would most likely just bounce off the heavily armored gunship. No, this was an act of defiance. The five soldiers standing firm, the Stars and Stripes flapping in the wind behind them. Suddenly the Tiger pilots knew what this was all about. . . .

These were the Crazy Americans—or five of them anyway. And in effect they were saying: *Do you really want to fuck around with us?*

The Tiger pilots didn't.

No one in the Persian Gulf did.

The pilots knew they could blow these five guys off the roof in a heartbeat. But if they did, some night soon they would surely awake to find more of the Crazies standing over their beds, and the beds of their wives and children, axes in hand. Only the most horrible end imaginable would come from that. That's the way the Crazies worked.

The Tiger pilots wanted no part of it. So they killed the weapons computer and veered off, just seconds before it would have fired automatically.

Then they made a call back to their commander and reported that the expensive new French helicopter had malfunctioned.

Reluctantly, the commander told them to return to base.

By the time Zangrelli ran back down to the penthouse, the Delta troopers had many of the hotel maids laid out on the floor, facedown.

The first thought through Zangrelli's head was: *God, they've seen our faces . . . but do we really have to shoot them all?*

The maids weren't being prepared for execution, though, as so many people on the bottom floor of the hotel thought. They were actually getting their fondest wish of the past two weeks. They were finally cleaning the penthouse.

Hunn had put the maids to work picking up all the paper scattered around the huge suite. There was so much of it, it would have taken the Delta team hours to go through it all, and at this point time was a luxury they could not afford. Once the maids had gathered up a sizable quantity of the refuse, they would lay it out as neatly as possible on the floor of the big room and, along with the young Delta troopers on their hands and knees, would begin scanning the individual sheets, looking for what the American team wasn't sure even existed. In all the thousands of old, overbooked airline tickets, were there really some that had yet to be used? And would it make any difference if there was?

By a quirk of the printing, it turned out to be a fairly easy thing to check. The first line on each of the multiline statements indicated what date the ticket being purchased could be used. Anything earlier than the present date was quickly discarded—in trash bags, at the maids' insistence. Still there were hundreds of sheets to go through, each one listing hundreds of tickets.

So Zangrelli didn't even have a chance to tell Hunn about the close encounter with the Tiger gunship. He wasn't four steps into the big room when the Delta squad leader dragged him down to the floor and started him looking through the paper debris as well. Meanwhile the noise and sirens were increasing down below. And even though the troopers had cut power to every floor except the one they were on, they knew it was just a matter of time before the police or the military or even the firefighters got enough gumption to climb nine floors in the dark to see just what the hell was going on. And that would only lead to another bloody shoot-out.

Zangrelli and Hunn were down on the floor no more than a minute when they heard a scream from the next room. They immediately had their weapons up and ready. *What now?* Zangrelli thought. One of the maids came running into the room, waving a sheet of paper over her head. She gave the sheet to Hunn and pointed to a group of receipts in the middle of many. Sure enough, it was a list of airline tickets purchased for flights that were leaving later that very morning, just a few hours away. Twenty in all. Just about what they were looking for.

The roller coaster was on its way up the hill again. . . .

The other troopers cheered. Hunn remained stoic, though. He pocketed the sheet and then began barking orders to his men. In seconds, the Delta guys started tying up the maids in earnest, binding hands together with duct tape and putting pillowcases over their heads, making them look more like prisoners than allies.

Why?

As Hunn explained to Zangrelli: "They might have just given us more help in catching these monkeys than the entire U.S. intelligence community put together. What do you think the mooks would do to them if they ever found that out?"

Aboard *Ocean Voyager*
1:00 A.M.

"You would have made a lousy burglar," Phelan was saying to Ryder. "Your hands are just too honest."

Ryder could not disagree. True, he had talent in his hands, at least for flying souped-up jet fighters. But he was not so good at picking locks and such. And yet that's exactly what he was trying to do now. He had a screwdriver, a pen, and a butter knife, and with all three he was trying to snap the lock off the drawer at the bottom of Bobby Murphy's desk.

The ship was still rolling; the rain outside was coming down in sheets. The heat had shut down throughout the vessel, and many of the lights were flickering, too. They were running out of fuel; there was just enough to keep the ship's engines turning and not much more. It was now just as cold and clammy in the upper decks as it usually was way down below.

The team leaders had not budged from Murphy's old stateroom, though. They were still here, going through his papers, even as the condensation was building up on the cabin windows and the big clock on the wall was ticking even louder.

Their quest in the stateroom had been a frustrating one up to this point. Murphy tended to write a lot of things down, but most of what they'd uncovered had to do with the operation of the ship: its logistics situation, the number of miles on the screws, the weight distribution of the containers. Items that were maddeningly routine. They did find one scrap of paper stuffed in a notebook, that read: *Profile on Ali M. due today?* But they had no idea what it meant.

Right about the time the lights began blinking, the team leaders turned their attention to the very ornate mahogany desk in the corner. It was the only thing in the large room they had not poked into, including the liquor cabinet. They'd discovered that every drawer in the desk was unlocked and empty—except for the bottom one. Why was it different?

What might it hold? They'd set Ryder, their senior man, to work on it. But after 10 minutes the drawer's lock had defied all methods of pushing, pulling, and twisting.

Ten minutes, wasted....

Finally Phelan nudged Ryder aside, drew out his service pistol, and fired at the lock, five times, at point-blank range. It disintegrated as expected, but the young pilot also succeeded in demolishing half the desk as well as filling the cabin with smoke.

It was a small price to pay, though, as they found something very tantalizing inside the drawer. It was a personal diary Murphy had been keeping, a small green journal, with a cheap clasp and a key dangling from its back cover. It had BOBBY MURPHY printed neatly in blue ink across the first page and it was time-stamped the day he'd first come aboard. At some point within, the little guy had jotted down, in his very conversational writing style, a few deep dark passages about what shape *he* thought the Next Big Thing might take.

They gathered around the bullet-ridden desk and read as Ryder turned the pages. The most intriguing scenario Murphy had come up with, and first on the list, had the terrorists taking local flights out of the Middle East, hijacking a number of U.S. airliners at their connecting points in Europe, and then crashing those airliners into prestigious or symbolic targets in the United States, a kind of "Super 9/11." In the margin, Murphy had scrawled the names of all of the bridges leading into Manhattan, the Empire State Building, the Statue of Liberty, the White House, the Capitol Building, and the Washington Monument as possible objectives, based on statements Al Qaeda had made in the past. He'd also written the words: *Coordinated or staggered?* beside this first entry. Also: *How will they dodge our fighters?*

The second group listed 10 nuclear power plants on the East Coast of the United States as potential targets, all of them close to population centers. The third group had 10 nuclear sites in the Midwest under the same bull's-eye. Next to this pair of entries Murphy had written two more notes: *747s and larger would be needed for nukes* and *even with enough warning, still no chance to evacuate?*

The fourth entry played out a scenario in which up to 10 U.S. airliners would be hijacked and then simultaneously blown up over the mid-Atlantic, certainly a death blow for what was left of the U.S. airline industry. The fifth entry detailed another massive attack against New York City, but this time with crashes specifically targeted around the Wall Street area. Next to this Murphy had written: *A real kick in the country's financial scrotum!*

It was the sixth entry that proved most perplexing. It consisted of just two words, both underlined several times and complete with multiple exclamation marks. The two words: *Or maybe!!!*

Reading this last entry, the team leaders could almost see their absent boss reaching what he might have considered the likeliest of scenario of all but, for whatever reason, not getting more than those two puzzling words on paper before being interrupted, perhaps by those who had come to take him away.

Not a minute after they finished reading Murphy's last entry, the sat phone came to life.

Once again Martinez answered the phone before the second beep. It was Hunn.

The Delta commander listened for a moment, then pumped his fist in the air.

"OK, Ryder was right—they found something," he said. He started repeating verbatim what Hunn was telling him: " 'Twenty tickets. All flights out of the same airport in Bahrain. Starting around 0800 hours this morning. Two tickets each flight. Local Arab air carriers. Ten connecting points. Ten different destinations, all in Europe. . . .' "

"Ten *different* destinations?" Phelan asked. "They're not all going to the same place?"

Martinez just shrugged. "I guess not."

"Actually, that's what most of them did on September Eleventh," Curry told them. "Just like it says on Murph's list, they flew somewhere else before hijacking the airplanes they used in the attacks."

"But why go through all that trouble?" Ryder asked him. "Why not go direct?"

Curry explained: "They wanted to get into the system early. They knew it was easier to move around that way. Back then there was less security flying out of a smaller place. Less suspicion. Plus, if one or two got caught or were delayed, the others could continue the plan. On Nine-Eleven, those that had to made their connecting flights; then the smaller groups all met up. Then they flew off to murder three thousand people."

"So if Murph was right then," Gallant said, "the mooks are still one step away from the big moment."

"Yeah, a baby step," Curry replied.

Martinez gave Hunn the go-ahead to finally leave the Royal Dubai hotel. He told the Delta team to get airborne, get out over open water, avoid the bad weather, and await further orders. Then he hung up.

Ryder was still puzzled, though. "But why would they buy up all those other tickets?" he asked. "They succeeded in knocking almost every U.S. airliner out of the sky. What did the radio broadcasts say? Only about ten percent of the planes are still flying between America and Europe? That's a whole lot of planes that *ain't* flying. So, when these guys reach their connecting points, what are they going to do? Hijack those few planes that are left?"

Blank faces all around the table. It did seem strange— because there were fewer airliners flying at the moment, the hijackers would have fewer planes to pick from. And certainly the security at those connecting terminals would not have decreased. Why then the flood of ticket buying over-booking and bomb threats?

No one knew.

"But what the fuck difference does that make?" Phelan said finally. "Wherever they're going, they'll never make it that far, because now we know what they are up to and all we've got to do is get our guys to that airport and blast them."

"The kid is right," Curry said. "It's the only thing to do."

But Martinez abruptly held up his hand. "Wait a minute," he said cautiously. "We can't be too hasty here."

Outside, the rain was splattering against the huge cabin windows. Thunder rumbled off in the distance. Martinez lit his cigar and let out a long troubled cloud of smoke.

"Like you said, these guys are still one step away," he began. "But we're still at least one step behind them. I mean, Ryder's question is a good one. Why would they go to such great lengths to ground nearly every U.S. airliner if they intend to use them in whatever they've got planned? And why are there only twenty tickets in the block Hunn found and twenty-two mooks on the CD?"

Another long stream of smoke.

"I think we have to be smart here," he concluded. "And not jump in the deep end too quick."

But Curry went ballistic. "I hope you're not suggesting that we hold off on these twenty guys," he challenged Martinez. "When we're so close? That's crazy. . . ."

"I'm not saying 'hold off,'" Martinez replied, not quite as calm as a moment before. "I'm saying that we use our heads. Sure, if we go in shooting, there's a chance we'll nail these particular monkeys. But we also might miss something going on somewhere else. We're not even sure if these guys are the real hijackers or just messenger boys. And let's face it. We've been trigger-happy since this whole thing began. We nailed those guys in Saudi, we nailed Zoobu in the electronics store, and we just nailed six more in that hotel and that Jamaal character before that. If any of them still had a pulse, he might have been a fountain of information."

He paused, as if to reach for a can of beer that wasn't there.

"Now, I know we're out here to mess these guys up, whenever and wherever we can," he went on. "But so far, going in with guns blazing has just made things more complicated. And besides, we're so strung out now, we're only going to have one last shot at them. We've got to make it a good one. . . ."

Curry was still furious. "But you might be letting them slip through our fingers!" he said. "This could be the only chance we have to redeem ourselves!"

Martinez finally exploded—something that was long overdue. He fired his newly lit cigar over their heads and against the far wall. It went by Ryder and Phelan like a rocket.

"It isn't about us anymore!" he roared back at Curry. "Man, when are you going to get that through your head? The time to think about saving our own sorry asses passed long ago. This is different. This is about saving the lives of the people those greasy assholes want to kill. Innocent lives. *American lives*. And God knows how many this time. In case you haven't noticed, I've come full circle here, Red. You had to convince me earlier, but now I'm finally onboard. They sent us out here to stop these guys—and that's what we're going to do, even if it means they'll be giving us our medals in jail. But, damn it, we've only got one bullet left in the chamber and we've got to be absolutely certain of when to pull the trigger. If not, then this whole thing really *will* have been a Chinese fire drill."

He took a moment, calmed down, and caught his breath.

"Now we still don't know what they are up to exactly," he began again. "But we know it's starting soon. If we can just get a hook into whoever is going to use those tickets, without their knowing it, we just might be surprised at what we find at the other end. It will also buy us time until the Spooks can break into the next level of the CD. . . ."

An uncomfortable silence descended on the room. Curry just stared at the floor. Gallant put his head in his hands. Ryder and Phelan slumped farther into their seats. It was impossible to tell if any of them were thinking straight. They were too tired, too drained, too punch-drunk.

"So, what you're suggesting," Ryder finally said, "is that we play it cool for once?"

Martinez just shook his head wearily, then began dialing Hunn again.

"There's a first time for everything," he said.

Manama, Bahrain
6:08 A.M.

The capital city police received the trouble call shortly after dawn.

There was something wrong at a domestics shop downtown, in an alley called al-Zakim Place. Customers arriving just before sunrise found the store locked and shuttered, unusual, as the owner was known to open at 5:00 A.M. every day.

A small crowd of women was waiting outside when the police van arrived, anxious to get material for the day's sewing. The cops were both fat and lazy, though, and insisted on having a smoke before they took any action. One did look underneath the shuttered window and saw the store's main products hanging from hooks on the other side of the glass. Bolts of black, white, and gray material, gold chains, cell phones, and sandals. The shop was dark within.

The cops finished their cigarettes, not any more quickly despite the murmured protests from the gaggle of women. Then one policeman retrieved a tire iron from the van's trunk and, after much grunting and groaning, snapped the shop's padlock in two. The front door slowly swung open.

A rush of incense and body odor flooded out. The cops waited for it to pass, then turned on their flashlights and tentatively stepped inside. Hearing muffled cries coming from the back room, they pulled their pistols and slowly walked to the cluttered storage area. Here they found the owner—an 80-year-old man named Barook Qadeen—and his three daughters. They'd been tied to chairs facing one another in a tight circle around a slowly boiling teapot, the steam from which had kept them warm for the past two hours.

The policemen untied the old man first. He began sputtering something about being robbed but got caught up in a hacking cough and could not be understood. The police then untied his oldest daughter. She was able to spit out only a few words before collapsing in tears. The next daughter was in no better shape. Soon the crowded storeroom was filled with coughing, moaning, and wailing.

The policemen finally untied the youngest daughter and at last found someone who could tell them what happened.

"The Crazy Americans were here!" she gasped. "They nearly scared us to death!"

But her story seemed unlikely from the start. She said she, her father, and her sisters opened the shop at 4:00 A.M. When they walked in, she claimed, two soldiers were waiting for them. They were soon joined by several more. Each soldier was carrying a huge weapon and was wearing a black uniform with a black helmet. Their faces were masked.

The daughter recognized the stars-and-stripes patch on each soldier's shoulder, though. It was the American flag.

And these Americans were indeed crazy. . . .

Why?

"They wanted to be fitted," the daughter said.

"Fitted? For what?" the police wanted to know.

"For women's clothing," was the improbable reply.

This made no sense of course, least of all to the two policemen. By this time, the father had managed to catch his breath. To the cops' astonishment, he confirmed his daughter's bizarre story.

"They wanted to be fitted with gowns of our material," he said. "Ten of them in all."

The police settled the man down, then asked him to explain what happened again, and this time very slowly. And honestly.

But the man did not budge from his tale.

"Ten of them came in," he said, voice still raspy. "Each one wanted us to sew a new *madras* for them—head to toe, one long piece of cloth. And we did it, quickly, and at the point of a gun. Then they tied us up, took a bunch of our cell phones and some money, and left."

He took a deep breath, collected himself again, and then said: "The Crazy Americans came in as soldiers. But they left as women. . . ."

Chapter 25

Heathrow Airport was like a ghost town.

It was raining, cold and foggy, as was usually the case at the huge international airport. It was inside the overseas terminal buildings where things were unusual. No bustling crowds. No long lines. No baggage stacked to the heavens. Just a couple bobbies, a dozing TV crew, and some cleanup men.

So many flights from America had been canceled due to the cyber-attack on the U.S. airline system, this part of the huge airport was all but deserted. This was particularly ironic because a week before the place had been a madhouse, with thousands of people stranded and sleeping on benches, countertops, and even the baggage carousels. The rest rooms and toilets had overflowed, food had run out at the concession stands, and tensions had become so high, the Army had been called in at one point to restore order.

This untidy situation had been the result of a massive transcontinental chain reaction. When the impact of the over-booking cyber-attacks first hit, the airlines could not muster enough airplanes to carry every American stranded in England back home again. The lines in Heathrow grew longer and the baggage piled up. One day passed, then two. Then three. Still no additional planes came. With every hotel in London already booked, many travelers had no choice but to camp out at the airport. Tempers were quickly shot, and fistfights between passengers and airline employees became routine. Eventually some people were lucky enough to catch a ride out on the few flights available, while others wound up flying to other destinations, like Canada and Mexico.

But many others simply did not want to fly at all, as it seemed like something catastrophic was going to happen over the Atlantic at any moment. Those who could found refuge in smaller hotels scattered throughout the United Kingdom to wait out the crisis. Others even booked passage on cruise ships and were waiting to sail home.

The crowd slowly petered out. By the sixth day of the crisis, the airport was virtually empty.

So it *was* a rare occasion that an airliner from America touched down here anymore. But one arrived at Heathrow around 11:45 P.M. local time this lonely night. It was United Flight 333—from Chicago.

It had carried essential businessmen, some government people, and a few celebrities across the Pond. The sleepy news crew was on hand to interview the passengers as they got off, especially the celebrities, so there was a flood of TV lights at the arrival gate. The policemen watched the commotion from across the terminal with bored indifference. The janitors hardly noticed at all.

Deplaning along with the people in the last four rows was Tom Santos. No one took his picture when he got off the flight though, thank God.

The international travel situation was so desperate, even Santos's tight-lipped government handlers had had trouble booking him a ticket to where he had to go. And still, he was only halfway there.

He'd finished his last flight-simulator exercise the day before. He hadn't graduated with flying colors exactly; it was more that the time frame for his training had run out. He wouldn't miss the long hours or the stuffy *faux* cockpit. But had he learned anything? It was hard to say.

If the question was, Could he start right away as an airline pilot? then the answer was, No. But could he take a big airliner off the ground and fly it safely?

Probably.

He arrived at British customs to find there was no waiting. Every station was open and there were more than enough agents to handle the people getting off the newly arrived plane. This was good. Santos wasn't feeling too well today. His stomach was acting up and his legs were weak. Standing in a long line would not have helped at all.

He almost lost his balance when he walked up to the open customs station. The customs agent did a quick search of Santos's bags and found nothing restricted. However, his eyes were drawn to the bottle of bright yellow pills that Santos pulled from his pocket. He asked Santos about them, and Santos explained he had a medical condition and these pills were helping to cure him. As proof, Santos swallowed one dry and claimed to feel better instantly. The customs man was unfazed. He was more concerned that the pill bottle did not have a prescription label or number for the medication within. If the pills were narcotics, then technically, carrying them into Britain unmarked was against the law.

But the customs agent could tell that despite his enthusiasm, Santos was unwell. Just to cover himself, he confiscated two of the pills with Santos's OK. He would have them analyzed later. Then he took down Santos's personal information, including his passport data, and let him go.

Santos thanked him, retrieved his bags, and wearily started off for the other end of the airport.

Once he was gone, the customs agent studied the two yellow pills. He broke one in half, wet one end, and sniffed it. It had no odor. He scraped a few particles off of it and put the granules to his tongue.

Tastes like nothing but sugar to me, he thought.

By the time Santos made his way over to the other side of the airport, where flights for the Middle East were leaving, he was barely able to walk. He was so tired, he was having trouble breathing. But he caught a break here, too. There were no lines at these counters, either. No customs, no security.

He walked right up to the ticket desk for Arab Gulf Air and bought a first-class seat to his next destination: Riyadh, Saudi Arabia.

He boarded the half-empty flight and took two more yellow pills shortly after takeoff.

But for the first time ever, they really didn't do him much good.

Chapter 26

Near Bahrait City, Bahrain

The new el-Salaam International Airport was nearly as empty as Heathrow.

The airport, the largest in this tiny Persian Gulf nation, had opened only three months before and was not yet up and running full-time. It did not have its night-flight instrumentation on-line, and it was operating off only two of its four major runways.

Nevertheless, when the airport *was* open it could handle a fair number of flights. On a typical morning, between the hours of eight and ten, roughly a dozen planes would depart, with about half that number coming in. Afternoons were usually much slower.

It was now 8:00 A.M. and passengers had begun loading for the morning flights out. A traditional month of prayer had just ended, so today was a busy travel day for Muslims, especially local women who could afford to go abroad. The first 10 planes, all regional Arab carriers, were flying to 10 different locations in Europe. The first four were going to Vienna, Bucharest, Munich, and Madrid. The middle four were going to Cyprus, Crete, Athens, and Rome. The ninth plane was bound for Istanbul. The tenth plane was going to Prague. Even if any were flying, there were no direct flights out of el-Salaam to the United States; the FAA hadn't rated the new airport yet. The destinations of these ten aircraft were typical for people connecting to flights to the United States, though. Nearly 100 percent of the people loading on them were Muslim, most of them women.

Just about the entire el-Habazz terrorist cell was here this morning, too. Nineteen members were on hand; Jamaal el-Habini, the odd man out, was missing. They were sitting far apart from one another in the large waiting area close by the loading gates. Some were dressed like businessmen; others were trying hard to look like tourists. At best, though, they all might have passed for elderly religious students. Abdul Kazeel was not among them.

Due to the flood of airline tickets the cell's moneymen had secured over the past two weeks, each man was now holding a golden pass of sorts: an actual ticket that had been purchased to use on a connecting flight to America. The thousands of others had been bought, cancelled, then bought again, over and over, to simply obscure the group's master plan, part of a long line of misdirections meant to throw off anyone who might be on to them. This elaborate, expensive smoke screen only had to last a little while longer.

Each cell member had checked in luggage that was appropriate for someone traveling a long distance. Each was also carrying a Saudi passport (courtesy of Prince Ali Muhammad), a high-powered satellite cell phone, and at least two weapons, including handguns, box cutters, banana knives, and old-fashioned razor blades. These weapons were either in their bags or on their persons, but this caused them no concern. There weren't any security checkpoints at el-Salaam International Airport. They hadn't been built yet. As it was, security was barely given lip service at many of the airports in the Arab Middle East. At el-Salaam, passengers walked directly from the waiting area to the airplane. They were not searched; their luggage was not screened.

The cell members rose calmly as their individual flights were called. Two men for each of nine flights; one man, Jamaal el-Habini's partner, would be flying alone. They barely looked at one another as they left to board their planes. They were composed but also very cautious, as they'd been trained to be. Still, none of them noticed that a lone woman, tall but stooped, in a black *madras* and *burka*, followed each pair onto their flight. But then again, why would they? Of the hundreds of people moving around the vast airport, many were wearing the traditional head-to-toe garb.

By 9:00 A.M., the first 10 flights of the morning had left. All of them were jet airliners, some bigger than others. Some filled near to capacity, others almost empty.

The weather was clear, with few clouds and very little wind.

It was a perfect day for flying.

Chapter 27

The Spooks were almost the heroes.

Because they'd cracked the CD-ROM's second level, and found the reference to the Royal Dubai, the American combat team had uncovered the sea of mysterious ticket receipts. Now the Delta guys were riding on the same planes as the *jihad* types, using their skills at impersonation and surveillance, following them to their connection points, dressed as women, in a sea of women.

But what would happen when the 10 planes reached those diverse destinations?

No one knew. There was still a piece of the puzzle missing: that elusive last part of the terrorists' plan. Would it be another all-out attack on America? Would it be a mass destruction of airliners over the Atlantic? Or the start of an incomprehensible nuclear disaster?

The targets and the timetable, that's all that mattered now. If the Spooks were able to find out those last two secrets and get word to the Delta guys, they would have thwarted the biggest terrorist attack since 9/11 and beyond. The answer, they hoped, lay inside the third and last level of the CD-ROM.

The trouble was, the Spooks couldn't get in.

The problem was simple. The encryption code to open the third level was actually double-sealed. It required *two* entries to get in, not just one. This meant the Spooks had to decipher two code phrases to break into it.

Getting the first of these two code phrases had been easy. Using the remaining clothesline letters, the Spooks found the key words *follow not desire* soon after punching through the second level. Bates recognized the phrase from a passage in the Koran that went: *Follow not desire, lest it lead you from the path.*

But even though he'd entered in these three words, the third level did not open. Instead, three more blank fields appeared.

That's when they realized it was a double seal.

"We're screwed," Bates said when it became obvious. He spoke for all of them. They had one last, unexpected barrier to crack, yet Jamaal's Koran could not help them anymore. The pinpricked letters had run out. They'd used them all up.

"The final code must have been given to the mooks verbally," Bates reasoned with his men as their dank compartment grew even colder. "It's probably a very common phrase they use among themselves, something that no one would mistake or get wrong. Like one of us saying, 'Go for it,' or, 'Whole nine yards.' Their last wall of security, the best of all, was the spoken word, the bastards. I'm sure the plan was to use it if the mission described on the rest of the CD-ROM ever got to the point of execution."

"But how the hell are we going to get it now?" one of Bates' men asked. "We got no more letters, no more mooks. No more time."

"That's why we're screwed," Bates replied.

Almost the heroes. History didn't recognize such things.

They had excuses. Despite their earlier success, decoding was not really the Spooks' expertise. Bates and his team were geniuses at tracking people and things, but not so in divining codes. The NSA, CIA, DIA, every U.S. intelligence agency, had people who lived, breathed, and slept decoding. It was an art as much as a science, one so intense, some of its top practitioners in the past had chosen suicide once they realized their best work had been done.

But it just wasn't the Spooks' thing.

This didn't mean they'd stopped trying. Just the opposite; they'd been beating their brains out for nearly two hours, taking turns sitting at the computer, trying to conjure up words from the ethers that might do the trick. The mood in the compartment was tense but weary. It had been that way ever since they made their unsettling discovery. There were doubts in here, too, creeping up on them, hanging by the edges. As smart as they were, as a group, the Spooks were also fairly neurotic. What if they *were* able to punch through the last barrier somehow, but instead of finding targets and timetables, they just found more useless backfill? What if the CD-ROM really wasn't the final mission briefing disk they'd convinced the combat team that it was?

What if they'd unwittingly sent the Delta guys on a fool's mission . . . .

All this was hitting Bates particularly hard. He already had the bank bombing weighing on his soul, his mortal sin of hubris and youth. Now the fate of the Delta team was in there, too. How bad was it for him? Since about 0800 hours, Bates imagined he could hear the nautical clock up in Murphy's cabin ticking . . . ticking . . . ticking away . . . like the telltale heart, even though it was at the opposite end of the boat.

Was there no better way to remind him that time was running out?

It was 0930 hours when Bates took his turn at the old battered keyboard again. White Room #2 was very dark now, with only one lightbulb working, and it just barely. It was also getting very claustrophobic inside.

His men had entered almost 500 different three-word combinations in the past two hours, none of which came close to breaking the last seal. Wild guesses, educated ones, random typing—everything was tried. Phrases contained on the same pages as the pinpricked letters were attempted, to no avail. The Spooks had even hung up the original 30 character sheets again, thinking that another phrase might be found by rearranging the old letters. A good idea. But it didn't work.

So the keyboard was back on Bates's lap now, as his guys collapsed into other seats nearby. He started typing, plugging in the most likely favorites again, just in case he messed them up somehow the first hundred times: *Allah is Truth, Praise to Allah, God is Great*. Nothing hit.

Just three words . . .

None the same as before.

Then an odd thought came to him. Maybe they were going about this the wrong way. He had three blank fields staring back at him. With the previous two barriers he had filled in all three encrypt words first, then hit the enter button—and the level popped open. But what if he came up with just the *first* word of the secret phrase? He would know it was right because if it fit, it would remain in the blank field when he hit the enter button. If it was wrong, it would simply disappear.

Wouldn't it be easier going for just one word at a time?

He began typing in single words at random, hoping to fill just the first blank. He tried: *You, I, We, They*. . . . Nothing happened. Each one went *poof* as soon as he hit enter. He tried *Life, Death, Live, Die*. Again, he got *bupkis*.

He took suggestions from his tired band of tweebs. *Get, Give, Don't, Will, Last, First*—all good Islamic words, just not the right ones.

A call from Martinez broke their concentration. It was a short, clipped conversation, the fifth one in the last hour. The Delta boss was reminding Bates that some of his men had been airborne for more than an hour and learning what was inside the third level was getting more critical with every minute. And Bates told Martinez the same thing he'd been telling him for the past hour: that he thought they were getting close. They were worlds apart, but just by listening to the background noise, or lack of it, during the phone call, Bates knew the tension up in the CQ was just as thick as it was down here at the bottom.

Thankfully, Bates's cell phone finally died at the end of the call. At least they wouldn't have that distraction any longer.

. . .

The search continued.

When, How, Never, Try. . . .

Nothing.

For, If, And, We. . . .

Again, all good words. But each one disappeared as soon as Bates hit the enter key.

Then he started to type in *Believe,* but suddenly—

"Wait!" he heard himself say.

Something made him stop at the first two letters. He didn't know what. His guys looked at him strangely. He rarely talked to himself.

"Try it like that," he said, aloud again. "Just try 'Be' "

He hit the enter key. The word remained in the first blank!

Whoops went up around the cold, dark room. Almost by mistake, they'd discovered the first word was "be. . . ."

Now the team gathered around the old PC, energized yet again.

Be something something.

Bates began typing madly. He started plugging in combinations like *Be Brave Today, Be Holy Today, Be with Heaven, Be Holy Forever.*

Nothing worked. *Be Strong Today. Be Strong Forever. Be with God. Be with Allah.*

Nothing. . . .

Bates banged his head against the computer screen. It didn't even hurt. He checked the time. It was now 9:45. His hands had begun to shake. His stomach was in knots. The ticking in his head grew louder.

Just two more words. . . .

He looked off into space, glasses pushed up to his forehead. His guys were shouting out suggestions, but Bates remained in his trance. *Think outside the box,* he told himself. *Beyond the envelope . . . Think laterally.*

Then a strange notion came to him.

What would Bobby Murphy's guess be if he were here? The enigmatic leader had spent many hours down in the White

Rooms with them, tracking the mooks, expounding on his theories of life, and just plain talking. He'd said so many things about the terrorists, about their *jihad* organization, about Al Qaeda. The way they ran their people. The way they ran their organization. Their faults, their idiosyncrasies. Murphy was an expert on them. He once claimed he could *smell* a terrorist if he was close enough. Knowing what he knew, what would Murphy think the magic phrase was?

That's when it hit Bates like a lightning bolt on the back of the head. He typed in: *Be Frugal Always.*

The last section opened immediately.

He let out a scream that sounded as if it had come from someone else's mouth. His men were beside themselves. Not just high fives all around this time, but there was backslapping and even embracing, this from a group of guys who, as individuals, had a hard time shaking someone else's hand.

Bates jumped from his seat, intent on dashing up to the CQ to tell the combat guys the good news. The *whole team* wanted to go with him. But then logic prevailed. Wouldn't it make more sense to find out what was *inside* the third level before making the long run upstairs?

Bates contained himself. The others did as well. They all sat back down and waited.

The third level took a very long time to download, nearly 10 minutes. But when it did, it was Abdul Kazeel's dirty face that appeared on the screen once again. A chorus of boos from the Spooks. He began speaking in Arabic, as more corny Muslim special effects swirled around him, just like the first level.

Bates felt some small measure of relief. At least they weren't staring at seven miles of Arabic text again.

He began taking down everything Kazeel said for translation, writing furiously, word for word . . . until the third sentence. That's when Kazeel started talking very strangely, about how *every* Muslim was really a martyr and how, at *any* time, God could call on them to give their lives for the cause.

Bates just stopped writing. His hand froze on the pen; the pen froze on the paper.

What Kazeel was saying began to sink in.

"Damn," he breathed.

They had made a terrible mistake.

Kazeel was laying out the final part of the plan—and at last, the Spooks had their bombshell. The el-Habazz cell, 19 members of which were now aboard 10 separate Arab airliners, *were not* proceeding to Europe or anywhere else in order to hijack American planes to throw at a target.

They were going to use the planes they were already on. . . .

"They're going to kill *their own people,*" Bates said out loud, just astonished.

They'd been fooled. By the perfect end-around play. While everyone was expecting Al Qaeda to jump through hoops to take over a large number of American planes, they were simply going to use Arab airliners instead. "Planes already under our control," was how Kazeel put it. *That* had been the secret all along. The Habazz gang wouldn't be flying into Paradise alone. They would be taking hundreds of their fellow Muslims with them, whether they wanted to go or not. The entire operation of buying up tickets, calling in bomb threats, disrupting the world's air transportation system, had all been part of a brilliant ruse, a misdirection, intended for nothing more than to get everyone looking one way while the terrorists were looking the other.

Bates felt sick to his stomach. The Delta guys were on those planes. . . .

But what was the target? Most of the planes that left Bahrain were medium-range models. None could fly as far as the United States on their own. Bates zipped past all of Kazeel's commentary to a section that plainly said: *Our One Pure Goal in God.*

The Spooks all watched in horror as an image, labeled "The Target," slowly downloaded. . . .

It was not a picture of Manhattan or a nuke plant or the Washington Monument. It was not a map of the mid-Atlantic Ocean or the bridges crossing into New York City or Wall Street.

It was a picture of an aircraft carrier.

Chapter 28

The USS *Abraham Lincoln* had entered the upper Gulf of Oman at 0800 hours, just about the time the first airliners were taking off from the el-Salaam Airport in Bahrain.

Twenty-two days before, the aircraft carrier had set sail from San Diego with more than 5,000 U.S. sailors onboard. Twelve ships made up her escort: cruisers, destroyers, frigates, refuelers, supply vessels. The battle group had been scheduled for this deployment for many months. Its intent was to add to the already-substantial U.S. military presence in the Gulf.

The carrier was huge, a real monster afloat. Its flight deck was as long as the Empire State Building was tall. It was 20 stories high from the waterline to its masts and weighed 97,000 tons. It was nuclear-powered. Two reactors provided the energy to turn four massive screws, each with five blades measuring 21 feet across.

There were 85 aircraft onboard: *F-14* Tomcats, *F/A-18* Hornets, *EA-6B* Prowlers, *S-3B* Vikings, *E-2C* Hawkeyes, *SH-60* Sea Hawks, and *C-2* Greyhounds. Twelve squadrons in all, the *Lincoln* alone carried more airplanes than many countries had in their entire Air Force.

Belowdecks were combat rooms, planning rooms, crews' quarters, officers' quarters, two huge hangars, four engine rooms, three mess halls, a post office, a ship's store—2,700 separate compartments, big and small. Two of these were ordnance magazines. One was crammed with thousands of the most high-tech munitions of the day: laser bombs, JRAM bombs, smart bombs, dumb bombs, every conventional type of bomb there was.

The second magazine was filled with nuclear weapons.

The ship entered the Strait of Hormuz just before 0900 hours.

The battle group was now coming to the trickiest part of its journey. At its narrowest, the strait was 34 miles across. However, it was very shallow in many places and dotted with islands, rocks, and other maritime obstructions. Passage had to be made through channels that were just two miles wide, leaving little room to maneuver, especially for a ship that was itself nearly a quarter-mile long. Yet much of the world's oil passed through the waterway, with supertankers and military vessels alike having to negotiate its crooked elbow shape, in drafts that were sometimes less than 200 feet deep.

These were not very friendly waters for U.S. ships, either. The coast of Iran dominated one side of the strait; Iranian troops held three strategic islands near the waterway's narrowest and shallowest points. And the waters of the Persian Gulf beyond were perpetually fraught with danger. U.S. Navy ships were always on high alert when passing through the strait.

The *Lincoln* carried Sea Sparrow missiles and CIWS guns for its own onboard protection, but it was the ships around it that were charged with keeping the carrier safe. The Aegis cruisers USS *Bradley* and *Philippine Sea* were always close by, their highly advanced air defense radars always burning hot. The battle group's air defense destroyers were doing likewise, farther ahead and well behind of the massive ship.

Almost half of the carrier's F-14s and F/A-18s were aloft as well. These warplanes had a supporting cast of electronic warfare craft, small AWACs and refueling planes. The combined effect was to create an electronic and visual umbrella around the battle group and most especially over the *Lincoln*. Indeed, the number-one priority of the battle group and the air wing was the protection of the carrier. This multilayer strategy of shielding U.S. carriers originated during the Cold War, to ward off an attack by forces of the former Soviet Union. These tactics had been endlessly rehearsed and modified over the years.

But they'd never been tested in a real attack.

By its size alone a supercarrier could inspire awe or defy a foe. But this was also the main criticism of these $5 billion ships. They were *too* big—as in too big of a target. No pinpoint, laser-guided bombs were needed to hit a carrier. Anything thrown at it had a large margin for error, nearly a quarter-mile of leeway in hitting the mark. The Soviets had built some of the earliest cruise missiles in history just for this purpose. They were big, dumb, and crude, but again, that's all they had to be.

For supercarriers like the *Lincoln*, size was both its greatest strength and its most glaring flaw. It took a long time for a ship so huge to speed up, slow down, or go into evasive maneuvers, especially in narrow waters.

Sometimes referred to as the Castles of the Sea, supercarriers had also been called the world's biggest sitting ducks.

Buried deep beneath the *Lincoln*'s superstructure was its combat information center, the CIC. The defense of the carrier was coordinated from here. One wall held a screen called the MRS, for Master Radar Suite. A relatively new add-on, it could show a real-time computer projection of the carrier's protective bubble, the ship's air defense as viewed in three dimensions. Its orbiting fighters appeared as icons, green for the Tomcats, yellow for the Hornets. The support aircraft were colored blue. The immediate protective bubble extended out to 60 miles. Should anything unauthorized enter this zone, it would show up on the screen in bright red. If this happened, the procedure was simple: the bogie would be labeled hostile/unknown and treated as such. That is, as a target, until proven otherwise.

This formula worked best in the open seas. It got tricky in places as tight as the Strait of Hormuz. Again, the waterway was very narrow as far as massive ships were concerned. Parts of the carrier's aerial protection zone spilled over into the airspace of Iran to the east and Oman and the United Arab Emirates to the west. The Navy did not want to have its jets caught inside another country's airspace, especially Iran's. So the zone of protection had to be pinched, as the waters in front of the carrier became more precarious.

Making this more problematic was something the sailors who worked the MRS called the O'Hare Effect. Once the carrier reached the narrowest part of the channel, all types of aircraft began showing up on the 60-mile-wide carousel swirling around its battle group. Small planes flying across the Omani interior. Airliners taking off from Iran. Commercial planes already in the air. Even air traffic as far up as Saudi Arabia could be picked up and displayed on the big screen. And at times like this, it *could* look like Chicago's *über*-frenzied airport, which made keeping the carrier's umbrella intact that much more difficult.

The sailors knew one missed icon, one missed radio call, and the results could be disastrous.

The mysterious blip didn't show up on the *Lincoln*'s MRS until it was just nine miles from the ship.

When it did appear, it only stayed on the big screen for a few seconds before dropping off again. Its ghostly presence lasted long enough, though, for the MRS to get a reading on its location, its speed, and its bearing. It was coming in from the west, appearing out of the haze of the upper Omani coastline. It was traveling at 110 knots and it was headed right for the carrier. Strangely, it was also just the size of a small bird, or at least that's what the pumped-up radar said.

This had happened 20 minutes into the passage, with the big carrier soon to begin its massive turn to port, a critical maneuver needed to get around the elbow of the strait's crooked arm. The battle group immediately went to advanced alert when the red dot popped up. Radio contact was attempted with the bogie but proved futile. The MRS was able to provide a probable prior flight track, which indicated whatever the object was, it had somehow managed to stay off the radar net by using the nape of the coast of Oman to mask its approach and then darting across open water once the carrier appeared in the strait. This, and the fact that the carrier's bubble was squeezed and there were many civilian planes on it at the moment, had further hidden its movements. For a little while at least, it had managed to penetrate the battle group's multilayered defense scheme.

This led to only one conclusion: if this was an aircraft of some kind, it probably had stealth capabilities and, no doubt, an extremely talented pilot at the controls.

A pair of Tomcats flying Combat Air Patrol five miles off the tip of Oman were alerted. They immediately went down to the deck, spotting the unidentified aircraft not 30 seconds later. They radioed back that the bogie was in fact a helicopter, an *American*-built Blackhawk helicopter varient. It had no discernible markings—at least not at first—and it didn't appear to be carrying any weapons. There was only one person aboard.

This made no difference to the pilots. In more peaceful times, every attempt possible would have been made to ID the bogie and somehow force it out of the carrier's protective zone. Under the prevailing combat conditions in the Persian Gulf, though, the rules had changed. Anything remotely suspected of threatening a U.S. carrier was fair game. So the F-14s were told to intercept the bogie and take appropriate action, carrier-speak for "blow it out of the sky." This could have been the papal helicopter; the pilots would still have to shoot it down.

But it wouldn't be easy. Whoever was flying the copter was managing to stay so low to the water, its struts were kicking up clouds of spray. The F-14 Tomcat was a long-range interceptor; it was more difficult for it to get a clear shot at a low-

altitude target than a high-altitude one. Plus, the copter was
already in among the support ships, all but ruling out a missile shot. It was flying so insanely low, the Tomcats would
have to try to bring it down using their cannons.

The F-14 flight leader went down to the deck leaving his
wingman up at 1,200 feet. He steered through the gaggle of
ships, some of which were firing at the rogue copter. The
sudden appearance of the Tomcat cut off all this fire immediately—no one wanted to hit the F-14 by mistake. The
Navy pilot pulled back on his throttles, causing his variable
wings to extend automatically. This slowed his speed but
also gave him less maneuverability. He managed to get on
the tail of the helicopter momentarily, but the chopper pilot
was shrewdly flying so close to the support ships, any cannon barrage from the F-14 would most likely impact on one
of them as well. The F-14 had to pull up and turn away.

The bogie was now just five miles out from the carrier.
Its pilot was jinking madly anytime he couldn't fly close to
one of the Navy ships. Someone on the destroyer USS *John
Hancock* let go with a shoulder-fired antiaircraft missile; it
missed the copter by just 20 feet before nosediving into the
sea. As the copter zipped by the combat stores ship, the USS
Westchester, the crew fired on it with their 20mm cannons.
They managed to get some hits up around the tail rotor, but
still the copter flew on.

By this time, the Tomcat had turned itself over and was
now coming toward the copter at a right angle. The helicopter ran the length of the Aegis cruiser *Normandy* but then
had no more cover for about two miles. The Tomcat closed
in, cannon ready. The fighter pilot slid the copter into his
gimbals, his finger poised above his trigger. But that's when
he saw the huge American flag plastered on one side of the
copter, its colors worn and faded but visible nevertheless.
He also couldn't help but notice what terrible shape the
copter was in. How could this thing be a stealth ship? It was
cored out inside and wasn't carrying such basics as navigation lights, antennas, or even glass in its door windows. All
this gave the F-14 driver pause just long enough for the

Blackhawk to zig once again, climbing sharply before nearly crashing back down toward the water. In that split second of hesitation, the Tomcat pilot gave up his best shot.

The helicopter was now just a mile away from the carrier. That's when the Tomcat backed away completely. He was too close to be dispensing any kind of ordnance that might hit something other than the target. The copter was probably being piloted by an American anyway, the F-14 pilot figured, someone who wanted to get to the carrier for reasons unknown. But it was out of his control now.

The carrier's Gatling guns would have to deal with it.

The *Lincoln*'s CIWS weapons opened up on the helicopter at 2,500 feet.

The role of these modernized Gatling guns was to fill a predefined area with so many projectiles, up to 600 a second, that practically nothing could get through. Two of the carrier's six CIWS had the copter locked in their sights.

But the copter pilot continued showing extraordinary skill. He did not take a direct route to the ship. Instead he began weaving back and forth, up and down, almost going inverted for a few moments. The CIWS guns were automatically aimed, automatically fired. Their real targets were incoming antiship missiles, projectiles that held steady to a course. By throwing his aircraft all over the sky, the copter pilot was confusing the guns' firing systems to a degree. Instead of sending out long streams of deadly rounds, the guns was stuttering, reaiming, stuttering again, and reaiming again.

But the copter could not avoid the Gatling guns forever. About five hundred feet out from the carrier, a barrage from the forward port CIWS hit it head-on. The helicopter seemed to come apart in the air. The tail section snapped off. The fuselage was blown in two. Trailing flames and thick black smoke, the copter, or what was left of it, took the brunt of another barrage about two hundred feet out. There was a tremendous explosion as the copter's fuel tank went up, certainly the *coup de grâce*. But those watching from the carrier deck were astonished to see the copter's forward fuselage emerge from the flames, its main rotor still spinning somehow.

Seconds later, this piece of flying wreckage slammed onto the carrier's deck.

Aboard *Ocean Voyager* forty miles away

Ryder couldn't find his crash helmet.

He'd looked for it everywhere in the makeshift pilot ready room, kicking aside empty beer cans and steak sauce bottles, searching through garbage bags filled with cigarette butts and used pep pill dispensers.

But with no luck. The helmet had disappeared.

"This is just fucking great!" he cursed.

He was otherwise suited up for flight; his Harrier was getting prepped and would soon be ready to go. His heart was pumping so fast, he could hardly feel his arms, his legs, his toes. His ears were burning red-hot.

He was furious. At himself. At every Muslim. At the whole goddamn world. When he was younger, things had always seemed to go his way. Had this adventure occurred 12 years before, he and his colleagues would have got the drop on the bad guys long before it had come to this. But luck and wisdom had arrived too late this time. As good as Murphy's team had been in its short heyday, they'd never managed to get any closer than one step behind the mooks.

Ryder had seen the CD-ROM's third level, *all* of it by this time. Kazeel's narration was just the beginning. Once his preamble ended, a computer-generated visual of the impending attack on the *Lincoln* had popped onto the screen. Many big planes arriving over the battle group at slightly staggered intervals, then raining down on the carrier from all directions, trying to overwhelm the AirCap of Tomcats and Hornets. It looked like something from a cheap video game but was chilling nevertheless, especially since those airplanes, the real ones, would all be turning toward the fleet soon, if they hadn't already. The plan of the Next Big Thing? To use about thousand innocent "martyrs" in an attempt to kill five thousand U.S. sailors.

A super-9/11.

Another unthinkable act.

The nightmare had begun in earnest about 30 minutes before.

That's when Gil Bates, running through the passageways and scaling ladders like a maniac, carried the old PC up to the CQ himself. When he arrived in the stateroom, disheveled and near cardiac arrest, Phelan had asked him: "Why didn't you take one of the pancakes up?"

Ryder had laughed; they all did. That was Phelan all over. But Ryder knew he'd never laugh quite that hard again.

They watched the computer-generated attack just once, Bates explaining that, by Kazeel's own words, the terrorists were going to try to overwhelm the carrier's protective bubble not by technology but by brute force. As the scenario played out, the Spook boss asked the one question on everyone's mind: "Can the carrier's fighters handle so many big planes, coming from all directions?"

No one knew. Bingo was on hand by this time; he and Phelan were both Navy guys. But Bingo had served only on cruisers and Phelan had never done carrier ops. He'd never even landed on one. The vision of World War II kamikaze attacks naturally came to mind—and sure enough, the terrorists' CD contained a segment showing old black-and-white footage of Japanese Zeros plowing into the deck of the USS *Lexington* off Okinawa. The message was clear: If just one small single-engine wooden plane could cause a massive amount of damage on a carrier, albeit fifty years ago, what would happen if something the size of an airliner hit a modern-day carrier? What if many of them managed to hit it? The damage would be beyond description.

"The F-14s will get some of them," Phelan had finally said. "And the escort ships might get a few more. But can they get them all? I don't know."

Then came the topic of nukes. The CD showed some

stock footage of a nuclear blast, something from back in the fifties, with Kazeel's voice-over promising if the planes were aimed right, a mushroom cloud for Allah would result.

Was this possible?

Gallant had asked: "What happens when an unarmed nuclear weapon is involved in an impact or an explosion? Isn't that what they used to trigger the original atomic bombs?"

"I think the first A-bomb was set off by nothing more than a couple thousand pounds of dynamite," Curry confirmed.

This was a highly disturbing possibility.

But it would be Ryder who asked the most painful and dumbest question of all: "What about Hunn and his guys? They're stuck on those planes."

He knew it was a mistake the second it came out of his mouth, and at that moment he wanted nothing more but to pull the words back in. More proof his timing was gone. The silence that greeted the question said it all. Obviously the chances of any of Martinez's guys getting out of this were slim.

The CD-ROM finally ended. Now came the big question: What should they do with this bombshell information?

"This could make Nine-Eleven look like a picnic," Curry had declared. "We've got to let those carrier guys know."

But how?

They had the same problem, for a different reason. This wasn't a matter of their trying to redeem Murphy's undoing. And where before they didn't want to involve anyone else in their undertakings, now it was essential they get word to higher-ups immediately.

But they just couldn't call the Navy up on the phone, could they? Ryder had asked. Actually, they could, because Bingo had a list of cell phone numbers for every Navy ship in the Gulf area. The trouble was, as before, there was no way anyone would believe them, at least at first. They'd be working against a military mentality where nothing ever moved fast and things frequently moved slow, even in a crisis.

How about a message via ship-to-ship radio then? Bingo would give that a try, too, but there wasn't much hope in that option either, for the same reason. Who would believe a voice on the other end of the line claiming that catastrophe was just minutes away?

"So what are we going to do?" Gallant had asked. "We can't just let the Navy sit out there and take the hit. Or hope they spot it on their own—and shoot down all of those planes. How the hell can we make them believe us, quickly?"

That's when Curry spoke up. "I'll go tell them," he'd said. "If you call them, and radio them—and I show up, too—then at least they'll know *something* is up."

They'd all looked over at him, his Raiders T-shirt now in tatters. Go *tell* them? How?

"I'll fly to them," he'd said. "In the old *Torch* rig."

The others almost laughed at him. "*Torch* is off the books," Gallant reminded him. "Its engine can barely turn the rotor. It has no gas. It doesn't even have a radio."

"I'll steal some fuel from the ship's engines," Curry said. "If that juice can make the thing fly, I won't need a radio."

Martinez started to argue with him. "You won't get within fifteen miles of the carrier. You could convince them that you're carrying the President in the back, they'd still shoot you down. Those will be their orders."

But Curry remained adamant. "There's no way I'm going to just hang around here and do nothing. I've got my brother's memory to think about."

A painful silence filled the stateroom at that moment. When Gallant offered to go with him, Curry said no. This would be a suicide mission, and he knew it. There was no sense in taking someone else along.

Finally Martinez just told him: "If you want to go, I can't stop you. . . ."

That's when Ryder and Martinez got into it. No sooner had Curry left, CD-ROM in hand, to warn the *Lincoln,* than Ryder insisted he be allowed to take off, too. Martinez flipped. Curry's mission was a one-way flight. Why would Ryder want to add to the death toll? The Navy was just as likely to shoot down a Harrier as they would a stray Blackhawk.

But Ryder, too, was insistent. He *could not* miss this, not if he ever wanted to sleep peacefully again. Besides, he wasn't going to warn the *Lincoln*. He was going up to search for the hijacked planes; that's how he would be of help. He'd seen the plan. He knew where the airliners were at the moment and even the flight paths they would use in their attempts to crash into the carrier. It was all on the CD-ROM.

Ryder also knew he'd be going up with just a couple dozen cannon shells in his aircraft's gun and less than a half-tank of gas. And he wouldn't have to worry about landing, because there probably would be no place for him to land and little gas for him to do it with. But . . .

"If I can intercept at least one or maybe two of them," he'd declared, "it might affect how this thing turns out."

"Do you realize what you're saying?" Martinez had countered. "Do you know what you'll have to do to stop one or two of them?"

"I do," was all Ryder said.

In the end it came down to rank. Ryder and Martinez were both colonels, though in different services. They canceled each other out. But Ryder was the senior man, by age and length of service. So there was no way Martinez could tell him *not* to go. Finally the Delta officer relented.

That's how Ryder won the argument to allow himself to go get killed.

He'd hurried downstairs to get into his flight suit. But now this helmet thing was holding him up.

He was just about to leave and fly the mission without it when he looked in his locker . . . and found it just sitting there. This was weird. The locker had been the first place he'd searched. Were the pep pills finally getting to him? The lack of sleep? Was he so pumped, he'd seen the helmet without realizing it was there?

He retrieved it from the locker and, in doing so, caught a glimpse of something tucked into its safety netting. It was a photograph of his wife. Ryder froze. He *was* getting old. He had no memory of ever putting the photo in there, though he must have, because it was his favorite picture of her. He'd surprised her one day with his camera while she was weeding her garden, and snapped a picture just as she was taking her hair down. Her expression was not the surprise he was going for but one of joy and good humor, blond curls and beauty.

He collapsed into the room's only chair now and stared at the photo. The world was falling apart all around him, yet he could not take his eyes off her. He missed her so much. He ran his finger along her face, her smile. He hadn't dreamed about her lately because he hadn't been to sleep in days. No matter. He brought the photo up to his lips, then let it ride along his unshaven face.

He might be seeing her again, very soon.

Two minutes later, helmet in hand, Ryder was banging on Phelan's cabin door.

The young pilot had disappeared shortly after Curry left on his mission. But Ryder knew the kid's Harrier was being prepped for flight, too.

When he got no response, Ryder pushed the cabin door open. He found Phelan sitting on the edge of his bunk, suited up, ready to go.

But he wasn't moving.

"You coming?" Ryder asked him.

Phelan was just staring straight ahead, intense and wide-eyed, his eyes zeroed in on his mother's photograph, hanging on the opposite wall. He looked scary.

Phelan finally acknowledged his presence. "I know this will be hard to believe," he said slowly. "But I just realized what's *really* been going on here. . . ."

Ryder was puzzled. "What do you mean?"

Phelan spread out his arms, indicating the ship, the whole operation. "What we've been doing out here. The things they've had us do. The missions we've run. The people we've killed."

He looked up at Ryder. There were tears in his eyes.

"You see it, don't you? And I'm just the dumbest one in this bunch? The last to understand what's been happening?"

Ryder could only shake his head. This was an unexpected turn of events. He checked his watch. Time was running out—for both of them.

"Think back to what Murphy did," Phelan went on. "What he told us, how he got us together. We'd all lost somebody to the mooks. We'd all been touched by it. He provided us the hardware, the gear, the ships, the bombs. No regulations. No oversight. No one to answer to. He made it strictly 'us against them,' and gave us a chance to fight back for our country."

He paused for a troubled breath.

"But what have we *really* done?" he asked. "We've lit off car bombs. We've blown up kids. We've wasted entire villages."

He put his head in his hands. "*Damn*—all this time, I thought I was doing my duty. I thought I was fighting a war . . ."

He looked back up at Ryder. "But we go out and kill children now without batting an eye. Just like the terrorists do. We blow up a bus full of innocent civilians in an instant. Just like the terrorists do. We collapse buildings. We poison food. We bring fear and terror and misery. Just like the terrorists do. . . ."

Another breath, deep, trembling. "Do you see what I'm saying? We've *become* them, for Christ's sake. We've become *terrorists* ourselves."

The words hit Ryder like bullets through a balloon. He deflated instantly. Phelan was right, of course. They'd been down in the muck for some time now, and it stunk as bad as the sewage they'd left spewing in the Rats' Nest.

Become like them. Murphy's plan all along.

But it was strange. At that moment, Ryder was painfully aware of two things. One, that he was nearly a quarter-century older than this kid who flew like a dream. But two, at last it dawned on him who Phelan reminded him of. It had always been in the back of his mind, unable to make its way to the front. But now he knew.

Talented but naive? More hot than cool? All talk, but all action, too? More lucky than not? Who did Phelan remind him of? No one more than himself: Ryder Long, 20 years ago.

He felt as old as Methuselah at that moment. He knew that Phelan would probably not heed what he was about to tell him, just like Ryder would have blown off some old fuck trying to talk sense to him when he was 24.

But he had to try anyway.

"OK, so Murphy knew what he was doing," he began, "He knew I lost my wife, just like you lost your dad and Martinez lost his kid and the chopper boys lost their brothers. He knew we wouldn't have any qualms about punching back, hard. But he also said something that stuck with me. Do you remember? He said the most important thing we had do was take care of our own. *Us*—and no one else. He knew no one in D.C. was ever going to get off the stick and *really* do something about the people who'd hit the World Trade Center that day. They can give speeches; they can pay off the families. They can invade entire countries. But they're just politicians. They don't have a clue as to how to deal with this the right way."

Now it was Ryder who took a troubled breath.

"The mooks kill our civilians because they want us to change," he went on. "We kill their civilians as a way of saying, 'Fuck you.' You can't drop a nuclear bomb on this problem and have it go away. The solution is not in air strikes, or cruise missiles, or turning Iraq into our own personal gas station. The solution is fire for fire and eye for an eye. The only way to make these guys pay is to come at them as mirror images of themselves. *That's* what scares them. And Murphy knew that, too.

"The night we saved that cruise liner—just before you flew onboard—I saw an amazing sight: The people on that boat went crazy when they realized who was actually saving them from the mooks. They saw the flag on the side of the choppers and they knew we were Americans and that we had delivered them. Old people pumping their fists—can you imagine what that looked like? Finally someone was *taking care* of them, *watching over* them. I could hear those people that night. My engine was cranking; my helmet was on—but I heard them. They were chanting, *'USA! USA!'* I still hear them. I'll *always* hear them. And if it means I've got to go to hell so they can go to heaven, then so be it. That's what all this means to me."

He took out his last two pep pills, placed them on the end of his tongue, but then just as quickly spit them away.

"Now there are about five thousand Americans who could be in body bags inside an hour," he concluded. "Or more likely at the bottom of the sea. Guys on that carrier. Guys on those support ships. *They're* the ones who need our help now. What little we might be able to give. Whether we're angels or devils, they're *our people*. We might be like the guys who dropped the A-bombs on Japan. Kill a lot of people, so a whole lot more *won't* be killed. Or maybe when history judges us, it won't be so kind. I don't know. But for now let's leave the psychoanalysis to the shrinks. We got one more thing we've got to do."

He gathered himself back up and sucked in some long, deep breaths. For the first time the sea air felt good going in. And he noticed the ship was rolling again, but it didn't bother him. He put his helmet on and turned back to Phelan.

"So what do you say, partner?" he asked. "Bump the jumpers, one more time?"

But Phelan still didn't move. There was no way Ryder could know if anything he'd just said had actually sunk in. He wasn't too sure he believed all of it himself. Even now he was thinking, *What the hell did I just say?*

But then finally Phelan put his helmet on, too.

"OK," he said softly. "Let's go."

Aboard the USS *Abraham Lincoln*

Lieutenant Commander Ken Gwinn had just reported to the bridge when the mysterious black helicopter crashed onto the *Lincoln*'s forward flight deck.

The impact had sent a violent shudder through the ship, but the crew recovered quickly. The intercoms were immediately screeching with fouled deck warnings. All flight operations came to a halt. The carrier's fire suppression teams were rushed to the top. The ship's flight surgeons were told to stand by.

There were 18 people on the *Lincoln*'s bridge when it happened. The floating behemoth was run from here, the place where all commands affecting the ship's movements originated. The helmsman steered the ship; the lee helmsman told the engine room how much speed to make. There were also lookouts and boatswains and the quartermaster of the watch who assisted in navigation, weather readings, and kept the ship's log. All flight operations were conducted one level up in the Primary Flight Center, essentially the air traffic control tower for the carrier.

Gwinn was the bridge communications officer, a new duty recently installed on the *Lincoln*. He was in charge of handling all messages flowing on and off the bridge. Stationed three feet to the right of the captain's chair, Gwinn was equipped with a secure laptop called a Q Fax, used in times of sensitive maneuvers or combat ops. Only the most important messages, from around the ship, from around the world, showed up here, printing out on long strips of bright yellow paper with the push of a button. It was Gwinn's job to make sure these messages got in front of the captain as quickly as possible.

From his vantage point high on the carrier's superstructure Gwinn had watched the rescue crews extract the pilot from the burning helicopter and then push the wreckage over the side. The fire crews washed down the deck and a quick foreign object sweep was done. All launchers were declared safe. Planes would soon be taking off again.

Not long after, an urgent message from the ship's surgeon blinked onto Gwinn's screen. The person flying the helicopter was seriously injured. He couldn't talk, but he could write. He was claiming to be a U.S. special operations agent, but his supposed outfit was not on a list of special commands held by the *Lincoln*'s intelligence officer. Still, the man came bearing some startling news: a large number of Arab airliners were in the process of being hijacked all over the Gulf. The hijackers would soon be trying to crash these planes into the *Abraham Lincoln*. What's more, he had a CD-ROM with him to prove it. Somehow, the disk had survived the crash.

Gwinn audibly gulped when he read the message. Could this be true? The carrier was not even halfway through its transit of Hormuz. There was very little room to maneuver, and the big turn to port would be coming up quickly, requiring the carrier to slow to less than 10 knots. This was the worst situation to be in if someone was trying to crash something into you, because this was when the ship was its most vulnerable.

Gwinn passed the message to the CO. The captain read it twice. At almost the same time, a report appeared from the carrier's radio shack. Someone was sending messages to the *Lincoln* over shortwave radio claiming the same thing, that a number of hijacked airliners were heading for the carrier. The person sending the messages did not identify himself or his location, for security reasons, or so he said. And now the ship was even getting phone calls from equally reticent persons, claiming to have the same information.

The captain took this all in and thought it over—for about two seconds. Had it just been phone calls or radio transmissions, he might have been of a different mind. But combined with the mysterious copter pilot's suicidal dash to get to the ship and his claim to have evidence on a CD-ROM . . . well, that was enough for the captain to act.

Nine F-14 Tomcats were on deck, standing by in case the CAP already airborne had some dropouts. The captain ordered these planes into the air immediately and told the Air Boss upstairs to prep and launch as many other fighters as humanly possible. Then the captain called the ship to a general alert.

Then he pulled out a secure sat phone and called the Pentagon, using a top-secret scrambled number given to him in the event of something like this. Gwinn could tell from the captain's side of the conversation that he was delivering unexpected and frightening news to Washington. The Pentagon told the captain to keep the sat line clear and open; the CO ordered the communications shack to make it so.

The captain called down to the carrier's air defense section next, asking for its status. The news here was not good, either. The *Lincoln*'s massive security bubble had engulfed so many different types of aircraft by now, the computers were having a hard time tracking them all. Blaring out over the comm speakers, this report only added to the tension building on the bridge. Minutes before, the fleet's vaulted defense had been unable to stop a lone helicopter from reaching the carrier. How were they going to stop a large number of airliners?

The captain sat back and began chewing on the end of his pipe. Gwinn noticed his hands were shaking. Not a good sign. His Q Fax screen blinked again. Another message was coming in.

It was from the ship's radar suite. An airliner had just been spotted straying off-course over Saudi Arabia, about sixty miles northwest of Hormuz. It had turned south and was heading for the carrier. Gwinn quickly handed the message to the captain. The pipe nearly fell out of the Old Man's mouth.

This airliner might be having engine problems. Or its navigation computer may have malfunctioned. But the captain couldn't take any chances. He directed two Tomcats to intercept the wayward airliner and take appropriate action. Those three words again. The moment the captain broke his radio connection, another report blinked onto Gwinn's screen. A second airliner had veered off-course, 30 miles to the north. It, too, was heading for the carrier.

Before Gwinn had a chance to pass this second report on, he received another message. A third airliner was now heading for the ship, coming straight down the Gulf. Gwinn hastily passed the two reports to the captain; his screen blinked yet again. A *fourth* plane had turned in their direction; this one was coming from the west.

The captain immediately called the ship to Condition Zebra. This meant an attack was imminent. Everything onboard was to be locked up tight. Thousands of sailors went rushing to predetermined positions, places they were supposed to be when a nuclear bomb, or something nearly as catastrophic, was about to hit the boat. Those last planes lined up on the carrier's catapults were launched; then the deck was cleared. Everyone on the bridge donned oversize helmets and life-saving gear, the captain included. Transparent blast shields were lowered over the bridge's huge windows, darkening everything inside.

The captain sent a message to every pilot in the CAP. It was the same order he'd just given the two F-14 pilots. Any aircraft, civilian or military, entering the carrier's protection zone was to be shot down, no questions asked. He then relayed the gist of his orders to every other ship in the battle group. They, too, began zipping up.

Gwinn was trying hard not to show his alarm. People up here were counting on him. Many more of the carrier's planes were in the air, thanks to the mysterious copter pilot and the ghostly radio and phone calls. And all those jets had the capacity to shoot down an airliner. But it was a question of time and numbers: Could the carrier's planes find all four airliners before the airliners found the ship?

Gwinn's comm screen blinked again. The radar team had detected a fifth airliner veering toward the battle group. As soon as Gwinn ripped this message, another one popped onto his screen. A sixth airliner was heading for them.

It was Gwinn's hands that were shaking now. He passed the new information to the CO. The captain immediately asked the navigation officer how much more time before the ship passed out of the strait. "At least another ten minutes," was the reply, and that was only before the carrier reached a point wide enough to start basic evasive maneuvers. Until then they had no choice but to keep going straight ahead, as fast as they could.

Gwinn could sense a fog of disaster starting to swirl around him. The tension on the bridge became very heavy.

Many people up here were equipped with binoculars; they were pointing them in every direction. The visibility was absolutely clear. *That's good, right?* Gwinn thought. Or did they want to see what was coming their way?

While all this was going on, Gwinn's screen began blinking yet again. A new message popped on-screen.

Two more airliners had been spotted heading for the carrier.

Above the Persian Gulf

Sergeant Dave Hunn knew something was wrong when he heard the awful scream.

It was a chilling sound, like from a woman but definitely coming from a man. High-pitched and mortal, it was cut off suddenly, the last vibrations from a set of torn vocal cords. The male flight attendant, his throat slashed, fell backward in the aisle about ten feet behind Hunn's seat, a tray of hot tea scalding him as he went down. Two men were standing over him. They were the al-Habazz cell members. One stepped on top of the dying attendant, put a gun to an old woman's head, and pulled the trigger. Her brains were blown out. Screams from the woman's family. Five shots later, they were all dead, too.

But none of this was computing for Hunn.

Why were the terrorists doing this? Why weren't they waiting until they made their connecting flights?

Why were they killing their own people?

There was only one explanation. *This thing is happening right now. . . .*

This was not good. Hunn hadn't expected to have a confrontation with the would-be hijackers, or at least not so soon. But here they were, carrying huge handguns, waving around banana knives, and killing passengers at random. Hunn, on the other hand, was armed with nothing more than a .22 handgun, one of the pistols from the shoot-out at the Royal Dubai. The Algerian popgun was small but was the only weapon he thought he could hide under his *madras*. Problem was, it only had two bullets left.

The terrorists began screaming at the passengers to stay
in their seats and that they were now in control of the airplane and that they were all going to make Allah proud of
them. At the same time, they stood up an old man right behind Hunn and shot him in the throat. He collapsed back into
his seat, bleeding furiously.

The plane itself was small, a two-engine job; this was the
flight going to Crete. It had a cramped compartment, with
very low overheads and narrow aisles. Plus, they were flying
at 22,000 feet, high enough where one shot-out window could
implode the plane. These were not conditions conducive to
gunplay, not that the inside of any aircraft was.

The terrorists had stood up another woman and were now
marching her backward down the aisle, heading for the
cockpit. They seemed to be carrying out a step-by-step plan:
kill a few passengers, suddenly, horribly, to stun everyone
else. It was a quick and economical way to get control, and it
was working. An eerie quiet came over the cabin as many
passengers saw their fervor for Islam go south. Literally losing their religion. Hunn had a very difficult choice to make
now. He didn't know why the terrorists had acted when they
did, but he had to do something. Yet for every bullet they
used on the passengers, that was one less bullet he would
have to worry about later on. The terrorists both had handguns, though, with a capacity for nine rounds in each clip
and probably more clips in their pockets. Hunn would have
given anything for his M16 right now.

The two cell members were not large men. They were
probably in their early twenties, and both bore a faint resem-
blance to the late Jamaal el-Habini. When the woman they'd
taken began to struggle, they shot her in the back. She fell
right next to Hunn's aisle seat. One more bullet gone. The
terrorists were now just five feet in front of him, still walking
backward towards the flight compartment, still screaming
about Paradise and Allah. Hunn really had no choice. He had
to stay frozen and let them get to the cockpit. Only then
could he think about making a move.

But then they grabbed a young girl. She was not wearing

Islamic garb; rather, she was dressed in Western-style clothes. She was about 10 years old, and in a strange way, reminded Hunn of his kid sister. The terrorists yanked the girl from the arms of her mother and pushed one of their pistols into her right ear. She screamed. She began to fight. Hunn could see the terrorist begin to squeeze his trigger.

Damn. . . .

Hunn stood up, pulled the pistol from his waistband, and shot the guy holding the young girl twice, right between the eyes. The man went over like a lead weight, pulling the girl down with him. His partner, like everyone else on the plane, was shocked to see a Muslim woman with a firearm. He fired two shots back at Hunn. Unaimed, the recoil almost knocking him over, the first one missed by five feet.

The second one went right into Hunn's chest.

The first indication the pilots of the airliner had that something was wrong was when the cockpit door flew open and the lone terrorist stumbled in.

The copilot in the right-side seat saw the gun and screamed.

"What are you doing? What do you want?"

The terrorist was shaking. This hadn't been as easy as he'd been told. "I want you to turn this aircraft due south," he said, his voice nervous, moving his gun back and forth between the two pilots. "Do what I say and you won't get hurt."

The pilots were instantly terrified—and confused. This man was obviously a Muslim. So were they.

"Sir . . ." the copilot asked him, "are you sure you're on the right plane?"

The terrorist replied by shooting him in the head. Then he turned the gun on the pilot.

"Turn south," he said. "Now. . . ."

"But, my friend . . ." the pilot said, *"we are brothers. . . ."*

The gun pressed deeper into his temple.

"South. . . ."

The pilot got the message. He started a long bank back toward the lower Gulf.

"But to where?" he asked the hijacker.

"To heaven, brother," the man replied.

The terrorist settled down a bit and wiped the sweat from his brow. He'd done everything he'd been taught to do. Terrorize the passengers quickly, get control of the outer cabin, then the pilots. He just didn't expect to be doing it all alone. He looked down to see the pilot had wet himself. No matter, they would have to fly for only a little while, just until they spotted the U.S. battle group. Then he would kill the pilot, get into his seat, and fly the airliner into the carrier himself.

He switched the pistol from his right hand to his left and wiped the sweat from his eyes again. Suddenly he was very hot. He could hear nothing behind him; the passengers were absolutely quiet, petrified into silence. At least that part of the plan had worked.

He closed the flight compartment door finally and then crouched beside the pilot, keeping the gun trained on his head.

Strangely though, no sooner had the door been shut than he heard someone knocking on it. Who could this be?

He stood up, opened the door, and saw a huge woman in a bloody *burka* standing in the doorway. The same woman who had shot his partner. But this woman had a goatee.

The next thing the hijacker saw was the barrel of a gun—his partner's gun. With all the strength he could muster, Dave Hunn pulled the trigger and shot the hijacker in the forehead. The man was blown backward. He hit the flight control panel, then slumped on top of the dead copilot. The plane started to dive. A chorus of screams rose up from the passengers. Hunn staggered into the cockpit and pulled both bodies away from the bloody controls, allowing the pilot to right the plane. Then he collapsed into the copilot's seat himself.

"Sorry, I fucked up," he began murmuring. "I'm really sorry. . . ."

The pilot was absolutely astonished. He wet himself a second time. It was only when Hunn reached up and took

what remained of the *burka* off his head that the pilot realized he wasn't a woman.

He was also bleeding heavily. Hunn reached inside his
shirt pocket and came out with a very bloody Koran. *Jamaal's*
Koran. It had deflected the bullet away from his heart, but not
by much.

The pilot began turning the plane to the west, towards
Oman, the nearest place he could land. Then he reached over
and touched Hunn's arm. This man who had just saved their
lives was already turning cold.

"Brother . . . . oh, brother," the pilot said, "is there anything I can do for you?"

Hunn slumped farther into the seat. He was fading fast.

"Yeah," he was just about able to say. "Fly this thing to
Queens, will you?"

Chapter 29

Contrails.

The sky above *Ocean Voyager* was filled with them when Ryder took off.

They reminded him of photographs taken during the Battle of Britain or, better yet, some gigantic piece of surreal art. The puffy white clutter might not have seemed so unusual on a normal day; the Gulf's air lanes were always busy. But after rising just a few thousand feet above the ship, Ryder could see that a half-dozen of those contrails, coming from a half-dozen different points in the sky, had cut across the normal lines of air travel and had abruptly ended above the same point: the Strait of Hormuz, 35 miles to the south.

Contrails were like the stars: they told you not what was happening now but what had happened sometime before. Ryder could read them, though; he knew what this meant: the six cross-cutting contrails belonged to hijacked airliners, probably those planes that had left Bahrain later in the morning and thus had a shorter distance to fly back once they'd been seized. And as he judged these peculiar contrails were at least 10 minutes old, this meant these planes were already falling on the battle group. The mass mayhem had begun, just over the horizon.

There was nothing Ryder could do about that now. He

was up here for a different reason. If six airliners were already close to the battle group, that meant four still were not.
And if the planes trying to crash into the carrier now were
the ones that had left Bahrain late, then the missing planes
were probably ones that had taken off early. Four in a row,
just around 8:00 A.M. They'd all headed toward Europe almost two hours ago, all flying roughly north by northwest.
They'd probably be coming back the same way. The Navy
would never make it out this far in time to intercept them.
No one would. It was up to him and Phelan to stop these
planes. Or at least that's how Ryder understood it.

He wouldn't need a wingman for this mission, though,
just as Phelan wouldn't need a flight commander. What they
were about to do was best done alone. They had a brief
phone conversation at 10,000 feet and then they split up.
The young Navy pilot peeled off due north. Ryder headed
northwest.

He was soon over land and rocketing above the rugged border area separating the United Arab Emirates and Saudi
Arabia.

No more than 40 miles inland, he spotted two airliners up
around thirty thousand feet, their contrails stretching back
to northwest. The airliners were flying side by side, a very
weird sight. When did you ever see two huge airliners flying
in formation? There was only one explanation: two hijacked
planes had linked up and were heading toward the battle
group together.

Ryder started climbing. The airliners grew outlandishly
in size as he ascended. One was an Airbus 300, silver and
shiny, with Islamic writing on its nose and tail; the other, a
Boeing 767, with a fuselage painted sickly yellow. If not
jumbo jets, both were still very large airplanes. They filled
Ryder's field of vision so quickly, he felt like a minnow approaching a pair of flying whales.

Even if each of these planes was only half-full, more than
500 people were riding inside them, women, kids, the old
and young, and, not to forget, a Delta guy in each. Yet Ryder

was here to shoot them down. What choice did he have? He
didn't want to do it. He didn't need *another* pack of ghosts
haunting him. He'd picked up enough demons on this trip already. But these people were doomed anyway. Either they
were going to get shot down by the Navy or they were going
to die if their airliner somehow managed to get through
the *Lincoln*'s air screen and hit the carrier. Every experience
Ryder had lived through in the past six weeks told him he
had to knock down these monsters and do it quick. Not to do
so would put those 5,000 American sailors on the *Lincoln* in
even graver danger than they were right now. Protecting
them was his mission.

He steeled himself and began prepping for the grim task.
Just how does one go about shooting down two enormous
airplanes? Ironically, he wasn't sure. This was not a hot-shit
fighter-interceptor he was flying here, not an F-14, -15, or -16.
He had no air-to-air missiles, the ideal weapon for this job.
The Harrier was an attack plane. It was built to drop bombs on
things on the ground. His tango with the Arab fighters that
night over the Med was proof: he was out of his league when
facing airborne targets.

Plus, he only had 24 rounds left in his cannon. Would
they be enough? It took 10 to 20 rounds to fuck up something like an APC or a tank. How many would it take to
shoot down a huge airliner? How many to shoot down two?
The absurdity of the situation hit him at that moment. This
was not the kind of pilot he was supposed to be. He was the
wrong guy in the wrong plane at the wrong time. *What the
hell was he doing up here?*

But then Fate arrived to make his situation a little simpler.
The big silver Airbus was flying slightly ahead of the yellow
767. Suddenly the Airbus banked wildly to the left, going up
on its wing and coming very close to tipping over completely. Ryder was only 1,000 feet below the planes now; he
banked sharply to his left, thinking the big plane was coming down right on top of him. Just as suddenly, though, the
Airbus regained control and dropped back to level flight. It
only lasted a few seconds, but it was a nightmarish thing to

watch. Ryder couldn't imagine any sane pilot trying such an extreme maneuver.

The Airbus stayed level, but only for a few moments. It went up on its left wing again, this time quicker, more violently, causing its contrail to cockscrew behind it. Just as it looked like the big plane was going to go over for sure, it returned to level flight again, but with so much force, its engines were nearly ripped from its wings. Surely this wasn't the hijackers doing this. They were still at least 20 minutes' flying time from Hormuz; they wouldn't be starting their death plunge so soon. Was there a fight going on in its cockpit? Was the Delta guy onboard trying to retake the plane from the hijackers?

Ryder would never know. The huge craft began bouncing all over the sky, nearly colliding with the 757 that was practically riding up its butt. It turned up on its left wing again, and this time it kept on going. Over onto its back, wings flapping so hard from the strain, both its engines finally fell off.

Then the plane began the long plunge down.

Ryder had seen some very disturbing things in his career. He'd seen combat and he'd been involved in secret warfare, which was always particularly nasty. But he'd never seen anything like this.

He watched the airliner all the way down. It took nearly two minutes to drop those six miles. It finally hit a mountain somewhere in the Saudi desert, vanishing in a cloud of fire and smoke.

A wave of nausea went right through him. The crash really shook him up. *Not so heroic now,* he thought. He took some quick, deep gulps of oxygen. It tasted stale, but it did the job. At least he stayed conscious. What had happened? He had to believe the Delta guy on the Airbus had somehow caused it to crash, just as the passengers on United Flight 93, the hijacked flight heading for the White House, had done on 9/11. If so, then the Delta trooper had indeed made the supreme sacrifice. He'd also done Ryder a big favor. Now he only had to kill 300 people, instead of twice that many.

He began climbing again. Finding the second airliner took only a few seconds. Painted in the garish yellow color scheme of Royal Gulf Airlines, it was cast by the rising sun in an eerie morning glow. Ryder was soon right below it, his cannon aimed for the place he knew its main fuel tank to be. He began to press down on his gun trigger, hoping a couple dozen shells would be enough to light it off. . . .

But suddenly he stopped. He wasn't sure why. Everything in his body was telling him to fire, now, and get this thing over with. But it was his head that was giving him trouble. Words were ringing in his ears, Phelan's words. Here he was, playing the Angel of Death again, a role he'd come to darkly embrace since joining Murphy's outfit. The kids in the camp in Algeria. The people in downtown Abu Dhabi. He'd even had a hand in the mass fruit poisoning. Who lives, who dies, was once again up to him, the fate of hundreds in his sweaty hands.

But just like every decision Ryder had made in the past six weeks, he'd been damn quick in determining that the people aboard this plane *had* to die. And wasn't that exactly what Phelan had been talking about? Fighting the mooks was a dirty business. But had they really lost that one last veneer of humanity? Was this really what he'd become?

Ryder's finger stayed hovering over the trigger. Many voices were in his head now. Phelan. Martinez. His wife, Maureen. Even his old partner, Woody. Being an American didn't automatically mean you were better than everyone else. It just meant you had a better opportunity to be that way. And there was *always* another option than to just go in guns blazing, right?

If so, then it was up to him to think of another way.

He banked hard right and then climbed. In seconds, he was on the airliner's tail. He booted throttles ahead full max and streaked right over the top of the big 767, so close he thought he felt an electrical jolt pass between the two planes. Just the noise alone would be terrifying for anyone inside the plane. That was his plan. A diversion might give the Delta guy onboard a chance to do something. If Ryder distracted the hijackers with his earsplitting, heart-stopping pass, maybe the American trooper would get the message and act.

Ryder peeled off to the left and looked over his shoulder. The airliner had dropped about one thousand feet, caused no doubt by sheer fright on the part of the person flying the airplane. But the 767 quickly recovered and leveled off at about twenty-nine thousand feet. Once back under control, it resumed its course toward Hormuz.

Ryder now banked hard left and went into a steep dive, streaking by the plane's right wing a second later. Not only was he making a tremendous noise; he was also disrupting the airstream in front of the huge jet, which usually led to some serious turbulence. But again, nothing happened. The jet bounced around a bit but still pressed on.

Damn, he really didn't want to shoot this thing down.

He did a quick check of his position. He was about thirty miles west of the strait, soon to pass back over the United Arab Emirates. With every second they were getting closer to the trouble zone.

He took another deep gulp of oxygen and buzzed the airliner a third time, streaking by just off its left wing this time. Once again, the big plane rocked around a little, but nothing more.

Clearly, this wasn't working. It was time to switch tactics.

He went full throttle again and rocketed ahead of the airliner. Two miles, three miles. Four. At five miles out, he went ass over end and turned 180 degrees, reversing his direction. Now the huge airliner was coming right at him.

If a distraction was still needed, then Ryder could think of no better one than to aim his plane at the airliner head-on. A game of chicken at 29,000 feet. That was bound to get someone's attention.

He increased power to 400 knots. The big plane was coming at him at least that fast. Ryder hunkered down farther into his seat. He and the airliner were closing on each other by a combined 800 miles an hour. Still, he pushed his throttle forward.

One second he was about 2,000 feet away from the 767. The next he was just 1,500, then 1,000—then just 750. Could they see him coming? That was the whole idea. He held the stick with both hands and fought to keep his eyes open.

Five hundred feet. Four hundred . . .

He was just seconds from a high-speed collision.

Three hundred . . .

Two hundred . . .

The airliner was not altering course and neither was he.

Hundred . . .

Fifty . . .

Did they see him?

He yanked back on the stick and roared up and over the airliner. As he streaked by, he could see right into the cockpit and in that instant, through the heavily tinted glass, he thought he saw at least a half-dozen people, faces white, looking back out at him. He'd come that close to colliding with the plane.

He fell away to the left and tore the oxygen mask from his face. His flight suit was soaked with sweat. His hands were shaking. Even 20 years ago, this would have been a heart-pounder.

He turned over again, checking his fuel load as he went. The noisy head-on pass had used up about a quarter of his remaining gas and taken a decade or two off his life, years that he dearly wanted to preserve.

But had he done anything at all?

He looked over his shoulder again and at last saw the airplane start to fall. Not like the first one, not like a B-17 falling on Berlin. The airliner's wings were level and it seemed under control.

But falling nonetheless.

More than five miles below, Habel el-Habella had just finished feeding his two camels when he heard a tremendous commotion off to the west.

Habel was a Bedouin, 85 years old, and he'd walked these

desert sands for nearly as long. But in all that time he could not recall hearing such a frightening screech as the one he was hearing now.

His camels bolted immediately, spooked to the point of relieving themselves. Habel grabbed for their reins and held on tight; they dragged him 100 feet before he got them to stop. Then somehow, he was able to look over his shoulder and was amazed to see a huge cloud of sand traveling at great speed, heading right for him.

Was this a *haboob?* No way. Habel had lived in the desert for so long, he could tell when a *haboob* was coming hours before it hit. They never came up this suddenly. So then what was this?

Before he could move, before he could think, the cloud was upon him. It was so loud it even drowned out the cries of his animals. The air became incredibly hot; it felt like flames going right through his lungs. So sure that he was about to meet his maker, Habel fell to his knees and let his camels go, something from childhood he'd been told never to do. But the animals must have felt as he did, because they both plopped down beside him. The noise was just tremendous. The sand was whipping around him so fiercely, it was cutting his face, his hands, his neck.

But then, suddenly, it was over. The calamity just went away. Habel stayed down on the ground, thinking this was death and death was very quiet. But finally, he opened his eyes and before him he saw an incredible sight. Rolling to a stop on the hard desert sand not 300 feet away was a huge yellow airplane.

Habel's mind was reeling. What sorcery was this! His camels were too stunned to cry; they could barely get back to their feet. How did this contraption get here? It was huge. And it was smoking all over, especially on its wings. And its tires beneath those wings had been torn to shreds. All through his many years, Habel had only seen airplanes passing over his head, *never* one up so close. It looked complicated and frightening.

Suddenly doors all over the airplane flew open and huge

orange balloons came bursting out. The balloons made a type
of slide and onto these slides Habel saw people start flowing out of the airplane. These people were all Muslims; Habel
recognized their dress. Many were women and children;
many were elderly. They were sliding down the balloon things
and running through the sand, away from the plane. Some
were laughing. Some were crying. Some were doing both.

As this was going on, Habel saw two bodies tumble out
of the front door of the airplane. They missed the slide completely and hit the ground in one thump. When this happened a great cheer went up from those who had already
exited the airplane.

Then came the strangest thing of all: a figure in a *burka*
came to the front door. Before Habel's eyes this person
stripped off the *burka* to reveal a military uniform beneath.
This was not a woman but a man who had been wearing
woman's clothing. And he was not an Arab. His skin was
white and he appeared huge and muscular.

This strange man finally slid down the orange balloon
himself. The people who'd come out before him met him at
the bottom and surrounded him and now were cheering him,
kissing him.

Old Habel didn't know what to make of this. Maybe he
was dead and the devil was trying to confuse him. That's
when some of the people who'd exited the airplane spotted
him and ran over to him. Again, they were all laughing even
though Habel could also see tears in their eyes.

They were shouting at him: "The Americans saved our
lives! We were dead, but now we are alive again!"

At that point, Habel determined this really was a trick of
Satan. He'd never heard anyone in this region talk kindly
about Americans. It was almost as rare as someone talking
kindly about the Jews. He quickly grabbed his camels and
tried to hurry away.

But then all the people on the ground were looking back
up into the sky again. Suddenly there came another earsplitting noise. And Habel heard the people cheering wildly and
saw them waving their hands in the air.

A moment later, the Harrier jump jet roared by, flying very fast and very low. It spun around on its wings once, a victory roll of sorts.

Then it turned southeast and rocketed off toward Hormuz.

The USS *Ballston Spa* had entered the Strait of Hormuz about ten minutes ahead of the aircraft carrier *Lincoln*.

It was a replenishment ship, lightly armed and filled with food and water rather than missiles and bombs. Minutes before, the ship's crew had been called to general quarters along with the rest of the battle group. Word was passed that terrorists had hijacked an unknown number of airliners in the area and that they were planning to crash them into the *Lincoln*. Some of the crew had seen a great flash off port side about ten minutes earlier. This was the first airliner being shot down by the fleet's F-14s. Trouble was, there were more commandeered airplanes out there, somewhere, and they were heading this way.

Ensign Alby Hirsch was the armaments officer for the *Ballston Spa*. He was at his position, the ship's forward gun mount, one of only two such weapons aboard the ship. Three young sailors were with him. All of them were equipped with binoculars and they were nervously scanning the skies around them. The air was filled with the sound of sonic booms and now more explosions; the sky above was a mad patchwork of contrails. It made for a frightening combination. Hirsch had completed his officer's training only a month before. This was his first deployment. He'd never imagined anything like this happening, at least not on his maiden cruise. At the moment, he was wondering if he'd ever see a second one.

He was trying to keep his wits about him, though. He continually checked his weapon, its ammo, its crew. The weapon was a .50-caliber machine gun, a peashooter compared to some of the hardware on the ships around him. It was intended to shoot at small boats that might menace the supply ship and certainly not to fire on adversarial aircraft. Or hijacked airliners. But Hirsch's training had taught him

that every head, every hand, every weapon, was important in
an emergency. He had to proceed on that point.

Suddenly he felt a hand on his arm, nails digging deep into
his skin. The youngest sailor on the gun crew, a kid no more
than 18, had grabbed him and was pointing off to starboard.
He couldn't talk. Hirsch looked north and soon saw why: an
enormous airliner, flying just 50 feet above the water, was
coming right at them. It was less than a half-mile away. Two
F-14s were on its tail, cannons blazing wildly. Ships in front
of the *Ballston Spa* were firing at the airliner, too. It was trailing two long streams of smoke and flame behind it.

The noise around Hirsch became deafening. Cursing,
shouting, the clatter of many guns, big and small, as the airliner, looking positively unreal, ran this gauntlet, flying so
low it was stirring up the surface of the water. Like a nightmare in slow motion, many of the shells being fired from the
Navy ships were hitting the airliner—but some were hitting
the pursuing Tomcats as well.

And the airliner just kept getting bigger. The plane
seemed to be adding power even as the flames about its
wings grew in intensity. Hirsch ordered his men to open fire.
The gun started chattering, but Hirsch could not hear it. He
could see the silver on the airliner's nose, the disturbingly
Arabic trim. It seemed to be moving along on a wave of exploding ordnance. It was being hit all over, yet it did not veer
one iota from its course. It was coming directly at the *Ballston Spa,* its nose pointing right at the midships.

Hirsch wasn't sure what to do. What could possibly stop
the huge plane from plowing into them? Should they keep
firing at it? Should he order his men to jump overboard? Did
they have time to do anything at all—except pray?

Suddenly a gray streak entered his field of vision from the
right. Incredibly, a Harrier jump jet had come out of nowhere
and appeared nearly on top of them. It swooped down into a
hover just off starboard bow, placing itself between the *Ballston Spa* and the oncoming airliner. A guardian angel sent to
save them was all Hirsch could think of, though he'd never
believed in such things. The Harrier began firing its cannon

at the airliner. Hirsch could see impacts all over the big DC-10. But would it be enough to stop the onrushing plane?

The Harrier hung there for what seemed like forever—though only a few seconds really passed. Finally the barrage of cannon fire took effect. The front of the airliner began to break off just 500 feet out, and for some reason this caused the huge plane not to plummet but to rise. A second later the Harrier moved out of the way, and a second after that the huge plane went right over the top of the *Ballston Spa,* tearing off its antennas, his halyards, and everything else above the bridge before plunging into the water on the port side.

The impact was so enormous, it created a backwash the size of a tidal wave. It swept over the deck of the ship, carrying Hirsch over the side with it. One moment he was in his gun mount; the next he was 10 feet underwater. Just him, no one else. Sheer fright pushed him to the surface. He came up gasping for air and nearly in shock. He couldn't believe he was still alive.

He had begun swimming furiously back toward the ship when he heard another tremendous roar. He turned in the choppy water to see an F-14 Tomcat, in flames, heading right for him. It was one of the planes that had been trying to shoot down the airliner. Again he couldn't believe it. Had he really survived one incoming plane, just to be killed by another? He went back under as the stricken fighter hit the surface not a hundred feet away. The waterborne concussion went through Hirsch like 10,000 volts, pushing him even farther into the depths. Once again he found himself madly swimming to the surface. By the time he reached air again, the Tomcat's fuselage was just starting to sink. Hirsch could see hundreds of perforations from the shattered cockpit to the horribly bent tail section. The two pilots, still in their cockpit, were both headless.

As the big fighter sank beneath the waves, it was obvious what had happened. The Tomcat had been shot down by gunners on the other Navy ships, even while it had been trying to shoot down the airliner. The pilots had been killed by their own troops.

A line was thrown from the *Ballston Spa,* now dead in the water, and with no little effort Hirsch was pulled back on-board. He was soaking wet and had a cut on his head, but he refused to go below. He retrieved his helmet and rejoined his crew at the gun mount instead. The pandemonium had not lessened any around them. The noise was tremendous, the multiple sonic booms twice as loud. There were so many ex-plosions going off high above them, the *Ballston Spa* was being barraged with shock waves blowing straight down onto its decks.

No sooner had Hirsch caught his breath than he was hit hard by something on the top of his head. It struck his hel-met with such force it caused a loud *ping!* Before he could react, something else hit him on the shoulder. Then again on his head. He managed to look up and saw an astonishing sight. It was raining airplane parts. Pieces of seats, chunks of plastic, rubber. They were falling out of the sky, into the water and onto the ship. Farther down the deck other sailors were getting hit by red-hot engine parts. A huge tire went right through the top of the bridge. Then Hirsch heard a loud *thump!* He turned to see that a body had fallen out of the sky and had landed just 10 feet away from him. It was a man, or what was left of him, middle-aged, in a suit and tie, still clutching a briefcase. He'd been horribly burned all over.

Then came another *thump!*—another body. Then another loud bang as a piece of jet engine came down on a group of sailors fighting a fire at middeck. One man had pieces of the engine go right through his body. He threw himself into the water, never to be seen again.

Hirsch began screaming into the phone attached to the gun mount, demanding medical personnel up on deck until he realized the phone's wires had been cut in the first rain of falling debris. His crew huddled all around him now as more airborne wreckage came down. The air was filled with horri-ble sounds and with smoke. Thick and putrid, it was swirling all around them.

What was happening? It could only be one thing: an airliner had been blown out of the sky high above the ship, and the

wreckage was now coming down on them. Hirsch screamed
for his men to take cover inside the gun mount and stay there.
In just the last two minutes, he'd come close to being killed at
least three times. He really didn't want to try for a fourth. He
squeezed himself in next to his crew and put his hands over
their heads. Then he started to speak to God in earnest.

Seconds later came another loud *thump!* Hirsch looked
up to see a body had fallen not an arm's length away from
where he was crouched. It was a woman this time, clad in a
burka. She had landed on her stomach and was bleeding
from everywhere. Her eyes were still open, though, and she
was looking right at him.

She seemed to be asking him: *Why me?*

There was only one super highway in Oman.

It was simply called the National Road. It stretched from
one end of the tiny country to the other, from the coast of the
Arabian Sea up to the tip of the Persian Gulf.

Because it passed mostly through desert, the highway was
long and straight; there was no need for curves here. It was
eight lanes in all, four going in each direction, a bit opti-
mistic perhaps on behalf of its builders, but a smooth ride
nevertheless.

The highway was used mostly by tanker trucks hauling
oil from the port city of Mirabet in the south up to Ṣuḥār in
the north. Occasionally citizens in private cars or SUVs took
advantage of the quick route between the two halves of the
country. There was also a bus that passed back and forth
once a day.

Amadd Amadd was a highway patrolman, Oman's *only*
highway patrolman, or at least on the National Road. He drove
the length of the lonely roadway twice every 24 hours. His
most frequent call was to help tank truck drivers who'd broken down, usually due to flat tires or engines overheating. Or
civilians who had run out of gas. The super highway had been
open only a year. In that time, Amadd had not once been
called to respond to a traffic accident. The road just wasn't
used that much.

That's why it was so strange when he got the call shortly after 10:00 A.M. In a bit of irony, he was eating a doughnut at the time, his car parked near the fifth exit of the highway, a place that had a slew of palm trees where he could stay somewhat cool without running his patrol car's air conditioner.

The radio call said there had been a massive crash on the north side of the highway just 10 miles from his location. The crash was so severe, it was blocking traffic in both directions. Amadd thought someone was pulling his leg. He made his dispatcher repeat the message three times before he was, convinced this was not a joke. Carefully rewrapping his morning delicacy, he started the engine of his patrol car—it was a Mercedes 601—pushed the air conditioner up to full blast, and roared off.

He was on the scene in just a few minutes, but after what he saw, he didn't know whether to laugh or cry. This was no huge smash-up of cars or trucks, though something was indeed blocking the highway in both directions.

It was an airplane. An airliner, to be more precise. An old 727 belonging to Southwest Asia Airways. It was straddling all eight lanes of the highway. But how did it get here?

Siren blaring, Amadd roared up to the plane. Many vehicles had stopped in both directions by now. Oil tank truck drivers mostly, a group of them had gathered beneath the nose of the 727 and were having an animated conversation with someone up in the cockpit. Then two water truck drivers appeared with an extension ladder. The plane's front door was open, but there was no means for anyone inside to get out.

Indeed, that's what the discussion between the ground and the plane had been about. The plane's emergency chutes had malfunctioned and the rear door was jammed; their landing had not been a smooth one. The plane had gone sideways at the last moment. The people onboard were trying to find a ladder in the middle of the Omani desert. And lucky for them, they'd found one, courtesy of the two water haulers.

The ladder was set in place and one of the drivers started to climb up. But Amadd quickly put a stop to that. He announced loud and clear that he was the police authority here. He would be going up the ladder first.

The driver stepped aside and Amadd began to climb. He didn't realize the ladder would become so shaky, though; he was not the thinnest of men. He was also amazed how high he had to go. His ascent was not pretty, and it was punctuated with frequent shouts to those below to make sure they held on tight to the bottom of the ladder.

Finally he reached the open door and, with much huffing and puffing, unceremoniously dragged himself inside.

He stood up and looked into the cockpit. The two pilots were still at their seats, in front of the controls. They both looked frightened but relieved. They stared blankly at Amadd; he stared right back at them.

"You gentlemen are going to have to move this airplane," he suddenly told them. His words sounded stupid coming out, but he really didn't know what else to say.

Both pilots simply pointed to the first seat in the first row of the first-class section; this was to Amadd's right. There were two men slumped in these seats. Both were dead. They had sharp bloody objects sticking out of their necks, their throats, and in one man's case his left eye socket. Amadd leaned over closer to them, filled with a sudden morbid curiosity. How had these men been killed? By nothing more than plastic knifes and forks, utensils given out with the onboard meal. These were the items sticking out of them.

Then Amadd became aware of a large individual standing next to him, almost hidden in the shadows, as it was very dark inside the plane. This man was wearing a desert camouflaged uniform.

Amadd didn't have to see any stars-and-stripes patch to know this man was a U.S. soldier. He *looked* American. Beyond him, Amadd could see the passengers. Unlike the pilots, they still seemed absolutely terrified. The passenger compartment was a mess.

The American soldier finally stepped out of the shadows and saluted smartly. There was blood on his hands.

In perfect Arabic, he said to Amadd: "I cannot tell you

anything more than my rank, my date of birth, and that I am part of a U.S. military special operations team.

"However, sir, as you are a representative of local law enforcement, I'd be most appreciative if I could turn responsibility for this aircraft over to you."

The gunfight aboard the DC-8 belonging the Royal Airways of Qatar lasted 20 long minutes.

This was the plane that was going to Vienna. The two Al-Habazz cell members had made their move just when they were supposed to. They'd quickly killed seven passengers in order to frighten the others, and their ruthless action had the desired effect. The plane was filled with women and children mostly, traveling after the month of prayer, another factor that had played into the terrorists' hands. Scaring them was almost too easy.

But the terrorists never expected a U.S. special operations soldier would be onboard, too. He was Corporal Rich Kennedy, one of the Delta guys who flew the old *Eight Ball* chopper on its last mission. He, too, was carrying one of the pistols from the Royal Dubai battle. It was fully loaded with seven bullets.

The DC-8 was a huge plane, though. And while Kennedy was sitting way at the back the terrorists had made their move farther toward the front. Kennedy knew something wasn't right as soon as he heard people in first class screaming. Then came the sound of gunfire and more screams. After that he concluded, for whatever reason, the terrorists were taking over the plane now.

He sat as calmly as possible until he heard the terrorists make their way into the cockpit. Only when he heard the cockpit door slam shut did he begin moving up to the front. He stripped off his *burka*, as there was no need for a disguise now. This elicited a huge gasp from the passengers, especially when they saw his American uniform and his stars-and-stripes patch. They were terrified that they were being hijacked by terrorists of their own faith. But they just couldn't believe that one of the Crazy Americans was riding with them, too.

By waving his pistol around, Kennedy coaxed several women to start wailing as one, this as the big plane began the long slow turn south, toward Hormuz. The women cried and screamed for nearly a half-minute before one of the hijackers finally appeared at the cockpit door. Their plan had been to take over the plane and then lock themselves inside the flight compartment, allowing the passengers to await their doom unattended. Only if there was a commotion would the terrorists reenter the passenger area; those were their orders. Six frightened Muslim women screeching loudly proved to be enough to lure one out.

The hijacker emerged from the cabin screaming loudly himself. Like all of the Al-Habazz gang, his way of dealing was to simply start shooting. Secreted in the forward galley, though, Kennedy surprised him, firing at him twice before the hijacker was able to kill anyone else. But while he hit the man both times in the shoulder, Kennedy's aim had been thrown off due to the turning of the plane. It had not been the quick death shot he'd been hoping for. Instead of returning to the cockpit, though, the hijacker panicked and ran toward the back of the plane, Kennedy in pursuit.

Thus the gun battle began.

It looked like something from a movie, the frightened passengers cowering in their seats or right down on the floor as Kennedy and his quarry traded shots. The terrorist was firing madly at Kennedy with his Glock 9mm, this while Kennedy did his best to use his remaining bullets wisely. So many bullets were fired by the hijacker, it was a miracle none hit a window or otherwise punctured the DC-8's airframe. Meanwhile the airplane seemed to be flying all over the sky, causing the lights to blink and the engines to make the most horrendous noises.

Back and forth, up and down the rear aisles, the two combatants fired, took cover, and fired again, this as passengers were screaming and the airplane continued to shake. In the end, though, it was Kennedy's first shot that actually killed the terrorist. It had hit a major artery in the man's shoulder. After running around the airplane for twenty minutes, the terrorist had lost so much blood, he literally dropped dead just as he and Kennedy were exchanging their last shots.

Kennedy immediately went to retrieve the man's gun, as his own pistol was empty by now. But the terrorist had emptied his gun as well, and he didn't have any more ammunition on him.

This was not good. Kennedy still had the hijacker up in the cockpit to deal with—or so he thought. When he rushed to the front of the plane again, he found this man was dead, too. How? He certainly hadn't been shot. He'd actually expired in a much more gruesome manner. While Kennedy was at the back of the plane trying to stop the one hijacker, a group of passengers, all women, had set upon this second terrorist, surprising him as he stepped from the cockpit looking for his colleague.

He was lying now between the cockpit and the forward galley. His face had been smashed to a bloody pulp; his arms and legs had been broken, their bones poking horribly through his skin. Even his eyes were gone. Kennedy was a Delta veteran, but he'd never seen anything as horrible as this. The women had beaten the man to death.

Kennedy finally stepped into the cockpit and began speaking to the pilots. Both were shaken up but still in control. When they told him of the hijackers' plans to hit the carrier, Kennedy immediately urged them to turn the plane around, as he knew full well if they came anywhere near Hormuz now, the Navy would shoot them down, no questions asked.

But in the confusion of the hijacking, and especially while the passengers were killing the second terrorist, the pilots had not been concentrating on what direction they were flying. Now they weren't sure where they were exactly or even how close the plane was to Hormuz. Kennedy looked below, expecting to see the Gulf waters, but discovered instead that they were flying over dry land.

That's when the two F-14s showed up.

They appeared suddenly, riding low off the left wing. Kennedy could barely see them through the cockpit window. One peeled off and began an attack profile on the airliner.

Kennedy couldn't believe it. He'd just saved the plane full of people—was it going to be shot down by the Navy anyway?

But then something very strange happened. The F-14 never fired its weapons. Instead it streaked by their nose and quickly returned to its former position to the left of the big plane. Then it began wagging its wings, the sign that the airliner should follow them.

Only then did Kennedy get a good look at the Tomcat's insignia and realize the big fighter didn't belong to the U.S. Navy at all. It belonged to the only other country in the world that flew the F-14: the Islamic Republic of Iran, leftovers from the regime of the former Shah.

Never did Kennedy think he'd be relieved to see an *Iranian* jet.

With a nod from Kennedy, the airliner pilots complied with the F-14's wishes. They followed the two fighters down to an airfield located near the Gulf coast. More Iranian warplanes showed up, making the DC-8's landing approach crowded and somewhat dangerous. The airliner's pilots did a good job setting the huge plane down, though, considering what they'd gone though in the past 30 minutes. They rolled to a stop at the very end of the runway, setting off a great burst of cheers from the relieved passengers behind them. The pilots kissed each other, then tried to kiss Kennedy. He declined.

He looked out the cockpit window and saw the plane was already surrounded by dozens of heavily armed Iranian soldiers. There were also tanks on hand with muzzles pointed at them, APCs, huge mobile guns, armed troop trucks, and many, many warplanes flying very low overhead.

Still Kennedy just shrugged and said: "Ain't no such thing as a bad landing."

Sixty miles to the south

It had been an unusual morning for Jean Rosseau and his partner, André.

Both Belgians, they worked as helicopter pilots in the massive Shell-France oil fields at Dakka Abbis, Iran. Just a half-mile inland from the shore of Hormuz, these fields were among the largest in the Persian Gulf. They were a little country unto themselves, carved out of the empty Iranian desert, a conglomeration of oil pumps, derricks, open wells, flames burning bright, highways, tank farms, employee towns, and two dozen gigantic man-made lakes containing the millions of gallons of water needed for this particularly arid pumping operation. And everywhere huge pipelines running off in every direction but especially toward the sea.

The day started with Rosseau's Bell-Textron X-1 helicopter being grounded due to the movement of a large U.S. naval force through the nearby strait. This was a relatively routine situation these days. Normally Rosseau and André spent their morning hours flying around the outskirts of the Dakka Abbis fields, checking for any leaks in the spiderwork of pipelines. This morning, though, they spent washing the grime from their aircraft.

Just after 10:00 A.M., they heard a series of huge explosions. At least six of them, right in a row. They were coming not from the oil fields but from the west, out over the Gulf. Soon after, Jean and André saw huge clouds of black smoke rising above the horizon. Their tiny helicopter base was located in one of the most isolated sections of the massive oil field. They tried using their shortwave radio to see if anything was being reported about the explosions but could find nothing.

Then, about ten minutes after spotting the smoke, they received a cell call from their boss back at the Dakka Abbis field headquarters, some twenty miles away. He was hysterical. Something incomprehensible had happened, he told them. An Arab airliner had been shot down by the American Navy and it had crashed into one of the oil field's artificial lakes, 16 miles north of their base. The boss ordered them to fly to the crash site immediately.

Rosseau and André were in the air two minutes later. They were both certain this was some kind of false report, though. What were the chances that a plane would crash into one of their fake lakes when there was nothing but sand everywhere else? But then again, they'd heard the explosions and seen the smoke out over the water. Maybe all that had something to do with all this.

The Bell was a fast aircraft, and they were coming up on their destination within five minutes. It was Cooling Pool #17, the place where their boss claimed the airliner had come down. But they could see no smoke, no fire, no wreckage. Nothing that would be associated with a plane crash.

They made one long sweep around the cooling pool just to be sure. It was about a quarter-mile long, 800 feet across, and in some places up to 50 feet deep. To their astonishment, at the very southern end of the lake they spotted pieces of debris coming up to the surface. Suitcases, seats, pieces of the plane itself. And even more amazing, in among that debris there were people.

Rosseau did not hesitate. He turned the controls over to André and told him to get down as close as possible to the debris field. Meanwhile Rosseau tied a safety belt around his waist. The next thing he knew, he was hanging out of the copter's right-side doorway.

Ten feet below him he saw an incredible sight. Floating somehow among the wreckage there was a man who either was bald or had his hair burned away. He was holding in his arms no fewer than six people, survivors, all injured but alive.

Rosseau couldn't believe it. There didn't seem to be any way anyone could have survived this crash. But here before him were at least seven souls. The man was holding one of them up to him.

Rosseau stepped onto the copter's strut, this while yelling for André to get lower—lower—*lower still!* It took several agonizing seconds for the aircraft to get low enough for Rosseau to grab the first person the bald man was passing to him. It was a young girl, maybe six or so. She was crying, bleeding, but quite alive. Rosseau grabbed the child and with one motion lifted her up and into the copter. Rosseau turned back to the water and now the bald man was lifting up an elderly Arab

lady to him. Where this man was getting his strength Rosseau
simply could not fathom. *But if he can do it, then so must I,*
he thought. He grabbed the woman and with all his strength
swung her up into the copter, too.

He leaned back out and the man had another child now,
a young boy, holding him over his head. Rosseau grabbed
the child around the shoulders and hauled him into the copter
as well.

But now, a problem. They were close to their weight limit,
as the copter was full of fuel and was suddenly carrying
three unexpected passengers. It was already beginning to
gyrate too much. Rosseau had no choice. He screamed for
André to back off. They would have to unload the three survivors on the edge of the pool and then come back for the
others.

By this time a truck full of oil field workers had arrived
on the scene. André maneuvered the copter as close as possible to them, and without even setting down Rosseau passed
the three survivors out to them.

Then he screamed for André to return to the pool. But
André now had another problem. The copter's engines were
overheating. No rotary craft liked hovering close to the
desert's surface; the heat was too intense. The Bell X-1 was
especially temperamental in that regard. But Rosseau
screamed at André to just do it.

And André did. He brought the Bell up and sideways and
soon they were over the patch of debris again. To Rosseau's
relief, the bald man was still there and was still holding the
three other survivors in his arms. Rosseau screamed again
for André to get as close as possible to the water's surface.
Timidly he did so. The spray from the water was even greater
now, but Rosseau could not feel it, though it was soaking
him. He climbed back out onto the strut and reached out, and
the man pushed another person up to him, a middle-aged lady,
in Arabic dress, wailing but alive. She landed in the cabin of
the copter with a thump.

Rosseau went back out onto the strut. The bald man was
holding up a boy of about thirteen. The kid had some life

in him. With just a boost from Rosseau, he climbed into the helicopter himself. The man was now holding just one more person, a girl, 20 years old or so, possibly a stewardess.

She was badly injured; both her legs were broken. Rosseau had to lean very far out to grab her. The bald man was practically lifting her over his head at this point. Rosseau just couldn't imagine how he was doing it. By grabbing onto her dress and under one shoulder Rosseau managed to get her halfway into the copter. The kid helped pull her in the rest of the way.

The copter was now unstable again, but Rosseau was no longer concerned. It was time to rescue the rescuer. He turned back to the water but to his horror saw the bald man was slowly drifting away. And for the first time Rosseau noticed the man was bleeding heavily as well. But Rosseau refused to just let him go. He reached out, twice nearly falling into the deep water himself, but the man just looked up at him, smiled faintly, and shook his head. That's when Rosseau realized the bald man was wearing a military uniform. An *American* uniform. He had an American flag patch on his shoulder, with the silhouettes of two tall buildings within. And Rosseau could see a name tag stitched above the man's left breast pocket. It read: *ZANGRELLI.*

Rosseau tried once more to grab onto the man—but it was no use. He looked up at Rosseau one more time and mouthed the word, *Thanks.* . . .

Then he slipped below the water for good.

Saudi Arabia

At about the same time this was happening, Tom Santos was checking into the Royal Ramada in downtown Riyadh.

His flight down from London had been extraordinarily quick, another asset of flying the half-filled skies. The cab ride from the airport to the hotel seemed to have broken the sound barrier as well.

Following instructions he'd received back in Chicago, he

registered at the hotel under the fictitious name of Richard Starkey. He discovered that his room had been booked and paid in advance for the past two months. He went up to the suite, exhausted from his flight and experiencing intense jet lag. It was a nice room, though, much bigger than his digs back in Chicago, with a great view of the Grand Mosque of Riyadh just a few blocks away.

There was a nondescript civil aviation uniform hanging in the room's otherwise empty closet. Dark pants, dark jacket, white shirt, dark tie. It had been left there earlier this day. It was still encased in dry cleaners' plastic and had Santos's real name written on a slip of paper pinned to the coat hanger. He pulled the uniform out of the plastic and found a letter in the jacket's inside pocket. It was addressed to him.

Santos read it—and started to cry. It contained instructions for the final phase of his mission, along with some perspective on this top-secret operation in which he had played just a small part, up until now. It also contained an apology from the guy named Bobby Murphy. The mystery man explained in great detail his unorthodox philosophy of fighting fire with fire and was so persuasive, Santos could not disagree with him, even though it called for him to make an enormous sacrifice.

The letter fell from his shaking hands. He sat on the edge of the bed, in shock. Finally he knew what was *really* going on, and that reality was devastating. But he also understood why he'd been chosen and what an important role he was still expected to play. In his note Murphy had told Santos that he could just walk away and no one would ever be the wiser. But he knew he would fulfill his mission, for two simple reasons: Because he was an American. And because it, in the end, was probably the right thing to do.

The letter also said he would be getting a very important phone call, one that could come at any time. When it happened, Santos was to climb into the uniform and follow the caller's instructions from there.

He finally composed himself and felt a strange peace

come over him. He took the bottle of yellow pills from his pocket and unceremoniously threw them in the wastebasket. He wouldn't be needing them anymore.

Then he climbed up on the bed, kicked off his shoes, and turned on the TV. The cable news stations were going crazy. Something was happening right here in the Persian Gulf. Another terrorism thing—a big one—though none of the newscasters knew exactly what. Santos couldn't have cared less. He was beyond all that now. He flipped through the channels, finally landing on a "truth is stranger than fiction" show. It looked about thirty years old, was brown and scratchy, and had very bad English subtitles.

Ironically, the show began with a segment titled: "Can the Dead Walk among Us?"

Santos just shook his head and actually laughed a little.

"Yes," he said to himself. "They sure can. . . ."

A moment later, the telephone rang.

Chapter 30

When Ryder reached the Strait of Hormuz, the scene almost defied description.

The waters below were churned up with so many ships, going full speed ahead, they looked like they were trailing tidal waves behind them. Thick clouds of smoke stretched almost the length of the strait's transit channel and at its narrowest point, on either shore as well. At least two Navy ships were on fire and dead in the water. Others were smoking heavily but still under way. Parts of the strait itself were aflame, as pools of aviation fuel were burning fiercely on the surface of the water.

But it was the airspace above the battle group that was like a vision from a fever dream. The sky was filled with warplanes. The carrier's F-14s and F-18s certainly—but also F-16s and F-15s, land-based U.S. Air Force fighters that had rushed to the scene. The Air Force planes were circling between 15,000 and 25,000 feet. The Navy guys were way down low, in the thick air around 12,000. The combination, seen by Ryder from 15 miles afar, looked like a kind of weird aerial carousel, its center of gravity being the *Abraham Lincoln,* that gigantic flat gray object among smaller ones, plowing forward now at 30 knots at least, kicking up the biggest waves in the narrow waters below.

This was what the U.S. military in the Gulf had been practicing for months: how to protect a carrier in a time of emergency. Saturate the area with warplanes and keep them moving as the carrier moved. It was a gigantic outgrowth of the battle group's own defensive umbrella really. The support planes were flying its periphery—ECM jammers, small AWACs, communications craft, and even big refueling tankers. And every Navy ship below was broadcasting warnings for all other aircraft in the area to stay away, that a state of war existed. This meant the airspace above the battle group was a free-fire zone. Anything coming near would be fair game.

Ryder counted the wreckage of at least three big airliners floating in the water as well. He saw more than a few downed U.S. fighters, too, all of them Navy planes. What happened to them? It wasn't like the airliners were shooting back. They had to be victims of friendly fire.

Ryder went into an orbit of his own, staying well away from the gigantic moving air screen. He'd expected to find Phelan down here by now, but the sky was so crowded, it was hard to pick out just one plane. Ryder began running through his VHF band radio channels, looking for one that might let him get a message to someone below. He soon came to one channel that nearly blew out his eardrums. It sounded like hundreds of voices speaking at once. Fighter pilots certainly, but all of them very excited.

Why the sudden anxiety? Another airliner was coming in.

It was a 737, a small Boeing regional carrier. It was green and white, the colors of Omani Civil Airways. Its original destination had been Malta. It was streaking in low now, around four thousand feet, out of the northeast. There was another flood of excited calls over the radio channel. Then Ryder saw four Navy F-14s break from the pack and pounce. The rest of the circling warplanes expanded their orbits to give the Navy killer squad some room. The F-14s quickly took up positions above and behind the airliner. No air-to-air missiles would be fired here. That's how some of the Navy planes had been shot down earlier. The Navy had learned that lesson fast, so this would be the work of cannons.

When the four Tomcats finally opened up, their resulting weapons' fire looked like a storm of lightning going sideways. The streams of high-explosive shells converged on the target at just about the same time. The airliner's tail fin was the first to go. Then the engines on its wings. Then the wings themselves. The more hits it took, the slower the 737 flew. The slower it flew, the closer the Navy jets could get to it, to fire into it further. It was eerily methodical. When it came, the airliner's explosion was tremendous. The smoke was black and hideous. There was only a cloud of ash and small debris left when it cleared, some of it on fire, to rain down on the ships below.

That's when Ryder's cell phone rang.

It was Phelan.

He could barely speak. "Man, did you see that?" he asked Ryder, huffing and puffing between deep gulps of oxygen. "I knocked two down myself, I think. And I was in on two more. . . ."

Ryder was shocked. He almost didn't recognize Phelan's voice. The young pilot was excited, certainly. Pumped up and out of breath. But there was something disturbing in his tone, too. Almost maniacal. He had been flying on the periphery of the carrier's expanded CAP, keeping pace with a couple of ECM Prowlers. Thirty seconds later, he was riding off Ryder's left wing.

Ryder quickly briefed Phelan on his encounter with the two airliners over the desert, then asked if he knew how to call the carrier. Phelan gave him the location of the UHF channel being used by the *Lincoln*'s CIC. Ryder broke in on the frequency and identified himself as being attached to an aerial special operations unit, just as Phelan had done earlier. The guy in the CIC didn't question Ryder's credentials. He briefly told him what had happened over the desert. The guy took the report, betraying no emotion, and told Ryder to stand by.

No sooner had Ryder done this than the VHF band erupted with voices again. At that moment, another 737 flew by him, not 1,500 feet below his right wing. It was painted in strange orange and green swirls, the colors of Arab Bali Airlines. The plane had already started a nosedive toward the carrier.

Without a word, Phelan peeled away. He caught up to the falling airliner and, coming at it from a right angle, fired his cannon directly into the cockpit. It exploded in flames. A quick loop and he sent another burst into the airplane's belly, shooting up either its fuel tank or a whole lot of luggage. At that same moment four Navy jets arrived on the scene, the designated hit squad. They started perforating the airliner with cannons, too. But Phelan was the most voracious.

The big plane started to spin; vast quantities of smoke began trailing behind it. The Navy backed off when the airplane went into a free fall. But Phelan continued to follow it down. He managed to sever one of its engine roots with his cannon fire. Half the left-side wing broke away. He shot off what was left of the tail wing, too. It disintegrated into hundreds of pieces. All this only made the jet's death spiral more severe, but Phelan never stopped firing. The massive piece of wreckage hit the water and exploded. But seconds later, Phelan was down on the deck, strafing the remains.

Ryder felt his stomach do another flip. Phelan's piloting skills were just astonishing. He was moving faster, turning quicker, and firing more accurately than the Navy's true fighter jets and pulling *beaucoup* G-forces in the process.

But what was happening here? Even now, Phelan was still down on the deck, still firing into the debris. Why the overkill to the *n*th degree?

Ryder called him, not on the radio but on the phone. That way he could talk to Phelan without fear of being heard by anyone else.

"What are you doing?" Ryder asked him sternly. "Are you OK?"

But Phelan answered him strangely. "I think I got three," he said, his voice still husky. Then he repeated: "And I was in on another two."

"But why are you wasting gas and ammunition?" Ryder asked him. "We're supposed to be smarter than that."

There was a short pause; then Phelan replied angrily, "It's just like you said. We got to protect our own. That's what I'm doing. What the hell are *you* doing?" With that, he hung up.

Ryder couldn't believe it. He tried calling Phelan back, but the young pilot didn't answer his phone. The dreadful silence made him think. Why was Phelan on this rampage? Just as Phelan's words to him back on the ship seemed to inject him with a much-needed dose of humanity, had his rah-rah words to Phelan created the opposite effect? Everyone in Murphy's group was suffering from battle fatigue in one form or another. Had Ryder's little sermon pushed Phelan the other way, and right over the edge?

Ryder switched back to the channel being used by the American fighter pilots; both Navy and Air Force guys were blabbing on here now. In among the cacophony of excited voices and radio calls, he heard Phelan, talking nonstop.

It took Ryder about thirty seconds of listening to this channel to learn what had happened down here in the strait while he'd been farther up north. No airliner had come within a mile of the carrier. The carrier's unusual defense had worked that well. But it was not just because the American pilots, both Navy and Air Force, were the best around. They also knew where the airliners were coming from. How? Because of Red Curry. The Navy had played the third level of the CD-ROM and learned just about all of the terrorists' plans just minutes after the attack had begun in earnest. This intelligence included the flight paths the hijacked planes were taking to attack the carrier.

The death and destruction that resulted was appalling. It brought to Ryder's mind another incident from World War II. Toward the end of the war with Japan, in June of 1944, swarms of experienced American fliers fell upon hundreds of Japanese planes being flown mostly by inexperienced pilots. The Americans knew where the Japanese planes were, knew from what direction they were coming. The result was a slaughter in the skies. The historians called it the Battle of the Philippine Sea. The pilots involved called it the Marianas Turkey Shoot.

Another burst of excitement exploded from the VHF channel. One last airliner had appeared. It was another 737, coming from the east, flying very low, almost on the surface of the water. Though it had caught some people off-guard, it soon had many fighters firing on it, with the support ships adding everything from SAMs to CIWS to the mix. The plane was coming apart one piece at a time along its two-mile death glide, but somehow it kept on going. Running this gauntlet, almost totally engulfed in flames, only caused more ships and more planes to fire at it. The voices on the radio reached a new crescendo as it seemed nothing could stop this one last airliner. It was now within a mile of the carrier.

That's when Phelan appeared from out of nowhere. He put a cannon barrage squarely into the airliner's left wing. There was a fuel tank here and it exploded, sending the airplane cartwheeling across the water. It finally hit so close to the *Lincoln*, the carrier was engulfed in a *tsunami* of smoke and flames. The big ship almost disappeared completely before finally emerging from the other side of the black storm.

And then, just like that, it was over.

The swirl of U.S. jet fighters slowly began to break up. The ships below had reached deeper waters of the Gulf and were in the process of dispersing. Suddenly everything got quiet on both radio channels.

Even Phelan had stopped talking.

A minute later, Ryder was down to just 500 feet, skimming the surface of the water. No one was paying any attention to him now. He was here because he had to experience for himself that almost indescribable moment just after a great battle has ended. The air down here was still full of debris. Pieces of lightweight flaming material were blowing like sparkling snowflakes in the wind. The water was still smoldering, full of oil and gas, pieces of airframes, tires, seats, safety vests, and, he was sure, many, many bodies.

Farther to his south, the airspace immediately around the

carrier looked like an airplane junkyard moving in three dimensions. The extent of damage from friendly fire was also more apparent near the water's surface. At least six Navy fighters had been shot down accidentally, either by the shipborne weapons or by missiles fired by other planes. Many more Tomcats and Hornets were gliding around, wings or engines smoking, not quite damaged enough to bail out of but obviously in need of a place to land as soon as possible. The *Lincoln* began recovering those aircraft most seriously damaged first. A traffic jam of limping airplanes quickly lined up behind them.

Ryder exited the area and climbed back up to 15,000 feet. He settled on a spot about five miles north of the battle group's current position.

He hit his radio again. So many Navy pilots were talking, Ryder couldn't understand any of them.

"How many?" one pilot kept yelling over the others.

Finally all the noise left the channel as the audio feed from a briefing aboard the carrier was piped in for all the pilots to hear. The carrier's CO came on. He began reading a tally sheet, his voice amazingly calm, almost eerie, it was so monotonic. Two planes were reported down in the Saudi desert, one crashed, one in a forced landing—those were the planes Ryder had dealt with. Then some unexpected good news: Delta guys had regained control of three other aircraft and had forced them to land, two in Oman and one in Iran. The Navy had shot down all the others. One of these had also crashed in Iran, but there were early reports of some survivors. The rest of the planes were now floating in pieces on the waters of the Gulf.

Then came a silence. It lasted for several long seconds.

Finally someone asked: "So we got them all?"

"Roger that . . ." the monotonic voice replied.

If there was any cheering, everyone must have done it with their microphone turned off. Ryder didn't hear a thing for the next 10 seconds. Then the carrier's CO resumed talking. There was no way around it, he said. Four airliners saved meant six had been destroyed. Grim by any standard. But even in this came a small victory, especially for Ryder's conscience. According to the *Lincoln's* CO, three of the four jets saved were fairly large planes, almost jumbo jets. They'd been carrying more people than all the other airliners combined. So, as he put it, more people were saved today than had been killed. But Ryder had to wonder: Was that really a victory?

Someone asked the CO to repeat the tally. Ryder counted on his fingers as the officer spoke. Four saved, six shot down. Ten for 10.

But suddenly Ryder realized there was something wrong here. Something that had been lost in the fog of war.

True, 10 planes had been hijacked in the unsuccessful attempt to sink the carrier. But on the terrorists' CD-ROM Kazeel had specifically stated "a dozen large airplanes" would be involved in the operation.

All 10 of the hijacked airliners had been accounted for.

But where were the other two planes?

Marty Noonan and his KC-10 Extender refueling craft had spent the last 30 minutes circling high above the strait. He and his crew had watched the astonishing battle from six miles up.

What had happened below still didn't seem real. The chaos of metal and men was frightening and not something for which Noonan was prepared. His tanker's UHF radio had become so cluttered with anxious and excited voices, Noonan had turned it off and had simply watched in silence as the fantastic events unfolded.

Aloft again on yet another double-up training mission, he and another tanker from Bahrain had been rushed to the scene as soon as the first reports of the hijackings had come in. Luckily, they were very familiar with the airspace due to all the flying they'd done above the Gulf recently. In those countless training missions with their Bahrani copilots, the American tankers had flown down to Hormuz, to go around in circles, sometimes for hours, before flying back to Bahrain

again. Now they were actually down here for a reason, or so
they thought. In all this time, not one of the U.S. warplanes
below needed to come up for a refueling. Everything had
happened that fast.

But that was OK, too. The two KC-10s just continued doing what they did best.

Circling and waiting. . . .

Once it appeared that everything was calming down below them, Noonan turned his UHF radio back on. There was
still a storm of excited voices and static, but now he thought
he was able to decipher what was going on. Ten airliners had
been hijacked; 10 had either been shot down or landed somehow. But now other people were coming on the airwaves and
saying that there were *still* two more planes out there. But
where?

Noonan almost laughed. He put this comment down to the
excitement of battle and how easily things could get confused. If there were two more planes, why weren't they
showing up on the Navy's hot-shit radar? Besides, he was flying the highest of any plane connected with the battle. He
searched the skies now and found they were clear to both
horizons.

"Two more planes?" he was saying. "There ain't two more
planes left up here."

That's when he saw a glint of metal off to his right. He
turned just in time to see his Bahrani copilot coming at him,
not with a pot of coffee but with a box cutter, its blade extended to its fullest length. . . .

Ryder had finally got through to a couple Navy pilots on his
radio. He'd explained to them who he was and why he
thought two more planes might be out there. They'd agreed
to pass his information on to the carrier's CIC.

The moment he broke off with them, he saw the huge
KC-10 tanker suddenly appear above him.

Ryder recognized the aircraft right away. It was Noonan's
Extender. He could tell by the image of the red Pegasus—
the Mobil Oil flying horse—emblazoned on its tail.

But what was it doing? Active refuelers rarely came down below 20,000 feet; at least that's how Ryder was familiar with them. This one, though, was falling like a stone.

And right behind it was another.

Ryder switched channels for his chin mike. For one foolish moment he thought he'd be able to radio the two tankers directly and tell them they had to clear the area immediately, that this was still a combat zone and nowhere for two planes full of gas to be. . . .

But that's when it hit him. *Could these be the last two airplanes?*

"Phelan!" Ryder roared into his cell phone. But the young pilot was already on the case.

"Those coffee-making bastards," he was cursing wildly. Then he added: "I'm climbing. . . ."

This was not good. The tankers were still about seven miles away from the carrier, but there was no doubt now that they were intent on crashing into it. But Ryder had lost contact with the Navy pilots and couldn't raise them again. Both UHF and VHF channels were still overloading, and any other U.S. aircraft not damaged in the great battle were at least two minutes away.

Bottom line: he and Phelan were the closest to the two refuelers. It would be up to them to stop them.

Ryder looked at his ammo counter. He still had exactly 24 cannon shells left. He was sure Phelan had less. In fact, the way the young pilot had been thoughtlessly blazing away earlier, there was a good chance his gun was completely dry.

"Ammo check!" Ryder called up to his wingman. Phelan was now about five hundred feet above and ahead of him.

There was no reply.

"Lieutenant Phelan . . . give me your ammo count!" Ryder said again.

Again Phelan did not acknowledge his request. Instead, he just said: "I'll take Noonan's plane. . . ."

Ryder had no time to argue with him. They were now about a half-mile behind the tankers, even as the tankers

closed to within five miles of the carrier. Ryder went left and
began lining up on the second refueler.

He thought he'd already spent his time in hell, but at least
in this instance things were more clear-cut. These weren't
airliners filled with innocent people. They were guided missiles filled with thousands of gallons of gas. The tankers *had*
to be shot down, simple as that. As for the American personnel onboard the planes, Noonan included—well, Ryder had
to assume just like the Delta guys on the airliners the Navy
had shot down, they'd fought the hijackers but lost. The
chances were great that they were already dead.

But Ryder knew he had to use his head. With only two
dozen shells left, he had to shoot this thing down well before
it reached the *Lincoln*. Even a near miss on the carrier could
prove catastrophic.

He booted full throttle and suddenly was going faster
than he thought possible in the jump jet. He came right up on
the tanker's tail and immediately fired off six cannon shells.
Only three hit, and they caused no discernible damage. He
fired off three more, but again to no avail. He smacked himself upside the head. What was he doing? He wasn't going to
take down this monster by firing on its rear end.

He pulled back on the throttle, then dived below the huge
aircraft. The tanker was full of JP-8 aviation fuel, highly
volatile. *Fuel,* the lifeblood of this crazy adventure, first not
ever enough of it and now too much. There was only one
place to hit this plane.

Ryder pushed 45-degree deflection nozzle and raised the
Harrier's nose 10 degrees, all in three seconds. It was a maneuver only a jump jet could do. His cannon was now pointing at the bottom of the descending aircraft, right where the
wings met the fuselage. He let off three more cannon shots.
Incredibly, they seemed to bounce right off. What were
they? Duds? He didn't know. He tried again, three more,
practically single-fired. Everything seemed to go in slow
motion even as the distance between him and his target was
shrinking. He could see these shells going right through the
center of the big plane—but so far to no effect.

He was running out of time. He kept the trigger depressed and watched his ammo count dwindle. Just nine shells left. Now six. Now just four. . . .

He let the last three go at once—and that's when the sky suddenly turned pearl white. Just for a second. Then it turned to yellow, and yellow to orange, then to nothing but red. Ryder had finally hit something on the big plane and it had caused a violent explosion. Again instinct took over. One of his hands yanked his plane up and over; the other went full positive deflection. In other words he went flat out, straight ahead.

He would retain a memory that he actually flew through all those flames, and maybe he did. But he also found himself going sideways over the top of the tanker's fuselage as the bottom half of the plane was falling away. He was moving at an incredible rate of speed, pushed along by the force of the huge explosion, but it was just too much for the Harrier to take. It flipped over and began spinning out of control. His panel lights were blinking like crazy. His engine was coughing and about to stall. For one brief moment he thought if he just let it go and plowed in, maybe he'd see Maureen again soon. But in the same instant he knew she would have disapproved. So he was able to dredge up an old test pilot's trick. He applied heavy right rudder and used just about the last of his gas to go full throttle. The Harrier began bucking as if it was being pulled in two directions at once. But that was the whole idea. The engine spazzed once, twice . . . but then came back on at full power.

He recovered flight, went wings level, and tried to get his bearings. He felt like he'd been hit on the head with a hammer. His stomach was turned inside out, too. But when his vision cleared he could see the tanker going down in four large pieces right below him. It hit the water with a mighty crash, causing yet another huge explosion, this one birthing a mushroom cloud of white smoke and water vapor. And then, just as quickly, it was gone.

Ryder took in a deep breath of oxygen and felt it run through his body. Then came a startling question: *Where the hell was Phelan?*

No sooner did the thought arrive than the other tanker went right over Ryder's head. It was bearing down on the carrier—and Phelan was riding right beside it. A bizarre moment ensued. It almost looked like Phelan was flying in formation with the big fuel plane, following it down. He had no ammo left; that much was clear now. And neither did Ryder. But for some reason the young pilot had pulled up almost level to the tanker's cockpit. He seemed to be looking inside. The two planes were now less than two miles from the carrier.

What was he doing?

Suddenly Ryder's phone rang. It was Phelan.

All he said was: "Go see my mom. Tell her what happened out here today."

"We'll both tell her when it's over," Ryder replied, not really getting what Phelan was saying.

That's when he saw Phelan bank his Harrier as sharp and clean as if he were coming in for another perfect landing. This time, though, he just kept on going—and slammed into the nose of the KC-10.

There was one long weird moment when the two planes flew along, almost cojoined. But then Phelan's Harrier blew up—and a moment later, the second refueler blew up, too.

Now just a mass of burning metal and igniting jet fuel, the wreckage went straight down and crashed into the sea about a mile north of the carrier.

Chapter 31

The Persian Gulf was in chaos.

The massive terrorist attack had been thwarted and the USS *Abraham Lincoln* had survived intact. Praise for the U.S. military was flooding in, but the world markets immediately began roller-coasting, even more so than before. Oil prices especially were all over the map, spiking both historic highs and lows within 20 minutes of the news coming out of Hormuz. Was the U.S. victory a good thing or not? No one could really tell. Al Qaeda had been dealt a serious blow, maybe its last. But hundreds were dead. Most of them passengers on the hijacked airliners, most of them Arabs. Cries of revenge were already coming from nearly every radical Muslim nation. But just who would pay the price was uncertain.

Suddenly the Middle East seemed more unstable than ever.

All this was certainly *not* good news for the six men who were at that moment leaving Prince Ali's palace outside Riyadh in a caravan of limousines.

The Next Big Thing had been a bust and their fingerprints were all over it, especially Ali himself. That's why he and the others had their trunks packed and were leaving the Saudi Kingdom as quickly as they could.

Their destination would be Switzerland, as they had many

friends there. The question of transportation had been a slight
problem, though. Once word of the foiled attack reached
them, they knew there was no way they could all fly off in
their private jets, making their way to Zurich individually.
That would have been way too suspicious. Plus the U.S. Air
Force and Navy were throwing every airplane they had into
the skies above the Gulf, acting as if they were expecting
another attack. Furthermore, American troops were being
rushed to just about every civilian airport in the region in order to scrutinize every passenger jet thoroughly and prevent
any further hijackings. Even the Saudi national police were
supposedly looking for the instigators of the plot, which
meant the government needed some warm bodies to arrest.
No, flying six Gulfstreams out of Riyadh anytime soon was
out of the question. There would be no better way to attract
attention to themselves.

Luckily, the half-dozen men had an alternate plan. Ali's
friend Farouk had many connections at the nearby Khalid International Airport. Six months before, he had made arrange-
ments to have a charter airplane on call, 24 hours a day, just
in the event of something like this. A lifeboat of sorts. As
soon as things started going badly around Hormuz, Farouk
called the airport and let it be known he would be needing
this plane immediately.

But how would it be able to fly when their Gulfstreams
could not? Because Farouk had arranged to lease the aircraft
under the guise of a UN agricultural team, one whose main
office was just an address, located in a very small town
somewhere in New Jersey. This gave the plane a sort of aerial diplomatic immunity. It would be able to leave despite
the immediate U.S. tightening on private and commercial
flights. Or the worst that could happen was that it would be
forced to turn around after taking off.

In any case, they knew the United States would never
shoot it down.

So now the six men were on their way to the airport. They
were escorted by a squad of Saudi National Guardsmen,

soldiers in their employ. Upon reaching Khalid, they were met at a private entrance by Farouk's personal bodyguards and taken directly to the airplane. It was a refurbished DC-9, owned by the Gulf Air Corporation; it was all white, almost like a real UN plane, except for the distinctive red flaring design of GAC on its tail. The big plane was already warmed up and waiting out on the runway.

The six men climbed aboard and took their seats in the deserted first-class section. They all said a quick prayer and laughed when the airliner took off. The ascent was a bit shaky, but as soon as the airplane reached 10,000 feet it leveled off and the seat belt sign went out. The six men sat back and relaxed for the first time in days.

The plane was luxurious. Farouk had done his job well. There were couches and reclining chairs and a buffet and of course a bar. The six men began to eat and drink and talk about what awaited them in Zurich.

That's when Prince Ali noticed the airplane appeared to be flying east, almost as if it was heading back to Riyadh, instead of north. He waved his hand at Farouk. His old friend got up and knocked on the flight cabin door. There was no reply. He tried again. Still nothing.

He opened the door and peered in. The first thing he saw was a man slumped over in the copilot's seat. He was an Arab. He'd been shot twice in the head.

Then at his feet was another man in a Gulf Air uniform. He, too, was dead.

Farouk was so horrified, he couldn't even cry out. There were two dead men on the floor of the flight compartment. Who the hell was flying the plane? He stepped into the cockpit to see a man behind the controls. Farouk screamed in his ear: *"What has happened here? Who are you?"*

Finally the man turned around. He seemed to have dark skin, not naturally but heavily tanned. His hair appeared dyed, as did his mustache. On a busy night or in the early-morning darkness he would have easily passed for an Arab. But he was not Arabic. He was an American.

It was Tom Santos.

And he was holding a gun.

"Please return to your seat, sir," Santos calmly told Farouk. "And enjoy the rest of your flight. . . ."

About 2,000 people worked in the Pan Arabic Oil Exchange building. All of them were men.

The retro-futuristic structure, whitewashed marble, 22 stories, with a postmodern bubble top and faux prayer tower, was among the most prominent in downtown Riyadh.

By myth, its location was a very holy place. Supposedly Muhammad himself had slept near here, when this area was still a desert, and predicted that someday great wealth would come from beneath the sands. It was a charming piece of bullshit and quite untrue. Yet many people in Saudi Arabia believed it as if it came directly from the Koran itself. And that's why the building was here, in all its gold and splendid glory.

Legitimate people with legitimate jobs worked at Pan Arabic. Its accounting department housed a small army of moneymen, many with MBAs from colleges in America. The company made millions and was worth billions. These accountants were the ones who kept it so.

There were also legitimate oilmen employed here. The trek sweet crude made from ground to gas tank was a long one, and money could be lost or made at every turn. The art of moving vast quantities of oil was practiced at Pan Arabic, day after day, month after month. Geologists, piping experts, supertanker captains, and Ph.D.'s in refining all worked here.

Of the two thousand employees, roughly half handled the actual product itself; the others counted the money. Of that thousand who worked on the money end, more than two-thirds had been involved in some way with helping fund Al Qaeda.

As word spread about the events in Hormuz, it seemed a very dark day for the state of Islam was at hand. Many people in the Pan Arabic Oil Exchange building were not at their desks or planning tables. They were in colleagues' offices or gathered in one of the building's six lavish lobbies, watching TV. Al Jazzier News was broadcasting the events in the lower Gulf practically as they were happening. Somehow the Arab TV network had received a piece of video tape, shot from very far away but still showing the height of the attack on the *Lincoln*.

The footage and the breaking news had just about everyone in the building glued to the TV sets.

That's why very few people ever saw the airliner coming.

The plane had been spotted by air traffic controllers at Khalid Airport shortly after 10:30 A.M.

It had arrived from the west and began circling the city at an altitude of just 2,000 feet, very low for such a large plane. There were two attempts to contact it from Khalid, but the plane never responded and Khalid never tried contacting it again. The ATC men would later claim that the events unfolding near Hormuz, just a few hundred miles way, combined with the Americans' sudden imposition of restricted airspace over the entire Gulf, had distracted them. Six of these air traffic controllers would later be arrested and executed by the Saudi government.

For the people inside the Pan Arabic Oil building, it was the noise that arrived first.

Jet engines, roaring from somewhere in the distance, coming from an airliner flying on a morning when there wasn't supposed to be anything other than the American military in the air.

It circled the building once, a huge white aircraft with a bright red tail and the letters GAC emblazoned on it. Then the plane began a long, slow, deliberate dive, its engines screaming and smoking, not unlike a B-52. The plane hit the building going 540 knots, nearly supersonic, and impacted about two-thirds of the way up the ornate prayer tower. It passed through the main structure, its fully loaded gas tanks exploding somewhere around the thirteenth floor. A massive fireball rained debris and burning fuel onto those unlucky to be caught below. Half the fuselage tore off within the building itself. The other half continued through to a courtyard and into the street beyond.

Everyone on the plane, and everyone in the building, was killed.

Near the Strait of Hormuz

Gallant and Bingo had been out on the fantail of *Ocean Voyager* for the past 30 minutes, scanning the skies above them while at the same time watching the rush of U.S. Navy warships flooding into the Gulf.

They were anchored off the coast of the United Arab Emirates, trying their best to maintain the cover of a simple cargo ship just staying out of the way. They'd watched the airliners' foiled attack from about twenty miles off. Even now, they couldn't believe it had been real.

But that's not why they were out here. They'd crept as close to the scene of the battle as they could and now they were looking for something. Something, up there, in the smoke and clouds.

Suddenly Bingo cried out: "Damn, here comes one of them!"

A Harrier had appeared almost directly above them, no more than 2,500 feet up. But it was coming down very quickly and making very little noise while doing so. It became obvious the Harrier wasn't so much trying to land on the ship as it was falling out of the sky. And it was not trying to set down on one of the ship's two exposed pancakes; they were actually too far away. Rather, it was heading for the ship's little-used helicopter pad.

"He's out of gas!" Gallant yelled. The two men immediately dived into a nearby hatch to avoid getting clipped by the falling aircraft.

The Harrier slammed onto the copter pad just a few seconds later. It bounced once, twice, and then almost fell off the platform completely. It came to rest only because its front nose and port outrigger wheel became entangled in the safety netting surrounding the pad. If this hadn't happened, it would have gone right over the side.

The two men scrambled out of the hatch and raced up to the stricken plane. Its canopy had blown off; its engine was not turning. Gallant had been right; the plane had run out of gas and crashed. Or, in jump jet parlance, it had performed a dead-stick, vertical insertion.

They climbed up onto the wing and found it was Ryder in the cockpit. He was conscious, but just barely. He was drenched in sweat and shaking. His hands were particularly white to the bone. So was his face. He looked terrible.

He somehow managed to take off his helmet and look up at his colleagues. His eyes were red.

"Did Phelan land yet?" was all he could say.

Ten hours later

The sun finally began to sink on this bloody, historic day.

The Harrier, near totaled in its controlled crash, was covered with pieces of canvas now, to keep it better hidden from prying eyes.

Ryder had been patched up by the Navy guys and injected with a large dose of morphine. It was the only way they could get him to sleep. He lay, not moving, on a cot in the sick bay for hours. Maureen did not appear in his dreams this time. In fact, he didn't dream at all. When he finally woke up, he felt worse than when he landed.

He was in a semi–state of shock. Whether it was exhaustion or the events he'd just lived through or the double whammy of morphine, he felt like he was sleepwalking. Some things made sense to him; other things didn't. Yet he insisted on being allowed to climb up to the fantail, where he hoped the others would still be.

Here he found Gallant and Bingo, leaning against the greasy rail, continuing their lonely vigil. Martinez was still

nowhere to be seen. Ryder would later learn the Delta officer
was locked in his cabin, refusing food, refusing to even talk.
What would have happened if he had allowed his Delta guys
to blast the hijackers while they were still on the ground at
el-Salaam Airport? It was a question destined to haunt him
for a long time to come.

Gallant and Bingo had the last six-pack of Budweiser on
the ship with them, but neither felt like drinking. Ryder
joined them at the rail. He was able to give them some scattered details on what had happened over Hormuz, but his
mind was elsewhere. As he spoke, he was continuously
searching the skies overhead, half-expecting Phelan to appear at any moment, circling the ship for a landing.

Bingo told him two of his guys had gone through Phelan's
cabin, once it appeared certain that the young pilot was not
coming back. They'd intended to gather his personal effects
but had found his billet practically empty. All his CDs, his
music player, his books, clothes, everything was gone, thrown
overboard, they supposed. Did this mean Phelan had intended
to commit his final act all along? Had he snapped? Or was he
just a brave kid who had seen too much? No one knew.

All that remained was his mother's picture, found hanging on the cabin wall. Bingo now handed the photo to Ryder,
who barely looked at it before putting it in his pocket.

Then the ship became ethereally quiet.

"God, was all this worth it?" Gallant asked softly. "Phelan, the Delta guys. Probably Curry, too. All gone. . . ."

"But look what they did," Bingo replied. "They helped stop
the mooks from hitting us big-time. *They helped save America*—at least for one more day. This thing would have played
out a whole lot different if we hadn't been on the case. Not
that it will settle everything. There are still plenty of mooks
left out there. Not just in this neighborhood either. I'm talking about Southeast Asia. The Philippines. Indonesia. There'll
be more blood in the water before this thing is finished. But
today, *this* day, we knocked them on their ass. And that's
what we were supposed to do all along."

More silence. Off in the distance, they heard a sound that

might have been made by a jet aircraft approaching. They all froze on the spot. But the noise quickly faded away.

Finally, Gallant asked the question that was still on everyone's mind: "So, what do we do now? We can't just float around out here forever. They're bound to catch up to us sooner or later. And I still don't think it will be to give us medals."

"Plus, we've run out of just about everything," Bingo added. "Including fuel for the ship's engines. We might be able to make a stop somewhere along the way, steal enough gas to sail back to the states. But then what?"

Ryder took a deep breath and finally took his eyes off the sky. Things were making a little bit more sense now.

"Then what?" he asked in reply. "Then we try to find Bobby Murphy."

The *Ocean Voyager* left the Gulf two hours later. Passing through the recently reopened Strait of Hormuz, it steered around the large pieces of wreckage still floating in the shallow parts and headed for the Indian Ocean.

A huge fog bank was lying off the coast of Oman, not unusual for this time of year. Fishermen close to the shore saw the containership emerge from the strait. It looked like any one of dozens of vessels that would pass this way on a typical day. They watched it follow a course parallel to the coastline for a few minutes.

Then, very slowly, it turned south and disappeared into the fog.

Three days later

It was a rainy morning in Illinois.

Ginny Santos had risen early, seen her youngest child off to school, and then sat down with the newspaper. Reading over all of the stories about the horror a half a world away, she scanned every page, looking for her husband's name. It was a game she'd played every day since Tom had left with

the men from the government. She told herself that if his
name was not to be found anywhere in the newspaper, then it
meant he was still alive and that she could sleep and breathe
and hope, for at least one more day.

When she did not find his name anywhere, she celebrated
with a cup of tea.

Then the mail came.

There was a large envelope, addressed to her, with a post-
mark Riyadh, Saudi Arabia. It was in Tom's handwriting.

Ginny hurriedly tore it open, and what seemed to be hundreds of letters fell out. They were love letters from Tom,
each written on plain white paper. Except one. It was written
on yellow stock. It stood out among the rest, as it was supposed to.

It was less than a week old. Ginny read it first.

My dearest Ginny,
*These are letters that I've written to you since I've
been away. I intended to give them to you myself, but
now that will be impossible because I won't be coming
home after all. In fact, by the time you read this, I will
be gone. Please have a good cry, but then a good
laugh. And please know I died in the service of our
country. Remember the places we've been, the things
we did. Tell the kids I love them very much and to be
proud of the place they live. Thank you for making my
life so complete. And if you ever feel sad, just remember that stream in the woods near our house. The one
you always said looked like it went on forever. It does.
And I'll be just up around the bend, waiting for you.*
                                        Love,
                                        Tom

Attached to the letter was a cashier's check. It was made
out to Ginny. For $10 million.

It was signed by Bobby Murphy.

Read on for an excerpt from Mack Maloney's next book

SUPERHAWKS

★ ★ ★

STRIKE FORCE BRAVO

COMING SOON FROM
St. Martin's Paperbacks

One Crazy Night

Singapore

The terrorists came dressed as waiters.

They arrived at the rear service entrance to the Tonka Tower Hotel at precisely 10:00 A.M. There were eight of them. They unloaded six food carts from their two vehicles. There was no security in this part of the building and the rear door had been left open for them. They rolled the carts up onto the kitchen's loading platform and simply walked inside.

It was checkout time and the lobby of the enormous hotel was packed. Hundreds were waiting in line; hundreds more were picking up luggage or trying to find cabs. The routine chaos gave the eight terrorists all the cover they would need. They walked right through the lobby, heads down, pushing their carts, and made for the service elevators. Once there, they pushed the button to call the largest of the hotel's 16 service lifts. It arrived a few seconds later. Loading the carts and themselves aboard, they quickly closed the doors and hit the button to go up.

The Tonka hotel was one of the tallest structures in the world. It was shaped like a futuristic pagoda, with a tower that soared 1,200 feet in the air. There were more than 3,000 rooms here, most of them expensive suites, plus many function areas, shops, and trendy restaurants. The hotel's grand style and downtown location made it a popular place for foreign businesses, especially American companies, to hold meetings and corporate events. The Singapore government encouraged such things and frequently picked up the tab.

The hotel was especially crowded with American citizens today, as it had been declared America Day by the city government, a fete for the families of U.S. business and foreign service people living in Singapore. Several gala events were being held at the Tonka. A huge breakfast for the American consulate was in progress on the sixteenth floor. A reception for U.S. Embassy employees was about to begin on the forty-fourth. Another for the Ford Motor Company was scheduled for 10:30 on the ninety-sixth.

But the disguised terrorists in the elevator passed all these floors. They were heading directly for the top.

They were members of Qeza al-Habu, a terrorist cell linked directly to Al Qaeda. Their destination was the building's penthouse, up on the one hundred and fortieth floor. There was an expansive banquet hall here known, simply enough, as the Top Room. A party for children of U.S. diplomats serving in Singapore had started in the hall around nine. There were 300 kids on hand, most under the age of 12, some as young as just a few months old. There were 22 adults watching over them.

The eight terrorists arrived on the top floor and unloaded their carts. Two stayed in the hallway and, using tools hidden in a steaming dish, disabled the hotel's elevator system by short-circuiting its main and auxiliary power panels, all of which were located here at the building's peak. This jammed more than 50 passenger lifts in place, trapping hundreds and making access to the top floor nearly impossible. It also knocked out every light in the hotel from the ninety-ninth floor down.

The six remaining terrorists proceeded to the Top Room function hall. They reached its one and only door and wheeled the food carts in. The large triangular room had a long dining table set up in the center. On it sat four gigantic chocolate cakes. Huge lime-tinted windows made up the three walls of the room; balconies went all around the outside. The Top Room was so high, wisps of clouds could be seen passing the windows.

The terrorists were met by several adults who greeted them quizzically. The children's party had already received their cake order from the kitchens downstairs. Why were these men here?

The terrorists didn't reply. They simply locked the door behind them, then uncovered their food carts. There were eight AK-47 assault rifles hidden inside. The terrorists pushed seven of the adults against the nearest wall and calmly shot each one in the head. Panic erupted. Children began screaming; some of the other adults tried to hide. The terrorists fanned out around the room, hunting down five more adults and killing them, including two shot at point-blank range found cowering under the banquet table. This thoroughly terrorized everyone in the room. The remaining adults froze in place. Many of the children went numb with fear. A few, however, did not. Some began crying. The terrorists walked around the room and shot each one. Soon enough, the room was deathly quiet.

The terrorists made their captives lie facedown on the floor. Some muffled cries could still be heard as the young hostages and the adults complied. Those terrorists charged with disabling the elevators joined their colleagues in the function room. Besides their tools and more weapons, their food carts were full of *plastique,* the highly volatile plastic explosive, nearly 60 pounds of it in all.

The leader of the terrorist group was a man known only as Moka. He was a tall, skinny Syrian Arab. He began shouting orders. While four terrorists watched over the hostages, three others began setting up the explosives. The Top Room had three immense pillars, one in each corner of the triangular hall. They were painted pearl white, with gold leafing. Exotic vines and flowers grew up their sides, and at night, under low light, these flowers became translucent. But the three pillars served a purpose beyond ornamental. Soaring right through the glass ceiling 35 feet above, they held the roof of the immense tower in place. The terrorists knew this because they had taken a complete set of building plans for the Tonka off the Internet. They also knew if the pillars were severed with enough force, the concussion of the blast and the weight of the debris would send the entire tower crashing to the ground.

The terrorists attached explosive charges to the three pillars 20 pounds each. Plastique was very pliable and the individual 2-pound packets stuck to the pillars like glue. Plastique was also easy to detonate. Two wires from a 20-volt motorbike battery would provide the spark for each pillar; a simple kitchen timer would throw the switch. The terrorists worked quickly, as they had been trained to do. This operation had been planned for six months. The participants had practiced for it every day for the past eight weeks.

Once the explosives were in place, the terrorists took out their third arsenal of weapons: cell phones. Each man had three, except the leader, Moka, who had five. Each cell had a set of phone numbers preprogrammed inside it, each number connected to a large news organization somewhere around the world. The terrorists began activating these numbers. In seconds, phones were ringing at the news desks of CNN, Fox, the U.S. broadcast TV networks, the BBC, the Associated Press, Reuters, and more. The message transmitted by the terrorists was short and grim: they had taken over the world-famous Tonka Tower and were planning to destroy it, with thousands trapped inside, in 15 minutes.

Moka's last call was to a local Singapore TV news station, Sing-One TV. It was the largest of the four news stations in the city. Moka was soon talking to an individual identified as Sing-One's executive manager. The man believed Moka right away, as reports that something was wrong at the Tonka Tower had already reached the TV station.

Moka made himself very clear to the TV executive. This was not a situation for negotiations or ransoms or diplomacy. This was an unfolding act of war. He and his men were dedicated to publicizing the plight of Muslim peoples everywhere. To this end, they were going to blow up the Tonka and kill everyone in it. Why was Moka personally calling Sing-One TV? Because he wanted the entire incident broadcast live around the world.

Sing-One's manager called Moka a bastard and a religious devil but then quickly complied with his wishes. Moka would allow only one news chopper to come close to the building. A camera onboard would be able to record everything happening inside the function hall. When the station manager pointed out there were other TV copters in the city and that a number of police and military helicopters would soon be heading for the tower as well, Moka assured him that only the Sing-One chopper would be allowed to approach.

The rest would have to stay at least 1,000 feet away, or Moka's men would start killing hostages.

In the next 10 minutes, the situation around the tower changed dramatically.

The city police cordoned off the entire downtown area, 20 blocks in every direction. Military police were flooding onto the scene. The government's Rapid Response Team arrived in six armed helicopters, landing just three blocks from the besieged tower. These special operations soldiers dispersed to buildings closest to the hotel, setting up weapons' positions and listening posts. The U.S. Embassy had also been alerted. Despite Moka's warning, an emergency diplomatic team was on its way.

Meanwhile thousands of citizens were streaming out of the area. They included the hundred or so guests who'd managed to get out of the tower simply by not being on an elevator when the terrorists first struck. Many more frightened guests were flowing down the stairwells of the hotel; most had a long, slow trip ahead of them, especially in the darkened stairwells. And hundreds were still trapped inside the building's fifty stalled elevators.

The sky above downtown Singapore had changed, too. As predicted, a small fleet of military aircraft, police copters, and TV news choppers had arrived. Thirteen in total, they were all orbiting the tower, except one: the bright yellow Bell Textron belonging to Sing-One TV.

So far the other helicopters had grudgingly obeyed Moka's orders, staying out at least 1,000 feet. The yellow Sing-One copter, however, was allowed to hover just 15 feet away from the Top Room's grand balcony, located on the east side of the building. This was a huge parapet, enclosed in glass except for a plant-filled open-air terrace. By floating just off its railing, the people inside the Sing-One chopper were indeed able to capture just about everything going on inside the function room, thanks to their computer-stabilized Steadicam. Inside two minutes of the copter's arrival, the horrifying images at the Tonka Tower were being broadcast around the world.

And it was all very clear for billions around the world to see: the hostages, the explosives, the terrorists, and the dead. It was early evening in the United States; the attack had been planned precisely for this hour so that it would be watched by a prime-time audience back in the states. A few minutes into the drama, Moka and three terrorists came out onto the terrace. Normally this would have been a very windy place, but glass valances installed around the balcony blocked most of the wind. Moka's men held up a banner. Scrawled in both Arabic and crude English letters, it declared the cell's intentions for all the world to see. At the same time, a phone connection was made between the Sing-One news copter and Moka. The conversation was conducted in Arabic, a common language between the head terrorist and at least one person inside the copter.

Moka reiterated his group's plans, and to prove his point, he signaled that four bodies be brought out to the terrace. Two children and two adults. They were unceremoniously thrown over the side of the balcony, twisting, turning, the smallest caught by the wind, all to plunge nearly a quarter of a mile to the ground below. It was a horrifying sight to see on camera and in person.

Then Moka read a statement, saying again that he had no demands, that he intended to destroy the tower at exactly

10:30 A.M. and that the timers to do this had already been set. This was going to happen, he said, and the world could only sit and watch. If anyone tried to interfere, Moka's men would start shooting hostages, children first.

A tiny clock popped up in the lower right-hand corner of Sing-One's broadcast screen.

Catastrophe was five minutes away.

More than two thousand people were still trapped inside the tower. To make matters worse, all of the lights had gone out in the building by this time, even inside the Top Room. Somehow a small fire had started on the thirty-first floor, filling the stairwells with acrid smoke. As the power continued to fail, many of the sinks and toilets began to overflow, too.

The people in the Sing-One news chopper asked Moka if he had any last statement to make. Moka responded that he'd already spoken his last word, as had his men. The people in the copter asked Moka if he wanted them to get final shots of the faces of his martyrs on TV, before the blast went off. To this Moka agreed.

He called all but three of his men to the balcony. Each man took out photos of loved ones he'd carried with him on the mission; they held the photos up to the copter's Steadicam. By the time the four terrorists got into camera position, the deadline for the explosives to go off was just 60 seconds away. Each man mouthed a short prayer, then raised his right arm above his head, with two fingers extended. Oddly, a peace sign.

Moka then signaled the copter that the explosives were about to go off. Sing-One TV had to back away. But the copter remained where it was, just 15 feet off the balcony. Moka signaled again. But the copter came in even closer. Moka became furious. He began shouting into the phone that the aircraft had to get away; it was important to him that the copter crew live to tell their tale. But with the explosives just seconds from going off, the helo kept coming in.

Now Moka was confused. He squinted his eyes, trying to see into the copter's open bay. *What was this?* The man who had been holding the Steadicam just moments ago was now holding a rather large gun. Men on either side of him were holding guns, too. Moka saw the muzzle flashes but never heard the shots that killed him. Six rounds, in rapid succession, went right through his head.

The same barrage killed the other four terrorists on the balcony, this while the copter's TV camera, now relocated to its cockpit, kept rolling for all the world to see. Then incredibly, and still on live TV, the helicopter touched down on the balcony's railing, an amazing feat of piloting. Six men burst from the copter's open bay. They were not TV reporters or cameramen. They were wearing combat suits—*American* combat suits. All black with armor plating, ammo belts, side arms, and helmets that looked like props from a fifties sci-fi movie. All with stars-and-stripes patches on their shoulders.

At the same moment, two of the Top Room's great plate glass windows came crashing in. Men swinging on ropes flew through the openings. The sudden change in air pressure created a minitornado inside the room. Some of the adult hostages screamed, kids began crying, but it was the remaining terrorists who panicked. They were stationed next to the explosive-packed pillars, but now the noise was tremendous, the wind like the devil. And suddenly a small army of armed men was coming at them.

Each terrorist backed up to guard his assigned pillar, but for what? The explosives were set to go off in 30 seconds. One terrorist boldly stood in front of his plastique charges, intent on protecting them with his body. He was shot five times in the head and there is where he died. His killers vaulted over the hostages and disconnected the explosive packs on the first pillar. But two remained, and only 20 seconds were left.

The terrorist in the northeast corner took cover behind his pillar and started firing at the soldiers in black. Everyone, hostages and soldiers alike, hit the floor. The men who had crashed through the window returned fire; a vicious gunfight erupted. The terrorist returned fire in three short bursts but turned too late to see the six men who'd just landed on the balcony. He was caught in their combined fusillade, taking more than 40 rounds to the stomach alone. He fell over in slow motion, his insides hitting the floor before the rest of him.

Now just one terrorist remained, with one pack of explosives—and 10 seconds before detonation.

Suddenly alone, this terrorist grabbed two small children and pulled them back against the pillar with him. The kids began screaming. Shrieks of horror went through the hall. *"Don't shoot!"* some of the adults started screaming.

Nine seconds.

The terrorist fired in the direction of his attackers. He was sure the soldiers would not shoot him, not as long as he was holding the two terrified children.

Eight seconds.

The soldiers kept advancing, moving quickly, but in a crouch. Their weapons were raised, but they were not firing.

Seven seconds.

The terrorist fired again, hitting the soldier closest to him, but still about twenty-five feet away. He watched in astonishment as his bullets staggered the man but then bounced off his armor plating.

"You cannot all be supermen!" the terrorist cried out.

Six seconds.

Most of the adult hostages were crying now; they knew the explosives were about to go off. One pack, 20 pounds, was more than enough to kill everyone in the room.

Five seconds.

The soldiers continued advancing toward the last terrorist. But would they sacrifice two children in order to save many?

Four seconds.

As it turned out, they wouldn't have to. . . .

Three seconds.

One armed man, undetected in the distractions around him, came up behind the terrorist and put a pistol to his head. He pulled the trigger and the terrorist's head was blown apart. He never knew what hit him, dead before he hit the floor.

Two seconds. . . .

The man with the pistol hastily reached down and began pulling wires out of the block of *plastique*.

One second.

Zero. . . .

There was one loud *pop!* as the last electrical wire was yanked from the explosive pack. The noise scared the hell out of everyone . . . but nothing happened except one long fizzle.

The bomb did not go off. The hostages were safe.

The crisis was over.

BOOTS
ON THE
GROUND

A Month with the 82nd Airborne in the Battle for Iraq

Karl Zinsmeister

Boots on the Ground is a riveting account of the war in Iraq with the 82nd Airborne Division as it convoys north from Kuwait to Iraq's Tallil Air Base en route to night-and-day battles within the major city of Samawah and its nearby bridges across the Euphrates. Karl Zinsmeister, a frontline reporter who traveled with the 82nd, brilliantly conveys the careful planning and technical wizardry that go into today's warfare, even local firefights, and he brings to life the constant air-ground interactions that are the great innovation of modern precision combat. Readers of this vivid day-to-day diary are left with not only a flashing sequence of strong mental images, but also a notion of the sounds and smells and physical sensations that make modern military action unforgettable.

Includes photos taken by the author while with the 82nd in Kuwait and Iraq!

"A fast-moving story of courage and competence, written by an observer who offers a far different picture from what was presented by our mainstream media. A moving tribute to what free soldiers united in a common cause can accomplish."

—Victor Davis Hanson, military historian

ISBN: 0-312-99608-X

**Available wherever books are sold
from St. Martin's Paperbacks**

BOOTS 04/04